About the Author

Diane Gaston's dream job had always been to write romance novels. One day she dared to pursue that dream and has never looked back. Her books have won Romance's highest honours: the *RITA*® Award, the National Readers Choice Award, Holt Medallion, and Golden Heart®. She lives in Virginia with her husband and three very ordinary house cats. Diane loves to hear from readers and friends. Visit her website at: dianegaston.com

Regency Rebels

Regency Rebels:

Love Bound

DIANE GASTON

MILLS & BOON

First Published in Great Britain 2023
By Mills & Boon, an imprint of HarperCollins*Publishers* Ltd,
1 London Bridge Street, London, SE1 9GF

www.harpercollins.co.uk

HarperCollins*Publishers*
Macken House, 39/40 Mayor Street Upper,
Dublin 1, D01 C9W8, Ireland

Regency Rebels: Love Bound © 2023 Harlequin Enterprises ULC.

Bound by Duty © 2015 Diane Perkins
Bound by One Scandalous Night © 2016 Diane Perkins

ISBN: 978-0-263-31969-9

This book is produced from independently certified FSC™ paper to ensure responsible forest management.

For more information visit: www.harpercollins.co.uk/green

Printed and Bound in the UK using 100% Renewable Electricity at CPI Group (UK) Ltd, Croydon, CR0 4YY

BOUND BY DUTY

To the memory of my mother, Teresa Gaston, a kind and gentle soul who was always quietly there for me, and who would never, ever hurt anyone's feelings.

Chapter One

February 1815—Lincolnshire, England

The winter wind rattled the windowpanes of Summerfield House as Tess Summerfield answered her older sister's summons.

Come to the morning room immediately, her note said.

More bad news, Tess feared. It seemed lately that the only time Lorene summoned her and their youngest sister, Genna, to that parlour was to hear bad news.

The wind's wail seemed appropriately foreboding.

The morning room on its best sunny days filled with light, but this day it seemed awash in grey. Lorene stood ominously by the fireplace. Genna sat sulkily in a nearby chair.

'What is it, Lorene?' Tess asked.

Lorene had been acting oddly lately, leaving the house on unexplained errands and remaining away for hours.

Their father's sudden death two months ago had seemed the worst of circumstances, but shortly afterwards they'd also discovered that he'd depleted their dowries before he died. Next, the distant cousin who was to inherit their father's title and property made it very clear he had no in-

tention of providing for them. After all, everyone believed
the scandalous Summerfield sisters were really not Summerfields at all. Rumour always had it that each had been
sired by a different lover.

Before their mother ran off with one, that was.

This heir to their father's baronetcy also made it clear
he wished to take possession of the entailed property as
soon as possible and that meant the sisters must vacate the
house, their home for all their lives.

What more could happen to them?

'Please sit,' Lorene said, her lovely face lined with
stress.

Tess exchanged a glance with Genna and sat as instructed.

Lorene paced in front of them. 'I know we all have been
worried over what would become of us—'

Worry was too mild a term. Tess expected they would
be split apart, forced to take positions as governesses or
lady's companions, if they should be so lucky as to find
such positions, given the family's reputation.

'I—I have come upon a solution.' Lorene sent them
each a worried look.

If it was a solution, why did she appear so worried?
'What is it, Lorene?'

Lorene wrung her hands. 'I—I discovered a way to
restore your dowries. A way to make you eligible again.'

It would take a sizeable dowry to erase the scandal that
had dogged them their whole lives. If their mother's aban-
donment were not enough, there was also their father's
scandal. Even before their mother left, he'd brought his
bastard son home to rear. Of course, Tess and her sisters
loved Edmund; he was their brother, after all, even if his
presence generated more talk.

'What nonsense,' Genna grumbled. 'Nothing makes us

eligible. Our mother had too many lovers. That is why we look nothing alike.'

That was not entirely true. They all had high foreheads and thin faces, even if Lorene was dark-haired with brown eyes, Genna was blue-eyed and blonde, and Tess was somewhere in between, with chestnut hair and hazel eyes.

Like their mother, Tess was told, although she did not remember precisely what her mother looked like.

A thought occurred to her. 'Lorene, do not say that you found our mother. Is she restoring our dowries?'

Tess had been only nine when their mother left.

Lorene looked surprised. 'Our mother? No. No. That is not it.'

'What is it, then?' Genna asked testily.

Lorene stopped pacing and faced them both. 'I have married.'

'Married!' Tess rose from her chair. 'Married!'

'You cannot have married,' Genna protested. 'There were no bans.'

'It was by special licence.'

No. Impossible! Lorene would never have kept such a big secret from Tess. They shared every confidence—almost.

'Who?' she asked, trying not to feel hurt.

Lorene's voice dropped to a whisper. 'Lord Tinmore.'

'Lord Tinmore?' Tess and Genna exclaimed in unison.

'The recluse?' Tess asked.

Since the deaths of his wife and son years before, Lord Tinmore had secluded himself on his nearby estate in Lincolnshire, not too distant from their village of Yardney. Tess could not think of a time Lorene could have met the man, let alone be courted by him. No one saw Lord Tinmore.

'He must be eighty years old!' cried Genna.

Lorene lifted her chin. 'He is only seventy-six.'

'Seventy-six. So much better.' Genna spoke with sarcasm.

Her adored older sister married to an ancient recluse? This was too much to bear. 'Why, Lorene? Why would you do such a thing?'

Lorene's eyes flashed. 'I did it for you, Tess. For both of you. Lord Tinmore promised to provide you with dowries and host you for a Season in London. He will even send Edmund the funds to purchase an advancement in the army and the means to support its expenses. He is a fine man.'

She married this man so they could have dowries? And Edmund, advancement?

'I never asked you for a dowry,' Genna said. 'And Edmund can earn advancement on his own.'

'You know he cannot, now that the war is over,' Lorene shot back. 'He does not have enough as it is. It costs him money to be an officer, you know.'

Genna shook her head. 'Did our dowries not provide Edmund enough?'

Their father had used the last of their dowry money to purchase the lieutenancy for Edmund.

Lorene leaped to Edmund's defence. 'Edmund has no knowledge of that fact, Genna, and you are never to tell him. He would be sick about it if he knew. Besides, Papa intended to recoup the funds for our dowries. He assured me his latest investment would yield all we would need.'

Of course, it would most likely go the way all his too-good-to-be-true investments went. If it paid off now, which was unlikely, the money would go to the estate's heir. Their father's will provided only for their now non-existent dowries.

But Lorene would say nothing bad about their father. Or

about anyone. She believed the best of everyone. Even their mother. Lorene would insist that abandoning her daughters had been the right thing for their mother, because she'd run off with a man she truly loved.

What of the love a mother should have for her children? Tess wondered.

Now Lorene was making the same mistake as their parents—engaging in a loveless marriage.

She glared at Lorene. 'You cannot possibly love Lord Tinmore.'

'No, I do not love him,' Lorene admitted. 'But that is beside the point.'

'Beside what point?' Tess shot back. 'Did you learn nothing from our parents? You will be miserable. You will make him miserable.'

'I will not.' Lorene straightened her spine. 'I promised I would devote my life to making him happy and I intend to keep my promise.'

'But what of you?' Tess asked.

Lorene averted her gaze. 'I could not think of what else to do. What would become of you and Genna if I did nothing?' Her question required no answer. They all knew what fate had been in store for them.

'Well, you did not have to fall on your sword for us,' Genna said.

'I thought about it a great deal,' Lorene went on, seemingly ignoring Genna's comment. 'It made sense. If I had done nothing, we all would have faced dismal lives. By marrying Lord Tinmore, you and Edmund have hope. With good dowries you can marry as you wish. You will not be desperate.'

What Lorene meant was that she, Genna and even Edmund could now marry for love. They could avoid the unhappiness of their parents and still have security. They had a chance for a happy life and all it had cost Lorene was her own chance for happiness.

A chance for love.

God help her, Tess felt a tiny spark of hope. If she had a dowry, Mr Welton could court her.

She turned her face away. How awful of her! To be glad for Lorene's sacrifice.

She composed herself again. 'How did you accomplish it, Lorene? How did you even meet him?'

'I went to him. I asked him to marry me and he agreed.'

Without telling her sister, the person closest to her? 'Without a courtship?'

Lorene gave Tess an exasperated look. 'What need was there for a courtship? We settled matters in a few meetings and Lord Tinmore arranged for a special licence. When his man of business procured the licence for him, the vicar of his church married us in his parlour.'

'You could have invited us,' Genna chided.

Genna was hurt, as well, obviously.

Lorene swung around to her. 'You would have tried to stop me.'

'Yes. I would have done that.' Genna spoke firmly.

The wind gusted and the windowpanes banged. Would Tess have tried to stop Lorene? She did not know.

The clouds that cast a pall on them parted and light peeked through.

They were saved. Lorene had saved them.

By sacrificing herself.

A mere two weeks later Tess Summerfield lounged on the bed in one of the many bedchambers of Tinmore Hall. This room had been given to Genna who stood behind an easel, facing the window. Lorene again paced nervously back and forth, which seemed to be her new habit.

'It is a lovely house party, is it not?' Lorene asked, looking hopefully at each of them.

'Lovely!' Tess agreed eagerly.

So much had changed so very quickly. Two days after Lorene announced her marriage, they moved out of the only home they'd ever known, taking with them no more than a trunk of belongings each. Now Lord Tinmore had invited several guests in a hastily arranged house party to introduce his new bride to his closest society friends. In another month or so they would travel to London for a whirlwind of dress fittings and hat shopping in order to show them off to best advantage when the Season began. Lorene's marriage was still a shock, but Tess could not help but be excited about what lay ahead.

She was also deeply, deeply grateful to Lorene—as well as feeling guilty.

Genna was not grateful, however. She remained as surly as the day Lorene had told them her secret.

'It is lovely, isn't it, Genna?' Tess, too, reeled from the loss of their home, but she was determined to show Lorene her support.

Genna threw her paintbrush into its jug of water and spun around. 'I hate the house party. I hate everything about it.'

'Genna!' Tess scolded.

Lorene made a placating gesture. 'It is all right. Let her speak her mind.'

Genna's face flushed. 'I cannot bear that you married that man—that *old* man—for money. His guests call you a fortune hunter and they are correct.'

'That is enough, Genna!' Tess cried. 'Especially because Lorene did it for us.'

'I did not ask for it.' Genna turned to Lorene. 'I would never have asked it of you. Ever.'

'No one asked me.' Lorene went to her and placed her hand on Genna's arm. 'Besides, the earl is a good man. Look what he has done for us already.'

He'd given them a new home at Tinmore Hall. He'd had them fitted for new dresses by the village seamstress. He was in the process of arranging dowries for her and for Genna and an allowance for Edmund whose regiment was somewhere on the Continent.

Tess sat up. 'It was a brave sacrifice. Don't you see that, Genna? We have a chance now. Lord Tinmore will provide us with respectable dowries. We're going to have a London Season where we can meet many eligible young men.'

Mr Welton would be in London. He'd said he would be there for the Season. Tess wanted so much to tell him of her changed circumstances.

Lorene squeezed Genna's arm. 'You will be able to have a choice of young men. You won't have to marry merely for a roof over your head and food in your mouth. You will be able to wait for a man you are able to truly esteem.'

'You can make a love match.' It was what Tess desired more than anything. That and to always be close to her sisters.

Lorene's tone turned earnest. 'I want you to have a love match, to have that sort of happiness.'

Tess was known as the practical sister. Sensible and resourceful. Would Lorene and Genna not be surprised to learn that she had a secret *tendre* for a man? To even think of him made her giddy with excitement.

Genna's face contorted as she faced Lorene. 'You married an ugly, smelly old man so that Tess, Edmund and I could marry for love. Bravo, Lorene. We're supposed to be happy knowing that because of us you must share his bed.'

Lorene blanched and her voice deepened. 'That part of

it is not for you to speak of. Ever. That is my private affair and mine alone. Do you hear?'

'What about your life, Lorene? What about your choices? Your love match?' Genna's voice turned shrill.

Lorene put a hand to her forehead. 'I did make a choice. I chose to do this. For you. And Lord Tinmore has been good enough to provide you with this lovely room, with your paints and paper. He's ordered us each a new wardrobe and soon he will take us all to London for even more finery—'

Genna broke in. 'And what must you do in return, Lorene?'

Lorene glared at her. She straightened and turned towards the door. 'I must go now. I must see that everything is in order for our guests. I expect you to behave properly in front of them, Genna.'

'I know how to behave properly,' Genna snapped, still recalcitrant. 'Did Papa not teach us to never behave like our mother?'

Lorene shot her one more scathing—and, Tess thought— pained look and left the room.

Tess leaped off the bed. 'Genna, how could you? That was terrible to say. About…about sharing Lord Tinmore's bed.' And about their mother.

Genna folded her arms across her chest. 'Well, it is what we think about, is it not? What she must do for him? Because of us?'

Tess felt a pang of guilt.

She took it out on Genna, walking over to her and shaking her. 'We cannot speak of it! It hurts her. You saw that.'

Genna pulled away, but looked chagrined.

Tess went on. 'We must make the best of this, for her sake. She's done us an enormous service at great sacrifice. She has given us a gift beyond measure. We are free to choose who we want to marry.' She thought of Mr Welton. 'We must not make her feel bad for it.'

'Oh, very well.' Genna turned back to her watercolour. 'But what are we to say when we hear the guests speak of her marrying Lord Tinmore for his money? Are we to say, "Yes, that is it exactly. She married him for his money and his title. Just like our mother did our father"?'

That was another truth best left unspoken.

'We pretend we do not hear anything.' Tess spoke firmly. 'We act as if Lorene's marriage to Lord Tinmore is a love match and that we are delighted for them both.'

'Hmmph. A love match between a beautiful young woman and a very old, smelly man.' Genna stabbed at her painting. 'And what do we say when they accuse *us* of exploiting Lord Tinmore, as well?'

'Us?' Tess blinked. 'Has anyone said that?'

Genna shrugged. 'Not to my face. Yet. So tell me what I ought to say when they do.'

Tess had not considered that possibility, but it made sense. In a way, she, Genna and Edmund stood to gain more from Lord Tinmore's money than Lorene. His money would open possibilities for them, possibilities that filled Tess with joy.

Until guilt stabbed at her again. 'We simply act grateful for everything he does for us, because we are grateful, are we not?'

Genna made a false smile. 'Very grateful.'

Genna bore watching. She was entirely too impetuous and plain speaking for her own good.

Tess changed the subject. 'I do not think Lord Tinmore has anything planned for us until dinner.'

The guests, all closer to his age than to his bride's, were in need of rest after travelling to Lincolnshire the day before. Tess supposed they had accepted the first invitation to Tinmore Hall in thirty years because they wanted to see what sort of woman caused Lord Tinmore to finally open his doors.

Tess dreaded their second meeting of the guests. The ladies' travelling clothes were finer than her best gown. Their dinner gowns took away her breath. The new gowns Lord Tinmore had ordered would not be ready for a week, but Tess could not bear for her and her sisters to look so shabby in the meantime.

'Would you like to walk to the village with me?' she asked.

Genna looked surprised. 'Why are you going to the village?'

'For lace and ribbons. I believe I can embellish our gowns so it does not appear as if we are wearing the same one, night after night.' They might be charity cases, but they could at least try not to look like ones.

'You are being foolish to go out.' Genna gestured to the window. 'It will rain.'

Tess glanced at the overcast sky. 'The rain should hold off until I return.'

'Well, I am not chancing it.' Genna dipped her brush in some paint.

'Very well. I can walk alone.' Tess always walked alone to Yardney, the village that once had been her home.

But it was only a few short miles from here. Obviously Lorene had walked the distance often enough to get married. Why not walk to Yardney instead of the village nearby? It would take only a little longer. If she went to Yardney she could call upon Mr Welton's aunt. If Mr Welton was still her house guest, she could tell him about having her dowry restored.

'You should take a maid or something,' Genna said. 'Is that not what wealthy wards do?'

If she wanted someone to know where she was bound, perhaps. Besides, Lord Tinmore was not their guardian. They'd not been appointed a guardian after their father died. There had been no property or fortune to protect. They were under Lord Tinmore's protection, though.

'Lord Tinmore will not care if I walk to the village when I've been walking the countryside my whole life.' At least Tess hoped he would not care. She and Genna had hardly seen him, only for a few meals. She opened the door. 'In any event, I am going.' With luck she could change their dresses by dinnertime and see to her future, as well.

Genna did not look away from her watercolour. 'Well, if it pours and you get soaking wet and catch your death of a cold, do not expect *me* to wipe your nose.'

That was much how their father had become ill. Surely Genna did not realise.

'I never catch colds.' Tess walked out of the room, closing the door behind her.

The rain did not begin until Tess left Yardney and was already on the road back to Tinmore Hall. The first drops that splattered the dirt road quickly grew to a heavy downpour. Moments later it was as if the heavens had decided to tip over all their buckets at once. In mere minutes Tess's cloak was soaked through. Even her purchases, wrapped in paper and string and held under her cloak, were becoming wet.

'Genna, you are going to gloat,' she muttered.

But it had been worth it. Tess discovered that Mr Welton had indeed left for London, but he knew about Lorene's marriage. She told his aunt about her changed circumstances.

He would find her when Lord Tinmore took them all to town for the Season. Only a few more weeks.

Mud from the road stuck to Tess's half-boots, and it became an effort merely to lift one foot in front of the other. Water poured from the drooping brim of her hat and the raindrops hit her face like needles of ice. She had at least two miles to go before she'd cross through the gatehouse of the estate.

The mud grabbed at her half-boots like some devious creature bent on stopping her. Trying to quicken her pace was futile, but at last she spied the bridge ahead through the thick sheets of rain.

But the stream now rushed over it.

'No!' Her protest was swallowed by the wind.

What now? She did not know of any other way to reach Tinmore Hall. There was no choice but to walk to the nearby village as she ought to have done in the first place. The rain was cutting into her like knives now, not needles.

She glanced at the wooded area next to the road. If this were home, she'd know precisely how to cut through the woods and cross the fields. She might be home already, sitting in front of a fire, letting the heat penetrate instead of this rain. Here she did not dare leave the road that she knew led to Tinmore Village.

Do not think, she told herself. *Just put one foot in front of the other.* Despair nudged at her resolve.

She walked and walked until she thought she saw a vague outline of the village church tower. She hurried on, but up ahead water was streaming across the road. She could not go forward. She could not go back.

But she could go home, home to Yardney, at least. Perhaps she would seek shelter at Mr Welton's aunt's house. Or knock at the door of Summerfield House.

She turned back, retracing her steps, passing the road leading to the blocked bridge. A short distance from there, the road was flooded. Turning back again, she walked until she found another road, not knowing where it would lead her.

If only she were closer to home. She would be able to turn in any direction and find someone's house who would welcome her, but she no longer knew where she was or how to find her way to anywhere familiar. She was lost, wet and terribly cold.

Chapter Two

Marc Glenville cursed the rain.

Why there must be a downpour while he was on horseback on his way to London was beyond him. Unless the gods of weather somehow caught his mood.

Returning to London was never a joy.

But there was nothing else for him to do. His business in Scotland was complete.

His horse faltered and his head dipped. A stream of water trickled down his back.

Business in Scotland. Ha!

That was the fiction he told his parents and would tell anyone else who questioned his whereabouts these last long months, but it was not the truth.

He'd been to France. Paris and the countryside, mixing with Bonapartists and others discontented with returning Louis XVIII to the throne, keeping an ear tuned to whether discontent was apt to erupt in insurrection.

All for king and country.

Unrest was not widespread. The French, like the British, were fatigued with war. Mark had made his reports. No more would be asked of him.

It was time to face more personal matters.

Time to face again the fact that his brother would never again grin at him from across the dinner table and his best friend would never again come to call. When he was pretending to be Monsieur Renard, *citoyen ordinaire* of France, he could almost forget that Lucien, his brother, had been gone for four years and Charles, not quite three. Whenever he returned, though, he half-expected to see them walk through the door when he was home.

Grief shot through him like a bolt of lightning.

Foolish Lucien. Reckless Charles. They'd died so needlessly.

Marc willed his emotions to cool, lifting his face to the rain that was already chilling his bones. Best to keep emotions in control. When deep in espionage, it could save his life; back in London, it might save his sanity.

Good God. Was the near-freezing rain begetting gloomy thoughts as well as soaking him to the bone? Concentrate on the road and on his poor horse. Slogging through muddy, rut-filled roads was a battle, even for the sturdy fellow.

The stallion blew out a breath.

'Hard going, eh, Apollo?' Marc patted the horse's neck.

He'd hoped to reach Peterborough by nightfall, but that was not in the cards in this weather. He'd be lucky to make the next village, whatever that was, and hope its inn had a room with a clean bed.

The rain had forced him off the main route and he and Apollo were inching their way through any roads that remained passable.

The delay did not bother him overmuch. No one was expecting him. He'd not informed his parents he was coming to town. Let it be a surprise.

Marc dreaded the family visit, always, but it was time to take his place as heir, now that duty did not call him elsewhere. He'd call upon Doria Caldwell, Charles's sister, and make official what had been implied between them since Charles was killed. He owed that much to Charles.

Besides, the Caldwell family, now consisting only of her and her father, was so ordinary and respectable—and rational—he would relish being a part of it.

Lightning flashed through the sky and thunder boomed. Was he now to be struck by real lightning, instead of being struck figuratively?

He must be near a village; he'd been riding long enough. Gazing up ahead, he hoped to see rooftops in the distance or a road sign or any indication that shelter might be near, but the rain formed a grey curtain that obscured all but a few feet in front of him. What's more, the curtain seemed to move with him, keeping him engulfed in the gloom and making his eyelids grow heavy.

Lightning flashed again and he thought he'd seen someone in the road. He peered harder until through the curtain of rain a figure took form. It was a woman on foot, not yet hearing his horse coming up from behind.

'Halloo, there!' he called out. 'Halloo!'

The woman, shrouded in a dark cloak, turned and waved her hands for him to stop.

As if any gentleman could pass by.

He rode up to her and dismounted. 'Madam, where are you bound? May I offer some assistance?'

She looked up at him. She was a young woman, pretty enough, though her face was stiff with anxiety and exhaustion. 'I want to go to Tinmore Hall.' It seemed an effort for her to speak.

'Point the way,' he responded. 'I'll carry you on my horse.'

She shook her head. 'No use. Floods. Floods everywhere. Cannot get there. Cannot get to the village.' Her voice shook from the cold.

He extended a hand. 'Come. I'll lift you on to my horse.' Her cloak was as wet as if it had been pulled from a laundry bath. Her hat had lost any shape at all. Worse, her lips were blue. 'We'll find a place to get you dry.'

She nodded, but there was no expression in her pale eyes.

She handed him a sodden parcel which he stuffed in one of his saddlebags. He lifted her on to Apollo and mounted behind her. 'Are you comfortable? Do you feel secure?'

She nodded again and shivered from the cold.

He encircled her in his arms, but that offered little relief from the cold. He took the reins. Poor Apollo, even more burdened now, started forward again.

'I am not from here.' He spoke loudly to be heard through the rain's din. 'How far to the next village?'

She turned her head. 'Lost. Yardney—cannot find it.'

Yardney must be a nearby village. 'We'll find it.' He'd been telling himself he'd find a village this last hour or more.

She shivered again. 'Cold,' she said. 'So cold.'

He'd better find her shelter quickly and get her warm. People died of cold.

She leaned against him and her muscles relaxed.

He rode on and found a crossroads with a sign pointing to Kirton.

'See?' he shouted, pointing to the sign. 'Kirton.'

She did not answer him.

A little further on, the road was filled with water. He turned around and backtracked until he came to the crossroads again, taking the other route. Someone was farming the lands here. There must be houses about.

If only he could see them through the rain.

The road led to a narrower, rougher road, until it became little more than a path. He followed it as it wound back and forth. Hoping he was not wasting more precious time, he peered ahead looking for anything with a roof and walls.

A little cottage appeared in front of them. No candles shone in the windows, though. No smoke rose from the chimney. With luck it would be dry.

'Look!' he called to his companion, but she did not answer.

Apollo gained a spurt of energy, cantering to the promise of shelter. As they came closer, a small stable also came into view and he guided Apollo to its door. He dismounted carefully, holding on to her. She slipped off, into his arms. Lifting her over his shoulder, he unlatched the stable door. Apollo walked in immediately.

Marc lay the woman down on a dry patch of floor. 'Cold,' she murmured, curling into a ball.

At least she was alive.

He turned back to his horse, patting him on the neck. 'She comes first, old fellow. I'll tend to you as soon as I can.'

He left the stable and hurried up to the door of the cabin. He pounded on it, but there was no answer and the door was locked. He peered in a window, but the inside was dark. Reaching in a pocket inside his greatcoat, he pulled out a set of skeleton keys—what self-respecting spy would be without skeleton keys? He tried several before one clicked and the latch turned.

The light from outside did little to illuminate the interior of the cabin, but Marc immediately spied a fireplace and a cot with folded blankets atop it. It was enough.

He hurried back to the stable.

Apollo whinnied at his return. 'You'll have to wait a bit longer, old fellow.'

He lifted the woman again, her sodden garments making her an even heavier burden. She groaned as he put her over his shoulder and hurried back through the rain to the cabin door.

His first task was to get her wet clothes off. He placed her on the floor where it would not matter if her clothes left a puddle. After tossing off his greatcoat, he worked as quickly as he could, cutting the laces of her dress and her corset and stripping her down to her bare skin.

She tried to cover herself, but not out of modesty. 'Cold,' she whimpered.

She was a beauty. Full, high breasts, narrow waist and long, shapely legs. He swallowed at the sight, but allowed himself only a glance before grabbing a blanket and wrapping it around her. He carried her to the cot and wrapped the second blanket around her.

By this time his eyes were accustomed to the darkness of the room. He saw a stack of wood and kindling and a scuttle of coal. On top of the fireplace were tapers and a flint. He hurried to make a fire. When it burned well enough, he flung his greatcoat around him again and ran back out in the rain to tend to Apollo.

The stable was well stocked with dry cloths and brushes. He dried off the poor horse as best he could, covering him with a blanket. There was hay, which Apollo ate eagerly, and a pump from which Marc drew fresh water to quench Apollo's thirst.

'There you are, old fellow.' He stroked Apollo's neck. 'That is all I can do for you. Soon the rain must stop and, with luck, we will be on our way before night falls. For now, eat and rest and I will check on you later.'

Marc ran back through the unrelenting rain to the cabin. He checked on his new charge. Her cheeks had some colour, thank God, and her skin seemed a bit warmer to the touch. Her features had relaxed and she slept.

He blew out a relieved breath and, for the first time, realised he, too, was wet and cold and weary. He stripped down to his shirt and breeches and pulled a chair as near to the fire as he could. He really ought to hang up their wet clothes to dry, but the warmth of the fire was too enticing. Instead he stared at the woman.

She was lovely, but who was she?

Hers was a strong face, with full lips and an elegant nose. Her brows arched appealingly and her lashes were thick. He could not tell from her clothing what her station in life might be. What sort of woman would be walking in the rain? She mentioned Tinmore Hall. Lord Tinmore's estate? Perhaps she was in service there.

If he could look at her hands, he might learn more. Were they rough from work? They were tucked beneath the blanket. Her hair was pulled back in a simple knot such as any woman might wear on a walk to the village. It would never dry that way.

He reached over and pulled the pins from her dark hair and unwound it from its knot. He spread it over the pillow as best he could. He leaned back.

Good God, now she looked like some classical goddess. Aphrodite, perhaps. Goddess of love, beauty, pleasure.

When she woke, would she wish for pleasure? His blood raced.

It did more to warm him than the fire.

Tess woke to the crash of a thunderclap and the constant keen of rain. She remembered walking. She remembered the rain soaking into her clothing.

Her clothing!

She sat upright. She was covered by a blanket, nothing more.

'You are awake,' a man's voice said.

He sat on a nearby chair. That was right—a man on a horse. She'd really seen him, then.

'Where am I?' she rasped. Her throat was dry. 'Where are my clothes?'

'I fashioned a clothes line and hung them.' He pointed behind her.

She turned and saw her cloak, her dress, her corset and her shift hanging from a rope strung across the room. Next to her clothes were a man's greatcoat, coat and waistcoat.

He continued talking. 'We are in a cabin somewhere in Lincolnshire, but blast if I know where. You fell victim to the cold. I had to get you dry and warm or...' He ended with a shrug of a shoulder.

'You brought me here?' And removed her clothing? Her cheeks burned at the thought.

'It was shelter. It was dry and stocked with firewood and coal.'

Tess blinked and gazed about her. It was a small cabin with what looked like a scullery in one corner. It was furnished with a table and chairs, the chair he sat upon, and a bed pulled close to the fire.

She was warm, she realised.

The man shifted position and his face was lit by the firelight. His hair was as dark as a raven's wing, with thick brows to match and the shadow of a beard. In contrast, his eyes were a piercing blue. She had never seen a man quite like him and he was dressed in only his shirt and breeches. Even his feet were bare.

A breath caught in her throat. 'Who are you?' The blanket slipped off her shoulder and she pulled it about her again.

He stood. He was taller than her half-brother and Edmund reached six feet. 'I am Marc Glenville.' He bowed. 'At your service.' His thick brows rose. 'And you are?'

Tess swallowed. 'I am Miss Tess Summerfield.' She frowned. She ought to have introduced herself as *Miss Summerfield*. Lorene was Lady Tinmore now, so Tess had become the eldest unmarried sister.

She touched her hair. It was loose! What had happened to her hair?

'I took out your hairpins.' The man—Mr Glenville— sat again. 'I did undress you, Miss Summerfield, but only because you were suffering from the cold. I give you my word as a gentleman, it was necessary. A person can die from the cold.'

He was a gentleman. His accent, his bearing, were that of a gentleman.

'I do not remember any of it.' She shook her head.

'A function of the cold. An indication that there was some urgency in getting you warm.' His voice was deep and smooth and soothing.

She ought to be more frightened, to be in a strange place, with a strange man. Naked. But it had been far more frightening to be wandering for hours in the chilling rain.

'I must thank you, sir,' she murmured. 'It seems I owe you my life.'

He glanced away as if fending off her words. 'It was luck. I found this cabin by luck. A groundskeeper's cabin, I suspect, used only when he works this part of the property.'

She looked around the cabin once more.

He stood again. 'Are you hungry? I have a kettle ready to make tea.'

She nodded. 'Tea would be lovely.'

He hung the kettle above the fire and reached over to pick up what looked like a saddlebag near his chair.

'Your horse!' She remembered a horse.

He smiled again. 'Apollo.'

Was the animal out in the rain? 'You must bring him in here.'

He made a calming gesture with his hand. 'Do not fear. Apollo is warm and dry in a stable, with plenty of water and hay. I've checked on him. He was quite content. I will check on him again in a few minutes.' He carried the saddle-bags over to the table, searched inside them and pulled out a tin and an oilskin package.

When he walked to the scullery and his back was turned, Tess rose from the bed and, careful to keep the blankets around her, went to check her clothing. Her dress was still very wet, but her shift was almost dry.

'Mr Glenville?' She pulled her shift from the line.

He turned. 'Yes?'

She clutched her shift to her chest. 'Will you please keep your back turned? I—I wish to don my shift.'

Without saying a word, he turned his back again and faced the window.

Marc watched her reflection in the window. Not very well done of him, but he was unable to resist. Her figure was every bit as tantalising from the back as from the front.

No harm in looking.

Except he could feel his body stir in response. He resumed his search for teacups and a teapot. He found the pot, but had to settle for two Toby jugs.

'You can look now.' Her voice turned low. Did she know how seductive it was?

'Is your shift dry?' he asked, trying to sound matter-of-fact rather than like a man battling his baser urges.

'It is a little damp, but I feel better wearing it.' She was still wrapped up in the blanket.

He lifted the jugs for her to see. 'These will have to do for tea. Who the devil knows why they are here?' He placed them on the table. 'Do you mind waiting for tea? I should check on my horse.'

'Apollo?' She remembered the name. 'Of course I do not mind. I should feel terrible if your horse suffered because of me.'

Was this sarcasm? He peered at her, but saw only concern on her face.

Consideration of his horse's well-being was nearly as seductive as her naked reflection and her lowered voice.

He took his greatcoat off the rope and threw it over his shoulders. 'I will only be a moment. I'll tend to the tea when I return.' He stepped outside.

The mud beneath his bare feet felt painfully cold, but that was preferable to wearing his sodden boots even if he were able to get his feet into them. The rain had slowed, but the sun was low in the sky. Even if the rain stopped, the roads would not improve before dark.

He and Miss Summerfield would spend the night together.

It would be a long, painful night. No matter what his body demanded, he would not take advantage of her. Besides, he well knew a man must keep his passions in check.

On the other hand, if she approached him…?

Apollo whinnied.

'How are you faring, old fellow? Are you warm enough?' He ran his hand down the length of the horse's neck.

He and Apollo had been through adventures more dangerous than this one, but Marc was sorry to have subjected the stallion to one more hardship.

He found a blanket to put over Apollo. 'This will keep

you warm.' He mucked out the stable and replenished the hay and water before returning to the cabin.

When he opened the door Miss Summerfield handed him a towel. 'I found this. You can dry your feet.'

The cabin was brighter. 'You lit lamps.'

'Only two, so I could see to fix the tea.' She walked to the table. 'It has been steeping. It should be ready.'

She fixed the tea?

'Come, we can sit.' She walked over to the table.

She still wore a blanket, but she'd fashioned it like a tunic and belted it with a rope. 'You've made yourself a garment.'

She turned and smiled, making her face even lovelier. 'I devised a way that the blanket will not fall off me if I wish to use my arms. I suppose I should leave a coin to pay for cutting holes in the blanket for my head and for the belt.'

He hung up his greatcoat. 'I would say you are resourceful.'

She smiled again. 'Thank you.'

He sat at the table and she poured him a Toby jug of tea.

'I could not find any sugar,' she said.

'No matter.' His fingers grazed hers as he reached for the jug. He glanced at her hands and saw no evidence of hard work in them.

She sat and poured herself some tea. 'I have never drunk tea from jugs like this. I have never drunk anything from Toby jugs. I have seen some like them in the village shop, though.'

He frowned. A well-bred young lady might not have used a Toby jug. Perhaps a woman in service would not have used a Toby jug either.

Who was this Miss Tess Summerfield?

He took a sip of tea and tapped his jug with his fingers. 'You said something about Tinmore Hall when I picked you up. Are you employed there?'

'Employed there?' She looked puzzled. 'No, I live there. Now, that is. We—my sisters and I—recently moved there.' She paused as if trying to decide to say more. 'My sister Lorene is the new Lady Tinmore.'

But this made no sense. 'I thought the old lord was still alive. He had a grandson?'

She met his eye. 'Lord Tinmore is still alive and he has no grandson. My sister married the old lord.'

His brows shot up. 'The old lord? The man must be in his seventies.'

'He is nearly eighty.' She lifted her chin. 'How do you know Lord Tinmore?'

He took a sip of tea. 'I do not know him. I know of him. My father went to school with his son and I remember my father mentioning the son's death. It was sudden, as I recall.' He stared at her. 'Your sister married a man in his seventies?'

'Yes.' Her gaze did not waver.

She was sister to Lord Tinmore's wife? Well, she certainly was not a housemaid, then.

He'd wager the old earl did not marry below his station— most men of his social stature did not. Most gentlemen were wiser than that.

'Who is Tess Summerfield that an earl would marry your sister?' he asked.

She met his eye. 'I am the second daughter of the late Sir Hollis Summerfield of Yardney.'

Sir Hollis?

Ah, yes. Sir Hollis. He'd heard of him. Or rather, he'd heard of his wife. It was said his wife had had so many lovers her daughters were sired by different men and none of them her husband.

Even so, they must have been reared as respectable

young ladies and now were under the protection of the
Earl of Tinmore.

He rubbed his forehead. 'This changes matters. We must
be very careful not to be discovered together.'

She sat up straighter. 'I have no intention of being found
with you! I assure you I hope to be gone as soon as the
rain stops.'

He did not have the heart to tell her that it would likely
be dark before then.

She took another sip of tea. 'I am sorry, Mr Glenville. I
did not mean to sound so ungrateful. You might have left
me in the road.'

He opened his eyes and gazed at her. Her expression
was soft and lovely.

'You did not sound ungrateful, Miss Tess Summerfield.'
He savoured the sound of her name.

She blushed, as though she had read his thoughts. 'I
know what you did for me,' she said quietly. 'You rescued
me. And I do realise that being alone with you in this
cabin, especially in my state of undress, is a very compromising situation.'

She was direct; he appreciated that.

'I have no wish to see you ruined,' he explained. 'That
is all I meant.'

She faced him again. 'All I need is to reach the road
back to Tinmore Hall. I will tell no one where I've been
or who I've been with. If you can help me get that far, you
can trust that I will say nothing of this. Ever.'

'I will see you to safety.' He'd always intended to do so.
'And I, also, will say nothing of this.'

She extended her hand across the table. 'Let us shake
on it.'

He placed his large, rough hand in her smaller, smooth
one. 'We have a bargain, Miss Summerfield.'

Chapter Three

Up so close, Mr Glenville's blue eyes shone with such intensity Tess could not look away. Nor could she move her hand from his strong grasp. Her face grew warm.

'Are you hungry, Miss Summerfield?' he asked, releasing her.

'A little,' she managed. She was famished.

He pulled the oilskin package towards him. 'I have some bread and cheese here.' He untied the string and unfolded the oilskin. Inside was a small loaf of bread and a wedge of cheese. He tore the bread in half and handed her a piece.

It was damp, but she did not care. She took an eager bite.

He broke off a piece of the cheese for her.

It was all she could do not to gobble it down.

'Do not eat too fast,' he warned, taking a bite of the cheese.

His manner had changed in a way she did not quite understand, but his gaze warmed her as effectively as the fire.

He'd shown her nothing but kindness. Indeed, he'd saved her life. How awful it would be to have someone discover them here. Some women might use such a situation to trap a man into marriage.

It would be dreadful to base a marriage on an accidental mishap. Even Lorene's marriage made more sense than that.

She took sips of tea between bites and held the doughy taste of the flour and the sharp tang of the cheese in her mouth as long as she could. If she had been served wet bread and cheese at someone's dinner table or at an inn, she would have been outraged.

'How can I thank you, Mr Glenville?' she murmured. 'This is ambrosia.'

He glanced at her and his eyes still filled her with heat.

He quickly looked away. 'Tell me why you were out walking in a rainstorm.' It was said conversationally.

She waved a dismissive hand. 'I had an errand in the village.'

'It must have been important.'

It had not been. It had been foolish. She'd hoped to see Mr Welton. And to buy ribbons.

Her ribbons! 'I had a parcel… Was I carrying a parcel when you found me?'

He lifted a finger and leaned down to pull something out of his saddlebags. He held it up to her. 'A parcel.'

She took it.

'The reason for your walk to the village?' He inclined his head towards the parcel.

She felt her cheeks burn. 'Ribbons and lace.'

He responded with surprise.

She shrugged. 'It may not seem important to you, but it was to me.' Even more important had been learning about Mr Welton. 'Besides, I thought the rain would hold off until later in the day.'

He took another bite of cheese.

She pulled off a piece of bread and rolled it into a ball in her fingers. 'So why were you out in the rain?'

He swallowed. 'I am travelling to London.'

She kept up the challenge. 'And set off even though there was threat of rain?'

He lifted his Toby jug, as if in a toast, and smiled. 'Point taken.'

If his eyes had power, so much more did that smile.

Tess lowered her voice. 'I am glad you set off even though there was a threat of rain. What would have happened to me had you been wiser?'

'Someone else would have found you,' he said.

She shook her head. 'I walked for hours. I saw no one else on the road.'

He held her gaze with those riveting eyes.

She glanced away. 'Why were you bound for London?'

'I finished my business in Scotland.' He lifted his Toby jug. 'So I am returning to London.'

'Do you have business in London?'

He sipped his tea. 'Of a sort.'

A sort of which he obviously did not want to discuss.

'I shall be travelling to London soon,' she said, trying to cover her sudden discomfort. 'For the Season. Will you be attending the Season's entertainments?'

His face turned serious. 'I am not certain.'

She felt as though he had withdrawn from her completely, but she did not know why. Perhaps he'd tired of her conversation. She felt suddenly as lonely as she had been when wandering in the storm. She missed her sisters. They would think she was in Tinmore. Tess hoped they would presume she was safe. If only she could get back to them soon.

She finished her piece of bread and cheese, and he wrapped up the rest of his food.

It turned deadly quiet.

'The rain!' she cried. 'I think the rain has stopped!'

She jumped from her chair at the same time as he and they hurried to the door. Both stood there for a moment staring at it.

He reached over and opened it.

The rain had stopped, but it was black outside.

She looked over at him. 'There is no chance we can leave now, is there?'

'None,' he responded. 'It is too wet and too dark. I am afraid we are here all night.'

All night.

Marc wished he could erase the disappointment on her face.

To her credit she said not one word of complaint, even though their situation was now clearly worse than before. Instead she busied herself pouring more hot water from the kettle into the teapot. She did not complain, but, then, she did not say anything.

A cold wind soon rattled the windows and put even more chill into the cabin. Marc rooted through the room again. He found two more blankets, stored in a chest tucked in a far corner. One for her; one for him. He handed her one and they pulled chairs from the table to be near the fire. They wrapped themselves in their blankets, sipped weak, but hot, tea and stared into the fire.

He felt as if he'd lost her company.

He wanted it back. 'Do you go to London for the marriage mart, then?' he asked.

She jumped. He'd startled her.

'I would not choose those words, precisely.' Her voice was hesitant. 'My younger sister and I will come out. We might even be presented to the queen, if Lord Tinmore requests it.'

'I am surprised,' he said.

'Why?' she shot back. 'Why should we not be presented?'

He held up a hand. 'I am surprised any lady would wish all that fuss.'

Miss Summerfield stiffened. 'It would be an honour.'

Did his sister wish it? If so, it would never happen for her.

'An honour, indeed, I suppose,' he said.

'As would procuring vouchers for Almack's,' she went on. 'Will you be getting a voucher for Almack's?'

He gave a dry laugh. 'Not likely.' The London Season was not a good time for his family.

She gazed into the fire. 'Why not? I thought you were high born.'

He sat up straight again. 'Why did you think that?'

'You said your father went to school with Lord Tinmore's son.'

He had said that.

'I am high born.' But he'd been deliberately evasive about who he was. Now that they were to spend the night together, she might as well know. 'You have likely heard of Viscount Northdon?'

She looked blank. 'No.'

She must be the one person in England who had not heard of Viscount Northdon. 'You see, Miss Summerfield, I come from a family with a tarnished reputation. Viscount Northdon is my father and, because he married my mother, our family is not accepted in the highest circles of society.'

He expected to see curiosity in her expression. Instead, he saw sympathy.

It touched him more deeply than he was willing to admit and made him go on. 'My mother is French and came from trade.' It pained him to say the rest. 'But that is not the worst of it. Her father became active in the Ter-

ror.' He cleared his throat. 'Hence we are not welcome at
Almack's.'

She lowered her gaze and spoke in a quiet voice. 'It is
likely our family will not receive vouchers to Almack's,
either, even if Lord Tinmore wishes it.' She raised her eyes
to him. 'I, too, have a scandalous mother.'

'I have heard of your mother,' he admitted. He'd also
heard she'd abandoned her husband and children to run
away with one of her lovers.

Pain filled Miss Summerfield's eyes. 'I suppose everyone has heard of our mother.' She pulled her knees up so
that her feet rested on the chair's seat. 'I expect they will
stare wherever we go. And whisper—'

He knew firsthand she was correct. 'Lord Tinmore's
reputation will ease matters for you.'

'Yes.' Her expression filled with resolve. 'Lord Tinmore
will do much for us.'

He could reassure her even more. 'Your sister will be
seen as having made a brilliant match. No reason you cannot do the same.' Especially with her face and her figure.

'I do not want to wish to make a brilliant match,' she
snapped. 'My parents made a brilliant match and look
what happened to them.'

And look what happened to his parents for making such
an unwise one.

She rested her chin on her knees. 'I do not care about
titles or position. I want to marry someone who will love
me for myself and who will not care what members of my
family have done.'

'Love?' His parents had married for love. Or at least
for the physical desire that so often masquerades as love.
'Better to make a marriage of mutual advantage.'

'My parents married for advantage,' she said. 'Believe
me, it does not work.'

Such a marriage had a better chance than one made out of love. Love led to rash acts and later regrets.

And constant discord.

'What say you of your sister's marriage, then?' The woman had not married the man out of passion, that was for certain.

She uncurled herself and leaned towards him. 'What can you know about my sister's marriage?'

'I can guess she thought it to her advantage to marry Lord Tinmore.' Why Tinmore might have married her was not a topic for the ears of a young lady.

'That she married him for his money, do you mean?' Her voice rose.

'Of course she married for money. And a title. And Lord Tinmore gained a young wife and a reason to emerge from seclusion. There is no shame in any of that.'

She settled back in her chair and crossed her arms over her chest. 'Lorene had no wish for a title or wealth any more than I do.'

That he very much doubted. 'Then what were her reasons?'

The pain returned to Miss Summerfield's eyes. 'She did it for us. For me and for Genna. And even Edmund. So we—so we could have a chance for decent, happy lives. So Genna and I could have dowries. So we could marry as we wish. And—and not be forced to accept just any offer. So we would not have to become lady's companions or governesses.' She took a breath. 'I assure you, Lorene married Lord Tinmore for the noblest of reasons.'

'Your situation was that dire?' he asked quietly.

She nodded.

'Then I commend your sister even more. I wish her well.' He'd sacrifice for his sister, if he could.

Her brows knitted. 'I fear she will be miserable.' Her

chin set. 'That is why I am determined that I should make a love match and be happy. For my sister.'

He peered at her. 'You would allow your heart to rule your choice?'

'I would insist upon it.'

He tapped his temple. 'Better to use your head, Miss Summerfield.'

She lifted her chin. 'How can you know? You are not married, are you?'

'Married? No.' But he did speak from experience.

When his father had embarked on his Grand Tour as a young man, he met Marc's mother and eloped with her. They continued his tour for a passionate year, but their wedded bliss ended almost immediately when they set foot back on English soil.

'Believe me, Miss Summerfield. A marriage is best contracted by one's brain, not one's heart.' Or one's loins.

She leaned back in her chair again. 'Then I pity the woman who becomes your wife.'

He shrugged. 'On the contrary. She is like-minded.'

She blinked. 'You are betrothed?'

'No.' He rose and put the last of their lumps of coal on the fire. 'But we have an understanding. She is the main reason I am bound for London.'

It ought not to bother Tess that there was a woman he planned to marry. It should not bother her that she might see the woman on his arm in London. Or dancing with him at a ball. She had dreams of dancing with Mr Welton, did she not?

But somehow it would have been a comfort to meet him in London without a woman in tow and to pretend they did not have a huge secret between them.

'Are you certain this woman will marry you, simply

because you offer her—what? That you are a viscount's son?' she asked him.

He shifted in his chair. 'I am heir to the title, not that I ever wished to be.'

'Why would you not wish for the title?' Both their father and Edmund would have been greatly gratified if Edmund had been the legitimate son and heir.

In fact, their father should have married Edmund's mother. She had been the woman he loved.

Mr Glenville turned his blue eyes on her. Grieving blue eyes. 'My brother had to die. Believe me, I would rather have my brother back than a thousand titles.'

She reached over and touched his arm. 'I am so sorry,' she said truthfully. 'It is a terrible thing to earn a title. Someone must always die.'

He smiled, a sad smile. 'Not always. One can earn a title from winning a war, like the Duke of Wellington.'

His smile made her insides flutter. She glanced back to the fire. 'You do not worry that this woman you wish to marry would marry you merely because you will be a viscount someday?'

'Mind?' His smile remained. 'That is what I have to offer. A title. Wealth. Why should she not want those things?'

A title did not keep a man from becoming a bitter person. Wealth could be fleeting, as well she knew.

'Why should you want her, then?' she asked. 'What advantage does she offer you?'

His expression sobered. 'She is the sister of a good friend. We've known each other since childhood. Her family is extremely respectable and that will do much to erase the damage my parents' reputations have done.'

'You will marry her for her family's reputation?' Was that not like marrying for social connections? Her father

had married her mother for her social connections, all of
which disappeared when she ran off with another man.

He gazed at her with understanding. 'Perhaps you and
your sisters never suffered the stigma of your mother's
scandals.'

She glanced away again. 'Our father never took us to
London.' There were, though, a few ladies around Yardney
who whispered when they were in view and a few gentlemen who'd spoken—rudely.

He added, 'You will benefit from Lord Tinmore's reputation in London, no doubt.'

She turned to him. 'I do understand that. Without Tinmore's wealth and reputation, we should be invited nowhere. But that does not mean that I would accept an offer
of marriage from a man for whom I do not feel great regard.'

'I feel regard for my intended bride, but I will not let
emotions dictate my choices.'

'You like her, then?' she asked.

He nodded. 'I like her well enough.'

Well enough. She was beginning to feel very sorry for
his intended. 'But you do not love her?'

He gazed at her and the firelight made his eyes even
more intense. 'Are you asking if I have a passion for her?
If my mind goes blank and my tongue becomes tied when
I am with her? The answer is no.' He turned back to the
fire. 'But I like her well enough.'

Perhaps if Tess's father had loved their mother, she
would not have sought lovers. Perhaps if her mother had
loved her father, he would have indulged her and flattered
her and cosseted her as she wished. Tess and her sisters
had discussed this many times.

'I hope you learn to love her,' Tess told Mr Glenville.
'I hope she loves you.'

His expression remained implacable.

She adjusted her blankets and stared into the fire. The chair felt hard and the wind found its way inside. The fire was losing its battle to keep the place warm.

They were silent for a while until Mr Glenville spoke. 'How old are you, Miss Summerfield?'

'I am two and twenty.'

His brows rose. 'And your sister, Lady Tinmore?'

'She is five and twenty.'

He peered at her. 'In your twenties and you have had no suitors? That is hard to believe.'

She straightened. 'I did not say we had no suitors. Our situation has not been such that those suitors could make an offer. We had no dowries.'

'Your father did not provide you and your sisters with dowries?' he asked.

If he'd heard of their mother, surely he could guess. Their father did not believe they were his daughters.

But she would not speak that out loud. 'Our father was fond of making risky investments. He wanted to be fabulously wealthy so our mother would regret leaving him, but his investments were terrible ones. He used the last of his funds—our dowries—to purchase a commission for Edmund.'

'Edmund is your father's illegitimate son?'

So he also knew that part of her family story, as well.

'Yes.' She added, 'Our half-brother.'

She and her sisters likely shared no blood with Edmund. The sisters shared a mother. He came from their father.

She went on. 'I do not disagree with you that one needs some fortune and reputation in order to make a good match. Lorene has given us this, but wealth and reputation are not enough for a marriage. It is love that is the answer. Love can get one over the inevitable hurdles of life.'

'Now you are sounding philosophic. There are some hurdles that mere emotion can't jump over.' He peered at her. 'Do you have a suitor?'

She felt her face grow red.

He frowned. 'You have a suitor. A man who would not court you because you had no dowry.'

She flushed with anger this time. 'Perhaps I do have such a suitor. Perhaps that is why I say the things I do.'

He threw off his blanket and stood. 'I am going to check on Apollo.' Before he reached the door he turned back to her. 'I hope it all works for you, Miss Summerfield. But before you make that final vow with your suitor, think with your head and forget your heart.'

She wanted to snap back at him, but his tone disturbed her. And what he said was true. Mr Welton could not court her when she had no dowry, but that did not mean his heart could not be engaged.

Did it?

He opened the door and the wind rushed in. The temperature dropped even lower in just that brief moment. Tess forgot about dowries or love matches or reputations. The air was freezing and they'd put the last of the coal on the fire. How would they stay warm through the night?

'I'll look for more firewood,' Mr Glenville said, as if reading her mind. 'What we have won't last the night.'

Chapter Four

Ice crunched under Marc's bare feet as he crossed the yard to the stable. His feet ached from the cold as he tended to Apollo. Why could he not have been stranded in June instead of February?

It was not only the icy cold that disturbed him. His conversation with Miss Summerfield did, as well.

It cut too close. All this talk of marriage. Love.

His parents had fallen in love and where had it led them? To shouting, accusations, recriminations, declarations that they wished they'd never set eyes on each other. They'd ruined their lives, he'd heard over and over.

Then there was Lucien and Charles. Where had love led his brother and his friend?

No falling in love for him. He'd control such runaway emotions.

'That is the sensible way, eh, Apollo?'

His horse snorted in reply and Marc leaned his face against Apollo's warm neck. He found another blanket to help keep Apollo warm and tried not to think of the icy hammers pounding on his feet.

'We'll be on our way in the morning,' Marc murmured. 'Stay steady, old fellow.'

He searched the stable for scraps of wood to burn and found a few pieces to add to the fire. They would burn quickly, though. He and Miss Summerfield were headed for a very cold night, he knew from experience. He'd spent many a cold night in the French countryside, hiding from men whose suspicions about him had been aroused.

Gritting his teeth, he crossed the icy mud again and entered the cabin. She was crouched by the fire, pouring water from the kettle into the teapot.

'I found some wood.' Not enough wood, though. He dropped it by the fireplace, coming close to her.

She looked up at him. 'I thought you might like more tea. It will be even weaker than before, but it might warm you.'

'Tea will be most welcome.'

Her eyes showed some distress. He wanted to touch her, ease her worry. Instead he moved away to hang his greatcoat on the line.

His feet hurt even worse as the blood rushed to them. He hurried back to his chair by the fire and wrapped his feet in the blanket.

'What is wrong?' she asked, gazing at his feet.

'Cold.' He rubbed his feet. 'I believe my wet boots will be preferable at this point.'

She rose and walked over to the clothes line. 'Your socks are fairly dry.' She brought them to him and knelt at his feet. 'I'll put them on for you.'

Her hands felt too soothing and his body came to life, precisely what he did not wish to feel.

'Perhaps this is not the thing for a lady to do,' he managed to protest.

She placed one sock on his foot. 'It is so little, after what you have done for me.'

At least now he felt warmer. He endured the pleasure

of her slipping the second sock on the other foot, gazing down at her as she worked it over his heel. Her hair was in a plait down her back, but tendrils escaped to frame her lovely face.

She was a woman a man could lose his head over. For once he wished he could be like his father had been— blinded by passion and unaware of the disaster ahead of him.

But his eyes were open.

She wrapped his feet in a blanket again and moved away to pour their weak, but hot, tea.

Take care in London, he wanted to tell her. There were men who knew how to play upon a young woman's heart. Love came in many disguises, some even more hurtful than the pain his parents inflicted on each other.

Perhaps he could watch out for her. Perhaps he could warn her away from the worst dangers of love.

No. He needed to stay away from her. She tempted him too much.

She handed him his jug. 'Such as it is.'

He nodded thanks.

She sat in her chair and they sipped the hot liquid that only retained the barest hint of tea. The fire dwindled to embers, but Marc held off on placing the last of their wood on it. He glanced around the room and wondered if he ought to try to break up the furniture.

It seemed an extreme measure and greatly unfair to the owner of the cottage.

Miss Summerfield yawned and curled up in her chair.

He reached over and touched her arm. 'You should lie on the cot and get some sleep. I'll move it closer to the fire.'

'Where will you sleep?' she murmured.

He shrugged. 'The chair will do.' He'd slept in worse places.

The wind found its way through the walls of the cabin. Miss Summerfield shivered. 'It is cold.'

And it would get colder. 'You'll be warmer on the cot.'

She did as he asked and she was soon tucked in under her blanket as close to the fireplace as he could place the bed.

He watched her as she slept and shivered as the temperature dropped even further and the fire consumed the wood. He scavenged the cabin and found a few more lumps of coal, but the room was very, very cold.

She woke, shivering, but not complaining.

There was only one way he could think of to keep her warm now, but it was a proposition that no young lady should accept. It was also a thought that consumed him much too often.

She rolled over and gazed at him. 'You should take a turn on th-the cot. You must be colder than I am.'

'I'm not going to trade places with you, Miss Summerfield.'

She got up and carried her blanket over to her chair. 'I'll sit here, then.'

He raised his voice. 'Get in the cot.'

She looked at him in defiance. 'No. It is your turn.'

'Do not be a damned fool, Miss Summerfield. Get in the cot.' There was no sense in them both sitting up all night, shivering.

She glared at him. 'The only way I'll get in that cot is if you are in it, too.'

The cold was addling her brain, he thought. But this was the answer, the consuming thought. He should not take advantage of it, but, if he did they'd both be warm.

'Very well.' He inclined his head towards the cot. 'Get in the bed and I will join you.'

An anxious look crossed her face and she hesitated,

but she carried her blanket over to the cot and lay down, facing the fire. He covered her with another blanket and crawled underneath it.

'Our bodies will warm each other,' he murmured in her ear. 'Do not fear. This is for warmth and nothing else.'

He hoped he could keep that promise.

Exhaustion helped where desire refused to waver. Even though she was warm and soft against him, the comfort of her had made him fall asleep almost immediately. He did not even wake to feed the fire the last lumps of coal. He knew nothing until the sound of muffled voices reached his ear.

The latch of the door rattled.

The worst had happened. They were discovered.

'Miss Summerfield!' He shook her, but had only time enough to bound from the cot when the door burst open.

'Halloo there!' a man cried.

Miss Summerfield sat up.

'I say,' said the man, a gentleman by appearance. 'What goes here?'

He entered the cabin followed by two men in work-men's dress.

'Is that you, Miss Summerfield?' the gentleman asked.

Marc took charge. 'Who are you?' he demanded.

Miss Summerfield covered herself with the blanket.

'I am Lord Attison,' the gentleman said indignantly. 'And, more to the purpose, who are you?'

Miss Summerfield answered before Marc could speak, 'He is Mr Glenville, sir. Allow us to explain.'

Marc put a stilling hand on her arm. 'First he must explain why he barges in without so much as a knock.' Put him on the defensive.

Lord Attison shot daggers at Marc. 'I was sent to find

Miss Summerfield.' He turned to her. 'You have caused
Lord Tinmore much worry, young lady, do you realise
that?'

Marc stepped between Miss Summerfield and Lord Attison. 'Do you have some authority here?'

Miss Summerfield answered, 'He is one of Lord Tinmore's guests.'

'Well,' Marc spoke sharply, 'you may tell Lord Tinmore
that it is a fine thing to let this young lady nearly freeze to
death. You should have come earlier.'

Lord Attison stuck out his chest. 'And you should have
returned her home, sir.' His gaze shifted to Miss Summerfield. 'Or would that have ruined your little tryst?'

'You have it wrong—' Miss Summerfield protested.

Marc seized Lord Attison's arm and marched him to
the door. 'We will discuss this outside and allow this lady
to dress.'

Once all the men were outside, Marc used his size to
be as intimidating as possible to the smaller Lord Attison.
'You will make no assumptions here, do you comprehend?
This lady has been through enough without your salacious
comments.'

'Lord Tinmore—' the man started to say.

Marc interrupted him. 'I will explain to Lord Tinmore
and to no one else. And, you, sir, will say nothing of this
until you are instructed by your host. Is that understood?'

Possibly, just possibly Lord Tinmore would have sufficient power and influence to allow this incident to blow
over without any damage to Miss Summerfield.

Or himself.

The cold of the morning finally hit him and it took all
Marc's strength to keep from dissolving into a quivering mess in front of this man. He wore only his shirt and
breeches.

And his socks, now damp from the frost on the ground.

Attison looked him up and down. 'Being undressed in front of an innocent young lady—' The man smirked. 'Or is she an innocent?'

Marc seized him again. 'Silence that tongue!'

Attison's eyes flashed with alarm, but he quickly recovered and pursed his lips. 'I will leave you to Lord Tinmore, as you wish.'

Marc released him and turned to the other two men. 'Do you know who owns this cabin?'

One man nodded. 'Lord Tinmore. It is a groundskeeper's cabin.'

'Are we on Lord Tinmore's property?' How close were they to the house?

'We are, sir,' the other man answered. He gestured to the south.

Against the milky-white sky rose a huge Elizabethan house with dozens of windows and three turrets adorning its roof.

They had been that close.

'The roads and bridges were flooded yesterday,' he said.

One of the men nodded. 'The water receded overnight.'

Miss Summerfield opened the door, glancing warily at their three early morning visitors. 'Mr Glenville, may I see you for a moment?'

Attison made a move to speak, but Marc silenced him with a steely glare.

He entered the cabin and closed the door.

'I have no laces,' she said to him, presenting her back.

'I cut them.' He looked around the room and found her packet of ribbons and lace. He pulled a long ribbon from the still-damp package and started lacing it through the eyelets on her corset and her dress.

'What do we do now?' she asked, her voice cracking.

He worked the laces. 'We tell what happened.'

'You will speak to Lord Tinmore?'

He tied the ribbon in a bow. 'I will speak to him. It turns out we are close to Tinmore Hall.' He turned her to face him. 'It is important that we make no apology, Miss Summerfield. We did what we needed to do to get through the storm. We did nothing wrong.'

Her jaw set. 'No apologies.'

At least she had fortitude.

He grabbed his waistcoat and coat and quickly put them on. He shoved his feet into his boots. 'We must leave now.'

She nodded.

They opened the door and walked out into the cold morning air.

Within an hour Marc and Miss Summerfield stood in front of a wizened old man in spectacles who nonetheless had a commanding bearing.

From his large wing-back chair, he glared at Miss Summerfield. 'You have caused your sister great worry, young lady.'

'It was quite unintended, sir.' At least she kept her voice strong.

Lord Tinmore, old and wrinkled, wielded his cane like a sceptre, obviously accustomed to authority.

Marc spoke up. 'We may dispense with this matter quickly if you will listen to what we have to say.' Men of strength usually respected strength.

Lord Tinmore glared at him over his spectacles. 'I want your name, sir.'

Marc bowed. 'Glenville.'

Tinmore tapped his temple. 'Glenville?'

'My father is Viscount Northdon. He was a schoolmate of your son's.' Maybe that connection would help them.

Pain edged the man's eyes, but the look vanished quickly. 'Northdon,' he scoffed. 'I know of him.'

Of course. Everyone, except perhaps Miss Summerfield, knew of his father.

Tinmore scowled at him.

Marc continued. 'Sir. Who I am, who my father is, has no bearing on this matter. I found Miss Summerfield near freezing in the storm. We took shelter in the cabin and it was impossible to leave until morning.'

'That is the truth!' Miss Summerfield added, with a bit too much emotion.

Tinmore's attention swung to her. 'The truth! The truth is you went gallivanting around the countryside without a chaperone, in bad weather, and wound up spending the night with a man!'

'We had no choice,' Miss Summerfield protested, still shivering and wrapping her arms around herself to try to stay warm.

Tinmore wagged a finger at her. 'You are a reckless scapegrace, girl! A discredit to your sister! And to me!'

'Enough!' Marc shouted. 'Miss Summerfield is still cold. And hungry. She needs dry clothing and food, not an undeserved scolding.'

'Do not dictate to me, young man!' Tinmore countered.

Marc glared at him. 'Give her leave to change into warm, dry clothes.'

Lord Tinmore glared back, but Marc refused to waver.

Marc lowered his voice to a firm, dangerous tone. 'Let her go.'

'Oh, very well.' Tinmore waved a hand at Miss Summerfield. 'Leave now, girl. But I am not finished with you.'

Miss Summerfield curtsied and started for the door. Before she reached it, she turned back. 'My lord, Mr Glenville is also cold and hungry—'

Tinmore snapped at her, 'I told you to leave. Do as I say.'

She did not move. 'That is little thanks for what he has done, sir. You could find him dry clothing.'

'Leave!' Tinmore shouted.

She remained where she was.

Marc spoke to her in a soothing tone. 'Do not fret over me, Miss Summerfield. Go now. Change into warm clothes. Eat something.'

She nodded and went out the door.

He turned back to Tinmore. 'That was poorly done of you, sir. She has been through an ordeal.'

Tinmore's eyes nearly popped out of his head. 'I'm out of patience with her. She caused her sister much worry and now more scandal. I will not have scandal in my house.'

Did this man not have any heart? 'She might have lost her life if I had not found her.'

He pursed his lips. 'Would have served her right.'

By God, would he have preferred her to die? 'She needs your help, sir. You have the power to stop any talk. If you stand by her, who would question it?'

'Much you know, Glenville.' Tinmore took off his spectacles and wiped them with a handkerchief. 'Attison is a scandalmonger of the first rate. There is no stopping him.'

'You invited him. And sent him on the search. You are more responsible for any scandal that results than Miss Summerfield. She should not have to pay.'

'Yes, I invited him!' Tinmore cried. 'So he could see firsthand that I am not in my dotage and that my wife is not a fortune hunter who duped me into marriage.'

Was he surprised that was what people would think?

'This chit has made everything worse. I suppose you know what people say about their mother?' He grimaced.

'If she thinks I'm still giving her a Season and providing her a dowry, she has another think coming.'

He would cut her off? 'You are being unfair.'

'It is my money to spend as I wish.' He fixed his gaze on Marc again. 'You are the one who wronged her, not me.'

Marc had not wronged her. He'd rescued her and kept her safe. But Tinmore was right about one thing. None of that would matter in the eyes of polite society, not if Tinmore refused to stand by her.

'If you will not protect her, I will.' Marc stepped closer to the man and glared down at him. 'I will marry her. That will silence the gossip. And she will need nothing from you.'

Tinmore's mouth quirked into a fleeting smile, but his scowl returned and he waved a hand. 'Marry her, then. Get her out of my sight.'

Marc stood in the hallway, outside the closed door of the private sitting room where Lord Tinmore presumably still sat in his throne-like chair.

He should be on his way to London, not offering marriage, but he'd had no choice, had he? It had been his duty.

The honourable thing to do.

Of all the reasons to marry, this must be the most foolish. Not out of passion. Not a love match. Not a well-considered decision.

So much for his pragmatic choice of marrying Doria. So much for paying the debt he owed to Charles. No comfortable life for him. Lost was the serenity marriage to Doria would offer. Lost was the respectability of her family. He, the son of the scandalous Lord and Lady Northdon, would marry the daughter of scandalous Sir Hollis and Lady Summerfield.

Tongues would wag.

He would not save her from gossip, after all. Perhaps he'd not done her so large a favour.

He must find her. Speak to her. Tell her what he'd done.

She needed to make the choice. The discredit of marrying him or the ruin of crying off.

But, if Tinmore made good his threat, she would also be impoverished.

A footman approached him. 'I am to show you to your room, sir.'

'Never mind my room,' he responded. 'I need to speak to Miss Tess Summerfield.'

The man's eyes widened in alarm. 'I cannot take you to Miss Summerfield.'

'Deliver a message to her for me, then.'

The footman shook his head. 'I do not think Lord Tinmore would approve.'

Marc gestured for him to lead the way. 'Lord Tinmore will not mind. The lady and I are going to be married.'

Tess sat in Genna's bedchamber again, like she had done only the day before, her two sisters with her.

It seemed an age ago.

Genna and Lorene had been waiting for her outside Lord Tinmore's drawing room. They'd hugged and cried and Lorene scolded her for giving them such a fright. While they walked to her bedchamber she filled them in on what had happened to her.

In her room a bath awaited. Tess bathed and washed her hair quickly, before dressing in warm, dry clothes. Hot porridge, bread, cheese and tea were set before her and the mere scent of it made her stomach ache with hunger.

Her mind, though, was on Mr Glenville. Would he convince Lord Tinmore that nothing happened between

them? Would Tinmore let him go? The whole experience had become like a dream. Would it fade from her
memory?

She did not want to forget him.

The maids came to remove the bath and straighten the
room. Tess and her sisters retired to Genna's room and her
sisters' relief at finding her safe had worn off.

'Tess, how could you have been so foolish?' Lorene
paced, as she had paced the previous morning. 'It is one
thing to seek shelter. Quite another to share a bed with a
man.'

'It was cold,' Tess explained. She remembered Mr Glenville climbing on to the cot, covering them both with his
blanket. She remembered the warmth of his body next to
hers, both comforting and thrilling.

'Do you know what the guests are saying?' Genna
offered. 'They are saying you met by design. That you
planned the tryst. Why else would you venture out on an
obviously rainy day?'

Lord Attison must have been very busy telling tales.

'That is ridiculous!' Tess cried. 'I told you how it happened. I never even met Mr Glenville before!'

'You might have met him some other time.' Genna settled herself on the window seat. 'You are known to take
walks alone.'

Tess glared at her. 'Are you doubting my word, Genna?
I went to the village to shop.'

Not to the nearby village, though. To Yardney. To see
Mr Welton, had he been there.

'No.' Genna spoke as if this were some interesting problem happening to someone else. 'But you did not bring any
lace or ribbon, did you?'

The lace and ribbon. She'd forgotten her parcel. 'I left
the parcel at the cabin. We could send someone for it.'

'It would not matter. What really happened does not matter.' Lorene still paced. 'Appearances. That is what matters.' She shook her head. 'I do not know what Lord Tinmore will do. This is such a trial for him and it has already put a strain on the house party.'

'A trial for him? A strain on the house party?' Tess rose off the bed. 'Goodness, Lorene. I did not choose to have this happen. I simply walked to the village and became caught in a horrible storm. Perhaps I should have tried to cross the bridge or continued down the roads even though water was rushing over both. Then I would have drowned. Or perhaps Mr Glenville should have left me on the road to freeze to death. Either way would have been so much less trouble for Lord Tinmore!'

Lorene grabbed Tess and hugged her. 'Do not say that. Never say that. That is what we all thought happened to you.'

Tess hugged her back. 'I had hoped you'd think I stayed in the village.'

There was a knock at the door and a maid stuck her head in. 'Pardon, my lady, but his lordship wishes to speak with Miss Summerfield immediately. In the library.'

Lorene released her. 'You must go.' She turned to the maid. 'Tell Lord Tinmore she will be there directly.'

The maid rushed off.

'I will accompany you,' Lorene said.

Genna rose from the window seat. 'I will come, too.'

'No.' Tess held them back with her arm. 'It is best you stay out of it.' Lord Tinmore would only become upset with them because of her.

Genna sat again and looked sulky. 'Well, you had better come back right away and tell us all about it.'

'I will walk with you, at least,' Lorene said.

As they walked the distance to Lord Tinmore's private

sitting room, Tess tried to quiet her nerves. Would Mr Glenville still be there? Goodness, she hoped Lord Tinmore allowed him to dress in dry clothing and get something to eat.

Had he been able to convince Lord Tinmore to let the incident pass? She hoped so. She prayed so.

'Tinmore is a reasonable man,' Lorene said when they entered the long hallway leading to his private rooms.

Lord Tinmore had seemed fairly unreasonable to Tess. Unlike Glenville, who had come to her defence.

At the stairs, a footman approached and handed Tess a piece of paper. 'A message for you, miss.' He glanced warily at Lorene, the new lady of the house, and hurried away.

Tess unfolded the paper and read the note. 'It is from Mr Glenville. He wishes to speak with me right away.' She folded the paper again and put it in a pocket. 'I should see him first.'

She turned around, but Lorene seized her arm. 'You cannot see Mr Glenville!'

'Why not?' She tried to pull away. 'He is waiting in the morning room. I can see him there.'

'No!' Lorene cried. 'You must attend Lord Tinmore first!' She pulled her along to Lord Tinmore's sitting room. Another footman stood at the door and opened it when they approached.

'Go to him.' Lorene gave her a little push.

Tess entered the room.

Lord Tinmore was alone, seated in the same chair where he had been before. His demeanour had not softened.

Tess curtsied. 'You asked to see me, my lord.'

His lips pursed. 'I trust you are comfortable now.'

'I am, sir. Thank you.' She remembered what Glenville had said. Make no apologies. They had done nothing wrong. 'I hope you allowed the same courtesy to my rescuer.'

'You need not concern yourself with Mr Glenville,' Tinmore snapped.

She straightened her spine.

He frowned. 'You have created a great deal of trouble for yourself, for my wife and for your younger sister.'

She looked him directly in the face. 'The rain caused a great deal of trouble for me. I was in danger and a gentleman rescued me. Surely you can make something sensible of that without a great deal of trouble.'

'Such as what?' He stiffened in his chair.

'Such as nothing.' Her heart pounded. Perhaps he could be convinced. 'Declare Mr Glenville a hero and allow him to go on his way.'

'A hero?' His expression turned shrewd. 'You seem immoderately concerned about Mr Glenville.'

Her hopes were shaken. 'Do not try to make something of that, sir. He saved my life and I am not so much a simpleton as to miss the fact that you are trying to punish him for it.'

'Punish him?' Lord Tinmore's rheumy eyes flashed. 'He was caught in bed with you. That cannot be ignored.'

'It can be ignored if you wish it,' she shot back. 'The world will believe what you, sir, wish it to believe.'

He stared at her before continuing. 'You have bedded a man and been caught at it. At least your paramour understands you must pay the consequences.'

Her heart pounded. 'What do you mean?'

'He will marry you.'

'No!' she cried. 'He will not.'

He half-rose from his chair. 'He will and that is that.'

Fear exploded inside her, but she could not allow it to show. Instead she moved closer to him and leaned down into his face. 'You know, sir,' she said in a low voice. 'You know that Mr Glenville and I did nothing wrong, nothing to truly compromise me. You know he rescued me. Saved my life. You know all you have to do is tell your friends the truth. Tell everyone the truth.'

'No.' He sat back in his chair. 'Glenville said he'd marry you and that will resolve matters nicely, with the minimum of scandal tainting my marriage.'

'Your marriage? Why should what happened to me taint your marriage?' she countered.

'It adds scandal to my wife's name,' he said. 'Your mother and father's carnal excesses are bad enough. I'll not tolerate more...' He shook his head. 'Stranded in a storm! Hmmph!'

She glared at him. 'You know it is true, sir.'

He waved her words away. 'You will marry Glenville and that is the final word.'

Her insides felt shredded, but she made herself lift her chin. 'What has Mr Glenville to say to this?'

Tinmore's mouth moved against his gums, an old man's gesture. 'Mr Glenville knows his duty. He made the offer.'

'No.' Her entire body began to shake. 'He does not wish to marry me. I cannot marry a man who does not wish to marry me.'

'He may not wish it.' Lord Tinmore smirked. 'But he'll do it. As will you.'

'You cannot force this marriage on him. Or on me!' she cried.

'Glenville made the offer. It is up to you to accept or not.' He leaned forward. 'But understand this. For you there will be no dowry, no Season.'

His words were a blow.

She swallowed the pain. And loss.

She lifted her chin. 'If you choose to break your bargain with my sister, it is no concern of mine.'

He worked his mouth as if unable to form words.

He finally spoke. 'If you do not marry Mr Glenville, I will also withdraw all funds and support from your sister Genna and your by-blow of a brother. Your sister will not have a dowry and your brother will not see a penny of mine.'

She felt the blood drain from her face. 'You would not be so cruel.'

He stared her directly in the eye. 'You will marry Mr Glenville after all, will you not?'

She fixed her gaze on Lord Tinmore and would not allow her voice to show her utter defeat. 'For my sisters' and brother's sakes, I have no choice. I will marry Mr Glenville.'

'Excellent!' Lord Tinmore clapped. 'Tomorrow I will send you with him to London in my carriage.'

'Tomorrow!'

'I want you out of sight of my guests. Once they know you are to be married, the talk will disappear. By the time I bring my wife and your younger sister to London, all will be forgotten.'

He was sending her away. She'd already lost so much. Her mother. Her father. Her home. Now she was to lose her sisters, as well.

And to be married to a man who would undoubtedly resent her and detest having been trapped into marriage with her.

As soon as Tess left Tinmore, she hurried to the morning room, but Mr Glenville was not there. If only she could speak with him. There must be some way out of this.

She waited there an hour, pacing back and forth. Finally

a footman opened the door and told her Lord Tinmore wished her to return to her room. She was not to come to dinner with her sisters and the house-party guests. She was expected to remain in her room.

And she was forbidden to seek out Mr Glenville.

Chapter Five

The next morning, Tess walked through the cavernous house, her sisters at her side. They made their way to the front door where Lord Tinmore's carriage and Mr Glenville would await her. One of the Tinmore maids, whom she did not know, was to accompany her to London, but return with the carriage.

Lorene had been scolding her every step of the way. 'I gave you the chance to choose who to marry and look what you do.'

Perhaps it was too much to hope that her sister would take her part against her husband.

Tess was beyond defending herself, in any event. She was sick with grief and trepidation. This was the very worst way to be married. Not out of love. Not even for status or financial gain. Mr Glenville was forced to marry her because he'd rescued her in the rain and taken her to a cabin to keep warm and dry.

If only she had been able to talk with him. Why had he not waited for her in the morning room?

Tess could not believe she would walk through Tinmore Hall's great door into a new life among people she did not know, in a place she'd never been before.

Genna had been in tears the whole morning. 'Why do you have to leave now?' She sniffed. 'Why can you not come to London when we go there?'

'It is better this way.' Tess was determined that her sisters not know how devastated she felt. 'Besides, I will see you in London in just a few weeks.' Although she had no assurances that Lord Tinmore would allow it. He might forbid her to call. Her sisters might be totally lost to her, as well.

Lorene had been so wrong about the reclusive earl. He was not reasonable. Nor benevolent. He went back on promises and wielded his power in the cruellest possible way. He had better not treat Lorene with cruelty or Tess would—

What could she do?

Nothing.

'You were supposed to marry happily,' Lorene went on. 'Now what was the use of my—my—' She could not say the words, but Tess knew—they all knew—what she meant.

They reached the hall. The arsenal of swords and pikes and other weapons hung on the wall surrounding the door seemed like a harbinger of pain and destruction.

She turned to Lorene. 'I will do very well, Lorene. I will be a viscountess some day. How grand will that be?'

'You will become like Mama,' Lorene rasped through her tears. 'You will be unhappy.'

She hugged Lorene. 'Do not concern yourself about me.'

Lorene held on to her. 'I meant something so different for you. A London Season. A chance to meet many fine young men, a chance to find your own true love.'

'I will still be there for the Season, will I not?' She pasted on a smile. 'Genna will have more fine young men to fall in love with her this way.'

'Do not look to me.' Genna wiped her eyes. 'I wanted nothing to do with this.' She turned to Lorene. 'This is your fault, you know. None of this would have happened if you had not married, Lorene.'

'I did it for you.' Lorene burst into tears. 'For both of you.'

'Stop. Stop.' Tess could not bear this. 'We must not fight and, for heaven's sake, do not cry. I will be fine. Mr Glenville is not a bad man. He rescued me, did he not? His proposal of marriage was honourable, was it not? I will do very well, I am sure.'

She hoped she convinced them, because she was having a great deal of difficulty convincing herself that all would be well.

The huge front door opened and a footman stepped in. 'The carriage is awaiting you, miss.'

Tess's heart jumped into her throat. 'I must leave.'

Her sisters followed her outside.

Tess looked past the carriage to the man on horseback— Mr Glenville astride his horse. Apollo.

'Is that him?' Genna asked.

His face was shaded by his hat and he sat stiffly in his saddle. What had Lord Tinmore threatened him with to make him offer to marry a woman he did not even know?

'Yes, that is Mr Glenville,' she responded.

Genna sniffed. 'Well, at least he is not fat.'

Nor ugly, Tess thought. On the contrary, he was handsome and tall and strong, and when his blue eyes fixed on her, something stirred deep inside her.

But he did not love her. How could he?

He had already selected his intended bride, a woman who could be an advantage to him, a woman who had the one thing Tess could never give him—a family reputation free from scandal.

He nodded to her and her cheeks burned. She hugged her sisters one last time before allowing the footman to assist her into the coach.

Marc followed the carriage, his mood nothing but dark. Anger seethed inside him. Anger at Lord Tinmore. Anger at Miss Summerfield's sister for marrying such a man.

Anger at himself for not waking before dawn and making certain he and Miss Summerfield were not discovered. Even more, he should have known better than to share her bed, even if he'd done nothing but warm her.

He'd waited as long as he could in the morning room where he'd been served his food, but she had not come. Eventually an elderly butler arrived and insisted he leave.

Not that it would have made any difference, although he might have reassured her in some way.

Damned Tinmore. If the man had stated that he believed them, the scandal would have faded quickly. Instead he'd been unnecessarily cruel. Miss Summerfield did not deserve cruelty. All she'd done was walk to the village to shop. Good God. Shopping was his mother's primary entertainment. How could any woman be faulted for wanting to visit shops? Miss Summerfield had also misjudged the weather. Well, so had he.

They reached Yardney, the village Miss Summerfield had tried to reach in the storm, the village where she had purchased her ribbons. From his seat on Apollo's back, he could see her face peeking out of the carriage window, looking desolate.

Fate was a cruel jokester.

If she had shopped an hour longer or an hour less, maybe even minutes more or minutes less, she would not have been on the road during the storm and she would be free.

Instead she was trapped into marrying him.

* * *

At least the coachman kept up a good speed, considering the roads were not yet dry. This trip would take them at least three days. Apollo was accustomed to hard rides.

The carriage changed horses when necessary and Marc made certain they did not resume the journey until Apollo had rested. When they reached a coaching inn in Bourne, it was past noon and time they stopped long enough to eat a meal.

It would be his first chance to speak to her.

He handed over care of Apollo to one of the stable boys and walked over to help her from the coach.

'Thank you,' she said. She looked tense and fatigued.

'Miss Summerfield, will you dine with me?' he asked. She nodded.

A maid who'd seen the better part of her forties had accompanied her in the coach. The woman scowled and sniffed impatiently. 'Will you be needing my services, miss?' She spoke in an overly solicitous and distinctly unpleasant manner.

'No, Ivers,' Miss Summerfield replied in a tight voice. 'Please have a pleasant repast. Do—do you need any money?'

Did Miss Summerfield have any money? Marc wondered. Had Lord Tinmore cut her off that completely?

The maid lifted her nose. 'His lordship provided for me.' The woman marched away.

Miss Summerfield blew out a breath.

'Well, she is certainly unpleasant,' Marc said.

Miss Summerfield sighed. 'That is couching it in the mildest terms.'

Marc did not offer his arm, because he did not think she would wish to take it, but she walked next to him into the inn. The public room was not crowded.

The innkeeper greeted them.

'Do you have a private dining room?' Marc asked him.

'I do indeed, sir,' the man said. 'Follow me.'

He led them past other tables and chairs, some with diners, some not, through a short hallway to a private room. It had a window overlooking the yard and a small round table with four chairs.

The innkeeper took their meal orders. Tea for Miss Summerfield, ale for Marc and meat pie for them both.

When the innkeeper left, Marc pulled out a chair for Miss Summerfield. 'Does the room suit you? It seems comfortable enough.'

She sat. 'It is wonderful. That detestable maid is not here.'

'Why is she accompanying you?' He took a chair across from her.

'Lord Tinmore sent her to travel with me.' Her voice was stressed. 'I do not know her at all. She is not one of the maids I'd met before.'

'You'd not met her?' Tinmore made her take this journey with a stranger?

She pulled off her gloves. 'She is quite disapproving. I suppose she was treated to the most sordid version of our time together.'

'Why did Tinmore not allow your own maid to accompany you?' he asked.

She met his eye only briefly. 'I shared a maid with my sister and I would not ask her to leave her home for me.' She glanced away again. 'Had I been given a choice, I mean.'

Damned Tinmore. 'Do you want to be rid of this one?'

'It is useless for me to want anything,' she said.

Their food and drink arrived and he remembered the last meal they'd shared. Sodden bread and cheese and Toby jugs. That day seemed pleasant compared to their present situation.

She looked up at him. 'Why did you offer to marry me?'

Her blunt question took him aback, but he had to admire that she did not shrink from the topic.

'It was my duty,' he replied.

She closed her eyes and averted her face as if his words had been a blow.

He softened his voice. 'It was the only solution. We were caught in a compromising situation, after all.' And, of course, Tinmore threatened to banish her and leave her penniless. Did she know that? If not, he would not tell her.

Her eyes grew bright with tears. 'I am so sorry, Mr Glenville.'

He was seized with a strong impulse to enfold her in his arms and assure her all would be well. He wanted to kiss away her tears and make her forget any unhappiness she'd ever experienced—

Wait. This would never do. No woman had ever stirred him the way she had done. He needed to keep a clear head.

She took a breath and smiled wanly. 'Do you think perhaps if we had a long engagement everyone would forget about us and you could marry the woman you wanted to marry?'

Was that her worry? Odd. He'd not thought of Doria since he'd made his decision. 'I doubt Tinmore is the sort who would forget.' He drank his ale. 'What would he do to you if we did not marry?'

'It does not matter what he would do to me.' Angry tears glittered in her eyes. 'Lord Tinmore said he would cut off Genna and Edmund without a penny. He would go back on his promise to my sister. Likely he'd make her life even more miserable.' She swiped at her eyes and took a sip of tea.

'Damned Tinmore.'

She glanced at him in surprise.

He took another long sip of his drink. 'Let's be rid of him and his threats.' He leaned across the table towards her. 'What say you to sending away Tinmore's carriage and with it that vile woman he inflicted on you? We do not need his transportation to London. I will arrange something for you.'

Her eyes widened. 'You would do that?'

He grinned. 'With pleasure.'

Mr Glenville acted quickly. As soon as he finished eating, he discharged the maid and sent her and the carriage back to Tinmore Hall. They'd reach there before the end of the day.

Tess wished she could see Lord Tinmore's face when they arrived. She hoped he choked on his outrage.

She'd not expected Glenville to be so kind. Certainly he must resent this forced marriage, although he'd be too much of a gentleman to say so.

He'd never wanted a marriage with love, he'd said, so perhaps it did not matter to him as much. But he did wish for respectability and that was something already lost. How long would his kindness last, as a result? Would he not begin to resent her as her father had resented her mother?

He secured rooms in the inn and found a village girl who worked for the local seamstress, but was eager to improve her situation. She presented herself to Tess for Tess's approval.

'Good afternoon, miss.' The girl, a pert, curly-haired blonde, curtsied. 'I'm Nancy Peters. What would you like to know about me? I would so like to be a lady's maid, if you find me to your likin'.'

The girl was bright-eyed and fresh-faced and so very eager.

'Do you want to go to London, Miss Peters?' Tess asked.

The girl pressed her hands to her cheeks. 'It is Nancy, miss. I am not old enough to be Miss Peters. Sounds like you are speaking of my aunt. She's old. Thirty, I think.' She took a breath. 'But you want to know if I want to go to London?' Her eyes grew huge. 'My dream is to go to London!' Her expression changed again. 'But do you not want to know if I know how to care for your clothing? And to dress your hair?'

Tess almost smiled. 'Do you know those things?'

Nancy looked earnest. 'I have been sewing clothes for as long as I can remember. I know how to care for cloth.' She frowned. 'I know a little about hair, but I can learn. Surely I will learn much in London just by looking at the ladies. I have good references and I'm an honest girl, I promise.'

Nancy made it feel as if spring had come early. She was so fresh. So happy.

'I believe you will do very nicely, Nancy.'

She jumped up and down. 'Oh, thank you, miss! Thank you! I—I must tell my mother and pack. But may I do something for you now?'

'Nothing now. Take your time.'

The young girl curtsied, grinned and danced out of the room.

Mr Glenville knocked and poked his head in. He'd been standing outside the room. 'Will she do?'

'Yes,' Tess said. 'Thank you, Mr Glenville.'

He walked towards her. 'It is Marc, miss,' he said, mimicking the new maid's voice. 'I'm not old enough to be Mr Glenville.'

'Marc.' She smiled, but her smile fled. 'I suppose it is acceptable to use given names since we are betrothed.' She looked up at him. 'I am Tess.'

'Tess,' he repeated in a low voice. 'I believe I've found a coach for hire that should be available tomorrow. We can proceed then.'

She met his gaze again. 'I feel as if you have rescued me again.' A third time, really. Was his offer of marriage not another rescue? He could have ridden away and forgotten her. 'Nancy is as delightful as Ivers was unpleasant.'

'I dislike being under someone else's thumb,' he said in a low voice. 'And I'd be a fool if I let that thumb's lackey spy on me.'

He was correct, of course. She'd not thought of it before, but obviously Ivers was supposed to report on her.

Glenville walked back to the doorway, but turned and faced her again. 'Shall I have your dinner sent up to this room?'

Did he not wish to dine with her? She felt disappointed. But she would not show him. 'Very well.'

The next two days on the road were much more pleasant for Tess with Nancy as a companion, but Marc spent little time with her. She rode with Nancy, ate with her, shared rooms with her at the inns where they stopped for the night. Nancy was so open and curious and eager to please that Tess was tempted to tell her everything about her family, her sisters and how it came about that she was going to marry. She missed her sisters so desperately. Confiding in someone would ease the loneliness, but it would not be fair to burden a servant with her trials. She told Nancy only that her betrothal had been sudden and that Marc's parents knew nothing of it. To the village girl it sounded all romantic and exciting.

It was exciting, Tess could not disagree, but obviously romance was not a part of it.

* * *

The morning of the third day, Marc appeared when Tess and Nancy entered the public room for breakfast.

He smiled at her. 'Good morning, Tess.'

Her heart skipped a beat. When had her heart skipped beats? With Mr Welton, perhaps, but that seemed an eon ago.

'Good morning.' She lowered her lashes.

He turned to Nancy. 'Nancy, I would like to dine with Miss Summerfield alone. Would you mind?'

Imagine him asking a maid.

Nancy curtsied. 'Not at all, Mr Glenville.' She grinned. 'Do not worry over me. I'll take care of myself.' She entered the room and took a seat at one of the tables.

Tess glanced at Marc. 'May we keep her in view? I do not like to leave her alone.'

'Indeed,' he responded.

He led her to a table nearby the maid.

Why did Tess feel so breathless? As if she'd run down the stairs to this room?

A tavern maid arrived and they ordered their food.

From across the table he gazed at her with his startling blue eyes. 'I expect we will reach London today.' His demeanour was serious. 'I should tell you what to expect.'

Her eyes widened. She'd worried about what would happen when they reached London. Would he leave her alone someplace, like in a hotel for ladies? Would she be alone in a city she knew only from magazines and books?

'I plan to take you to my parents' house.'

Tess released a relieved breath.

This plan appeared to make his brow furrow deeper, though. 'I cannot predict how they will welcome you. I can only warn you that my parents are…' He paused as if he had to consider carefully what to say. 'Well, their situation—not being as socially connected as you might wish—'

She interrupted him. 'Do not concern yourself over that. I am not at all certain I wish to be connected to society.' Not if such people were as unreasonable as Lord Tinmore.

A defensive tone entered his voice. 'I told you that my mother was not born to society. She may not be accepted by the *ton*, but she is a fine person.'

Tess almost reached for his hand, only inches from hers on the table. 'Yes, you did tell me. I am the last person who would judge your mother from the situation of her parents. I can only hope your parents do not hold it against me for being the daughter of Sir Hollis and Lady Summerfield.'

He shook his head. 'That is what I cannot predict.'

She blinked. 'You had hoped to marry a respectable woman. I expect that was their wish, as well. I am so sorry.'

He frowned, but his blue eyes still pierced her. 'No more apologies, Tess. What is past is done. We can only look to the future.'

But the future was like the sheets of rain from the storm that led to this day. She could not see where she was headed. To Tess the future seemed grey and cold, a place where she would be lost and alone.

By midday, much to Nancy's sheer glee, the buildings of London came into view. Tess recognised the dome of St Paul's Cathedral from engravings of the church in books. She'd imagined this moment, her first sight of London, many times, but her actual arrival brought trepidation.

Not that Nancy noticed. Nancy leaned out the window and remarked on everything she saw. A building with a red door! A street vendor selling ginger cakes! A man dressed in purple livery!

Tess glimpsed Marc from time to time as he led the

coachman to his parents' house. It was located in Mayfair, he'd told her. An excellent address on Grosvenor Street near the square.

She was nervous about meeting his parents. Perhaps it would be better to leave her at a hotel, or even at a bench in the park to wait while he explained to his parents that he was forced to marry the daughter of the infamous Sir Hollis and Lady Summerfield.

The rows of shops turned into rows of town houses with doors painted bright red, green or blue. The carriages on these streets were of finer make. Fashionable phaetons were driven by elegantly dressed men, a young boy perched on the back, ready to attend to the horses.

'Have you ever seen the like!' exclaimed Nancy.

'I never have,' Tess answered truthfully. The genteel people who called upon her family were neighbours or friends of her father's passing through and they wore travelling clothes. Lord Tinmore's carriages came from another age—nothing she'd ever seen outside of books or fashion plates was as sporting and new as what passed them.

'We must be in Mayfair,' Tess said.

They were close to the end of her journey and the beginning of a life of unknowns. Would Lord and Lady Northdon accept her or would they be furious that their son was forced to marry her?

The carriage came to a stop by a row of town houses.

They had arrived.

Marc dismounted from Apollo and opened the door of the carriage. 'We are here,' he said.

He looked as grim as she felt.

She nodded and gave him her hand so he could assist her from the carriage. Could he feel how her hand shook?

He gazed directly into her eyes, a silent communication that might have been intended to reassure her, but merely revealed he was as uncertain of their reception here as she was. It was a scant second of intimacy, though, and that in itself heartened her a little.

'Wait here,' he said before he walked up to the door and pounded the wrought-iron knocker.

A footman answered. 'Mr Glenville! Welcome. Were his lordship and her ladyship expecting you?'

'Not at all,' Glenville said. 'Good to see you, Staines.'

Why had he not written his parents that he was coming? He could have sent a letter from any of the inns where they'd stayed. He could have prevented making her presence such a surprise.

'Are they at home?' he asked.

'They are, sir.' He opened the door wider for Marc to enter.

'I am not alone.' He gestured to Tess and Nancy and to the coachman who was lowering trunks and travelling bags on to the pavement. 'I will discharge the carriage, but I need someone to bring in the luggage and tend to my horse.'

'Indeed, sir.' Staines stared wide-eyed at them before disappearing inside the house. Soon two other footmen hurried out. One took Apollo's reins and the other picked up one of the trunks and headed for a servants' entrance below street level.

Marc returned to Tess. 'Come inside.' He turned to Staines again. 'Do you know where in the house my parents are?'

'I cannot say for certain, sir, but your father is likely in the library and your mother in her sitting room.' Staines picked up two of the smaller bags. 'Shall I announce you?'

'No,' Marc replied. 'I'll find them.'

He took Tess's elbow and escorted her inside. He helped her off with her cloak and laid it on a chair in the hall. 'Come this way to the drawing room. I should not be long.'

Nancy stared up at the painted-and-plasterwork ceiling as she followed.

They entered an elegant drawing room that looked straight out of Ackermann's prints of the latest furnishings. Not the worn but genteel furniture of Summerfield House, nor the opulence of a bygone era in Tinmore Hall.

'I'll return soon.' He hurried out the door before Tess could say a word.

She closed her eyes and tried to quiet her nerves.

'This room is so grand!' Nancy twirled around. 'And it is so big.' She walked around, peering at everything. 'Look! Little porcelain people.'

There were Meissen figurines on a side table.

Tess only half-listened to her inventory of items in the room.

'I cannot believe I will live in this house!' Nancy exclaimed.

'Do not be hasty,' Tess said. 'We may not be able to stay. Remember Lord and Lady Northdon know nothing of us.'

Nancy spun around to face the door, as if Lord and Lady Northdon might enter at any moment. 'I wonder what Mr Glenville is saying to them.'

Chapter Six

Marc knocked on his mother's sitting-room door.

'*Qui est là?*'

The familiarity of her voice warmed him. '*C'est moi, Maman.*'

'Marc?'

She was already on her feet when he opened the door. Still thin, still white-haired, still beautifully fine-boned. As lovely a woman as ever.

'Marc!' She threw her arms around him.

Her embrace was strong and firm, the embrace of the woman who had soothed all his childhood hurts, the woman who valiantly did not complain of having no friends and few social contacts.

She continued to speak in French. 'We did not expect you. Come. Sit with me and tell me all about where you have been and what you have been doing. You spent Christmas in Scotland, no?'

He answered in French. '*Oui.*' That was about as much as he could tell her of his doings. 'Come with me to Papa. He is in the library. I have something to tell you.'

'Must we, Marc?' Her mouth pursed. 'Tell me here, *s'il vous plaît*. I do not wish to leave this room.'

'No. I want to speak with you and Papa together, Maman.' Here he was, in the middle of them again.

'He does not like to be disturbed, *cher*.' She frowned.

She meant they spent their days apart as much as possible.

'I insist, Maman.' He extended his hand to the door. 'Come with me. It is important.'

'Very well. If it is important.' She sighed, taking his arm.

When they reached the library, she walked in first.

'John!' she snapped, switching to English. 'Look who is here.'

Her father scowled at her sharp tone, but broke into a smile when he saw Marc. 'My boy! What a pleasant surprise. A pleasant surprise.'

Again Marc was engulfed in a hug. 'Papa.'

His father seemed smaller than Marc remembered. Marc embraced him back, but the old resentments nagged at him.

'What brings you here? Are you staying? You have not been home in a very long time.' His tone, of course, turned to a scold. 'You should stay awhile.'

He'd been in his father's presence for less than a minute and already the man was scolding and issuing orders and reminding Marc he was not his brother who could do no wrong in their father's eyes.

Marc moved out of his father's embrace and tried to keep the rancour out of his voice. 'I might extend my visit.' He gestured to the sofa nearby. 'Please, both of you sit. I have something to tell you.'

They sat—in separate chairs.

Marc sat on the sofa. He'd had nearly three days to prepare for this conversation and still had not decided what to say.

Better to lunge than parry. 'I have brought a lady with me, a lady I will marry…'

Both his parents stared back in shock.

'Marry!' his mother cried, but her eyes kindled with excitement.

His father frowned. 'Who is this lady?'

Marc took a breath and began his explanation. His father would know who Tess's parents were, so there was no sense withholding that information. He would withhold the reason he and Tess were marrying, though. Eventually, when Lord Tinmore's guests made their way to London, the story might come out, but telling it now would only make Tess's introduction to his parents more difficult for her.

'She is Sir Hollis and Lady Summerfield's daughter?' his father cried when Marc finished.

'Who is this Sir Hollis and Lady Summerfield?' his mother demanded.

His father gave her a peeved look. 'Sir Hollis was a fool who threw away a fortune on bad investments, but not before marrying a wife who cuckolded him repeatedly before she finally ran away with one of her lovers. She had so many lovers, no one knows who fathered her children.'

'Pfft!' Marc's mother waved away her husband's words. 'Lovers. What does that matter?'

'Fidelity matters very much to some people,' he countered.

'Does it?' His mother glared at his father.

Good God. Was one of them—or both—taking lovers now?

His father cleared his throat. 'In this situation, however, it matters that we don't know what blood flows in this young lady's veins.'

'Yes!' His mother nearly bounded from her seat. 'She

might have common blood in her. Would that not be *très tragique*!'

His father's face turned red. 'I did not mean that and you know it. I meant there could be insanity in the family. Or deformity.'

Marc stood. 'Silence!'

They both looked at him as if surprised he was there.

'It does not matter who her parents were or what blood is in her, I am marrying Miss Summerfield, not her parents.' He glared at them both.

'Good God.' His father rubbed his face. 'It is bad enough your brother—' He broke off and it took a moment for him to renew his attack on Marc. 'What is the urgency of this marriage? Is she increasing?'

'Increasing? Say what you mean.' His mother turned to him. 'Is she *enceinte*?'

'No!' Marc responded. 'There is no child. She is a virtuous, respectable young lady and I have treated her as such.'

'Well, her family is not respectable.' His father huffed. 'Her mother. Her father. And did I not read that a sister married old Tinmore? That could not be respectable.'

'Pah.' His mother's eyes flashed at his father. 'You put too much on respectable. You always did.'

He glared back at her. 'Not always.'

They stared at each other and Marc felt he might as well not be in the room.

'You could have stopped Lucien,' she whispered.

This again. Were they still battling over his brother's death? This was the most painful of all.

His mother, though, returned to the topic at hand. 'What is it with this Tinmore? Is he not *respectable*?'

His father's tone turned almost civil. 'He is eighty, if he's a day, and he's been a recluse for years.' He glanced away in thought. 'I wonder if he is in his right mind. Must not be if some chit duped him into marriage.'

'You think it is the woman who is at fault?' his mother countered. 'More likely this Tinmore forced her to marry him.'

Marc broke in. 'Never mind Tinmore! Will you welcome Miss Summerfield into this house or must I put her up in a hotel some place until I can arrange to marry her? I need to know this minute because she is waiting in the drawing room.'

Nancy finally settled in a chair against the wall and Tess sat where she could view the drawing-room door. From the window she'd seen the last of their luggage carried away and the carriage driving off. It was disconcerting to not know precisely where she was or how to get anywhere. If she were on the streets of Mayfair, she'd be as lost as she'd been in the storm.

The door opened and she braced herself.

But it was not Marc, nor his parents who entered. It was a young blonde beauty, so much Genna's size and colouring that Tess ached to see her sister again. The girl, though, looked even younger than Genna's nineteen.

Tess stood and Nancy popped up, as well.

'Hello,' the girl said. She had the same piercing blue eyes as Mr Glenville, complimented by a stylish day dress of nearly the same hue. 'Staines told me my brother was here. And that we had visitors.' She walked over to Tess and curtsied. 'I am Amelie Glenville.'

Brother? Marc had not mentioned he had a younger sister.

Tess curtsied in return. 'I am Miss Summerfield. Tess Summerfield.' She gestured to Nancy. 'This is my maid, Nancy.'

Nancy's curtsy was deep. 'Miss.'

'You came with my brother, did you not?' Miss Glenville asked, her tone hesitant.

She was shy, Tess guessed. 'Yes. Yes, we did.'

'I ordered some tea for you.' Miss Glenville lowered her gaze. 'Please do sit. Both of you.'

Tess lowered herself into the chair again.

Miss Glenville took a seat nearby. 'Where is my brother now?' she asked.

'With your parents, I think.' He'd seemed gone a long time. A bad sign.

Staines entered carrying a tea tray with some little cakes. Miss Glenville, with the deliberateness of an unpractised hostess, poured for them both. Nancy, still wide-eyed, but suddenly bashful and perhaps even more desirous of refreshment than Tess, retreated to a far chair along the wall to consume her tea and cakes.

'You came in a carriage,' Miss Glenville said timidly. 'Where did you come from?'

'From Lincolnshire, actually,' Tess responded.

'Lincolnshire!' the girl exclaimed. 'You must have travelled for days.'

'Yes.' Home was very far away.

Miss Glenville seemed to search for what else to say. 'You must be very tired.'

They'd left with the morning's first light and the clock in this room just chimed three times. 'We stopped along the way.'

Miss Glenville fell silent, but she looked as if she were trying to decide something. She finally blurted out, 'Are—are you a friend of my brother's? Why did he leave you in the drawing room alone?'

Tess would not take it upon herself to explain why Glenville arrived at her home with a strange woman, luggage in tow. 'He wished to speak with your parents first.'

Miss Glenville made a puzzled frown, then smiled shyly. 'It is nice to have a visitor, in any event. We do not have many when we come to London.'

Tess very much wanted to put the girl at ease. 'Then many people are missing a lovely house. This room looks the very height of fashion.'

'It is.' Miss Glenville brightened. 'Maman likes very much to make a room pretty.'

'She succeeds very well.'

There was another long silence. Tess felt the pain of Miss Glenville's meekness. She had Genna's beauty, but lacked Genna's confident outspokenness.

Finally Miss Glenville stood. 'Shall I see what is keeping my brother?'

Tess smiled. 'Yes, please. I would so appreciate that.'

Miss Glenville curtsied again and fled the room.

When the door was closed, Nancy spoke in a hushed tone. 'She is a beautiful lady!'

'Very beautiful.' Amelie Glenville was as beautiful as her brother was handsome, as fair-haired as he was dark.

Tess considered herself passable, but not a beauty like honey-blonde Genna or mahogany-haired Lorene. Or like their mother, who was renowned for her beauty, even though Tess could barely remember what she looked like.

Was the woman Marc wanted to marry a great beauty?

Tess sighed. There was no use dwelling on such matters. She would do what she must for Genna and Edmund. And Lorene.

Footsteps sounded outside the door. Several footsteps. Tess stood again.

The door opened and Marc entered first. His gaze caught Tess's right away, and she saw no reassurance in it. Behind him came an unsmiling but graceful lady whose white hair showed the vestiges of having been blonde like Miss Glenville. Next entered an equally sober grey-haired gentleman. Miss Glenville, who walked in last, was the only one smiling.

Mr Glenville came to Tess's side. 'Let me present you to my parents.'

She raised her chin as his parents came to stand in front of her. They exchanged glances, their expressions grim.

'May I present Miss Tess Summerfield.' He gestured to his parents. 'My parents, Lord and Lady Northdon.'

She curtsied. 'I am honoured.'

'Yes,' uttered Lord Northdon.

Lady Northdon made a nervous laugh.

This was a horrible moment. Tess was desperate to survive it. 'I realise I am a great surprise to you. For that I apologise. I assure you I will certainly endeavour not to be a problem—'

'Problem?' Lady Northdon responded in a French accent. 'A surprise, yes, but we are quite able to accommodate a guest, even on short notice.'

'Then I am to stay?' she asked.

Lord Northdon cleared his throat. 'We did not even expect our son, so you will forgive us if we need time to accustom ourselves to you.'

Or was she not to stay?

Tess glanced at them both. 'Your son has told you of… me.'

To her surprise Marc took her hand and squeezed it. 'I told them of our betrothal. That we wish to marry as soon as I can arrange it.'

Even though her senses flared at his touch, she knew the gesture had been a signal, nothing more. He was trying to tell her he'd not explained everything.

Miss Glenville's eyes grew huge. 'You are to be married?'

Tess smiled at her. 'Yes. I could not tell you before your parents knew.'

'Married.' The girl's voice turned dreamy.

Lord Northdon scowled.

Lady Northdon glanced at him and laughed. 'My husband thought you were *enceinte*.'

'What was I supposed to think?' Lord Northdon snapped.

'It would have explained much, would it not, sir?' Tess mollified. 'But, no, I am not *enceinte*.'

The word hung in the air until Lord Northdon said, 'Well, are we going to sit or are we going to stand here all day?'

Lady Northdon swooped over. 'That is no way to speak to a guest, John.' She took Tess's arm. 'Come, sit with Amelie and me. Would you like some refreshment?'

Tess felt as if she'd fallen between two fighting cats. 'Miss Glenville served us tea.' She sat where Lady Northdon asked her to sit. 'May I ask if my maid and I are to stay in this house?'

'Oui.' Lady Northdon pursed her lips. 'If my son asks it, you must stay.'

That was not precisely a welcome. 'Then may I request my maid be shown our rooms? And be introduced to the rest of the staff and to the customs of the house?'

Miss Glenville piped up. 'I can take her to the housekeeper, Maman.'

Her mother waved her hand. 'Yes. Do that, Amelie.'

Nancy sent Tess an anxious but excited look before following Miss Glenville out of the room.

'Pour me some brandy,' Lord Northdon demanded of his son.

Marc crossed the room to a cabinet. He turned. 'Maman, some claret?' He paused. 'Tess?'

Tess waited for Lady Northdon to say yes before she agreed. 'I would very much like some claret.' A whole bottle of it, perhaps.

With glasses poured, Lady Northdon clapped her hands. 'Now we must plan a wedding, no? What church? Grosvenor Chapel? I know the fashion is to marry at St George's, but Grosvenor is closer.'

'They do not want a church wedding, Ines,' Lord Northdon shot back. 'The fashion is to marry at home by special licence.'

'I do not know such things.' She pouted. 'Marry at home. Pah! A wedding is for a church.'

'A church wedding is for the country where there might be many guests,' Lord Northdon countered. 'There will be no guests here.'

Marc drained his brandy in one gulp. 'Tess and I will decide, but we are not deciding now.'

Had Tess landed in Bedlam by mistake? 'Perhaps I might retire to my room until dinnertime?' she asked. 'I am a little fatigued from the journey.'

'Bien sûr,' Lady Northdon said. 'The room should be ready.'

Marc strode over to Tess. 'I will take you.'

Marc nearly pulled her out of her seat and out of the room.

Once in the hall, he slowed. 'I am so sorry, Tess. They were even worse than I feared.'

'How could you expect them to approve of me?' Tess asked.

'There is no reason they should not approve of you.'

Did he truly think that?

He led her up the stairs. 'My father knows of your parents, of course, but he is not in a position to object on that score.' He stopped at the first landing and faced her, holding her arms almost as if she were a true fiancée. 'I did not tell them the whole story. I said only that we were betrothed and will be married as soon as possible.'

She gave him an ironic smile. 'And that I am not *enceinte.*'

He rolled his eyes, but flashed a smile. 'That, as well.'

She could feel the tension in him even after he released her. He was trying so very hard to ease matters for her. Marc Glenville was a kind man.

'Come. I'll show you to the room.' They continued to the third floor. 'Your room is likely to be rather plain, I'm afraid. I do not think my mother's interest in decorating reached this floor.'

'I need nothing fancy.' Her room at Summerfield House had been very pleasant, but had not approached the opulence of the one Lord Tinmore allotted to her. 'Am I alone on this floor?' she asked.

'My room is here, too.'

Her insides fluttered.

As they approached the door, they heard voices. Nancy talking happily to someone.

When they opened the door, Nancy looked up. She and another maid were making the bed. A third girl was wiping the furniture.

'Goodness, miss!' Nancy exclaimed. 'We are almost done with the room, if you do not mind.'

Passing the time watching two cheerful maids doing their work seemed the best the day had to offer. 'I do not mind. I just wish to rest from the trip.'

'I will leave you.' Marc merely nodded and walked away.

Tess lowered herself into a chair by the window and rubbed her brow and wished she could be back in Lincolnshire.

* * *

Marc left Tess and went in search of Staines to help him change into fresh clothes. Clean linen and a coat and waistcoat not covered with the dirt of the road were almost reviving, but he was too stirred up to savour the experience. He wanted fresh air. A quick turn in the park would calm him enough to face the rest of the day.

On his way out, he met Amelie on the stairs. He embraced her. 'I did not have a chance to say a proper hello, little sister.'

'I am so glad you are here,' she answered, hugging him back so tightly his guilt at leaving her alone with their parents rushed back at him.

'I was away too long, I know.' He held on to her.

'I understand, Marc. Really, I do.'

She did not know any of it. His reasons for leaving his family, usually without a word, were hidden from them.

He released her, but held her at arm's length. 'By God, I believe I've been gone longer than I thought. You have turned into a beautiful woman while I was away.'

She blushed. 'Do not say such silly things.'

'I mean it.' He examined her again. How could she miss attracting suitors with a face like that? 'You should have a Season.'

Her smile turned sad. 'Maman and Papa do not receive many invitations.'

None, she meant.

'I'll do something about that, I promise.' He was filled with resolve.

Doria Caldwell, the woman he'd planned to marry, would have opened doors for Amelie. The Caldwells were not in the highest circles, but they received plenty of invitations. What he could do for Amelie now, he did not know. He'd brought on more scandal, not less.

Amelie pulled on his arm. 'Come. Talk to me a little. Tell me about Miss Summerfield. How you met her. Everything.'

He glanced away. 'There is little to tell. We met in Lincolnshire and I decided to marry her.'

Her pretty mouth opened, as if she were going to ask another question, but she shut it again. After a moment or two, she smiled again. 'Tell me about Scotland and anywhere else you've been.'

He put an arm around her. 'I have a better idea. Fetch a warm cloak. Let us take a walk in the park. Who knows? Perhaps you will catch the eye of some handsome young man.'

She pushed him away. 'I do not care about that, but I would love to walk in the park with you.'

It was the fashionable hour, but too early in the year for a turn in the park to be considered a social event. Too bad, maybe all she needed was to be seen in the park.

Marc resolved to think of some way for Amelie to be introduced to society. In the meantime, he would merely enjoy a walk with her.

Chapter Seven

When it was time for dinner, Marc knocked on Tess's door. The least he could do was save her from having to walk to the drawing room and face his parents alone.

Nancy opened the door and greeted him with a smile. 'Mr Glenville! Have you come to collect Miss Summerfield for dinner? She is ready.' She stepped away and revealed Tess. 'I tried to dress her hair like your mother's and your sister's, but different. And did we select the right dress?'

The maid had succeeded very well. Tess was a vision. Her hair was pulled high on her head and cascaded around her face in shiny chestnut curls. Her gown was simple and unembellished, a pale pink that might have been worn many times, but it flattered her. In fact, it made him all too aware she was a woman and that he soon would share a wedding night with her.

'You look…nice, Tess,' he managed.

She looked down at herself. 'This was one of the dresses I intended to alter with that lamentable lace and ribbon.'

The lace and ribbon she'd purchased on the day of the storm.

'I could alter your dress!' Nancy piped up. 'If I had

lace, I could put it around the neckline and perhaps at the sleeves and maybe around the skirt in some way. Beading would look wonderful sewn into the lace. If I had beading.'

Bless this maid. Her diversion interrupted Marc's too-carnal thoughts. 'I will ask my sister. I suspect there is plenty of lace and ribbon and beading in this house.'

'That would be wonderful!' Nancy beamed.

'I will ask her tonight.' Marc offered Tess his arm. 'Shall we go?'

She nodded, her expression a cross between tense and sad. He could not make this right for her, no matter how hard he tried.

When they entered the corridor, Tess sighed. 'She is so effortlessly happy.'

'Nancy, you mean?'

She nodded.

Unlike the two of them, he thought.

They reached the stairs and she hesitated. 'Are you certain I will not be underdressed? Your mother's and sister's day dresses were finer than this.'

He gazed at her and again was stirred into baser urges that turned his voice raw. 'It flatters you.'

Her eyes grew wide.

Finally she moved forward. 'I do not know why I asked. It was my only choice.'

They walked down the stairs.

'If it pleases you, buy as many new dresses as you desire. I am well able to pay for them.' His father provided an allowance made even more generous because of his brother's death but, even without that, he had money of his own.

She stopped and stared at him again. 'Thank you, Marc,' she murmured.

She looked so vulnerable at this moment all he wished

was to hold her in his arms. At this moment she could ask
him for anything and he would provide it for her.

She affected him. Strongly.

He pulled away. 'It is the least I can do since we are
to marry.'

She lowered her lashes and continued to walk down
the stairs.

Tess entered the drawing room with emotions disor-
dered. She'd felt drawn to Marc in those few moments together, almost as though they'd regained the camaraderie
they'd shared in the cabin, but, inexplicably, he withdrew
from her again.

She might have spent the entire evening disturbed by
his manner, but, as soon as Marc's mother discovered Tess
needed a new wardrobe, there was no chance to think of
anything besides fabrics, modistes and the latest fashions,
which Lady Northdon was determined Tess should have.
Fashion, it turned out, was Lady Northdon's consuming
interest.

She said, 'My father was—what is the word in English—'

'A linen-draper, Maman,' her daughter responded.

'*Oui.* A linen-draper.' She made a sound of disgust.
'Before he entered politics, that is.' Her expression brightened again. 'I grew up around the most marvellous fabrics
and I knew all the best modistes in Paris, because they
purchased only from my father, you know. I always wore
dresses that were *au courant.*'

During the meal Lady Northdon and her daughter
talked of nothing else but Tess's new wardrobe. Marc and
his father held their own conversation and Tess could almost forget he was there.

Almost.

After dinner when the men remained in the dining room with their brandy, Lady Northdon sent tea up to her private sitting room where she pulled out a collection of fashion prints that would put Yardney's lending library to shame. She had the latest issues of *La Belle Assemblée*, and *The Ladies' Fashionable Repository*, as well as the *Journal des Dames et des Modes* from France.

Marc and his father never joined them. Tess told herself it was easier that way. She could almost pretend she was with her sisters, planning their next gowns, talking of what hats and shoes would go with them. Unlike discussing fashion with her sisters, however, this time no one ever discussed how much it would cost.

By the time Tess retired to her bedchamber, Lady Northdon and Miss Glenville were calling her Tess and she was calling Miss Glenville Amelie. She would not dream of addressing Lady Northdon as anything but Lady Northdon, but dropping the formality made it a little like having a family again. It should have given her enough peace to fall easily asleep.

Sleep did not come so easy, though. Alone, under the bedcovers, she thought again of Marc.

Perhaps love was impossible, under the circumstances, but could they at least be the friends they'd become when stranded in the cabin?

The next morning Tess found her way to the breakfast room with some assistance from the footman attending the hall. When she entered, though, she was alone.

Another footman stepped into the room.

'Am I too late or too early?' she asked him. 'When does the family eat?'

'Lord Northdon rises quite early and has already break-fasted,' the man responded. 'The ladies tend to eat late.'

'And Mr Glenville?' Why must her heart pound when she spoke his name?

'I believe he rose early and went out without eating, miss.'

What could it mean that he left early?

'Thank you.' She approached the buffet and glanced at the food. 'I am happy to serve myself, but I would love a cup of hot tea.'

He nodded. 'Right away, miss.'

A generous array of breakfast foods was spread out on the sideboard. Not only the breads, butter and jams she was used to at home, but also oatmeal with cream, pound cakes, ham and kippers. It was almost as varied and generous as the breakfasts at Tinmore Hall. She took a little of each offering, which filled her plate rather fully.

She sat and the footman poured her tea and withdrew.

The good spirits with which she'd filled her plate ebbed in the stillness and loneliness. She picked at her food and wondered if she could abandon her plate without the footman reporting it to the cook and housekeeper and ultimately reaching the ear of Lady Northdon.

The door opened and Marc entered the room.

She flushed with pleasure.

He paused and in that moment her spirits plummeted again. He might not be pleased to see her.

Then he smiled.

'Tess, you surprised me.' He bowed to her. 'How nice to see you up this early.'

His pleasure sounded genuine. She relaxed a little. 'I am used to country hours, I fear.'

He glanced at the footman. 'Coffee, Wilson, if you would be so good.'

Marc walked to the buffet and filled his plate. 'I rarely sleep late.'

They shared that trait, at least. Of course they'd both slept too late that morning in the cabin. How different everything would have been, if they had not.

He sat adjacent from her. 'I've given Apollo a bit of a run on Rotten Row.'

Dear Apollo, who'd carried them both through the storm and who'd travelled three days to reach London. 'Poor Apollo. Did he not deserve a day of rest?'

He glanced at her, but she could not read his expression. 'I think he appreciated the run. He dislikes holding back.'

She looked down at her food. Why could she not hold her tongue?

He started eating. The footman came with a pot of coffee for him and withdrew again.

He took a sip, then smiled at her again. 'I must tell Apollo sometime that he has a champion in you.'

When he smiled like that, he made it hard for her to breathe.

He cut a piece of ham. 'I have an errand to perform this morning. I am sorry to leave you alone.'

He did not sound all that sorry. 'Do not concern yourself. Your mother and sister are taking me to the shops for new clothes.'

'Are they?' He nodded. 'That should please Maman very much. There is nothing she enjoys more.'

'She is very knowledgeable.' Tess took a sip of her tea. 'She is taking me to a modiste on Petticoat Lane. A Madame LeClaire. Apparently Madame LeClaire is someone she knew in France when she was a girl.'

He frowned. 'Poor Maman. I did not realise she once knew the modiste. No wonder she likes to buy new dresses.' He speared a piece of ham and chewed it. After he'd swallowed it, he went on. 'She's had a difficult time of it.'

'It is a shame, really,' Tess said. 'She is a lovely person and so fashionable. There is much other ladies could learn from her.'

'You like her?' he asked.

Of course she liked her. 'She's been very kind to me.'

He reached over and took her hand. 'Let her order all the clothes she wants for you. As I said before, the cost is of no consequence.'

He cared about his mother. Another thing to like about him.

He released her and she was unsure what the gesture had meant.

'I am certain I will enjoy your mother's company and assistance. I only hope that I will look well enough for London.'

His blue eyes pierced her. 'You look well enough for London already.'

After breakfast, Marc set off on the first of his errands of the day. A visit to Horse Guards to an office of a gentleman he'd called upon several times before. The visit was a formality, an official end to the clandestine activities of which Marc had been a part these last few years of the war. Now that Napoleon had abdicated, though, his days as a British spy in France were over.

When Marc's brother died his father insisted he not return to his regiment. Marc had been forced to give up the dream he and his friend Charles shared since they were boys. But not long after, he'd been recruited for another sort of service to his country—as a spy.

On several occasions he crossed the Channel in secret and entered enemy territory. He watched the coast for naval activity, spent time in Paris meeting French contacts, keeping his eyes and ears open, passing for a Frenchman named Renard. Thanks to his French mother, Marc spoke the language without an accent and, with a simple change of clothes, he easily passed for a common Frenchman. The information he had gathered saved many a British soldier's life.

It was some consolation for not being at Ciudad Rodrigo to keep Charles from volunteering for the Forlorn Hope. Charles was one of the first to storm the walls; one of the first to die.

Marc walked up to the office of Lord Greybury, his superior, to say his final goodbye and receive his official release from duty. Only a select few, no more than he could count on one hand, knew what Marc had done for the war effort. That was all well and good. Marc had not risked his life for the glory of it.

He'd always known his days as a spy would come to an end. How different this end was than what he'd planned. He'd planned to help take Charles's place in Charles's family, and, in return, abide in a house that scandal had never touched, where rational thinking and calm discourse existed instead of shouted words and deliberate misunderstandings.

He and Tess would begin their marriage in scandal. Would they, like his own parents, wind up without having a civil word to say to each other?

The mere thought of her, though, stirred him. His rational mind might bemoan this scandalous marriage, but another part of him was in a hurry to wed her.

His next stop would be to Doctors' Commons at the office of the Archbishop of Canterbury where he would arrange a special licence. He and Tess would be able to marry within days.

He told himself this would be the best way to minimise the gossip that would ensue when word escaped that they'd been caught in a compromising situation. When they presented themselves as a married couple, there would be little to talk about.

Was that truly his reason? Or was he merely eager for the wedding night?

After his visit to Doctors' Commons, Marc had one more call to make.

He walked through Mayfair to the street where Mr Caldwell's town house was located. Likely Caldwell would be at the Home Office where he worked for Lord Sidmouth. That was for the best. It was his daughter Marc needed to see.

This house had been as familiar as his own ever since his school days when he and Charles became the best of friends. They'd both been mad for the army and obsessed by anything to do with it. Even as young boys they plotted to purchase commissions in the same regiment. For years the two of them had debated which regiment it should be and what part of the world they most wanted to see. India? The Colonies? When the time came, though, the Battle of Trafalgar had just been fought and both Charles and he were keen to fight Napoleon.

He and Charles joined the Eighty-Eighth Regiment of Foot, Connaught Rangers. The Devil's Own.

Marc reached the town-house door and sounded the knocker. The butler, who'd known him since those early school days, greeted him warmly. 'Glenville. Come in. Come in.'

A few minutes later, he was in the drawing room waiting for Doria. He'd known her nearly as long as Charles.

She entered the room as serene as always. 'Marc. How delightful. You are back in London. It is good to see you.'

She was, he realised, quite an attractive woman, dark and intense, with thick, grave brows framing fine, intelligent eyes. There was no reason for her not to stir his blood.

But she did not.

She extended both hands and he clasped them. 'Are you well, Doria?'

'Very well.' She smiled and led him to the sofa.

'And your father?' he asked.

She sat. 'He is in good health. But tell me about you. Did you enjoy Scotland?'

Her question seemed more out of politeness than genuine interest. 'Scotland was pleasant.'

'Would you like some tea?' she asked.

He joined her on the sofa. 'No. I cannot stay long.'

He'd never discussed marriage with her, not specifically, not since they were children and she had insisted in all seriousness that she would marry him. She was much like her father. Practical, intelligent and impassive. Their house had always been serene—unlike his—and he'd always preferred being there instead of his own home.

Charles had been equally as quiet on the outside, but his heart had always been full of big dreams and strong emotions admirably held in check—unless Marc pushed him to unleash them. Marc's emotions always seemed to burst from the seams, exploding from him like they constantly did from his mother and father. He taught Charles to let loose sometimes, to get into adventures. And scrapes. They'd had great fun.

And when they went too far, they could always return to this house. Here Marc learned he could keep his emotions in check, as well as his wild schemes. Charles, his father and Doria were masters of control. They taught him serenity.

So what had happened that Charles so lost his good sense? How had he allowed his emotions to go unchecked? Too soon after losing his brother, Marc had lost Charles, as well.

The grief of losing Charles washed over him, but Marc tamped it down. It was in this house where he'd gained that skill.

'I have something to tell you,' he said to Doria.

She gazed at him in friendly interest.

He took a breath. 'I am to be married.' He paused. 'Soon.'

Her thick brows rose. 'Married? What a surprise.'

Did she have any emotion beyond surprise? He could not tell. 'It is sudden, I realise.'

She blinked, then shook her head as if tossing away an unwanted thought. 'Who are you marrying?'

Had he hurt her? She would never allow him to see it, if he had. 'She is Miss Summerfield, daughter of Sir Hollis Summerfield of Yardney. You do not know her. She has not been to town before.'

'No, I do not know her.' She spoke so softly he barely heard her.

Her father would certainly have heard of the scandalous Sir Hollis and Lady Summerfield. She'd soon learn of it from him.

'I wanted to tell you before an announcement is made.' He wanted to spare her feelings as much as possible.

'How kind of you.' Her voice seemed composed. 'Is Miss Summerfield in town now?' she asked.

He nodded. 'She is staying at my parents' town house. We will be married by special licence.'

Her brows rose again. Whatever she assumed was his reason to act with such haste, she would soon learn, as well.

'Yardney is in Lincolnshire, is it not?' Doria was well versed in geography as well as most other subjects. She was well practised in making conversation, too. 'Will you be returning there or staying in town?'

'I do not know.'

A silence fell between them, a silence he had no idea how to fill. Had she been Charles he would have told the whole story, even down to his confused emotions regarding Tess Summerfield, but he and Doria had never been confidantes, and the very thing he most valued about her made it impossible for him to tell how his news had affected her.

She smiled politely. 'My father is giving a dinner party. Perhaps you and Miss Summerfield might join us.'

He could not think of anything worse. 'I could not attend and leave my sister and parents.'

'Then they must attend, as well,' she said.

'Please do not feel obligated, Doria.' The Caldwells had kindly included Marc's parents in invitations before. They were among the very few who did.

'Nonsense. They will be welcome,' she said. 'Your sister, too, of course. Is Amelie not of an age to be out?'

'She is.' Amelie had turned eighteen, an age most society daughters made their come-out.

'Then coming to my party will be a treat for her. There will be other young people there. My cousin and some of her friends. It will be good for Amelie to be introduced to them.'

He could not refuse. This party might be the very thing for his sister. It might lead to more invitations and more opportunities to meet potential suitors.

'Very well, Doria. We will attend your dinner party. It is exceedingly kind of you to extend the invitation.'

'It is tomorrow night,' she said.

Tomorrow night?

'Do you have another engagement?' she asked.

'No. No.' Certainly no other engagements.

'Good.'

'I must go.' He stood, suddenly too uncomfortable in the place he'd once always felt at ease.

She stood, as well. 'Wait a moment. I will pen a note to your parents and Miss Summerfield.'

She walked out.

He glanced around the room. He'd once counted on spending many more peaceful hours in this room. He'd always imagined he'd feel Charles's presence here, but the room seemed empty and strange.

She returned and handed him a folded piece of paper. 'We will see you tomorrow, then.'

He placed it in his pocket said goodbye to her there, walking out to the hall alone. The footman brought him his hat and greatcoat and he stepped out into the street.

He'd thought perhaps this was to be his last visit to the house where so many of his happy childhood memories resided. Now he would return. This time he'd squire his new bride to the home of his once-intended bride, with his parents in tow.

All for the sake of his sister.

Tess's morning had been filled with trying on dresses, discussing alterations and embellishments, and planning for other gowns. Lady Northdon and Amelie took her first to the modiste, who had several dresses already sewn that could be altered to fit her. After purchasing four gowns and ordering more, they went on to a linen-draper, a hat shop, a glove shop, a shoe shop.

In each shop, Lady Northdon knew the shopkeepers. She conversed with them happily, asked after their families, oohed and ahhed over their merchandise and appeared to thoroughly enjoy herself.

They were her friends, Tess realised, although the lady was not free to invite them to her home or call upon them at theirs. Tess's heart went out to her, a woman caught between two rungs of society and not belonging to either one.

It was a shame, really, that the aristocracy would not give Lady Northdon a chance. Amelie, as well, could be such a success with her beauty and style and pleasant manners. Gentlemen on the street noticed her. Some even turned around for a second look at her. In a ballroom, how could she not fail to have gentlemen standing in line to be her dance partner?

If Tess thought about it, her own place in London society was equally in question. She already felt as though she did not belong in this fashionable, busy city. She no longer belonged in Lincolnshire, either, though.

It was nearing two o'clock when they stumbled back into the Grosvenor Street town house. The three ladies retired to their bedchambers for a much-needed rest. Only Nancy, who had accompanied them at Tess's request, seemed to have gained energy from the expedition.

She'd been a proper servant during the expedition, staying in the background, not speaking unless spoken to, carrying parcels. Now, however, she was bursting with words.

'I never saw such beautiful fabrics!' Nancy gushed. 'And the designs! So clever! I could make you one of those dresses, miss. The modiste gave me so many wonderful ideas.' Her eyes grew huge. 'Perhaps I could make your wedding dress! I could make it out of some of those lovely silks we saw. An ivory-silk gown with a silver net over it? And beading. And lace! I know I could make it.'

A wedding dress? Tess had not thought about what she would wear. 'I am sure you could make a delightful dress, but you have your maid duties and you will not have much time.'

'I will. I know I will.' Nancy's eyes pleaded. 'All your dresses will be new. They will not require much care. Everything will be new. I will not have enough to do, I am sure of it. Will you please allow me to sew the wedding dress?'

Tess did not care what she wore—that was not true. She wanted Marc to admire her in it.

And it would make Nancy happy—happier, she meant. 'Very well. I will ask Mr Glenville for the money and you may go purchase everything you need.'

'Oh, thank you, miss!' Nancy jumped up and down. 'If I had paper and a pencil, I could make a sketch to show you.'

Paper and pencil. If Tess had paper and ink, she could write to her sisters. She should at least let them know she had arrived safely in London. 'Perhaps you could ask one of the servants how I might have paper and pencil for sketching and pen and ink, as well. Tell them both are for me.'

Nancy bobbed into a curtsy. 'Right away, miss!' She rushed out the door.

After she left, Tess collapsed in a chair and pressed a hand against her forehead. Wedding dresses. Writing to her sisters. The reality of her situation struck Tess anew. She was to be married to Marc Glenville, a man trapped into marrying her, a man she hardly knew.

A knock sounded at the door.

'Come in.' She expected Lady Northdon or Amelie.

The door opened. 'Tess?'

She spun around. It was Marc.

'I heard you were back,' he asked from the doorway. 'How was your shopping expedition?'

Her heart pounded. 'Expensive for you, I am afraid. I purchased a great deal of everything.'

He held up a hand. 'Do not worry over the cost. Enjoy your purchases.'

'At least I will not look shabby.' She gestured to herself. 'Your mother made certain I will wear the latest fashions.'

He smiled. 'She would know.'

His smile gladdened her.

She liked that he cared about his mother and was protective of her. Tess could not pretend to know Lady Northdon well, but after only a day, she knew that Lady Northdon was fiercely devoted to her son and daughter.

What would it be like to have such a mother? Marc spoke. 'I was about to take a walk in the park. Would you care to join me?'

Her fatigue fled. 'Certainly.' She grabbed her bonnet, gloves and pelisse.

Soon they were out of doors, walking down the pavement to the Grosvenor Gate of Hyde Park. He led her through the gate and on to one of the walking paths. The afternoon sky was bright, but overcast. The air was chilly, but Tess did not mind. It felt wonderful to walk with him. Such a normal thing to do. There were a few other people in the park, but so far away it was as if they were alone.

'It is a bit early for the fashionable hour,' he explained as if reading her thoughts. 'Both in the day and for the Season.'

The path took them across a long expanse of grass edged with trees and shrubbery.

'It is almost like a walk in the country,' she said.

He glanced at the sky. 'But one without a rainstorm.'

She smiled at him. 'I sometimes do take walks when there is not a raging storm.'

He smiled back. 'As do I.'

Her heart lifted.

'Do you know about the park?' he asked.

'Only that it is where London society goes to be seen.' She'd learned that from magazines.

'It was created by Henry VIII in the fifteen hundreds for hunting and was not open to the public until more than a century later. Most of the landscaping, including the Serpentine, was created about one hundred years ago. We'll walk to the Serpentine.'

The Serpentine was the small lake in the park.

They reached the water. It was serene, cool, rippling gently in the light breeze. Such a contrast to the rushing, white-foamed water flooding the bridge to Tinmore Hall that fateful stormy day.

'It is peaceful here,' she commented.

'I should tell you of my errands today,' he said.

Somehow Tess's sense of peace fled. 'Where did you go?' she asked politely.

'To the Archbishop of Canterbury's office for the special licence.'

The licence for them to marry. 'Oh?' she responded.

'It will take a few days.'

She did not know if that was good news or not. She could not tell what he thought of it, either.

'I also called upon a friend,' he added in an ominous tone.

'A friend.'

His words came in a rush. 'Miss Caldwell. Doria. The sister of a school friend of mine who died at Ciudad Rodrigo.' The terrible siege where so many soldiers died.

She turned to him, now understanding completely. 'Speak plainly, Marc. Was this the woman you planned to marry? The sister of a friend you spoke about in the cabin?'

He met her gaze. His eyes, reflecting the sky and water, appeared grey. 'Yes.'

She turned away and watched a brown-and-white duck swim in circles near the shore.

He spoke softly. 'I needed to tell her…about us. I could not chance her finding out in another way.'

'Of course you could not.' She understood. Really, she did. 'It must have been a difficult speech to make to her. And for her to hear.'

He rubbed his forehead. 'The whole experience was unsettling. It was like being in a strange place, but one that was once as familiar as my own image in a mirror.'

That was precisely how she had felt when Tinmore's carriage drove through Yardney. Everything familiar had suddenly turned foreign.

He went on. 'I cannot tell you how she reacted. She was completely self-contained. But I must tell you, she has invited our family—and you—to a dinner party tomorrow night. I do not know how many guests are expected, but several, I imagine. Her cousin and some friends among them.'

'A dinner party!' She turned to face him. 'Did you accept?'

'I did.'

She turned away again.

He touched her arm. 'We can cry off, if you wish it, but let me explain why I accepted.' He wrapped her arm around his and started walking again. 'Miss Caldwell's cousin is around Amelie's age. If we attend, it will give Amelie some social time with people her own age. I have no doubt Amelie will be a great success, so this might lead to more invitations.' He paused. 'You must know my family does not receive many invitations. I cannot stand in the way of her having some enjoyment, like other girls her age.'

Or the chance to meet potential suitors, Tess thought.

'Besides this, my mother and father so rarely are seen out socially. This would be good for them, as well.' He stopped and looked down at her. 'What say you?'

She did not want to attend any dinner party, especially one given by the woman he wished to marry. 'You do not think it cruel for me to attend? You were to marry her, Marc.'

'I would not be cruel to you, Tess. If it would be too uncomfortable for you, I will send word we will not attend.'

And have her be the means of depriving his sister of a party? 'I meant cruel to her, not to me.'

He shrugged. 'She extended the invitation, which she certainly did not have to do.'

Perhaps this Miss Caldwell wanted a look at the woman who'd stolen her prospective husband. She straightened her spine. 'I suppose I must face people sometime.'

Chapter Eight

The next day was a flurry of dressmaking.

Marc had not considered that Tess might not yet have a suitable dinner dress. Or that his mother and Amelie would tear through their wardrobes searching for the perfect gown to wear. Nothing they had was perfect. Everything required work.

Worse, his father loudly protested the commotion, insisting all the fuss was nonsense. That simply fired up his mother's temper. There had been nothing to do but insist his father take him to his club and introduce him to his cronies.

His father sometimes retreated to Brooks's Gentlemen's Club, the club that attracted members of the Whig party and others a bit more tolerant of his choice of a wife and his liberal political views. Not that their tolerance resulted in the club members' wives inviting the Northdons to many social events, but at least Marc's father was accepted and comfortable among the other gentlemen in the club.

They sat in the dining room where three or four other gentlemen sat alone with their faces hidden behind the *Morning Post*. Marc ordered a coffee; his father, a Spanish brandy.

'Not too many members here today,' Marc commented.

'Hmmph.' His father sipped his drink. 'I'd wager there are still some tables full in the game room.'

Brooks's was known for its gambling. At least his father never gambled. In fact, his father did not practise any vices, not that Marc knew of.

His father swallowed and took another drink. 'I cannot abide all that fuss about dresses.'

'It makes Maman happy, you know. What else has she to be happy about?'

His father frowned. 'She is not happy. She blames me.' He downed the brandy.

Marc peered at him, still a handsome man even with his silver hair and sagging skin. An unhappy man. 'Is there more trouble between you and Maman?' he asked.

'More trouble?' His father scoffed. 'Do you mean her accusing me of your brother's death? That is hardly new. How was I to know he would be so reckless?'

Lucien had fallen in love with an earl's daughter, but her father refused his suit and the foolish couple eloped to Gretna Green. They never made it, however. Her father's men went in mad pursuit and Lucien overturned his phaeton.

His father's complexion turned grey and he stared into his drink. 'She is right, though. I should have stopped him.'

'Enough, Papa,' Marc said gently. 'Do not blame yourself.' He put his hand on his father's arm.

His father pulled away and took another sip of his brandy.

Marc felt the slap of rejection, but, then, nothing Marc did pleased his father.

He lifted his mug of coffee in both hands and leaned back in his chair. 'The trouble I meant was—when I came home—you and Maman seemed to be accusing each other of infidelity.'

His father waved a dismissive hand. 'Words.' He signalled for another brandy. 'There is no infidelity.' He leaned closer to Marc. 'What about you? Hmm? Why the devil are you marrying Sir Hollis's daughter? You are being as foolish as your brother.'

Was he being as foolish as his brother? Perhaps, but he'd had no other choice, had he?

His father pointed a finger at him. 'Have you lost your senses over her?'

No. But he certainly had the feeling he was battling against losing his senses over her.

The servant returned with more brandy and poured it in his father's glass. His father swirled the nut-brown liquid. *'Thus grief still treads upon the heels of pleasure: Married in haste, we may repent at leisure.'* He downed the entire contents of the glass and gazed up at Marc with a bleak expression. 'At least your brother was spared the repentance.'

That evening Marc's father nursed another glass of brandy in the drawing room while he and Marc waited for the ladies to be ready.

His father tapped impatiently on the side table. 'Your mother will probably change gowns ten times. We'll be late. God knows how long your sister will be.'

'I'm certain someone will be more fashionably late than we are.' Marc felt anxious, too, but one family member needed to at least appear to be calm. His mother and Amelie would be nervous. And Tess? How could she not be?

His sister walked in the room. Her white dress seemed to float about her. Her blonde hair was all in curls like a halo around her head.

His father stopped in his tracks. 'Amelie.' His voice

was hushed. 'You look like—like your— You look like an angel.'

Marc rose and approached his sister to put a kiss on her cheek. 'Papa is right. You are a vision.'

Amelie blushed. 'You are both speaking nonsense, of course, but it is kind of you.'

His father continued to stare at her, almost as if he were seeing a ghost.

The door opened again and this time his mother entered. His father, for an instant, looked upon his mother with that same awed expression. It changed quickly to one that seemed devoid of all emotion.

Marc greeted his mother with a kiss, as well. 'You are in fine looks, Maman. You look glorious.'

His mother's dress was very simple and understated. It relied on colour for its beauty, a deep blue that accented her pale skin and blue eyes.

His mother smiled, but her smile turned uncertain when she glanced at his father.

'Mother looks as lovely as Amelie, wouldn't you say, Papa?' Marc asked.

'They both look fine,' his father answered, but his gaze was averted.

Curse his father! One kind word and his mother would have been over the moon. Marc turned away and saw Tess slip into the room.

He lost his breath.

She did not appear ethereal like Amelie, nor elegant like his mother, but something that pleased him more, something real and warm and female. Her gown was simple, like his mother's, but suited her perfectly, causing nothing to distract from her beauty and her presence. It was a deep, rich green that turned her eyes the same shade and accented the red tones in her hair. Perhaps he had nothing to worry over at this dinner. Surely when this woman entered the room, no one could possibly find fault with her.

There was no fault with her.

'You look beautiful, Tess.' His voice felt raw.

'Thank you,' she said tightly, obviously not believing him. 'I am sorry to keep everyone waiting.'

The others noticed her then.

'Ma chérie!' his mother exclaimed. 'You are perfection.'

Amelie smiled. 'Tess, the dress looks so lovely on you. I am sure everyone will be impressed.'

'Do you think so?' Tess gazed at Amelie and her mother. 'I think no one will notice me with the two of you there.'

Tess was kind to his mother and sister. How could Marc not value that?

He smiled. 'Papa and I will be the envy of all the gentlemen at the party.'

His father started for the door. 'Let us get underway, then.'

His mother held back. 'We will not look out of place?'

Marc put an arm around her. 'Maman, your taste in fashion is unsurpassed. You will not look out of place.'

'I agree,' said Tess with a reassuring smile. 'Although I cannot know what ladies wear to a London dinner party, I would wager you have struck the perfect tone.'

His mother looked mildly heartened.

'Come on,' his father snapped. 'We do not want to be the last ones arriving.'

The ride to the Caldwell town house was silent and thick with tension. Tess was nervous enough, but it made her sad to see Lord and Lady Northdon and Amelie this frightened to attend a dinner party, all because Lady Northdon had been a merchant's daughter and the daughter of French Jacobins.

Would the guests at this dinner party be willing to overlook Tess's scandalous family? Surely someone there would know all about her mother's many lovers and her father's foolish financial dealings. How many would have read of Lorene's marriage to Lord Tinmore? Tess provided plenty for the guests to whisper about even if they would not yet know the circumstances of her betrothal to Marc.

At the town-house door a footman ran out to open the carriage door and help them alight. This was not as prestigious an address as Grosvenor Street, even Tess could tell. The town houses were smaller, the streets narrower. Another footman met them at the door and took their cloaks and the men's topcoats and hats.

The butler walked them to the drawing-room door where he announced them. 'Lord and Lady Northdon, Mr Glenville, Miss Glenville and Miss Summerfield.'

All heads turned and some turned quickly away.

A pleasant-looking man in his fifties approached them and right behind him, a pretty young woman.

'Ah, Lord Northdon. Lady Northdon. How good of you to come. You know my daughter, Doria? Of course you do…' The man's smile was a little forced.

This was Mr Caldwell, obviously, and the young woman, his daughter.

Miss Caldwell looked at Tess with some interest. She was lovely. Dark-haired, fair-skinned, intelligent.

Mr Caldwell fussed over Amelie and the girl's face turned bright pink. Miss Caldwell greeted the family warmly, as if these were old, dear friends.

Finally they came to Tess.

Marc presented her. 'Mr Caldwell, Doria, may I present Miss Summerfield.'

'How nice to meet you.' The young woman seemed remarkably composed. She quickly turned to her father.

'Father, do you recall I told you Miss Summerfield and Marc are to be married?'

'Yes. Yes.' Mr Caldwell's cordial tone turned a bit sharp. 'Welcome, Miss Summerfield.' He turned to Lord and Lady Northdon, quickly dismissing Tess. 'Come meet the other guests.'

Marc offered his arm to Tess and leaned close to her ear. 'I apologise for Mr Caldwell. He was rude to you.'

'Perhaps he is disappointed,' she whispered back.

Marc looked exceptionally handsome in his black coat. His blue eyes were even more riveting than usual in the candlelight of the drawing room. How could Miss Caldwell not despise Tess for taking him away?

They followed Marc's parents and Amelie to where the guests were gathered. During the introductions, some people were kind and polite; some barely acknowledged them. Some guests' faces sparked with recognition when meeting Tess. Were they remembering her scandalous mother? Or her father? Or the new Lady Tinmore?

Amelie earned surprised stares and some frankly admiring ones from the gentlemen present, some envious ones from the ladies. Miss Caldwell's cousin took Amelie under her wing and included her in the group of younger people amusing themselves with a peg board in a corner of the room. Lord Northdon crossed the room to speak to someone and Marc was pulled away by Mr Caldwell.

Miss Caldwell found seats for Lady Northdon and Tess and sat with them, making pleasant conversation, mostly to Lady Northdon. She asked about Lady Northdon's gown and soon drew another lady into the conversation about modistes and linen-drapers and the latest dress designs.

That left her alone with Tess. She smiled politely. 'How long have you known Marc?'

Tess thought perhaps the question was not asked out

of politeness. 'Not very long.' Less than a week, actually. 'And you? You and your father seem like old friends of the Glenvilles.'

Miss Caldwell's smile faltered a bit. 'Old friends of Marc's. He and my brother were in school together as boys and were inseparable. Marc spent as much time in our house as his own, I think. Through him we have been acquainted with his family.'

'Yes,' Tess said. 'Marc told me of your brother and about his tragic loss.'

The young woman lowered her gaze. 'He died at Ciudad Rodrigo.'

'I am so sorry,' Tess said honestly. 'My brother is a soldier and I worry over him constantly.'

Miss Caldwell's gaze shot up. One brow lifted. 'Yes. Of course you do.'

Tess met her eye. 'You have heard of my brother, I see.' Her half-brother, that was. Tess could not remember a time when people did not talk about *Lord Summerfield's bastard* growing up with them.

Miss Caldwell looked almost approving. It was not the reaction Tess expected.

'Do you have any sisters?' Tess asked, grasping for conversation.

Miss Caldwell seemed lost in her own thoughts for a moment. 'Sisters? No. It was just my brother and me.'

At that moment two gentlemen appeared in the doorway, their faces not visible.

'Excuse me. More guests.' Miss Caldwell rose to greet them.

'Mr Pemperton and Mr Welton,' the butler announced.

Tess's gaze snapped to the doorway. Mr Welton—*her* Mr Welton—stepped into the room to be greeted by Miss Caldwell and her father. Tess's heart pounded. She'd heard that everyone knew everyone in Mayfair, but to encounter Mr Welton at her first party? Impossible.

But there he was.

She turned towards Lady Northdon again and pretended to listen to a conversation about sleeve length.

What was she to do? Walk up to him and say hello? Or avoid him?

She was saved from the decision by the dinner announcement.

Marc and his father came to escort Tess and Lady Northdon to the dining room. Amelie had a couple of gentlemen vying for her arm. Mr Welton disappeared somewhere behind Tess and she was certain he had not seen her.

As the group of about thirty people assembled, Miss Caldwell raised her voice. 'We are not being strict about precedence at the table, you will notice. We sat people where they might find most enjoyment.'

Once inside the dining room, though, Lord and Lady Northdon earned places at the high end of the table. How very astute of Miss Caldwell. To have placed them anywhere else would have felt like a snub, even with the caveat of her announcement. Tess's name was further down, but she was seated next to Marc. Again, Miss Caldwell had been exceedingly kind—and generous—to seat Tess next to Marc.

Luckily, Tess was not in Mr Welton's direct line of sight. He sat on the other side of the table, but several seats away from her.

As the dinner progressed, Marc seemed to be doing his best to make conversation with her. He talked about the food and the wine and was solicitous of her needs. He also included her in conversations with the guests who sat next to them.

When those guests were occupied in other conversations, Tess leaned towards him. 'Your mother seems to be doing well. I was worried for her.'

He nodded. 'I was worried, too.'

Tess looked to where Marc's parents sat. 'Miss Caldwell has been kind to me and to your family. She seems to be a fine person.'

He glanced down at his plate. 'Yes, she is.'

Tess gripped her fork. 'Oh, Marc. I feel dreadful. She would make you a fine wife.'

Marc stabbed at a piece of meat. 'Do not think about it, Tess.'

Tess attended to her own plate. How could she not think about it?

Another course was served and they fell into silence with each other, speaking only when the guests next to them required it.

After some time, Marc lightly touched her arm. 'There is a gentleman who keeps looking at you.'

She knew whom he must mean. 'Oh?'

'Blond dandy-looking fellow on the other side of the table.' He tilted his head in the man's direction.

She glanced quickly. 'Mr Welton.' Welton's fine tailoring did seem a bit excessive. Especially if compared to Marc's ease in his clothes. 'I am acquainted with him. He visited his aunt recently in Yardney.'

'In Yardney.' Marc frowned.

He made her feel as if she'd been caught in some indiscretion, which was ridiculous.

'He might not recognise me,' she said. 'Your mother and Nancy have transformed me.'

His gaze pierced her. 'You would not be so easy to forget.'

She felt her cheeks flush with pleasure.

* * *

After dinner the ladies returned to the drawing room for tea. This time the ladies grouped themselves with their friends. Tess sat with Amelie and Lady Northdon.

Amelie was bursting with talk. 'The people here are so kind. I've felt so very welcome.'

'They ought to welcome you, *chérie*.' Her mother patted her arm.

'Some of the young men seem to enjoy your company,' Tess added.

Amelie, as isolated as she was, must not be used to such attention. If only Genna were here to help her.

Amelie coloured and lowered her lashes. 'I have been paid some pretty compliments, but surely the gentlemen are merely being polite.'

'Pah!' Her mother's eyes flashed. 'You are a beauty, but you must be on guard. If they are gentlemen, they will court you properly, no?'

'Oh, no one has said anything untoward, I assure you, Maman,' Amelie responded. 'I do not think I have ever felt so much friendship.'

Was it genuine friendship or some goodwill manufactured by Miss Caldwell?

Tess turned to Lady Northdon. 'You have been received with kindness, have you not?'

Lady Northdon lifted her teacup. 'For the most part.'

Miss Caldwell joined them. 'Is there anything you need, ladies?'

'Non,' answered Lady Northdon.

Good for Lady Northdon. She maintained her dignity.

Miss Caldwell smiled at Amelie. 'You have been quite a success, have you not? My cousin assures me several of the gentlemen are smitten already.'

Amelie blushed again. 'Surely you exaggerate.'

What man would not admire Amelie? The girl outshone all the other young ladies.

'I assure you they were lovestruck.' Miss Caldwell glanced at each of them. 'In fact, the ladies are all impressed by your fashion. What is your secret, *madame*? A new modiste?'

'Not new to me,' Lady Northdon replied.

'Well, you all look very lovely.' Miss Caldwell pressed Lady Northdon's hand and moved on to another group of ladies.

After she walked away, Lady Northdon took another sip of tea. With the cup next to her lips, she murmured, '*Quelle horreur!* She feels obliged to be kind to us.'

Amelie's eyes widened. 'Maman! What a horrid thing to say.'

Lady Northdon lifted a shoulder. 'I do not like to feel someone needs to make an effort to be civil to me.'

Yes. There was an air of forced solicitude when Miss Caldwell spoke to them, now that Lady Northdon called her attention to it. Even so, Tess wondered if she could have forced herself to be as kind as Miss Caldwell had the tables been turned.

Amelie protested more and listed all the nice things Miss Caldwell and her friends had said or done this night. Tess could hear no more praise for this fine woman.

She rose. 'Excuse me for a moment.'

Let them think she was in need of the lady's retiring room, but all she truly wanted was a few moments alone. She peeked inside the room set aside for the ladies and found several others there. She tried another door and found a small library where she sank into a chair.

She must not think only of herself and the strain of this evening. She must also think of Marc. How much worse it must be for him. And for Miss Caldwell. Tess had ruined their plans.

The truth of it was, she could see a marriage between Marc and Miss Caldwell working very well. Miss Caldwell would never impetuously walk to the village when rain threatened. She would never become besotted by a gentleman from London visiting his aunt in Lincolnshire. Miss Caldwell could provide the serene, respectable married life Marc desired.

What could Tess offer him?

More scandal.

She heard men's voices in the hallway. They must be rejoining the women. She waited until the voices died away to return to the drawing room. She tried to slip in unnoticed. As soon as she walked through the door, though, Mr Welton approached her.

'Miss Summerfield?' He bowed.

'Mr Welton.' She curtsied.

She'd once felt breathless at just the sight of him in Yardney; giddy when he spoke to her. She felt nothing now. His handsome face, blond hair and pale brown eyes were still striking, but she was unaffected.

He smiled. 'I confess I did not know you at first.'

'I am newly arrived in London,' she said.

'Did I not hear your sister married old Lord Tinmore?' He gave her a knowing look. 'Such a change of fortune for your family.'

His tone was polite and conversational. And utterly indifferent, such a contrast to his flirtation and pretty words in Yardney.

'I understand you are betrothed to Mr Glenville,' he continued in that uninterested manner. 'My very best wishes to you.'

'Thank you,' she managed to say.

He glanced over to Amelie. 'Is Miss Glenville out, I wonder? She is a lovely young lady. If only—' He cut himself off. 'Well, never mind that. Is your sister in town? Your younger sister?'

Genna. Beautiful Genna. 'No, she is not.'

'Tinmore has been generous to your family, I hear.' He meant Tinmore had restored Genna's dowry, she'd wager. 'I heard he planned to break his exile and come to town for the Season. Your sister will come as well, will she not?'

'Yes,' she answered through gritted teeth. 'But, I assure you, Mr Welton, my sister will be looking so much higher than you. After all, Lorene married an earl and I will be a viscountess some day. I believe Genna has hopes to best us with a marquess.'

He was the mere younger son of a baronet.

She curtsied again. 'If you will excuse me, sir. I must return to Lady Northdon.'

She turned away and crossed the room, taking her seat next to Lady Northdon again and attempting to look as unaffected by the interview as possible.

Mr Welton was nothing but a fortune hunter. He'd been toying with her in Yardney. It all had meant nothing to him. How could she have been so fooled?

Across the room Marc sat with Doria Caldwell, watching the scene between Tess and Welton.

'They appear to know each other,' Doria said, as impassive as always.

'She is acquainted with him.' Marc felt consumed with jealousy. 'They met in Lincolnshire.'

'Did they?' She turned to him. 'My father told me about her mother and father. And of her sister's recent marriage.'

He nodded. 'Both our families have scandal in them.

I'll not fault her for the sins of her mother and father if she does not fault me for mine.'

She placed her hand on his arm. 'You are quite right.' She lowered her voice. 'Our family has always loved you for yourself.'

The truth of that felt like a stab in the heart.

He wanted to apologise to her, but that would imply that he'd made her a promise and he had not, not when he'd known he'd be riding into danger at any moment. He'd been careful not to make any promises, although he'd wanted to when Charles died.

He averted his gaze from her and saw Tess return to sit next to his mother.

From the moment Tess said she'd met Welton in Yardney, Marc realised who the man was. Welton was the man Tess had wanted to marry, the man who needed her to have a big dowry to make it worth his while. Marc disliked Welton on sight—well—as soon as he'd seen the man looking at Tess.

Marc's father, standing across the room, gestured for Marc to come.

He rose. 'You'll have to pardon me, Doria. I believe my father wishes to leave.'

'So soon?' She stood, as well. 'I am glad you and your family came. And Miss Summerfield, too, of course. I wish you happiness.'

He took her hand. 'You are a fine lady, Doria. Charles would be proud of the woman you've become.'

Tears filled her eyes. 'Say no more.'

He squeezed her hand and turned away from her.

His father reached him before he'd taken more than a few steps. 'Your mother is ready to leave.'

Marc would bet it was his father who'd tired of the party, who'd tired of pretending the guests weren't forcing themselves to be civil to him. His mother was made of sterner stuff.

'I will say goodnight to Mr Caldwell and arrange for the footman to get our coats.'

A few minutes later they stood outside the town house in the chilly February air, waiting for their carriage. Marc's father was pacing the street, impatient for its arrival. Amelie was excitedly talking with their mother about all the people she'd met—all the young men who'd noticed her.

Marc's thoughts were with Tess, though. It was all he could do not to demand she tell him what she and Welton spoke about.

'How was it for you?' he asked instead.

'The party?' she responded. 'Quite splendid for my first town entertainment.' She did not sound as if it were so splendid. 'How was it for you? It must not have been so easy.'

He gazed down at her, her lovely face illuminated by the rushlights mounted outside the town-house door. 'Not so easy for you, either.'

She glanced away. 'I assure you. It was a lovely party.' Her eyes darted back. 'Not nearly as difficult as a freezing cabin with dwindling firewood.'

He laughed softly and his heart warmed to her. 'I believe I would have preferred the cabin.'

Her brows rose. 'Would you?'

He took a breath. 'There is something to be said about shutting out the rest of the world for a brief time.'

She seemed to search his face. 'Especially when the world outside is so cold.'

Was she talking about the party or the cabin?

'I shall always remember the cabin. It was the place you brought me after saving my life.' She held his gaze.

'Although your life might have been better if you had ridden right by me.'

'I could not have done so.'

She nodded. 'Yes. That would not be in your character, would it? And look how I thank you for it.'

'We are both in this fix.' He touched her arm. 'Do you wish to marry him?'

'Who?'

'Mr Welton.' He spat out the name.

She blinked in surprise. 'Mr Welton? Not at all.' She paused, then lowered her voice. 'What of you? Your attachment to Miss Caldwell was the stronger.'

Truth was, he could not imagine marrying Doria now. He was sensible that he'd broken a promise to her, though, even if it was a promise unspoken.

'Do you wish me to cry off?' she asked, her voice no more than a whisper. 'Because I will, if you wish it.'

He closed the short distance between them and gently touched her face. 'I am marrying you, Tess.'

She looked up at him, her eyes dark, her breath quickening.

'Where the devil is the carriage?' his father bellowed.

Tess jumped back.

Chapter Nine

Marc could not sleep.

He was on fire for her.

Tess had looked so beautiful this night, like a jewel cut and polished to perfection. His eyes kept straying to her and it had been all he could do to remain composed. He'd wanted to take her by the arm and leave the Caldwell town house, return here and make love to her. When that dandified Welton approached her, he'd wanted to plant the man a facer. He'd managed to hide his runaway emotions until they were waiting for the carriage. Then he'd almost kissed her.

How would it have felt, to seize the woman to whom he was betrothed and take possession of her mouth?

His father's words pounded in his head—*Thus grief still treads upon the heels of pleasure...*

Did any good come from so totally losing one's head and acting out of passion?

Not for his father, certainly.

Nor his brother.

Nor Charles.

How could this work to marry her? She did not wish to marry him, after all. She had been forced into it. She'd wanted a husband to love her.

Marc knew this consuming desire for her was not love, but something more primal, something that had robbed his father and mother of happiness and robbed his brother and friend of their lives.

He must conquer this, control it before it controlled him.

He glanced out the window into the starless night. If it were dawn, he'd dress and take Apollo for a long run in the park. Dawn was a few hours away, however.

He paced in his room.

He'd wanted a peaceful and scandal-free life, hadn't he? He'd wanted to marry Doria. They each had an esteem for the other, an admiration. Marriage to her would have been calm and sane, without this churning lust that did him no credit at all.

The memory of Tess's hazel eyes flew into his head. Her eyes were so beautifully expressive. How might those eyes appear in the heat of passion?

He went to the window again and opened the sash. The cool air rushed in like a good slap on the face.

This was madness. Stop thinking, for God's sake.

Marc shut the window again and strode to the door. He left his bedchamber and made his way to the drawing room. A decanter of brandy might quiet his insanity. Make him sleep. He opened the cabinet. The decanter was full. He poured a glass and downed it right there. He grabbed the decanter and glass and returned to his room. Two glasses later, he was only more restless.

He remembered the reflection of her lithe body in the glass of the cabin's window as she had donned her shift. He remembered her creamy, smooth skin, her full breasts and narrow waist.

He poured another glass and downed it in one gulp. Damnation!

There was only one way out of this. Call off the wed-

ding. So what if Tinmore withheld funds from her sister
and her brother? Marc could make up for that. He could
support Tess, if she so desired. He could give her an in-
come and a dowry. Enable her to marry a man she could
love.

He'd do it!

Marc threw the glass down, wanting to hear it shatter,
but, instead, it bounced off the curtain and rolled across
the carpet. He retrieved it and poured the remains of the
brandy into it, finishing it off.

Why had he not thought of this before? Give them
money. Free Tess and free himself from this insanity.

He'd tell her. Tell her now. It seemed as good a time as
any. Why not? Her room was just a few feet away from
his door.

He placed the empty glass on the table and walked carefully out of his room, his gait unsteady from the brandy.
Still in bare feet, he padded over to Tess's door and raised
his arm to pound on it.

That would not do. He'd wake the whole house.

He rapped lightly. 'Tess. Are you awake? Want to speak
with you.'

He heard her voice faintly through the closed door.
'Marc?'

'Let me in. Need to say something.' He swayed and
steadied himself against the door jamb.

'One minute,' she said.

His head spun, but he ignored it.

Finally she opened the door. 'What is it?'

In the dim light of the hall sconce, she appeared little
more than a shadow. The scent of lavender wafted around
her and intoxicated him even more than the brandy. Lavender. The laundress always scented the bed linens with
lavender. Now whenever he lay between the sheets, he'd

think of her. Her feet were bare, too. Like in the cabin. The memory of her warm against his body slammed into him.

He lowered his voice. 'May I enter?'

She opened the door wider and he stepped inside.

The only light in the room was from the fireplace. It turned her nightdress and robe a ghostly white, like an apparition. A dream. A pleasant dream. Marc shook his head.

He watched as the apparition took a taper to the fire and used it to light a lamp on a nearby table.

She blew out the taper. 'What is it, Marc?'

She was so lovely, so much like the woman in the cabin and the beauty who'd dressed in green for the dinner party. His senses flared with desire.

Why had he come to her bedchamber? He tried to remember. All he could think of was making love to her. She looked like a woman who needed to be well loved.

He shook his head and remembered. He'd come to talk about money.

He came closer. 'Wanted to tell you…' The scent of the bed linens reached his nostrils again and the words disappeared.

He touched her shoulder and fingered a lock of her hair. 'You look lovely, Tess.'

What would it feel like to slide his hand down her body and explore the softness beneath her nightclothes? He remembered her curves when they'd lain together on the cot in the cabin.

A sound of discomfort came from her throat. 'You came to tell me something?'

He nodded. By God, the drink affected him. He couldn't stand without swaying. He couldn't think. 'We have to marry, Tess.'

She stood very still. 'Did you come here to tell me that?'

No, it felt more likely he'd come to feel her hair beneath his fingers. To taste her lips.

He leaned close, so close those lips were a mere touch away. He had almost tasted her lips earlier. If he kissed her, would it ease this sudden hunger for her? How would she taste if he plunged his tongue inside her mouth? If he plunged himself inside her?

Why not? They'd be married within days.

He closed his eyes and his mind cleared for a moment. He leaned away.

She stepped back. 'I think you should go back to your room, Marc.'

He nodded and, still gazing at her, backed away.

'We will marry,' he said again when his hand was on the latch of the door. Before he weakened and changed his mind, he walked out and closed the door behind him.

Tess stared at the closed door, her body a-tremble. What had happened?

He'd been drinking, clearly.

What did it mean that he'd come so close, touching her hair, her arm, making her senses come alive? She was quivering with the mere memory of his touch.

Had he wanted to bed her? Before marriage? Her old governess used to lecture Tess and her sisters to beware of men who'd imbibed too much wine or brandy. Too much drink drove men and women into bed with each other, the governess said.

It was true. Tess had seen her mother drinking wine with a gentleman who'd called upon her. She'd been in her mother's sitting room, a place she'd been forbidden to enter, so she'd hidden behind the curtains. Through a slit in the curtains, she'd seen them kiss. And undress. And—and—

She'd never told anyone of that.

But now all she could think was that Marc had wanted to do that with her. She should have been shocked. Appalled.

Instead, she'd wanted to feel *his* hair between her fingers, put her hand on his shoulders. She'd wanted him to kiss her. She'd wanted him to lie with her in the bed like her mother had lain with her gentleman.

Perhaps she was more like her mother than she ever dreamed she could be.

Tess extinguished the lamp and walked back to her bed. She climbed in. Sleep would be difficult to achieve when every part of her seemed on fire. Was this what her mother had felt when gentlemen came near?

She had never felt this way when Mr Welton shook her hand or leaned close. This was something carnal, something with a power all its own. Something she wanted.

It was unforgivable for Marc to come to her in such a state, was it not? Tess tried to muster up anger or outrage or even embarrassment, but, even now, she wished he would come back.

If Marc Glenville returned to her room this moment and wished to be carnal with her, she would not stop him.

The next morning Marc slept later than usual. When he roused himself, his head ached and his stomach roiled. He washed, shaved and dressed, all the while hoping Staines could not tell he was trying not to cast up his accounts.

In the dining room, the smell of kippers and cheese nearly set him off. He quickly took a piece of toast and poured a cup of coffee and was very glad he was alone in the room.

Not for long, however.

Tess entered.

He thought he must look like hell, but she was as fresh as the air after a storm. Her hair was simply dressed atop her head. She wore a dress of sprigged muslin, blue on white, with blue flowers embroidered on the shoulders and around the hem.

She paused when she saw him.

He stood. 'Good morning, Tess.'

She did not look at him. 'Good morning.' She went directly to the sideboard.

The footman appeared, but only long enough to bring her a pot of tea. Marc was drinking coffee. Lots of coffee.

She sat not too close to him, but not as far away as she might have. She kept her attention on her food, a piece of bread with jam.

He needed to say something. 'I owe you an apology, Tess.'

She gave him the briefest glance.

'I came to your room last night.'

She finally gave him a direct gaze. 'I know.'

He met her eye. 'It was unforgivable of me to wake you and to come to your room. I had too much to drink.'

'Why did you come?' she asked.

He did not wish to tell her of his brandy-laced plan to buy her off. It would not have worked. It would have left her in more scandal, with a ruined reputation and little chance of making a respectable marriage.

He shook his head. 'I do not remember.'

Her brows rose.

'I will say,' he went on, 'that I am not in the habit of drinking to excess. It will not happen again.'

She nodded and glanced back to her food.

A footman came in. 'Lord Northdon wishes to see you in the library, sir.'

A summons from his father never meant anything good. 'Thank you. I'll see him directly.'

He stood again. 'What are your plans today?' he asked Tess.

She looked up at him. 'Your mother wishes to take me shopping again.'

'Do you mind?' Not everyone shared his mother's passion for shopping.

'No. I enjoy it.'

He was not sure if she was being completely honest, but her kindness to his mother meant a great deal to him.

He walked over to her, needing to touch her, just a little, before he left the room.

He touched her shoulder. 'You should have spending money of your own. I will make sure you have some before you leave.'

She grew quite still under his hand. 'Thank you.'

He lifted his hand, his fingers still feeling the warmth of her. He bowed to her and left the room and made his way to the library.

When he stepped into the room, his father swung around in his chair. 'About time. What took so long?'

'Eating breakfast.' And touching Tess.

His father looked him up and down. 'Your colour is poor. Are you ill?'

'Not ill.' He was not going to explain that he'd consumed an entire decanter of brandy and almost seduced his fiancée. 'You have need of me, sir?'

His father picked up a rolled document and handed it to Marc. 'A messenger brought this earlier. Your special licence.'

Marc's stomach protested.

He took the document into his hand and unrolled it. 'It

seems in order.' He took a deep breath. 'I must tell Tess it is here.' He turned to the door.

'Wait,' his father cried. His expression looked strained. 'No one else knows. If you need more time—'

Marc shook his head. 'There's no need to wait.'

Truth was, he did not want to wait. He'd search today to find a clergyman to perform the ceremony as soon as possible.

'Why the devil are you marrying this woman, Marc?' His father sounded exasperated. 'Why the hurry if she is not with child? It does not make sense. There is something you are not telling me.'

He owed it to his father to hear the truth from him. 'There is more to it.' He hoped his breakfast would stay down. 'When I was riding back from Scotland, I came across Tess on the road in a rainstorm. She was suffering greatly from the wet and the cold. I found a cabin and took her there to get her warm. We were forced to spend the night. In the morning Lord Tinmore's men found us and Tinmore declared I had compromised her.'

His father's face turned red. 'You compromised her? How could you be so foolish?'

Marc stared at him. 'I did nothing you would object to. If I had not taken her to the cabin, she would have died from the elements.'

His father averted his gaze, then gave Marc a sceptical look. 'There must be more to it than that.'

Only that Tinmore had threatened to impoverish her, her sister and brother, but what purpose would it serve for his father to know that? 'I am honour bound to marry her.'

'How many knew of this? Could it not have been kept quiet?'

Marc shook his head. 'Tinmore was having a house party at the time. With luck most will have forgotten it by the time those guests and Tinmore arrive in town, but there may be some gossip about it.'

'More talk…' His father spoke more to himself than to Marc.

'I am sorry, Father.' Marc meant it. He never wanted to cause anyone to talk of his family.

'You need to do this, then.' His father's voice sounded more resigned than dictatorial.

'I do, Papa.'

His father rose from his chair. 'If only she came from a better family. Her parents—'

Marc cut him off. 'Do not say a word about her parents.' Surely his father could see the hypocrisy in complaining about *her* parents.

His father walked up to him and gripped his upper arms. 'I did not mean that. I meant—well, I thought—I thought you were marrying her because she had a pretty face.' He looked earnestly into Marc's eyes. 'I feared you would make the same mistake.'

'As you did with Maman?' Marc shrugged him off. 'You have told me many times of your regret at marrying my mother. I do not need to hear it again.'

His father shot back, 'Credit me with wanting to save you pain.'

Marc grimaced. 'Now you are saying marriage to my mother gives you pain. You cause her pain, too, you know.'

His father looked as if Marc had slapped him. 'I think of it. Every day.' His expression turned to concern. 'I do not wish you to have regrets, my son. Perhaps if I had said these things to your brother—' He broke off and waved those words away. He pointed to the special licence. 'Let me lock the paper up in a drawer. We can think of a way out of this.'

'I will marry her. It is the only way.' Marc rolled up the

special licence again and put it in a pocket inside his coat. 'We'll be married as soon as I can arrange it.'

His father nodded. The man suddenly looked smaller and older than he had a moment before.

Marc patted him on the back. 'It will work out, Papa. It is not like Lucien.'

He wanted to marry Tess and there was nothing impetuous about it. He must marry her to spare her reputation. There was no reason they could not do well together.

Especially if he banked his passion and kept it under tight control. There was no reason they could not have the rational sort of marriage he'd planned with Doria.

If he could indeed bank his passion and keep it under tight control.

He left his father and went to get Tess some spending money. He'd venture out that very morning and search for a clergyman to perform the ceremony.

Later that day Marc walked through Mayfair on his way back to his parents' town house. He'd spent hours searching for a clergyman. Finally he found a man from St Clement Danes who agreed to perform the ceremony in three days' time.

It should not have been so difficult, but, as it turned out, many men of the cloth were not eager to perform a service for Lord and Lady Northdon's son. He did not know why he should have expected a different reaction. Such treatment he'd experienced his whole life.

He turned down Berkeley Street from Piccadilly and decided to stop in Gunter's Tea Shop for some sweets for his mother, sister…and Tess. He entered the shop and who should be there, peering into the glass-covered cases displaying treats of all kinds and colours, but Doria, attended by her maid.

He had not expected to see her so soon. Or even at all, for that matter.

She looked over and smiled. 'Marc. What a surprise.'

'Indeed.' He walked over to her. 'How are you, Doria?'

She continued to smile. 'I am well.'

They stared at each other until he turned to the case. 'I came in for some sweets.'

'As did I,' she said.

A clerk approached and she made her order.

Another waited on Marc.

Their packages were ready at the same time and he walked out with her, her maid following.

'What did you select?' she asked.

'Ginger candy, sugar drops and some French nougat,' he responded. 'My mother is particularly fond of French nougat.'

She gestured to the maid who carried her package. 'And my father adores liquor comfits.'

They stood outside the shop. 'I want to thank you again for inviting my family to your dinner party. I think Amelie will talk of nothing else for weeks.'

'I am glad,' Doria responded.

They stepped aside for a gentleman and lady to enter the shop.

She went on. 'Your Miss Summerfield seems like a lovely person.'

He did not know what to make of that. 'I am glad you think so.'

She glanced across the street to the square where there were benches for Gunter's customers to enjoy his ices during the summer months. Most were empty this day.

'Would you sit with me for a minute?' she asked. 'I wish to say something to you.'

'Of course.' He escorted her across the street.

Her maid sat a discreet distance while he shared a bench with Doria.

She seemed to steel herself. 'I think you realise that everyone expected you to make an offer to me—'

He interrupted her. 'We never spoke of it. I never offered marriage to you.'

She held up a hand. 'Yes, I know you did not. There was a time I assumed it would happen, though.'

'I am sorry, Doria,' he said.

'Wait.' She shifted her posture. 'This is difficult to say. I want you to know that I would have refused you.'

He leaned back in surprise.

Her brows furrowed and her voice turned very low. 'The truth is, you are too much a reminder of Charles. Every time I look at you, I remember he is gone. My father very much wanted me to marry you, but he and I must move on from Charles's death. I know we cannot do that if you—if you are constantly present.'

He took her hand. 'I miss Charles, too.' He quickly released her. 'I want you to know, no matter what gossip you hear, that I want to marry Tess. We will be married in three days.' He gave her a wan smile. 'You are the first to know that.'

She took his hand back. 'I am genuinely happy for you.'

Tess gazed out of the carriage window as Lady Northdon and Amelie discussed what to do with the pieces of fabric they'd purchased. Nancy sat in rapt attention to their every word. Tess could barely attend to any of it. She was tired from a fitful night's sleep and a lot of shopping. This day they had visited a corset maker and ordered several types of corsets for her, as well as looking in on yet another linen-draper where Nancy found a silk ivory fabric she declared perfect for Tess's wedding dress. To Nancy's great pleasure, Lady Northdon and Amelie heartily agreed.

Tess's thoughts drifted to Marc. How it felt for him to be so close, to touch her, to have his blue eyes look at her in such a way that made her know he wanted to bed her. Could a man who did not want to marry her still want to bed her?

It must have been the drink. That was the only explanation.

The carriage drove slowly by one of the squares that seemed to be everywhere in Mayfair. This was Berkeley Square, she remembered. They were only a short distance from the town house, thank goodness.

The square was lovely, with trees starting to sprout leaves and plenty of grass and benches for people to sit on.

A lady and gentleman sat on one of the benches, their hands clasped.

Tess gasped.

It was Marc and Miss Caldwell.

Chapter Ten

Tess quickly glanced at Lady Northdon and Amelie to see if they noticed the couple, but both ladies and even Nancy were still wrapped up in the discussion about fabric.

Her throat tightened.

Why would Marc be with Miss Caldwell?

Why else but that he still felt an attachment to her?

How often had she heard her father lament that he'd married her mother instead of the woman he truly loved—Edmund's mother. He'd kept Edmund's mother as a mistress and she'd borne him a son. He'd spent more time with her than with his own wife, more time with his son than the children his wife eventually bore, the ones everyone said were fathered by her lovers.

They all wound up unhappy. That is what happened when two people did not marry for love.

That is what would happen to her and Marc.

The carriage entered Grosvenor Street and brought them to the door.

When they were inside the town house, Tess said, 'I am suddenly very tired. I believe I will retire to my room for a little while.'

'Mon Dieu, ma chérie,' exclaimed Lady Northdon. 'You do look pale. Go. Rest. We do not wish you a *maladie*.'

Her kindness made Tess's eyes prick with tears.

She gave Lady Northdon a quick hug. 'Thank you, *madame*.'

She felt like running up the stairs and flinging herself on the bed as she did when she was little and Lorene or Edmund teased her. Instead she forced herself to walk at a normal pace.

Once in the room, she still could not dissemble. Nancy would enter any minute and how would she explain her tears to the maid?

Nancy came into the room, carrying the packages from the shopping trip. 'Oh, miss, I must say that I adore London! I had no idea there could be so many shops. I do believe Lady Northdon knows them all!' She set the packages on a table. 'So many corsets! Did you ever see the like? I understand now how the right corset might enhance a gown. It is like discovering the New World, is it not?'

'A whole new world.' Tess sank into a chair. 'Of corsets.'

'So.' Nancy faced her, arms akimbo. 'What may I do for you? You look very tired.'

'Help me into a morning dress.' She rubbed her eyes. 'I may even nap a little.'

Nancy sprang into action, pulling one of Tess's new morning dresses from the wardrobe.

As she helped Tess out of her walking dress, Tess asked, 'Did the shopping not even tire you today, Nancy?'

'Oh, no, miss!' Nancy pulled the dress over her head. 'There is too much to see.'

She helped Tess into the morning dress and brushed out her hair and put it into a plait. 'There. That should be more comfortable for you. When you are finished resting,

summon me and I'll rearrange your hair. I'll come to help
you dress for dinner, as well.'

It was comforting to be fussed over.

The girl tied a ribbon to hold her plait. 'Unless there is
something else you need for me to do, I'll work on your
wedding dress.'

Her wedding dress. A dress she should not wear.

'It will be so pretty,' Nancy went on. 'I hope you will
like it. It will be the best gown I've ever made.'

'I am certain it will be lovely.'

How could she let Marc marry her, if the woman he
wanted was Miss Caldwell?

'Then I'll go,' said Nancy brightly. 'Have a nice rest.'

Tess remained in the chair, gazing out the window that
looked down upon the small garden in the back, the stor-
age sheds and the gated wall. There was a bench facing
flower beds, a nice place to sit when the weather was warm
and dry, like the bench in Berkeley Square.

She rose from the chair and climbed on to the bed, bury-
ing her face in the pillow.

Be strong, she told herself.

Refuse to marry him. It was her right to cry off, after
all, and his reputation would not suffer overmuch for refusing, not under the circumstances. She would seek employment. She would put her name in with an agency that
found positions for governesses and ladies' companions.
There were many such agencies in London, she'd heard.

She rolled on to her back and covered her eyes with
her arm.

But what of Genna and Edmund? And Lorene?

A rap on the door made her jump.

'Who is it?' Please, not Amelie or Lady Northdon. She
could not pretend to be cheerful.

'It is Marc,' came the voice from the other side. 'May I speak with you?'

Marc?

This was too much like the night before, waking to his knock. Her senses flared with the memory.

And plummeted and hardened in resolve.

She climbed out of bed and walked to the door.

Like the night before, she opened it a crack. 'What is it?'

'May I come in?' He smelled of fresh air. He must have come straight from Berkeley Square.

She opened the door wider and he entered the room. She left the door ajar.

His demeanour was altered from the night before. Then he'd looked wild, emotional, sensual. Now he appeared steady and calm.

'Forgive my appearance,' she said. 'I was resting.'

'I woke you?' He frowned. 'I am sorry.'

'I was not asleep.' She took a chair. 'What do you want?'

He sat in an adjacent one and handed her a small wrapped package. 'I bought you something. A trifle.'

She untied the string and unfolded the paper. 'Oh. Sweets. How nice.' Her voice rang flat in her own ears.

'I walked by Gunter's Tea Shop and purchased some for you, and for Maman and Amelie.' He smiled.

'Gunter's,' she repeated woodenly.

'On Berkeley Square,' he added.

Berkeley Square. She tried not to flinch.

She set the sweetmeats aside. 'I shall save them for later.'

He reached into a pocket in his coat. 'I also have the special licence.' He pulled out the paper.

'Oh' was all she could manage.

'And I've arranged for a clergyman to perform the ceremony here in three days, if that is to your liking.'

'Three days?' She rose and faced the window. 'Are you certain this is what you want?'

'How many times must I say it, Tess?' He left his chair and stood behind her. 'I know this is not the sort of marriage you desired. I know you marry me for your sisters' and brother's sakes and for no other reason. I know it is not your choice.'

'It is not your choice, either,' she said.

He turned her to face him. 'You are wrong there. I did have a choice and I chose to offer you marriage.'

She would not look at him.

'What is it, Tess?' He shook her gently. 'Is this about my behaviour last night? I told you, it will not happen again.'

'It is not about last night.' The look of him coming to her room, wanting her, was too painful to remember. She raised her gaze to him. 'I know last night was nothing to you, nothing but drink. Please be honest with me now. Do you still wish you could marry Miss Caldwell?'

His expression turned exasperated. 'Why ask this of me again? I told you, that was in the past. I do not think of it now.'

'But you met her at Berkeley Square.' It still hurt. 'I saw you.'

A muscle in his cheek twitched. 'I met her by happenstance and we spoke together a short while. Nothing more.'

Her mother's excuses to her father rang in her ears. *I just happened to encounter him. It was nothing.* Or that day her mother's lover visited her sitting room. *He came to call upon you. I offered him some sherry.*

Lies.

Was Marc lying to her? She'd been completely fooled by Mr Welton, after all. And Lord Tinmore lied about giving her a dowry. Even Lorene had kept the truth from her, the truth about getting married to Tinmore.

Their father lied to them so many times, it became a joke among her and her sisters.

Her own mother had lied to her. She said she'd come to their bedroom to say goodnight. She said she would see Tess the next day.

She never came back.

How was Tess to believe Marc?

Somehow Tess managed to get through the next three days. Marc was especially attentive to her, making time to show her some of the sights of London. They walked through the tombs at Westminster Abbey. Toured the Tower. He even took her to Gunter's Tea Shop where she again saw the bench upon which he had sat with Miss Caldwell.

The wedding was set to take place in the afternoon, because the clergyman Marc found to do the ceremony was not available until the afternoon. Because of the special licence, they did not need to be married in the morning, though, so the time was of no consequence. Tess's preparation for the ceremony started two hours before the scheduled time. As Nancy and Amelie joined her in her bedchamber, it started to rain outside, a heavy, constant rain that reminded Tess of the storm not even a fortnight before, the one that brought her and Marc together.

It seemed fitting that it should rain for this day, as well.

Amelie had begged to help her dress so Tess had to keep up a facade of good cheer for both Amelie and Nancy. Nancy spent at least an hour arranging Tess's hair in curls tied up with ribbon that matched her dress. Amelie tinted Tess's cheeks and lips the lightest pink, which was good because otherwise Tess feared she would have no colour in her face at all.

She felt as if this were someone else's hair being arranged, someone else being dressed like a doll. A part of her was again lost in the storm, wandering one road after another.

Nancy's hands shook as she helped Tess step into her wedding gown and put her arms through its sleeves. Nancy buttoned the long row of buttons she'd sewn on the back of the dress. Then Amelie turned the mirror on Tess.

'Do you like it?' Nancy asked nervously as Tess shook herself back to reality.

In the full-length mirror was the image of a woman dressed in a beautiful ivory-silk gown with embroidery and lace adorning the bodice, sleeves and hem. Tess gasped.

'It is quite the loveliest gown I have ever worn,' she answered truthfully. 'I hardly know myself.'

Amelie clasped her hands together. 'My brother will love it, I am certain, and Maman will be so very impressed.'

Nancy looked awed. 'If her ladyship approves, I can ask for no greater compliment.'

'She will approve, do not worry, Nancy,' Amelie said.

Tess slipped her feet into shoes that matched the ivory silk and picked up her prayer book, the one piece of her past that could accompany her to her wedding. 'I suppose we should go.'

Already waiting in the drawing room were the clergyman, Lord and Lady Northdon, and Marc. The only other people who would witness the wedding would be the servants, who were included as members of the household. Tess was glad for Nancy, who had always been much more excited about the wedding than Tess could ever be.

Nancy fussed with the dress one more time, then nodded and smiled. 'I am ready, miss!' She laughed. 'This is the last time I shall call you miss. You will be ma'am from now on!'

She'd be Mrs Marc Glenville and, someday, Lady Northdon. It felt like the end of Tess Summerfield, the end of her connection to home, a fraying of her ties to her family, who were not even present to see her married.

Her past washed away in the rain.

Amelie walked down the stairs first and Nancy trailed behind Tess, attending to the train of the dress. Amelie slipped into the drawing room to alert them that they were ready. Nancy peeked in and gestured to Tess when they all stood in their places. Nancy opened the door and everyone turned.

The furniture had been moved out of the way and Tess's path to where the clergyman and Marc stood was lined with jardinières of flowers. Lady Northdon's idea, no doubt, and such a dear gesture that a lump formed in Tess's throat.

The servants stood along the walls and Lord and Lady Northdon were joined by Amelie near where Marc stood waiting for her. He was dressed in buff-coloured breeches and a black coat and waistcoat. He might have been attending the finest ball, he looked so handsome, but the expression on his face was unreadable and she faltered before making the inevitable walk towards him. His gaze followed her every step. She clutched her prayer book tighter as she took her place next to him. Marc turned to face the clergyman, a kind-faced man with a smiling demeanour that was almost enough to put her at ease.

'Dearly Beloved,' he began. 'We are gathered together here in the sight of God, and in the face of this congregation, to join together this man and this woman in holy matrimony; which is an honourable estate...'

An honourable estate? It wasn't honour that brought

Tess to this moment. It was love. Not the romantic love for which she once yearned, but love of her sisters and brother. Perhaps there was honour in that.

He went on, not in a style as if he were reciting some memorised passage, but as if he were talking to them in conversation, serious at times, smiling at others. All the while, Tess heard the rain in the background.

The clergyman spoke to Marc as if he'd known Marc for years. 'Wilt thou have this woman to thy wedded wife, to live together after God's ordinance in the holy estate of matrimony? Wilt thou love her, comfort her, honour and keep her, in sickness and in health and, forsaking all other, keep thee only unto her, so long as ye both shall live?'

Marc answered, 'I will.'

Did he hear the rain, as well?

It was her turn.

'Wilt thou have this man to thy wedded husband, to live together after God's ordinance in the holy estate of matrimony? Wilt thou obey him, and serve him, love, honour and keep him, in sickness and in health and, forsaking all other, keep thee only unto him, so long as ye both shall live?'

She answered, 'I will.'

In the distance, thunder rumbled.

The ceremony continued. It was astonishingly personal, and very intimate with just Marc's parents, sister and servants there, all cocooned by the rain.

At the end, the clergyman smiled. 'I pronounce that they be man and wife together.' He finished with the blessing, in like manner, as if he were a friend come to have conversation with them.

And it was over.

After the ceremony, there was punch and cake for the servants. Marc had known some of them since childhood and their congratulations were heartfelt. His mother seemed in her element, basking in praise for how she'd transformed the room into something special for the occasion. She and his father were on good behaviour for once, but, then, they did not speak to each other overmuch. His father talked mostly to Reverend Cane, and his mother, to Amelie.

He and Tess accepted the good wishes of the household, but said little to each other.

She looked stunningly beautiful. No woman on her wedding day could have looked more beautiful. Her silk gown caught the candlelight, making it shimmer as she moved. Her hair was a luxury of curls that appeared as if they would all tumble down with one tug on the ribbon threaded through them.

Tess smiled and accepted the servants' congratulations with grace. She thanked his mother and Reverend Cane for making the ceremony special.

How sad, though, that this was not the wedding of her dreams, a wedding to a man she could love. Marc would try to make it up to her. He vowed to do whatever was in his power to make her life pleasant.

'How are you faring?' he asked her during a break in the congratulations.

'Very well,' she said unconvincingly. 'I am touched by all the care that was taken by your mother and the servants to make this—this—special.'

'You have given my mother a great deal of happiness. And doing this for you brings her much pleasure.' Marc was grateful, so very grateful to Tess for accepting his mother and befriending her. His mother knew so little of friendship.

'I should add Nancy,' Tess said. 'Nancy made this splendid dress.'

His gaze swept over her. 'You look magnificent in it.'

Her expression stiffened. 'That is kind of you to say.'

Any compliment he gave her seemed to have the opposite of what one would expect. Instead of helping her to warm towards him, it made her withdraw even more. At least her distance cooled his ardour, like a cold rain cooled the warm earth.

It was good, though. It helped his head rule his heart. Only by using his head would he avoid any missteps. He was determined to make this marriage pleasant for both of them. He wanted them to regain the camaraderie they had shared when stranded in the cabin.

Eventually the cake and punch were consumed and the servants returned to their duties. Marc, Tess, his parents, the reverend and Amelie sat together in the drawing room until dinner was announced. The wedding breakfast of tradition became a wedding dinner, not unlike dinner every other night of the week, except they had Reverend Cane as a guest and Marc's father served his best wine. The reverend had a gift of making everyone comfortable and Marc experienced perhaps the most pleasant dinner ever with his family. Tess was polite but reserved, but perhaps no one noticed except him.

When dinner was over, it was quite like any other night. The men stayed in the dining room for brandy and the women retired to the drawing room for tea. The reverend did not stay long after the men rejoined the women. He bid them all goodnight and wished Marc and Tess a happy life together. Marc walked him out to the hall where he donned his greatcoat and hat and armed himself with his umbrella. Marc's father had ordered the carriage for the man. When it pulled up to the door, he said goodnight and left.

Marc returned to the drawing room and his father suggested they all retire.

They walked up the stairs together, Marc and Tess leaving his parents and Amelie on the first floor. He followed Tess up to the second floor. Staines was waiting for him as, Marc expected, Nancy would be waiting for Tess. Let the servants ready them for bed. Let them think this would be a typical wedding night.

But nothing was typical about this marriage.

Chapter Eleven

'Here you are, miss—ma'am!' Nancy clapped her hands in excitement when Tess entered the bedchamber. 'This is the wedding night!'

Tess wished she could feel such high spirits. She wished she could feel anything but gut-turning anxiety. She made herself smile. 'I am glad you are here to help me out of my dress.'

Nancy grinned. 'Oh, I'll help you out of your dress and make you very presentable to your new husband!'

Tess did not even know if she would see her husband this night. She pressed her fingers on her brow.

Nancy peered at her, a look of concern on her face. 'Miss—ma'am! Do you know about the wedding night?'

Daughter of the infamous Lady Summerfield not know of such carnal matters? She squeezed Nancy's hand. 'I'm a country girl. I do know about the wedding night.'

She'd seen the act performed, after all.

'Whew!' Nancy's eyes grew wide. 'I was afraid I'd have to tell you. That would have been very strange, would it not?'

'Very strange.' Tess smiled, this time in genuine amusement.

Nancy chattered on while she undid the buttons down

the back of the dress, helped Tess out of it and unlaced her corset.

Dressed in just her shift, Tess washed her face and hands and sat at the dressing table so Nancy could pull the pins from her hair. 'I'll brush out your hair and tie it in a ribbon.'

Having her hair brushed was so soothing that Tess thought she might actually sleep this night. Would it not be wonderful if she could wake up in the morning in her room at Summerfield House? Her sisters would be there and all would be as it had been before their father died. She closed her eyes and again saw that room, bright with sunlight, its pale blue walls and white-skirted tables, her keepsakes lovingly arranged on a shelf. Where were her little treasures now? She'd packed them for Tinmore Hall, but never unpacked them. Would they be lost, like the life she'd once enjoyed?

Nancy wrapped her hair tightly with the ribbon and tied it in a bow. 'I have something for you, ma'am,' she said as she dabbed some lavender scent on Tess's neck and arms. 'Stay right there.'

From the reflection in the mirror, Tess watched Nancy remove a white, neatly folded garment from the clothes press.

'Turn around,' Nancy said.

Tess swivelled in her chair and Nancy held up the white garment and let it loose of its folds. It fluttered down like a billowing cloud.

It was a nightdress made from soft, thin muslin and adorned with lace around the neckline and hem.

'Oh, my!' Tess exclaimed. 'It is lovely! Where did you get it?'

'Lady Northdon gave me the muslin and lace and told me exactly how she wanted it made.' She threw it over her arm and returned to the clothes press for another garment in the same fabric. 'It has a robe to match it!'

Tess rose from her seat and fingered the fabric. 'I cannot imagine how you sewed all these garments. You are a marvel, Nancy.'

Nancy beamed with pride. 'It was a pleasure, ma'am, truly it was.'

Tess hugged the girl. 'I do not know how to thank you. First the beautiful wedding dress and now this. I must also thank Lady Northdon for suggesting it.'

'Let's put you in it,' cried Nancy. 'You want to be ready. Your husband might come any time now.'

Tess took off her shift and Nancy helped her into the nightdress. She turned to the full-length mirror.

It was so sheer that she could see her flesh beneath it.

She added the robe and it was marginally better, but even by lamplight in her room, she could see the outline of her body under the gown and robe.

'What do you think of it?' Nancy asked as she picked up Tess's shift and put it away.

It is too sheer, she wanted to say. Instead, she said, 'I think it is the loveliest nightdress there ever could be.'

Nancy grinned. 'Now, is there anything else I can do for you? I've turned down the bed already.'

Tess did not want the girl to go, but there was no reason for her to stay, except to keep Tess from thinking too much. 'You've done more than enough.'

Nancy stepped forward and gave Tess a quick hug. It was not the proper sort of behaviour for a maid, but Tess found she was hungry for such warmth.

'I'll bid you goodnight, then,' the girl said. She winked. 'A very good night!'

She was gone and Tess was alone. She remained where she stood. As still as a statue, she listened to the sounds of the house. The hiss of the fire, footsteps above her—Nancy going to her room, no doubt. No sound of rain, though. It must have stopped.

He would not come to her, she knew. She wore a woman's nightdress, as alluring as any her mother had possessed, but he would not see it, because theirs was a forced marriage.

All the days in her future stretched before her, empty like land washed bare by a flood.

She strode over to the window and opened it, sucking in the cool air. The air retained that damp chill that so reminded her of their night in the cabin. She stood at the open window until the chill seeped into her skin. She could feel it on her cheeks, in her lungs, on her eyelashes.

They'd worked together well in the cabin, had they not? Of course, Marc had done most of the work, but she had made herself useful, fixing tea and such. The point was, she could act now. She'd not remained passive and helpless in the cabin and she did not need to think of herself as helpless now.

They were husband and wife. It was time she started acting like a wife and not like a little girl pining for her dolls and wishing for things to be different. So what if her keepsakes were lost to her? She could find new ones in her life with him.

She also did not have to wait for him to cross the hall and knock on her door. She could cross the hall and knock on his. He might refuse her this night, but she could offer herself. Or perhaps they could lie together as they'd done in the cabin?

It would be a start.

Tess closed the window and touched her face, reassured that it still felt the bracing chill. She strode to the door and opened it.

As she stepped into the hall she saw him coming towards her, not in breeches and coat, but the loose fabric of a banyan. He was almost as apparition-like as he'd been riding towards her in the rain those few days ago, just the silhouette of him, but she felt that same rush of relief she'd felt that day.

If he welcomed her, she would no longer be alone.

Marc hesitated when Tess appeared before him. She looked as alluring as she'd appeared the night he visited her bedchamber. Only this time he was clear-headed. It helped a little. Only a little.

'What is it, Tess?' He'd not expected her to seek him out. He'd been on his way to her door to reassure her he would not expect anything from her until she was ready.

'I wanted to see you.' She reached out her hand. 'Talk with me, Marc. Please. For a little while?' Her voice was uncertain. 'In—in my room or yours.'

He took her hand. 'I have some claret in my room.' He'd had Staines bring it up earlier in the day when he'd been dressing. A little wine right now might be a good thing.

'Your room, then,' she said.

He held her hand as they entered his room. He had only two candles lit, which bathed the room in a soft light. He led her to a chair near the window. It rattled in the wind like the window of the cabin they shared. He poured the claret and handed it to her.

'You wanted to talk?' Perhaps he would like what she wished to say.

She took a sip of the wine. 'We should—' She began determinedly, but her courage seemed to flag. She gazed out the window. 'Did you hear the rain earlier? It sounded so much like that rain at the cabin.'

'I was reminded of the cabin when I heard it.' He was

reminded of the cabin right now and all his resolve to let his head rule was rapidly being washed away.

She turned her lovely eyes on him. What colour were they at this moment? At the wedding ceremony they had been grey. Like the rain. 'We did well in the cabin, did we not?'

Until he overslept and allowed them to be caught in bed together. 'You did well,' he said.

Her scent distracted him, the lavender scent of bed linens. She looked soft and warm, like she belonged between the sheets, but he'd already promised himself he would not consummate their marriage this night. His head said he would wait until she wanted it, if she ever did, but now the idea of waiting did not appeal to him at all.

He sipped his drink.

She toyed with her glass. 'At the cabin you said you would marry sensibly, that marriage should be to the man and woman's advantage.'

Had he said that? He could not feel less like being sensible right now.

She went on. 'You cautioned me about marrying for love.'

'I remember that.' Men and women mistook love for passion and passion meant allowing one's emotions to dictate actions, as his parents had done.

'If you had married sensibly.' She smiled faintly. 'I assume you intended to—to have a real marriage.'

Of course he had. He was obligated to produce an heir, was he not? 'Certainly.'

She rose and moved towards him, kneeling at his feet. 'Then I think we should have a real marriage. We could make something good of this. What, after all, is the difference between having a sensible marriage and a forced one?'

Was the question rhetorical?

She rested her hands on his knees and gazed up at him. She was offering herself to him? Good Lord, he wanted her beyond all sense. He tried to pull back. Did she truly wish this?

'Tess, you must not feel under any obligation—'

She pushed away and stood, glaring down at him. 'I did not come out of obligation. I wanted to try to make something good out of this, but I can do nothing alone. You must also want me, which you obviously do not.'

She turned on her heel and headed towards the door.

'Wait!' he cried.

He bounded from the chair and caught her by the wrist. He pulled her back and made her face him. Having her in his arms drove words right out of his head.

He took a breath and gazed down at her. 'I never said I did not want you.'

'Then why not?' Her mouth parted and her lashes fluttered. 'I am willing, Marc.'

She had pluck, he must say.

'You want me to show you about making love, Tess?' His blood was surging through his veins as he spoke.

She looked him right in the eye. 'Yes. That is what I want.'

Those words were the only permission he needed. He picked her up and she wrapped her arms around him and did not break her gaze while he carried her to his bed.

He sat her on the bed and stood in front of her. 'How much do you know of this, Tess?'

Her breath quickened. 'Enough. More, than most, I think. I know what happens.'

He still was unsure of her. His head said she offered herself out of duty. His heart wanted to make something good of this, as she suggested.

Her fingers untied the ribbon of her robe. 'I know I must undress for you.'

He watched as she took off her robe. As she moved, the thin cloth of her nightdress clung to her skin. It was so sheer he could see her flesh beneath it. His fingers longed to touch that smooth skin.

Her look was more determined than passionate as she reached for the skirt of her nightdress, but he felt proud of her courage. Slowly she raised the skirt, revealing herself in inches. Glorious inches. Finally she lifted the nightdress over her head and tossed it away and, still looking directly into his face, sat before him, fully revealed.

His eyes drank in the sight of her. Her breasts were high and firm, her nipples dark against her pale skin. Her waist was accented by the fullness of her breasts and hips. The triangle between her legs was tinged with auburn, like her hair. Her legs were long and shaped as if a sculptor had carved them.

She displayed her nakedness almost defiantly. This woman he married would face any situation with admirable fearlessness. She'd already done so and was doing so now. Would she be as bold in lovemaking?

His blood surged in his veins in anticipation of it.

He stepped back and mimicked her undressing, removing his banyan and letting it fall to the floor. He, too, revealed his nakedness, his arousal. She, as he expected, did not avert her gaze.

'Lie back on the bed, Tess,' he instructed.

As she did so, he climbed on to the bed and lay next to her. 'I must touch you, to help ready you.'

She nodded, her eyes widening as he stroked her arms and shoulders. His head was still working enough that he knew it would be best for her to become used to his touch. His loins wished to awaken her body, like his had awakened. He wanted to join her. They were made one in matrimony; now let them be made one in the flesh. Put the past behind them and forge something together.

Her limbs relaxed and he grew bolder.

She gasped as his hand slipped over her breast. He moved gently, though it cost him something. His desire was pushing him and her skin felt so very soft. He moved his hand further down.

Tess did not expect a man's touch to feel this way. His hand was strong and sure, but gentle, and the sensations he created radiated throughout her. She thought she would come apart when he stroked her breasts. The intimacy of it astounded her. Who had touched her there since she'd been a little girl in need of help bathing?

The touch was not all pleasant. His fingers, no matter on what part of her body, created an ache at the womanly parts between her legs. With each stroke the ache grew more intense. Not a pain, exactly.

A need.

His hand moved down her body, closer, and she wanted to push it down *there*, as if his touch would relieve the ache.

Finally his fingers reached the place.

'I need to touch you here. To make you ready. To make it easier for you,' he explained.

He fingered her most sensitive place and the aching surged. Her back arched and she moaned, the sound not unlike those her mother made when Tess had watched her with her lover.

'Do you feel the pleasure?' he asked, his voice rough.

'Not pleasure.' How could she explain? 'Not quite.' She did not have the words.

He was a magnificent man. Tall and as well formed as the Greek statue at Tinmore Hall. Better formed, in fact.

Leaner and hard-muscled. Was it wanton of her to think so? To enjoy his touch so very much?

He rose above her. 'Now,' he uttered, 'I will enter you.'

A wave of fear joined the potpourri of emotion and sensation flowing through her. His male member was large; she could well imagine pain, but she did not want him to stop. She wanted this need, this aching to come to its end, even though she did not know what that end would be.

'Don't stop,' she cried. 'Don't stop.'

It seemed as if her body opened to him and he eased himself inside her, with stroke after stroke. Her muscles responded of their own volition, moving with him, meeting and separating, meeting and separating.

The ache grew even more intense, so all consuming, so needful, that she lost the capacity to think. She was all feeling, all sensation, all merged with this glorious man. Her husband.

He moved faster, his breath came faster and she moved with him, wanting to cry out with each thrust.

Then something remarkable happened. Sensation exploded inside her, filling her with an unimagined pleasure. A moment later, a growl escaped his lips and he trembled inside her. Spilling his seed, she realised.

This was consummation, she thought, as her body drifted into a pleasant languor. Joining.

He collapsed atop her, but immediately lifted his weight off her and rolled to her side. 'You felt it,' he said.

She could not speak, so she nodded her head, and blinked back tears that suddenly filled her eyes.

He rose on an elbow and peered at her, looking puzzled.

She swiped at her cheeks. 'I'm not weeping. Not hurt. Not sad.' She couldn't explain.

He wiped the tears with his thumb and stared into her face. She tried to smile. She wanted to smile.

His expression turned soft and tender. He leaned closer and placed his lips on hers.

She realised then that this was her first kiss. By him. By any man.

And it had come after lovemaking.

Chapter Twelve

Tess woke with the dawn's first light. Through the window she could see a piece of sky, a glorious and joyful shade of pink.

She smiled. Even the sky matched her mood.

After that tumultuous first time of making love, Marc made love to her again. To her delight, the sensations were every bit as wonderful. Different, though. Slower and sweeter.

She, Lorene and Genna had been warned of the temptations of the flesh by every governess they'd had. Considering their parents' excesses in such temptations, it had been good advice. When Tess watched her mother and her mother's lover on the sofa in her sitting room, she'd not understood the appeal. It had not looked at all like something one would desire to do.

Now she understood, though. She understood her mother better, as well, how her mother could crave this wonderful experience, how she could want to repeat it, over and over. She understood precisely how like her mother she was.

Tess gazed at her husband, face relaxed in sleep, hair tousled, thick, dark lashes casting shadows on his cheeks. He took her breath away. She could not imagine lovemaking with anyone else. Ever. She felt connected to him in a way even stronger than her connections to her sisters, as if the consummation of their marriage had indeed made them one.

Did he feel that, as well? How could he not?

She'd felt herself open to him in their lovemaking. Surely now he knew everything there was to know about her; she'd felt that unguarded.

Her heart surged with hope. Surely such a profound experience provided a strong foundation for a marriage. They could build upon this night and perhaps create a marvellous future together. He was a decent man, after all, a good man.

He stirred and opened his eyes. To merely call them blue did them no justice. They were rimmed in navy with flecks of light and dark radiating from the pupil. Having his eyes focused on her was like being pinned with a sabre to the chest.

She could not tell what he hid in the depths of those eyes. Would he open himself to her?

'Good morning,' he murmured, his lashes lowering. 'How do you fare?'

She smiled tentatively, suddenly needing to pull back from the intensity of her emotions. 'I fare very well. And you?'

He moved towards her, taking her in his arms and pulling her naked body against his. 'I'm well.'

His arousal pressed against her and the delicious aching returned.

He drew her into a kiss, opening his mouth. Her lips parted and he touched his tongue to hers. She gasped and dug her fingers in his unruly hair, holding him in the kiss.

He eased her on her back and, still kissing her, climbed

atop her. His hands stroked her. How could she have known how wonderful his hands would feel on her body? How glorious a kiss would feel?

She opened herself to him again and he entered her and drove her again to the unimaginable pleasure. While she still quivered from her release, he spilled his seed inside her.

When he lay next to her again, his arm around her, all the stress, anger and regret she'd lived with since being discovered with Marc in the cabin washed away. Like the day after a rainstorm, everything seemed fresh, bright and new. They would make this a good marriage, in spite of being forced to marry. Perhaps they had just made a baby together.

How more wonderful could life be?

Marc lay with her in his arms, sated and satisfied, but with his heart racing as if he'd just run a league. He already wanted her again, needed her again. He wanted her all to himself. Wanted their own rooms, their own household, away from his family, away from everyone.

And he wanted to flee.

The power of his need for her shook him to his core. Surely this is what his father had felt, what Charles and Lucien felt?

Thus grief still treads upon the heels of pleasure: Married in haste, we may repent at leisure.

His father's words again.

Had he married her for this—this explosive lovemaking? Was this lovemaking the pleasure in that line from the Congreve play? He cared nothing of grief and repentance. He only wanted her.

And he would do anything to have her again.

Anything.

Were these the sentiments that drove Lucien and Charles to their deaths?

Some wiser part of him threw off the covers and rose from the bed.

His abrupt movement woke her.

'Are you rising already?' she asked in a raw, sleepy voice.

All he heard was an invitation to return to the bed, make love to her again, but he needed to get himself under control.

'I had better get up.' Some hint of good sense made its way to the fore. 'Too much could make you sore.'

She patted the bed where he'd been lying. 'I do not mind.'

Good God. 'No!'

Her face fell. His sharp tone wounded her, obviously.

He dared to lean over her. 'Do not be distressed, Tess,' he managed. 'I—I sound as I do because I want you so strongly and I know we must not...' He paused, almost forgetting what he needed to say. 'Overdo.' He stroked her cheek with his finger, not willing to risk touching her with even his whole hand.

She softened again, but moved towards his touch in a way so alluring he was tempted to tell his head to go to the devil.

He straightened. 'I think I will take Apollo for a run.' He made himself smile at her. 'That should cool me off.'

She looked disappointed, but she said, 'Apollo will be happy. Will I see you at breakfast, then?'

'Better not wait for me.' Who knew how long it would take to sort himself out? 'I would not wish you to be hungry.'

She smiled. 'Hungry enough for soggy bread and cheese?'

The reminder of the cabin pierced him like a sabre thrust. 'Never that hungry again,' he murmured.

'No food ever tasted so delicious,' she said.

He gathered up his riding clothes and dressed himself, all the while very aware that she watched his every move. After he was dressed, he started for the door, but instead turned and walked back to the bed where she was now sitting up and holding the linens over her lovely breasts.

He leaned down and kissed her. She reached for him and held him in the kiss and passion throbbed inside him. He drew away.

He ought to tell her how captivating she was, how she had pleased him, but he said only, 'I will see you later.'

He hurried out and soon stepped out of the door on to the street.

The cool, fresh air filled his lungs and cleared his mind.

What was this foolishness overtaking him? Why should he and Tess not forge a happy marriage? The passion they shared should bode well for it. And she was a woman worthy of loving and deserving of happiness. Why could he not give them both that? He could make it happen. He'd do it for Lucien and Charles—and even for his mother and father. He'd be happy for all of them.

He stepped on to the pavement with renewed hope. Renewed resolve.

A man approached him. 'Mr Glenville?'

'Yes?' Marc frowned. Something in the man's manner put him on alert.

The man handed him a letter. 'This is for you. I am told it is urgent.'

Marc accepted the letter, broke the seal and unfolded the paper.

It read:

*Come immediately. It is vital. You must come. Some-
thing has happened that cannot be written in a letter. Do not delay. I will explain all.*
    Yours, etc.
    Lord Greybury

Hope turned swiftly to foreboding.

Marc looked up at the messenger. 'I will come straight
away.'

He hurried on to the mews, but he'd not be riding Apollo
for pleasure.

The stable boy saddled Apollo quickly and Marc set out
for Horse Guards. Even the horse seemed to sense the urgency. The streets were filling with carriages, wagons and
other riders, but Apollo pulled through. Marc announced
himself to the sentry and handed Apollo's reins to a waiting attendant. The building seemed to be a-bustle and the
air filled with tension.

He made his way quickly to Greybury's office. The
clerk waved him by before he could say anything.

He knocked on Greybury's door and opened it. Two
other men Marc recognised as working for Castlereagh
stood with Lord Greybury. This must be something important.

They all turned when he entered.

'Ah, gentlemen, here is Renard.' Greybury gestured
Marc forward.

The other men likely knew Marc's true identity, but
since Greybury used his code name, it sounded like he
was back on the job.

'What is this about?' Marc asked.

Greybury glanced from one gentleman to the other and

back to Marc. 'We received word today that Napoleon has escaped.'

'Escaped!'

Napoleon had been exiled to Elba after the Treaty of Fontainebleu.

'He's making his way to Paris,' said one of the men.

'Castlereagh warned the Allies this could happen,' the other gentleman said. 'He warned them.'

'We need you in France, Renard,' Greybury said. 'Napoleon will seek power again and we need to know all that transpires as a result.'

'Suffice to say that every nation on the Continent and our United Kingdom are at risk!' the first man added.

The stakes were high, that was for certain.

Marc's insides turned cold. 'I cannot go.'

Greybury straightened. 'You must.'

'I cannot,' Marc insisted. 'You must choose another man. I was married yesterday. I cannot leave my new wife.'

'You will leave her. There is no other man to replace you.' Greybury glared at him. 'Recall that you made a vow to serve your country when needed. You are needed.'

No. He could not do this to Tess. Make love to her and leave her?

Greybury leaned towards him. 'I cannot stress how vital this is. I am sorry that your private matters impinge on this situation, but your duty is to your country. Napoleon will take up the sword again. He is not a man of peace. Without the information only you can gather, countless men will no longer be able to return to their wives.'

Marc was bound by duty. He could not refuse.

'Very well,' he said. 'I can be ready by tomorrow.'

'Not tomorrow.' Greybury spoke firmly. 'Today. Now. There is a boat waiting at Dover to take you across the Channel.'

Tess would be hurt. How could she not be?

It was all his fault. If he'd maintained his distance from her, not shared his bed with her, he would not hurt her nearly as much. But, no, he let passion rule, just as Charles and Lucien had done and, because he'd done so, he'd grievously injure Tess.

How more monstrous could he be? Love her and leave her.

Better he'd lost his own life than wound her so.

Perhaps it was better not to spend another night with her. It would be cruel of him to make love to her another night.

And it would be cruel of him not to.

'Very well. Today. I can be ready in a few hours—' With hard riding, he should be able to reach Dover before nightfall.

'No!' Greybury pounded a fist on his desk. 'You must ride to Dover now.'

'Even a few hours can make a difference,' added the second man. 'We must know immediately Napoleon's whereabouts and his plans.'

'The usual network is in place,' Greybury said. 'Your trunk has already been sent to Dover.'

The office kept a trunk packed with weapons, clothing and such so he could easily slip into the role of Renard.

An announcement of his marriage would appear in the *Morning Post* this very day. As soon as all of society learned of his marriage to Tess, they would also learn he had left her. What could he say to her?

He felt sick inside. 'I cannot leave without speaking to my wife.'

'Write your wife a letter.' Greybury pushed paper and pen towards him. An inkpot was on the desk.

'No.' Marc pushed them back. 'I speak to my wife or I do not travel to France.'

Marc started for the door.

'Wait!' Lord Greybury cried.

Marc stopped and turned towards him.

Greybury stood. 'Very well. We will do it your way. Speak to your wife. But be quick about it.'

He'd take whatever time was necessary.

Greybury rubbed his face. 'Say nothing to your wife about where you are going or why, though. Remember Rosier.'

Rosier had confided in his wife, but a clever French spy tricked her into talking. Rosier's deception and his mission were discovered. And worse, Rosier and several colleagues were killed.

Marc would not tell Tess the truth. If she knew nothing, she could divulge nothing. What would he say to her instead?

'I know my duty.' Marc bowed and left the room.

After breakfasting alone, Tess spent her morning writing letters to her sisters and brother, informing them of her marriage.

Would they write her back? She'd received nothing from them so far, but perhaps not enough time had passed for them to answer her first letters. She'd tried to tell them she was well, but this morning she'd been tempted to write to them about how wonderful marriage with Marc would be. How could she put in a letter that it had been his lovemaking that filled her with hope? Or that something in his manner this morning brought her worries back?

If she could talk to Lorene and Genna, it would be different.

Even if there were some things she could never tell them.

Maybe they would reassure her that Marc had not been eager to be away from her this morning. Maybe they would say it was merely due to a morning mood or something.

She ought not to worry, in any event. Marc had been her steadfast protector since that moment he'd found her in the rain. He'd never failed her. Never lied to her. She even believed him about Miss Caldwell.

Hadn't she?

At least through her letter to Lorene, Tinmore would learn Tess kept her part of his bargain. If he kept his word this time, Genna and Edmund's futures should be secure.

Marc would never break his word.

Would he?

She sent a footman to post the letters and waited in her bedroom for Marc to return from his ride. If he did not knock on her door, she'd at least hear him go to his room to change from his riding clothes.

Then she'd learn her worries were baseless.

Nancy came in and out of the room, always hiding a smile and obviously trying very hard not to ask about the wedding night.

Tess blushed to think that the servants would all know she and Mark had made love. The evidence would be on the bed linens.

Had her mother been concerned about such things? Tess wondered. Did Lorene think of such things?

She could not imagine Lorene and Lord Tinmore—

She thought of the pleasure Marc created in her, a pleasure she'd never dreamed she would experience. Her body came alive again and she ached for his return.

Tess paced the room, restless and more uncertain with every tick of the mantle clock.

When the knock sounded at her door, though, she jumped in surprise.

She swung around. 'Come in.'

A last shaft of agony sliced through Marc as his hand gripped the latch. He took two deep breaths and opened the door.

'Tess!' He walked in with a firm step. 'I have something I must tell you.'

She took a step towards him, but seemed to think better of coming closer. 'What?'

'I encountered some friends of mine when I was out. At the park.'

She blinked. 'Some friends?'

He faced her and tried to keep emotion out of his voice. 'They are bound for Switzerland today and I am going with them.'

'Going with them?' Her expression turned confused. 'To Switzerland?'

He crossed his arms over his chest. 'I realise the timing is not ideal, but I cannot pass up this opportunity. I have always had a strong desire to hike through the Alps.' This was at least true. 'The possibility was denied to me during the war, but now there is no reason not to go—'

'No reason?' Her voice raised an octave. 'You were married yesterday.'

Yes. And his leaving would hurt her.

'Ordinarily I would not leave,' he explained. 'But I cannot pass up this opportunity.'

'Walking in mountains is so vitally important?'

He made himself look directly at her. 'It is what I wish to do.'

'You wish to leave me!' Her face turned red with anger.

'For a few months.' He acted as if it were a trifle. 'I do

not even need to pack much. We will purchase what we need when we reach the mountains. Sturdy boots and such. These are the same men I travelled with through Scotland. They will not make this trip again.'

'You choose them over me?' Her voice trembled.

'I am not choosing them over you.' Good God. He did not want her to think this had anything to do with her. 'It has nothing to do with you. I merely wish to take this trip.'

She swung away from him. 'I do not believe this. This does not sound like you. You would not do this to me.'

'Would I not? You do not know me.' He kept his voice steady. 'Heed this, Tess. I will do as I please. And it pleases me to take this trip. Ask my parents if I do not leave when it pleases me to leave. It is something to which you must become accustomed.'

'Must I?' Her eyes flashed.

He pretended to be severe with her. 'You will do very well without me. You've settled in here, especially with my mother and sister. Soon your sisters will be here. You will be invited to social events, events I would not wish to attend. You will be well entertained.'

She blinked. 'I do not care a fig about all that!' She swallowed, as if she were trying not to weep. 'What do you think people will say about you leaving me the day after our wedding?'

He shrugged. 'People will talk no matter what. Besides, it is not as if we can pretend this is anything more than a marriage of convenience, not when Tinmore and his guests come to town.'

Likely she would never forgive him for this. When he returned to her, what could he expect? A marriage of estrangement like his parents?

'Do not make light of this, Marc,' she shot back. 'You are leaving me to bear the scandal of our marriage alone.

And you add the additional humiliation of leaving after the wedding night.'

He cursed himself. If only he had not given in to his desire for her, her pain would not be so great. He'd been right to have been so shaken when he left her bed this morning. He ought never to have been there.

Her voice dropped to little more than a whisper. 'How could you make love to me and then leave me so callously?'

Misery swept through him. He could not answer her. He fancied he felt every bit of her pain.

'Go, then,' she rasped. 'Leave me. It is not as though I have not been left before. I dare say your absence will not be as devastating.'

Marc had no choice but to turn and walk out of the room.

As soon as he closed the door, though, he leaned his whole body against it. 'Tess,' he murmured. 'I am sorry. I am so very sorry.'

Chapter Thirteen

June 1815, three months later—Brussels, Belgium

Tess, with Amelie at her side, glimpsed the Parc de Brux-elles for the first time and gasped.

'It is magnificent!' Amelie exclaimed.

As soon as they'd arrived in Brussels, nothing would do but for Amelie to see the park. So while Lord and Lady Northdon rested in their rooms at the Hotel de Flandre, Tess and Amelie walked to the park.

The park was a magnificent space, indeed, a huge formal garden enclosed with iron rails and bordered by the Royal Palace and other grand public buildings. Inside the park were gravel walkways, crisscrossing each other in symmetrical patterns. Large, leafy trees, green shrubbery and flowers grew in grassy spots between the walkways. In every direction something interesting could be found. Statues and fountains and benches.

And men in uniforms of all types and colours, strolling with elegant ladies or conversing in groups of twos or threes.

It is madness to be here, Tess thought.

When Napoleon was exiled to Elba, the English flocked

to the Continent where travel had so long been denied them. Brussels especially had become a fashionable destination, as well as a place to live in luxury for significantly less than it cost in Britain. Now, though, all was changed. Napoleon had reclaimed his empire, and the British, Prussians, Austrians and Russians declared war, not on France, but on Napoleon himself.

Impending war brought even more people to Brussels—thousands of soldiers, their officers and others who had official duties made necessary by the inevitable war. The Allies were planning to march into France any day now.

There was no reason for Tess, Amelie and her parents to be in Brussels, though. Lord Northdon had no official duties and he certainly had no need to economise. He and Lady Northdon came to Brussels simply to indulge Amelie.

Amelie had become enamoured of a young captain in the Scots Greys to whom she'd been introduced at one of the London entertainments. The Scots Greys, a prestigious cavalry regiment, was sent to Brussels to prepare for the battle with Napoleon's forces. Amelie could not bear to be parted from her Captain Fowler, so Lord and Lady Northdon agreed they could all follow him here.

Here in the Parc de Bruxelles people seemed as festive as if this were the London Season. Was Tess the only one who worried about why the soldiers were here?

Amelie talked excitedly. 'Would it not be beyond everything if I should run into Captain Fowler here in the park? He could be here at this moment! Papa said he would send a message to him that we have arrived, but would it not be exciting if he found us here before he reads the message? He will call as soon as he is able. I am sure of it.'

Tess, too, scanned the park, but to look for Marc, not for Captain Fowler.

Because Marc, too, could be in Brussels.

The one letter Tess had received from him in the three months he'd been gone had been posted from Ostend, the port at which she, Amelie and Lord and Lady Northdon had landed just the day before. It had arrived just days before they'd left and merely stated that he was well, but was remaining on the Continent.

If Marc had been in Belgium when he'd penned the letter, he could very well now be among the English visitors to Brussels.

Apparently he was no longer in the Alps. Most likely he had never been there. He'd lied to her about his travel plans. If he had indeed been planning a hike across the mountains, he would not have taken Apollo with him.

His whereabouts ought to be of no consequence to Tess, but the pain of his abandoning her had not abated, even though she'd become very skilled at not showing it.

In London she'd had plenty of practice hiding the wounds he'd inflicted. She'd done so at every social event she'd had to attend. Either Lord Tinmore had arranged for invitations or Amelie's success at the Caldwells' party had made her a desirable guest, Tess did not know which. Amelie was quite a success wherever they went. Tess, on the other hand, received stares and whispers and sympathetic looks. At least she did not experience the cut direct as Lady Northdon occasionally did. Lady Northdon always held her head high and refused to be cowed by cruel treatment. Tess emulated her. Tess had become quite fond of Lady Northdon, who treated her as if she were another beloved daughter. Lord Northdon was not quite so generous. Tess suspected he blamed her for Marc's abrupt departure. None of them spoke to her about Marc's leaving her, though.

Tinmore brought Tess's sisters to London, as he said he would, and they were often at the same events. Her sisters insisted she explain why Marc left her. Tess told them only what Marc told her, but that was not enough for Lorene. Lorene lectured Tess on how she might have been more accommodating to her husband. Or Lorene lamented that Tess's marriage was not the sort Lorene had wanted for her. It was not the marriage for which Lorene sacrificed herself. Genna argued with both of them for expecting any marriage to solve their problems.

This was more blame Tess could leave at Marc's feet. By abandoning her, he'd widened the breach between her and her sisters. If he'd stayed, they might have at least pretended to have a successful marriage. She would not have to endure her sisters' grief for the shambles she'd made of her life. Tess and her sisters rarely called upon each other and mostly saw each other at social events where Lord Tinmore was also present. What that man thought of Marc leaving her, Tess could only guess.

Mr Welton also appeared at some of the London events, making straight for Genna, who just as swiftly sent him packing. How was it that Genna could see through Welton when Tess had been unable to? Tess could not trust her judgement of anyone any more.

She'd been so terribly wrong about Marc.

Marc's lovemaking had made her believe he loved her. Instead, he'd wanted to be a continent away from her.

No one would hurt her like that again. She built armour around herself to keep her safe and to hide how shattered she was inside.

'Shall we walk together a little?' Amelie asked, rousing Tess from her reverie.

'As you wish.' Tess smiled and tried to sound cheerful.

They strolled down one of the paths and all the men they passed paused for a moment to gaze at Amelie.

Amelie took Tess by the arm. 'Let us make our way to the centre and see the basin with the fish.'

Their guidebook said there was a huge basin in the middle of the park with silver and gold fish, but it seemed like they must pass through a gauntlet of staring men to reach it.

As they walked, Tess remarked, 'I do not see how you can be so at ease. Every gentleman turns to look at you.'

'Oh, they are not looking at me,' Amelie insisted, walking on serenely.

Was the girl that deluded? She was a beauty.

When they neared the basin, Amelie ran forward. 'It really does have fish!'

Tess joined her, acutely aware of the interest Amelie created. As Amelie circumvented the basin, Tess kept her gaze firmly on the fish and not on the staring men.

'Oh, my goodness!' Amelie suddenly exclaimed. 'He's here. Look. Look.'

Amelie ran ahead. Had she found her Captain Fowler? Tess glanced across the basin to see.

And froze.

Marc stood on the other side.

He must have seen her the instant she'd seen him. He looked directly into her eyes.

His sister reached him and threw her arms around him. 'Marc! Marc! Are you truly here?'

He embraced Amelie, but his eyes never left Tess.

When he released her, Amelie turned and called across the basin, 'Tess! Look! It is Marc!'

Tess made her way slowly to where they stood.

'Marc,' she said, trying to keep all emotion from her voice.

'Tess,' he whispered.

'So you came to Brussels, too?' Amelie cried. 'You

should have told us you would be here. We just arrived today. Where are you staying? Papa procured rooms for us at the Hotel de Flandre and Maman has been speaking nothing but French since we arrived. She cannot wait to visit the *magasins*. Every shop calls itself Magasin de—something, she said...'

While Amelie chattered, Marc continued to gaze at Tess, but he suddenly collected himself. 'Forgive me. There are others here who would wish to greet you.'

He was standing with three men and a woman.

The woman stepped out from behind one of the men. 'Mrs Glenville. Amelie.' It was Doria Caldwell, looking serene as ever. 'What a surprise. I do hope you had a good trip.'

Tess's glance darted to Marc. Had he lied about Doria Caldwell after all?

Amelie ran over to clasp Miss Caldwell's hand. 'Doria! We had no idea you were coming to Brussels, too!'

Miss Caldwell smiled at her. 'Papa was asked to come. He is assisting one of the diplomats.' Her gaze slipped over to Tess. 'We just ran into Marc a few minutes ago.'

Mr Caldwell stepped over to Amelie. 'My dear, you look as pretty as a picture. What a delight to see you here.' He turned to Tess. 'And you, of course, Mrs Glenville.'

'What a coincidence!' Amelie said brightly. 'It is almost like being back in London.'

Tess felt suddenly sick to her stomach. Her husband was here, conversing with the woman he once wanted to marry, and was about as happy to see Tess as she was to see him.

She depended upon her armour to keep her rooted to this place when she wanted to run back to the hotel and hide herself in her room.

'Good afternoon, sir,' she said to Mr Caldwell.

Marc turned abruptly. 'I am being remiss. Let me present my two companions to you.'

Tess attended to the two men standing near Marc. One was dressed as a gentleman like Marc, the other, in an officer's uniform. Marc presented them and Tess promptly forgot their names. She did notice their surprise when he introduced her, saying, 'This is my wife, Mrs Glenville, and my sister, Miss Glenville.'

Their attention quickly turned to the beautiful Amelie, though. Mr Caldwell and his daughter discreetly stepped back and she was left to speak with Marc alone.

'What are you doing here?' he asked in a gruff tone.

He'd certainly made his feelings known.

She lifted her chin. 'I am in Brussels only because your mother and father wished me to come. They are here because Amelie has a suitor here. He is the reason.'

'A suitor?'

Better to talk of Amelie's suitor than to ask Marc to explain why he was in Brussels, or why he was in the company of Miss Caldwell.

'He is Captain Fowler of the Scots Greys,' she said.

The man in uniform overheard her. 'Scots Greys? A prestigious regiment.'

'Oh, yes!' exclaimed Amelie. 'Captain Fowler considers it quite an honour.'

'You have a suitor?' Miss Caldwell asked Amelie.

Amelie lowered her lashes and looked even more beguiling. 'I suppose you could say he is my suitor.' She began to explain to Miss Caldwell and Marc how she'd met him.

Tess turned to the officer, because she did not want to be a part of Miss Caldwell's conversation. 'What regiment are you, sir?'

He bowed. '28th, ma'am.'

'The 28th is here?' Tess's eyes widened. She forgot about Miss Caldwell and Marc for the moment. 'My brother is in the 28th. Do you know him? Lieutenant Edmund Summerfield. Is he here?'

'I know him and, yes, ma'am, he is here,' the man answered.

This was beyond wonderful! 'Would you tell him his sister Tess is at the Hotel de Flandre? Tell him to call on me and ask for Mrs Glenville.'

Her brother Edmund was here! With him here she would not feel so desperately alone.

Her high spirits deflated. Edmund was here to fight in the new war against Napoleon. He could be killed.

The officer bowed again. 'I will inform him with pleasure, ma'am.'

The other man clapped him on his back. 'Come. Let us leave them all to their reunion.'

The two men bid them good day.

Amelie seized her brother's arm and pressed her cheek against his shoulder. 'I cannot believe you are actually here. And Doria and Mr Caldwell, too!'

Marc looked straight at Tess. 'This is no place for you. The Allies are preparing for war. It may become dangerous to be here.'

Was he trying to scare her away? 'Tell your father, not me. It was not my decision to come.'

Miss Caldwell broke in. 'But, Marc, the soldiers are not going to fight here. They will march to France.' She turned to her father. 'Is that not right, Papa?'

'That is indeed what is expected,' he replied.

'Oh, let us not think of the war right now!' Amelie cried. 'Come back to the hotel with us. Maman and Papa will be so glad to see you!' She turned to Miss Caldwell.

'You and Mr Caldwell must come, too. We shall all eat dinner together!'

'No, no, my dear,' Mr Caldwell said. 'We would not interfere in your reunion. But send a messenger to us at the Hotel de Belle Vue if your parents would indeed like us to join you for dinner.'

Marc looked hesitant, as if coming with Amelie and Tess was the last thing he wished to do. Or was it that he wished Tess were not a part of it?

Amelie nodded. 'We will send you a message.' She took her brother's arm. 'But you will come with us now, will you not, Marc?'

He smiled at his sister. 'Of course. I'll come with you now.'

Marc offered Tess his arm, but she acted as if she did not notice and merely walked by his side. Silent. Amelie happily took his other arm and talked on about their trip, about Captain Fowler, about the Season's entertainments she'd attended before travelling here. He'd never seen his sister so happy and so full of life.

Such a contrast to the woman carefully avoiding touching him or speaking to him. She looked beautiful in the light of the June sun on this fine Belgian day, but she was like some distant dream. Was there anything he could say or do to close the gulf his abandoning her had created?

Having her find him with Doria did not help.

When they reached the hotel, Amelie ran ahead to tell their parents.

Marc and Tess walked more slowly, still not speaking.

He'd hurt her terribly, though, and there was no way he could explain.

'How were the Alps?' she asked in a sarcastic tone.

He must lie to her again. 'Quite nice.'

She gave him a very sceptical look.

He wished he could tell her the truth.

Within two days of that meeting with Greybury in London, Marc arrived in Calais and was on the road to Paris. His task was to locate Napoleon, learn of his plans and gauge whether or not the people of France would support him. The French people, unhappy with Louis XVIII, welcomed Napoleon's return and Napoleon planned to rule France. He sent word to the Allies that he'd give up his empire, if they left him in peace.

As if the Allies would believe him.

The information Marc gathered was sent back through the network of agents scattered around the countryside and throughout the Continent. Marc learned that Napoleon had quickly raised a fully equipped army of two hundred thousand men. In fact, Marc had almost been conscripted into that army. He'd had to flee France to escape it.

Napoleon's army was readying for battle and Napoleon was intent on victory.

Marc made his way to Brussels and briefed his contact of everything he'd learned in France. His contact informed the Duke of Wellington, who had been appointed Field Marshal over the forces of British, German, Dutch and Belgian soldiers assembling in Brussels. The Allied plan was to orchestrate a coordinated invasion of France.

Marc had no hard facts, but he believed Napoleon would not wait for that invasion and he feared Napoleon would march straight for Brussels.

Now his family was here? And Tess? He must convince them to leave, but how? Why would his family believe him?

He certainly had lost his wife's trust. Tess would not even allow him to touch her.

He and Tess turned down a hallway and saw Amelie open a door to their parents' rooms. 'Maman! Papa!' she cried. 'Look who we have brought with us!'

His parents greeted him with surprise and delight, his mother kissing his cheeks, his father shaking his hand and pulling him into a hug.

'Why did you not let us know you were in Brussels?' his father asked.

'You know I am a terrible correspondent.' That much was true.

They had more questions for him to answer with evasions and lies. Through it all Tess sat at a little distance, her posture stiff, her face like stone.

As soon as Marc could manage it, he cut them off. 'I am certain I may see much of you here,' he said. 'There will be plenty of time to discuss...whatever you wish to discuss. At the moment, though, I would like some time alone with my wife.'

His father immediately stood. 'Of course.' He turned to Tess. 'Tess, take Marc to your room. We will see both of you later.' He turned back to Marc. 'You will join us for dinner?'

Marc had plans—work, actually—but he could delay until after dinner. 'Certainly, I will join you.'

'Papa,' Amelie broke in. 'You remind me. You will never guess who else we found on our walk.'

Tess rose while Amelie told of the Caldwells also being in Brussels. Marc moved to her side and gave her no choice but to lead him to her room.

She acted as if she were marching to the gallows.

She opened the door and her maid turned from unpacking clothes. 'Back so soon, ma'am?' She noticed Marc then. 'Oh! Oh, Mr Glenville!' She made a hurried curtsy.

'Nancy.' He smiled at the girl. 'How good to see you. You are looking well.'

She stared from Marc to Tess, obviously full of curiosity. 'Thank you, sir.'

Tess spoke to her in a strangled voice. 'Nancy, would you mind leaving us alone for a while?'

'Yes, ma'am!' She dropped the folded clothes she'd been holding and, glancing back at Tess, left the room.

Marc turned to her. 'Tess—'

She recoiled as if his speaking her name was a blow.

He went on. 'I hardly know what to say to you.'

She would not look at him. 'Does it matter what you say? I have lost the ability to believe you.' She walked towards the window. 'Tell me, did Apollo enjoy climbing the mountains?'

'Apollo?'

She continued in her biting tone. 'Your horse. I confess, I never knew horses climbed mountains.'

She'd surmised he'd lied about the Alps and he could not counter with the truth of where he'd been and what he'd been doing.

He had no choice but to play the role he'd created the day he'd left her. 'You may think whatever you like about my activities,' he said sharply. 'I wanted to leave, to be away. I may desire to leave again in the future.'

Her voice dropped. 'You wanted to leave me, you are saying.'

He made himself glare at her. 'I am saying I will come and go at my pleasure. I suggest you accustom yourself to that habit of mine.'

She returned his gaze. 'I've had several weeks to accustom myself.'

He wanted to ask her how it had been for her, but she would never believe he cared about such things. 'Like it or not, we are man and wife and we are together in Brussels. We must act like man and wife while we are here.'

She recoiled. 'Do not expect me to perform my wifely duties. I performed them once and you left me.'

He understood. He truly understood. It must have been excruciating to open herself to him so intimately, only to be abandoned. But he could not say so.

Instead he said, 'We will address that issue at a later date. As it is, I am housed in a different hotel. I will not require you to move from here.'

'You will not require me!' she cried.

He lifted a hand to silence her. 'Suffice to say we will make the appearance of marital harmony, if for no other reason than it will cause talk if we do not and it will upset my parents and Amelie.'

'I am used to talk.' Her chin trembled. 'I have endured much talk already.'

That was like a sabre thrust. 'Well, then, let us put a stop to it.'

She'd probably think he wanted to be rid of her if he sent her and his family away from Brussels as soon as possible. His father would never turn around and leave the day after arriving, in any event.

He took a breath. 'There is to be a ball in two days' time. We will attend together. I will see that you and Amelie receive invitations. My parents, too, if I can manage it. And Captain Fowler.'

The Duke of Richmond and his secretary were Greybury's men. Marc could manage the invitations.

'And Miss Caldwell and her father?' she asked scornfully.

'I do not include them.' Why would he? He tried to get her to look at him. 'My encountering them in Brussels was as unexpected as encountering you, Tess.'

'Possibly more welcome though,' she said.

He did not want anyone he cared about to be in Brussels now.

'You will come to the ball with me,' he commanded. 'It will be the place to be seen.'

Once they were seen together at the Duchess of Richmond's ball, the gossip should abate. He could at least give that to her.

Chapter Fourteen

Dinner was early in Brussels. Not enough time for Tess to collect herself. Oh, she had time to dress, but not enough time to master the emotions spinning around inside her.

All because of encountering her husband after all these weeks.

The Caldwells were added to the dinner party, much to Tess's dismay, as was Captain Fowler.

They supped at the Café de l'Amitié. Café of Friendship. Was that not a farce?

Tess sat at Marc's side and was forced to watch the family and the Caldwells delight in his presence.

How odd they all were, to act as if Marc had merely been on a trip to Switzerland. He had deserted a new wife, not that any of them seemed to take him to task for that.

Or perhaps they were simply on good behaviour. Lord and Lady Northdon were always on good behavior when Captain Fowler was present. They were extremely eager that Captain Fowler think well of them, even to the point of refraining from their constant bickering. They doted on Captain Fowler. If this man did not make Amelie an offer, Amelie would not be the only one crushed.

At least the conversation at dinner did not require Tess's

participation beyond the occasional expression of interest or nodding of the head. While Tess seethed inside, though, Miss Caldwell was the epitome of serenity. It did no credit to Tess to resent Miss Caldwell for it.

After dinner they all walked back to the hotel on the Rue Royale, four couples, one behind the other. Lord and Lady Northdon led the way followed by Mr Caldwell and his daughter. Amelie and Captain Fowler trailed last and Marc and Tess were caught in the middle.

Amelie called to her parents, 'Maman, Papa, it is still so fine a day. May I take a turn in the park with the captain?'

'An excellent idea!' Lord Northdon stopped for a moment, so the whole parade stopped. 'In fact, let us all walk in the park.' He turned to Lady Northdon. 'Would you like to see the park, my dear?'

Amelie looked crestfallen.

Her father chuckled. 'Do not fear, Daughter. We will not stay in your pocket.'

But they certainly could keep an eye on her.

'Marc!' his father bellowed, though they were not at a distance. 'You will come with us.'

Tess saw her chance. 'Yes, do, Marc. Take a promenade through the park with your parents and the Caldwells. I can manage to walk the few steps to the hotel alone.'

Marc did not respond to Tess, but to his father. 'Thank you, Papa. I will stay with Tess.'

Lord Northdon's brows rose, as if he could not believe Marc would pick Tess over a few minutes with his parents and his good friends. 'If you wish it,' he said tersely.

'Let them go, John. They do not wish to be with us right now.' Lady Northdon smiled knowingly, as if she thought Marc and Tess were eager to be private together. She turned to Marc. *'Adieu, mon fils.'*

While Marc said goodnight to the others, Tess started walking to the hotel. Marc caught up to her.

'You should have stayed with your parents and your friends,' she said to him through gritted teeth.

'I would not leave you,' he replied.

She laughed. Surely he caught the irony of that statement.

She did not look at him to see, though. Looking at him was too painful. It reminded her of how he had looked in their marriage bed, how he had looked upon her with his intense blue eyes, how she'd been filled with hope and happiness.

'I cannot stay, however,' he added. 'I have somewhere else I must go.'

She shrugged as if she did not care where he went.

He held open the grand door of the Hotel de Flandre for her. She entered the lobby and strode determinedly towards the stairway. He seemed to have no difficulty keeping pace with her.

She stopped. 'I am going to my room and I do not need your escort. Go on to your next…entertainment.'

He gave her a firm look. 'I will walk you to your door.'

She turned to face him. 'I do not want this attention from you, Marc. Play the devoted husband when your family is around or other people who might matter to you, but there is no need to do so when no one of consequence is looking.'

'I can still be a gentleman,' he said.

'A gentleman!' She swung away from him and quickened her pace.

'Tess!' she heard a man call. 'Tess!'

A red-coated soldier hurried towards her.

'Edmund?' Was it truly her brother? 'Edmund!'

She rushed towards him and he caught her in a hug.

Tears immediately sprang to her eyes. Her armour was no match for seeing Edmund.

'Edmund,' she repeated. 'I wanted so badly to see you!' Her brother who loved her was here!

'What are you doing in Brussels, Tess?' He sounded unhappy to see her.

She stepped back.

A furrow of worry creased his brow. 'Are you in a financial fix?'

'Not at all,' Marc answered for her. He had followed her. 'Allow me to present myself. I am Marc Glenville, Tess's husband.'

'You are the husband?' Obviously Tess's letter had reached Edmund—the one that told him she was married; she'd not followed with one that said she'd also been abandoned. 'I am Edmund Summerfield, sir, Tess's brother.'

'Summerfield.' Marc extended his hand and Edmund shook it.

'My father acknowledged Edmund and gave him his name,' Tess explained.

Marc glanced at her. 'I was not questioning his name, Tess.'

'Indeed.' Edmund shifted uncomfortably before giving Marc a puzzled look. 'Why are you in Brussels, then, if not to escape debt? Do you have an official function?'

It was a blunt question, Tess thought.

'No debt. No official function.' Marc answered without apparent offence. 'I have been here for several days, but Tess and my family arrived today.'

Why did Marc not leave? It felt to Tess as if her brother was all she had left. She did not want to share his company with Marc.

'Never mind why we are here,' she said. 'Tell me, are you well? Do you need anything? Where are you staying?'

He took both her hands in his. 'I am very well. I need nothing. And—and I particularly wanted to tell you where I am staying.'

She hoped it was nearby so she could see him often. Perhaps he would be free from duties, like the officers in the park. Perhaps she could spend a day with him.

His expression turned serious. 'I am staying with your mother.'

Did she hear him correctly? 'My mother!'

'Yes,' he responded. 'I am staying with her and Count von Osten. They have a large house on Rue Sainte Anne.'

Count von Osten was the man her mother had eloped with.

'My mother and Count von Osten.'

Edmund released her. 'I shocked you, Tess. I am sorry.'

'I do not understand.' She shook her head. 'You—and my mother?'

He shrugged. 'I discovered she was in Brussels a long time ago. I've been corresponding with her for years.'

'For years?' Tess's voice rose. 'You've written to her? About us?' About Lorene and Genna and herself?

'Of course,' he admitted. 'But mostly about me.'

'You never told us!' It felt like a betrayal.

Her mother had no right to know anything about her! Or about Lorene and Genna. How could he write to her about them? Thank goodness they'd never told Edmund about their father's financial ruin or about him stealing their dowries to purchase Edmund's commission. Thank goodness she kept the mess of her own life secret.

'Why did you find her? Why write to her? Live with her? She is not your mother!' She trembled.

A strong, comforting arm wrapped around her shoulders. Marc.

Edmund faced her. 'Your mother was always kind to me.'

'She hardly saw any of us!'

'Maybe so,' Edmund responded. 'But she always treated me well. She treated me as if I were of value and when I was a boy, I greatly needed that.'

Her mother had been charming, that was true, but she could not have valued any of them. She left them, after all.

Edmund's expression turned earnest. 'She wants to see you, Tess.'

'She knows I am here?' Tess did not want her mother to know anything of her.

'She was with me when Upton told me you were here,' he explained. 'Will you call upon her, Tess? She would like you to.'

'Call upon her!' Never.

'She even invites you to stay.' He turned to Marc. 'You, too, sir.'

'Tess is here with my parents and sister,' Marc explained.

'I am certain they would be welcomed, too,' Edmund said. 'It is a very big house.'

'No!' Tess cried.

She pulled away.

'Perhaps we should bid you goodnight, Lieutenant,' Marc said. 'Tess is weary from travelling.'

Edmund nodded. 'May I call upon you again, Tess?'

He was still her brother, after all. Even if she could no longer trust him. 'Of course you may call upon me.' She walked back to give him a quick hug. 'But I do not wish to hear more about my mother.'

'I will call again tomorrow.' He turned to Marc. 'Goodbye, sir. I hope to see more of you.'

Marc again offered his hand to shake. 'I do, as well.'

Tess hugged Edmund once more before Marc led her up the stairs and out of sight of the lobby.

She pulled away then, and turned to face him. 'How dare he! Did you hear him? He acted as if I should not mind that she abandoned us!' She started down the hallway, talking to the walls now. 'Why is it that everyone who abandons me thinks it perfectly acceptable to do so? I am expected to greet them as if they'd merely been gone an hour. Am I supposed to feel nothing?'

That day when she'd been nine, her mother came flying into the nursery, waking up her, Lorene and Genna and kissing them and saying she would see them later. Since that day she'd not sent one letter, not one message, to them. The only news they heard of her after that was through their father when he ranted about how she'd ruined his life.

'She asks to see me as if it did not matter.' Tess fought angry tears.

When they reached her door, she pulled the key from her reticule. Marc took it from her and wrapped his arms around her, holding her close.

His warmth, the solidness of his body, his scent, was comfort itself, as if he were pouring some of his strength into her. He simply held her, giving and demanding nothing. She wanted to stay in his arms forever.

But this was Marc. He'd abandoned her, too.

She pushed him away.

'Do not touch me,' she snapped.

He merely bowed and backed away. She hurried into the room, but stopped and opened the door a crack to watch him walk down the hall, away from her and to wherever it was so important he go.

Marc descended the stairway with his own set of churned-up emotions. He had indeed abandoned her, just as her mother had done.

Could he ever make it up to her? Or had their marriage been doomed from the start?

When he reached the lobby, her brother still stood there and looked surprised to see him.

'I am off on an errand,' Marc explained, walking towards the door.

Edmund walked with him. 'Is Tess all right?'

Marc met his eye briefly. 'She has had a very difficult day.'

Marc had made it difficult.

Edmund looked regretful. 'Please convey my apologies to her. I should not have told her about her mother so abruptly.'

'It is done now.' What else could Marc say?

A footman opened the door.

'I do not think Tess will call upon her mother,' Marc told Edmund as he walked outside.

'She should do so.' Edmund shook his head. 'I knew this news would be a surprise to her. I thought she might be happy about it, though. As children we sometimes talked about her mother leaving. She and my sisters always said Lady Summerfield had done the right thing.'

'Sometimes you can still hurt someone even if you do the right thing.' How well Marc knew this.

Marc liked this brother of Tess's. Edmund was loyal to Tess and caring, even if he had brought Tess unwelcome news. Marc even liked Edmund's loyalty to Lady Summerfield. Edmund had apparently forgiven her for abandoning her family.

Would Tess ever forgive him?

They parted ways shortly after and Marc walked the half-mile to Le Double Aigle at the old Halle aux Blés. It was an inn of an inferior type where he could be somewhat unobtrusive. It was also packed with billeted soldiers.

Marc climbed the stairs to his room and changed into the clothes of an ordinary Belgian.

He took care to leave the inn again without anyone noticing and made his way to a part of town where no Englishmen thought to visit. There he entered a public house, one he'd been visiting frequently. He took a seat and ordered the beer this country brewed so well. Like previous nights, he settled down to listen to the conversations of those around him. He'd stay until late at night, listening to men's tongues loosened with drink.

He suspected, though, that his thoughts would turn to Tess, even more often than they'd done before while on his travels. With any luck, he would not miss some useful information that might come his way from the many Belgians who would welcome Napoleon's return.

The next morning Marc woke early, his head aching more from lack of sleep than the beer he'd consumed. He'd promised his father he would breakfast with the family and he did not want to disappoint them. He forced himself out of bed and dressed quickly. Soon he was out in the cool morning air that finally revived him. He walked briskly to the Hotel de Flandre.

Would Tess wake so early? he wondered. Would she breakfast with the family? Would he have any time alone with her?

He would wager any amount of money that she'd not let on to his parents or Amelie or even her maid Nancy that her mother was in Brussels. He hoped she'd regained her composure.

He'd not wanted to leave her last night, but he had his duty to perform.

And she did not want him.

His night had been productive, at least. He'd wound

up befriending a couple of Bonapartists and they wanted him to meet someone this afternoon. Apparently a group of men was planning to help Napoleon gain back Belgium. Marc would shout *Vive l'Empereur* if it would help them accept him as one of them and tell him what they knew.

He entered the hotel and asked the steward to have him announced to his father. Instead of the steward returning with permission to call upon his father, his father appeared in person.

'Your mother is not yet awake,' his father said by way of greeting. 'Let us take a turn in the park.'

They walked the short distance to the Parc de Bruxelles. Even at this early hour they had plenty of company, soldiers in uniform, some arm in arm with willing women who'd undoubtedly warmed their beds the night before.

His father was silent a long time before speaking. 'I would be remiss if I did not address what you have done, my son.'

A lecture. Marc supposed he deserved it, at least from his father's viewpoint.

'You know I am not at all happy about this marriage of yours. It caused plenty of talk in town. The gossips made much of you and she being caught *in flagrante*.' He made a disparaging sound. *'In flagrante.'*

Marc sliced the air with his hand. 'We were never *in flagrante*, Papa, so say no more. I told you what happened.'

His father stopped and looked straight in Marc's eye. 'Why the devil did you leave her, then? To travel to Switzerland? God knows you've run off willy-nilly plenty of other times, but this was not the thing to do.'

'I could not refuse,' Marc said truthfully.

'Could not refuse. Of course you could refuse,' his father muttered. 'Well, you've done a lot of harm by leaving.

A lot of harm. To her and the family. What are you going to do about it now?'

'Whatever I can,' he answered honestly.

They continued to stroll down one of the walkways, passing a copy of the statue *Apollino*.

'You have to tend to a marriage.' His father's voice took on a philosophical tone. 'A wife needs your consideration.'

This was his father talking?

'You need to consider her desires, if you are married to her. And if you must do something that she cannot like, you must tell her in the gentlest way possible—'

Marc would hear no more of this. 'Papa! Are you speaking from experience? Because I have seen little of what you describe in your marriage.'

His father stiffened. 'I am not talking of my marriage.'

'Obviously not.' Marc continued walking. 'When have you considered Maman's wishes above your own? When have you been gentle with her?'

'Your mother and I should not have married!' Marc had heard his father say this many times. 'We were carried away by—by—well—those visceral feelings that lead to—to—carnal desire. She has been unhappy with me ever since coming to England where she can never belong. She blames me for it.'

'Is that so?' Marc continued. 'I dare say Tess's and my marriage began even more problematically. Before you tell me what I must do, you ought to try it yourself.'

'Your mother would not accept it.'

'Do you think so?' Marc was not letting this go. 'You and she were on excellent terms last night. Both of you refrained from picking at each other. It was quite pleasant.'

His father waved a hand. 'That was nothing. We are eager that Captain Fowler think us a good family and we are always civil in front of the Caldwells. We are anxious to see your sister well settled. Amelie seems to like this fellow very well and Fowler would make an excellent husband for her.'

Like Fowler? Amelie seemed to think Captain Fowler hung the moon and stars. And his parents had travelled to Brussels because of it.

'Did you find the evening pleasant when you and Maman were acting civil to each other?' Marc asked instead.

His father did not answer right away. He pretended to examine the busts of Roman emperors on the terrace surrounding the basin.

Finally he said, 'It was pleasant enough.'

'Then heed your own advice before you pass it on to me. Show me you can make my mother happy and I'll attempt the same with my wife.'

His father averted his gaze. 'I cannot make your mother happy.'

And Marc probably could never make Tess happy. But he could try.

He changed the subject. 'Father, I wanted to warn you about being in Brussels. It is not safe if there is to be fighting soon.'

'Ridiculous!' his father snapped. 'Brussels is as safe as London. Look at everyone who is here.'

'You should return to England as soon as possible.'

'After just arriving here?' his father scoffed. 'I have it on good authority that the march on France is a couple of weeks away at least.' He swept his arm across the park. 'Look at those men in uniform. They do not look as if this is the eve of battle. They look as if they are on holiday. Besides, your mother likes it here. We will stay as long as it suits her and your sister.'

'I realise that.' Marc felt none of the leisure of the soldiers in the park. 'But when the soldiers march, you must return to England.'

'Bah. What do you know about it?'

Marc would know more very soon, he hoped. Something was afoot and the Bonapartists he'd met in those public rooms were his best bet on learning what it was.

His father went on. 'You probably want to get rid of us so you can continue your affair with Doria Caldwell.'

He turned on his father. 'I am not having an affair with Doria Caldwell!' He tried hard to contain his anger. 'You do us all a disservice by saying so, and if you've implied anything of the sort to Tess, you are cruel indeed.'

'I have said nothing,' his father snapped, but his expression turned to concern. 'Then, why, my son? Why did you leave? Where did you go and why?'

'I went to the Alps.'

'I do not believe you,' his father said. 'You are hiding something.'

Marc looked him directly in the eye. 'Do not believe me, then. But when next I tell you to leave Brussels, take me seriously.'

His father looked back at him, his eyes widening. He slowly nodded.

Tess's sleep had been fitful, filled with dreams, not only of Marc and Edmund, but also of her mother. She dreamed of being suddenly alone in Brussels, finding her mother's house an empty ruin, but hearing her mother's laughter, watching Marc come towards her in the rain, but disappearing. She dreamed of cannon fire and soldiers on horseback galloping through the town, no one noticing she was alone.

When she'd finally fallen into a deep sleep, Nancy came in the room to wake her.

Tess sat up in the bed. 'What time is it?'

'It is eight o'clock, the time I was supposed to wake you,' Nancy said cheerfully.

Tess fought the urge to send Nancy away and burrow under the covers again. Instead she swung her feet over the edge and searched for her slippers. 'I hope you slept well.'

Nancy shared a room with Lady Northdon's and Amelie's maids. 'Lady Northdon's maid snores, but otherwise it was very comfortable.' She opened the curtains and sunlight poured into the room, such a contrast to the gloom of Tess's dreams. 'What would you like to wear?' she asked, walking over to the clothes press.

'The blue, I think.' Her blue gown always reminded her of Marc's eyes and she wore it often in the hopes that she could attach the colour to something else. The sky. The sea. Something.

Tess walked over to the washstand and poured some water into the basin. She washed herself and brushed her teeth before donning a fresh shift. Nancy brought her a corset and laced her into it, then they moved to the dressing table so Nancy could brush out her hair and pin it up. It was a familiar routine for them, even in this unfamiliar place.

'Will you see Mr Glenville today?' Nancy brushed through a difficult tangle. 'Or your brother?' Tess had confided only the bare facts of the previous day to Nancy.

'I do not know,' she answered. How could she know if she would see Marc? She did not even know the name of his hotel. If he wished, he could easily disappear again. 'I do hope to see my brother.'

In the mirror Tess saw Nancy's usual cheerful expression change to a frown. 'I know it is not my place to say, but it wasn't right for Mr Glenville to leave you the way he did and then not to let you know he was here in Brussels. He should not have surprised you so.'

'I fear it was we who surprised him.' If he'd known they were coming to Brussels, would he have left?

Nancy pinned Tess's hair into a simple knot and helped her into her dress. 'Do you remember that Lord Northdon wanted you to breakfast with them in their sitting room?'

Tess nodded.

'When will you be needing me today?' Nancy asked.

'Goodness,' Tess exclaimed. 'I have not thought that far ahead.'

'The thing is, I would like to visit the shops, if I may. The maids who work here in the hotel said that Brussels is known for its lace and I should want to look at lace.'

Tess reached for her reticule and took out several coins. 'If you see something worthwhile, purchase it, for yourself or for me. No matter what, buy yourself something.'

Nancy's eyes sparkled. 'Oh, thank you, ma'am!'

'And take one of the other maids with you. Or Staines, if you can. Do not go out alone. There are soldiers everywhere.' Nancy's sheer good spirits would attract the men to her.

'Oh, do not worry over me, ma'am. I have brothers. I know how to handle myself.' She made a fierce face. 'But Miss Glenville's maid wants to see the shops, too.'

There was a knock on the door, but it opened before Tess could speak.

Amelie stuck her head in. 'Tess! May I come in?'

She was halfway in already. 'Of course, Amelie.'

The girl practically danced into the room. 'It is such a lovely morning, is it not?'

Nancy grinned. 'Only one thing makes a girl that happy!'

Amelie gave Nancy a quick embrace. 'A man, you mean. A special man! The most handsome man you have ever seen and the most gentlemanly, too.'

'It is lovely to see you so happy, Amelie.' A man, a special, handsome man, a gentleman, was on Tess's mind, too, but to think of him made Tess feel wretched.

Amelie floated over to where Tess sat and hugged her, as well. 'I am so very happy! Captain Fowler is calling upon Papa this morning. He will ask if he can marry me!'

'Oh, miss!' Nancy exclaimed. 'That is so exciting! We must see if we can find some beautiful lace here for your wedding dress.'

Amelie plopped herself down in a chair. 'A wedding dress made of Belgian lace. Does that not sound beautiful?'

Tess could feel happy for Amelie. 'It sounds very beautiful.' But was it wise, she wondered, to become betrothed to a soldier when war was expected?

Amelie smiled beatifically. 'And now you might be happy, too. Marc is back with us.'

Tess tensed. 'Marc is in the hotel?'

'Oh, I do not know if he is in the hotel, but he is to have breakfast with us. Do you not remember?' Amelie sighed. 'I wonder what time Captain Fowler will arrive?'

Tess wondered when Marc would arrive. *If* he would arrive. She could plead a sick headache and remain in her room all day, but what good would that do? She must face him inevitably.

'I am certain Captain Fowler will arrive at the perfect time,' Tess said. Any time he arrived would be perfect in Amelie's eyes. She rose. 'Shall we go to breakfast?'

She and Amelie walked down the hall to Lord and Lady Northdon's set of rooms, which consisted of two bedchambers and a sitting room where breakfast would be served to them. When they walked into the sitting room, three gentlemen rose.

Marc, his father and Edmund.

'Edmund!' Tess hurried over to him, clasping his hand.

It was the vision that was Amelie who caught Edmund's eye, though. Tess noticed he forced himself to look at her.

When he did, he smiled. 'Your husband and Lord Northdon found me in the park and invited me to breakfast. I would never have called so early otherwise.'

'Your brother is *très charmant*,' Lady Northdon remarked. 'We were just becoming acquainted.'

'It was kind of you to include him.' Tess's gaze fixed on Marc, but she looked away quickly.

He looked fatigued, as if he'd not slept. Had his other entertainment kept him up late?

'Good morning, Tess,' he spoke in a low, smooth voice.

Amelie stepped towards Edmund. 'I have not been introduced.'

Marc spoke. 'Amelie, may I present Tess's brother, Lieutenant Summerfield.' He turned to Edmund. 'My sister, Miss Glenville.'

Edmund's face seemed full of colour. He bowed. 'My pleasure, Miss Glenville.'

'Shall we all sit and eat?' Lady Northdon said.

The breakfast was pleasant because Edmund was there and, because he was there, Tess did not have to talk to Marc or the others, even though Tess noticed Edmund's attention often strayed to Amelie. Captain Fowler joined them when the meal was almost finished and, while Amelie's and Lord and Lady Northdon's spirits rose, Edmund became more withdrawn.

Poor Edmund. What chance would he ever have with Amelie, even if it weren't for Captain Fowler? He was the illegitimate son of a disgraced baronet and Amelie was a viscount's daughter.

'Do you have time to spend with me today, Edmund?' Tess asked him.

'Later in the afternoon, perhaps.' His gaze moved to

where Amelie and Captain Fowler sat with their heads together.

'I want you to come with me this morning, Tess,' Marc said.

Tess could barely look at him. 'I have something else to do.'

Marc spoke firmly. 'No, you do not. Come with me.'

Her brother and Lord and Lady Northdon were all staring at her, waiting for her to respond.

'If I must change my plans for you, I will.' Not that she had any plans.

Chapter Fifteen

Breakfast ended. Tess, her brother and Marc quit the rooms, leaving Amelie and her captain with Lord and Lady Northdon. Undoubtedly, the betrothal was imminent.

Tess said goodbye to Edmund and she was left alone with Marc.

'Come with me, Tess,' he said. 'I want to call upon someone.'

'Who?' Tess was not willing to endure more surprises. 'I will not go unless you tell me.'

'Do you recall the gentlemen I was with yesterday in the park?'

Do you mean the gentlemen who stood with Miss Caldwell and you? she wanted to say. 'Not their names,' she admitted instead.

'One was Captain Upton, the man who knew your brother. The other was Mr Scott, who is secretary to the Duke of Richmond. We are calling upon him.'

'The Duke of Richmond?' Whatever for?

'Not the duke. Mr Scott.'

'Was he one of the fine fellows traipsing through the Alps with you?' she asked sarcastically.

'No,' he answered quietly.

Tess did not wish to call upon anyone, especially if he

was a friend of Marc's, even if he had not been a part of the fictitious trip to the Alps.

'Marc, would you please call upon this gentleman without me?' she asked. 'I am certain your mother would like for me to visit the shops with her.'

'My mother is wrapped up in Amelie and Fowler at the moment,' he said. 'Come. How many opportunities do you receive to see a duke's house?'

'How far is it?' she asked.

'About a mile,' he responded.

She acquiesced in the end.

As they set out, she had to admit that it felt good to be outside in the brisk air and to stretch her legs and walk. There was so much activity. So much to look at. All the street signs were in French and they heard more French spoken on the street than Dutch. Everywhere they walked, there were soldiers, some dressed in red coats, some in dark blue. Marc pointed out buildings of importance on the way and talked about the history of the city. It almost felt normal, like the few walks they'd taken together in London, if those could be considered normal.

They reached a very grand house on Rue de la Blanchisserie. Marc sounded the knocker and they were soon admitted to the hall. A footman explained that Mr Scott was to be found in another building. He led them to it through an anteroom and announced them to Mr Scott.

Scott strode over. 'Glenville! Ma'am.' He bowed to Tess. 'How good to see you. He gestured into the large room, its walls papered with roses and festooned with draperies in the royal colours of red, gold and black. 'This is where the grand event is to take place. The duchess has given me the task of seeing to some of the arrangements.'

Workmen were putting the finishing touches on some sort of platform. Others were carrying in sofas and chairs.

Crystal chandeliers hung from the ceiling and huge cande-
labras, taller than a man, were arranged against the walls.

Mr Scott laughed. 'Can you believe this used to be
where a coach builder displayed his wares? The children
were using it as a schoolroom—or, more likely, as a place
to play shuttlecocks—until the duchess took it over for
the ball.'

The ball? Surely this was not the ball Marc had spoken of the day before. Why would a duchess condescend
to invite Lord and Lady Northdon, or the equally scandalous Tess Glenville?

'That is why we have come,' Marc said. 'Were you able
to do what I asked?'

'I was.' He leaned forward with a conspiratorial look.
'With a little assistance from our friend.'

What friend? Of course, Tess would know nothing about
Marc's friends.

Mr Scott reached into the inner pocket of his coat and
pulled out white cards. 'Invitations for all of you. Your parents. Your sister. Captain Fowler.' He winked at Tess. 'And
you and your husband, ma'am.' His smile grew wider. 'His
Grace the Duke of Wellington promises to attend, as well.'

'We are invited to this ball?' Tess could not believe
it. 'The duchess's ball?' A ball Wellington would attend?
'Does the duchess know of our invitations?'

Mr Scott handed the invitations to Marc. 'She does, indeed.' He turned suddenly and shouted to some workmen,
'No, not there! On the other side.'

Marc put the invitations in his pocket. 'We should take
our leave. You are busy.'

Mr Scott made a wry smile. 'A tad busy at the moment. I, for one, shall be glad when this ball is over.' He
gave Marc a significant look. 'I will hear from you later?'

'Later,' Marc agreed.

They bid Scott farewell and walked back out to the street.

'Where shall we go next?' Marc asked.

Tess whirled on him. 'You did not tell me the ball I must attend would be a duchess's ball.'

Marc lifted a shoulder. 'It was an invitation I had at my disposal to arrange.'

'How could you have it at your disposal? A friendship with a duke's secretary is hardly a reason to be invited.'

'There was more to it.' He blew out a breath. 'What difference does it make, Tess? It is a very much sought-after invitation and I was able to arrange it.'

'Did you think arranging an invitation to a ball would make any difference to me?' Telling her the truth would be vastly better.

Not leaving her would have been ideal.

'This invitation will lead to others,' he said. 'It should at least please Amelie and my mother and make your time in Brussels more pleasant.'

The invitation did not please Tess. She would never have sought it. 'They talked about me in London after you left me,' she told him. 'Let them talk about me in Brussels, because you are forced to be with me.'

'I am not forced to be with you, Tess.' He paused. 'And I am profoundly sorry you were the object of gossip because of me.'

He looked at her with regret in his eyes, but should she trust how he appeared?

'Oh, how can I ever believe you?' She stepped away. 'About anything.'

He caught her and forced her to stop. 'We must learn to get on together.'

She raised a brow. 'Must we?'

He squeezed her arms. 'I know I hurt you by leaving,

but it was an unhappy accident of timing.' Caused by Napoleon, as a matter of fact.

She gave him a scathing look. 'I am certain leaving me right after our wedding night seemed like a sensible choice to you.'

'Let us drop this.' His tone turned soft. 'I have thought of another site to show you.'

They started back the way they'd come and he resumed his discourse on Brussels.

When they again passed the Cathédrale des Saints Michel et Gudule with its imposing two towers reaching to the sky, she asked, 'Why do you know so much about Brussels? Have you been here the whole time?'

He paused before answering. 'No. I have spent time here before, though.'

'When?' He'd been in Scotland before they met. Before that was the war. Who could have travelled to Belgium during the war?

'Some time ago,' he answered non-committally.

Was there no end to what he would not tell her? Secrets and lies had been a part of her parents' marriage and now it was part of hers.

They did not turn back to the Parc de Bruxelles, but continued to the Grand Place. The Grand Place was a square surrounded by buildings that might once have been grand, but now looked as if they had seen better days.

'This used to be in better repair, they say,' Marc told her as they walked through the square. 'But revolutionaries sacked the buildings a couple of decades ago.'

The buildings reminded her of herself. When she was little her life had seemed so shiny and perfect, but time chipped away at what was once beautiful, leaving mere memories of what was now gone.

She was glad when they continued past the Grand Place.

'Was that what you wished to show me?' she asked rather peevishly. Sad, neglected buildings? 'May we return now?'

'Oh, no.' He smiled. 'What I want to show you is meant to amuse.'

She wished he would not smile like that. It made her insides flutter as if thousands of butterflies were trapped inside her. He looked even more handsome when he smiled, less like a buccaneer and more like someone who could make the sun shine brighter.

She did not want to think of him as handsome. She did not want to remember how it felt for his arms to hold her, his fingers to stroke her skin. He seemed to be trying so hard to please her. It would be so much easier if he simply left her alone.

She pressed her lips together.

They turned a corner and after a few steps he said, 'Close your eyes.'

'This is nonsense,' she muttered, but she did as he demanded, mostly as an excuse not to look at him.

He led her further. 'Now open.'

She opened her eyes and laughed aloud.

Before her was a fountain made from a statue of a little boy, the water shooting out in a stream from a very particular part of his body.

'He is relieving himself!' she exclaimed.

He stood behind her, his hands resting on her shoulders. 'He is called Mannekin Pis and he has been in this spot for two hundred years.'

His hands almost made her forget anything else. She forced herself to speak. 'Why would anyone erect such a fountain?'

His voice turned deeper. 'The true meaning is lost, but

there was a statue before this one dating back to the twelfth century.'

He moved closer. Or had she been the one to move? She could feel his breath on her neck. He smelled of lime and bergamot—and a fragrance that made her body ache in response.

She did not want to feel this way. And she did not want to move away from him.

A church bell rang the noon hour.

He released her and stepped back. 'I must return you to the hotel.' An urgent tone entered his voice.

'You have somewhere else to go?' she asked.

'Yes.' He offered her his arm.

They started walking. 'Where?'

He frowned. 'To meet someone.'

Her throat tightened. Someone? If it was not a woman, then why not simply tell her?

Let him go, then! She wanted to be rid of his disturbing company.

'Why did you have me accompany you?' she snapped after they'd gone several steps. 'I do not understand at all.'

His muscles tensed under her fingers. 'We must start somewhere, Tess.'

Marc's spirits plummeted. As soon as matters calmed between them, he did something that drove her away again.

Damned meeting. He could not explain to her why it was so important or why the information he was likely to gather might help keep her and his family safe.

If he could be honest with her, it would help a great deal. The Tess he knew would understand how duty could take him away from her, even the morning after their wedding night.

He'd spent many a night thinking about her, yearning

for her and fearing he'd lost her forever because he could not be honest with her. Her delight at Mannekin Pis filled him with a little hope.

Even though she stopped speaking to him.

What would heal the wounds between them? Time? Time certainly had not healed his parents. They were as angry at each other today as when he'd been a child.

Tess held his arm as they walked, but in a perfunctory way that was like a knife thrust to his heart. He hated this silence between them, but he'd exhausted his knowledge of Brussels. What else could he talk about when almost everything about him must be kept secret?

It left too much to the imagination. His father, for one, imagined he was being unfaithful to Tess with Doria. He hoped Tess no longer believed that, but who knew what she thought he was hiding from her?

It would solve everything if he could simply tell her he was employed as a spy, that his contacts in Brussels were Mr Scott and the Duke of Richmond, that his need for secrecy had to do with duty to his country, not infidelity, not rejecting his wife. He'd come perilously close to saying too much to his father. Marc understood now how Rosier could have broken his oath of silence. It merely cost Rosier his life. Somehow Marc felt his choice, to honour his oath and do his duty to his country, might cost him something more precious. His marriage. Tess's happiness.

Was it futile to hope to win her back? As they walked together through the beautiful streets of Brussels, she would not speak to him.

He grasped at straws, or rather at a topic he knew she would dislike, but at least answer. 'Will you call upon your mother?'

Her hand tensed. 'No.'

He pushed. 'Even though your brother resides there?'

'He can call on me.' She took several steps before speaking again, but, then, it was more to herself than to him. 'I cannot understand him. She was not his mother. He was only there two or three years before she left. I never noticed her pay much mind to him at all.' She slowed and glanced to some unseen place. 'She did not spend much time with us. A visit to the schoolroom when she was home.'

'The time she spent with him meant something to him, apparently,' he said—to keep her talking.

'She was always charming.' Tess continued to walk. 'I suppose it drew even little boys to her.'

'And little girls,' he dared to add.

Her hand on his arm tightened.

'Yes,' she said in a hushed voice. 'When Mama was there nothing else mattered.'

Poor hurt little girl!

He wanted to keep her talking. 'When Amelie, Lucien and I were children, my parents were always too busy fighting each other to pay a great deal of attention to us.'

She glanced at him with a surprised expression.

He looked at her. 'Surely you have noticed that they skirmish all the time.'

'They are unhappy,' she admitted. 'But I am surprised you say they did not pay attention to you. They dote on Amelie.'

He nodded. 'I guess they do. Coming to Brussels certainly is greatly indulging her.'

She actually went on. 'They have been remarkably in concert about Captain Fowler. And they do not bicker when he is around.'

Marc was encouraged. This was almost comfortable conversation. 'What do you know of this Captain Fowler?'

'He's the younger son of Lord Ellister, a man your father esteems a great deal, apparently. From your father's account, it is a good family.'

'No scandal?' he asked with a wry smile.

To his delight she answered in like manner. 'No scandal.'

His spirits rose.

'Do you like Fowler?' he asked.

She shrugged. 'He seems besotted with Amelie.'

He frowned. 'But you are not certain of him?'

She looked into his face. 'How can one ever be certain?' That dagger thrust was meant for him.

They walked on.

'Is Amelie equally as besotted?' he finally asked.

'More so, I am afraid,' she responded.

'Wait.' He stopped. 'What do you mean *afraid*? I thought you believed in such love.'

She looked away. 'Not any longer.'

The dagger twisted.

This talk of love was too painful. Tess wished he would stop.

'Should I be concerned about Fowler?' he asked.

'Of course you should,' she snapped. 'He has the power to hurt her terribly.' Just as Marc had hurt her. 'Love, I've learned, has that sort of power.'

He frowned.

Did he even realise she spoke about how he hurt her?

They walked in silence after that. Good. She did not want him to say anything to her.

But she hated his silence.

What did it matter? Soon he would leave her to meet this mysterious someone he refused to tell her about. She would be free of his company.

He suddenly asked, 'Do you know why my friend Charles volunteered for the Forlorn Hope?'

He'd startled her. 'Why?'

They walked a few more steps. 'Charles became besotted with a Spanish woman. He was mad for her—at least that is what he said in his letters about her.' He took a breath. 'She threw him over for another man, so he volunteered for the Forlorn Hope. He wrote to me about it. Said he might as well, because he no longer cared if he lived or died.'

How awful! She'd felt close to that level of despair because of him, not that she'd ever let on.

'Charles thought himself in love,' he said in a bleak tone. 'He was so obsessed by her, he lost all reason.'

Her brows knit. 'Sad. But why—'

He did not let her finish. 'My brother was no different,' he went on. 'Lucien lost his head over a young woman whose parents refused his suit. He eloped with her and was racing to Gretna Green when his carriage wheel broke and pitched him to the ground.' He swallowed as if it became difficult to continue. 'He lingered for several weeks. I was called home from my regiment.' He could not finish.

Her voice softened, 'So you concluded love kills?'

'Well, love killed my brother and my friend. It doomed my parents to unhappiness—' He stopped abruptly as if his emotions prevented him from saying more.

No wonder he did not believe in love.

She wished he had not shared this with her. It chipped away at her defences against him. If she allowed herself to feel his pain, her protection could vanish. She could be hurt once more.

They reached the Place Royale before she spoke again. 'Do not worry too much about your sister and Captain Fowler. They seem to have the happy combination of being well suited in temperament and situation. I suspect they will be the lucky ones.' She paused. 'That is, if he is not killed in a battle.'

Neither spoke more. They reached the Hotel de Flandre and Marc escorted her to her room.

At her door, she took out her key and put it in the lock.

He reached into his pocket and handed her the invitations to the Duchess of Richmond's ball. 'Here are the invitations to the ball. Will you pass them on to my parents and Amelie and Captain Fowler?'

She looked at him with suspicion. 'Why? Will you not be giving them the invitations yourself?'

'In case I do not see them…'

She felt her entire body turn rigid. 'Are you planning on disappearing again?'

He seized her shoulders. Their bodies were mere inches from touching. 'I will come back for the ball.'

She raised her gaze to his eyes. 'But not dinner tonight?'

He looked away. 'If I am able, I will escort you to dinner.'

She could not believe him. 'Unless a trip to Switzerland comes your way.'

She opened the door and slipped inside before he could see that holding her so close had caused her face to flush and her body to come alive with sensation.

Marc tore himself away from Tess's door. He'd not planned to hold her so close. His body had ached for more of her. Would he ever earn that right?

He hurried to his hotel to transform himself into a Bonapartist with no ties to the British aristocracy and on to the meeting where six other men gathered. One claimed to have some news from another man who was in communication with Napoleon's aides-de-camp. Marc said all the right things and was apparently accepted, because this man spoke openly.

He said they must prepare for Napoleon's triumphant return to Brussels. Napoleon might appear at any moment, he said, while the British and their Allies attended parties and staged military revues rather than preparing for battle.

His information was second hand at best, but these Bonapartists took it seriously enough to design handbills and set in stores for a victory dinner.

Marc promised he would be ready to pass out fliers or help in any way possible when the time came. There was much shaking of hands and clapping each other on the back and shouts of *'Vive l'Empereur!'*

When Marc left he was careful not to appear suspicious, or to lead them to Mr Scott or the Duke. He spent an hour visiting shops, stopping for ale and otherwise looking as if he were having an ordinary day.

Eventually he made his way to Rue de la Blanchisserie and found Scott.

Scott summoned the Duke and the three of them met in the Duke's library.

Both Scott and the Duke were grim-faced as Marc told them what he had heard.

'Can we reach you at your hotel?' Mr Scott asked.

'At my hotel or my wife's.' But would she want him to stay? He could hope. 'She is at the Hotel de Flandre.'

'If what you report is correct, Glenville,' his grace said in a grim tone, 'Brussels may soon become a very danger-ous place for Englishmen.'

And everyone Marc cared about—including the woman he loved—was in Brussels.

Chapter Sixteen

That afternoon Tess brought the invitations to Lord and Lady Northdon, finding them in their sitting room. Amelie was there, as well.

'The Duchess of Richmond's ball?' Lady Northdon exclaimed.

Lord Northdon looked sceptical. 'Marc arranged this? How could he?'

'He arranged it through the duke's secretary,' she explained. 'A man who, I gather, is a friend.'

'The duke and duchess know of this?' Lady Northdon asked.

'The duke's secretary said they do.'

Amelie stared at the invitations. 'This is the most wonderful invitation I ever received. Everyone is talking about this ball and we actually will attend.' She clasped the invitations to her breast. 'Even Captain Fowler!'

Lord Northdon crossed the room to where his wife was seated. He lowered himself into the chair next to hers and leaned towards her. 'Do you wish to attend, Ines?' His tone was surprisingly mild.

Lady Northdon glanced at him in surprise. 'Do you?'

He actually touched her hand. 'Only if it pleases you.'

Amelie stared at her. 'Maman! Please say yes!'

Lady Northdon glanced from her husband to her daughter and smiled, showing every ounce of her beauty. *'Bien sûr.'*

Amelie ran over to her and hugged and kissed her, then hugged and kissed her father.

She covered her cheeks with her hands. 'What will I wear? Maman, come look at my dresses and tell me which will do for a duchess's ball.'

Lord Northdon stood and extended his hand to Lady Northdon to help her up.

She looked at him with adoring eyes. *'Merci*, John.'

Tess gaped at them. They were acting civil to each other even though there was no one to impress. Had the world gone topsy-turvy?

'If I may have your leave,' she asked, 'I should speak with Nancy about a gown for me.'

'Oui, chérie,' Lady Northdon said. *'À bientôt.'*

When it came time to dress for dinner, Tess dragged her feet. It was silly of her, she knew, because Marc would not show.

'You are quiet today, ma'am,' Nancy said as she pinned up Tess's hair.

'Am I?' She'd said nothing to anyone, not even Nancy, about Marc wanting to share dinner with her. Why would she?

Nancy twisted a strand of Tess's hair and secured it with a hairpin. 'What would you say to my sewing an overdress of Belgian lace for your ball gown?'

'In one day?' She spoke to Nancy's reflection in the mirror.

'I could do it,' Nancy insisted. 'It is just a few seams and I sew seams very fast.'

Tess sighed. 'If you wish to try.'

Nancy pushed one last hairpin into Tess's hair. 'What dress do you wish to wear to dinner?'

'It does not matter,' Tess said.

Nancy walked over to the wardrobe and pulled out the blue gown, the one that reminded Tess of Marc's eyes. Of all her gowns, why that one?

She said nothing, though. What would it matter what gown she wore?

Nancy helped her into the dress and she slipped her feet into her shoes. There was nothing left to do but appear at Lord and Lady Northdon's sitting room and go have dinner with them.

A knock sounded at the door. She was probably late and they'd sent a servant to collect her.

Nancy hurried over to open the door. 'Oh, Mr Glenville!'

Marc?

'I've come for Mrs Glenville. Is she ready?' he asked.

Nancy stepped aside to allow him to enter.

Tess stood. 'Oh. You are here.' In spite of herself her heart pounded at the sight of him.

He remained near the doorway. 'I said I would try to come for dinner.'

Tess picked up her shawl. 'Well. We should go then. Your parents will be waiting.' She turned to Nancy. 'Goodbye, Nancy.'

Nancy bobbed a quick curtsy. 'Goodbye, ma'am!'

Tess swept past Marc and crossed into the hallway. She started towards his parents' room.

He caught up with her. 'We are not dining with my parents.'

She halted and faced him. 'Not dining with them?'

He stood too close to her. 'I know you will not believe me, but they told me they were dining alone.'

'Alone?' She did not believe him. 'What of Amelie?'

'They have apparently given Captain Fowler permission to take Amelie to one of the nearby restaurants.'

She peered at him. 'Why do I think that you are tricking me?'

He took her by the arm and walked with her to a sofa at the end of the hallway.

He sat her down and his blue eyes held her in their grasp. 'Tess, I admit I have not always been able to tell you the truth, but I am telling the truth now. I want you to trust me. I want to begin again with you.'

She felt weak under the power of his gaze and his soft words.

'I will go to dinner with you,' she told him. 'But I do not trust you.'

He nodded. 'Dinner is enough at the moment. Will the Postillon be acceptable?'

'I know nothing about where to dine in Brussels.'

He stood and extended his hand to help her up. She accepted it, but he did not release her even when she was out of her seat. 'Thank you, Tess.'

She pulled her hand away and wrapped her shawl around her. They walked down the stairs and out of the hotel on to the Rue Royale.

Marc's hopes soared. He'd not been at all certain she would actually agree to dine with him. He was determined to put her at her ease.

But they'd walked halfway to the restaurant, near the cathedral, before she even spoke to him. 'Your mother and Amelie were very pleased to receive the invitation to the ball.'

'I am glad,' he responded. Mostly he was glad she decided to converse with him.

'It was odd, though,' she went on. 'Your father was quite solicitous of your mother. And there was no one about to impress, merely Amelie and me. Your mother opened like a flower in the sun under his kindness. It was quite remarkable.'

'He was kind to her? I should have liked to see that.' Had his father actually listened to him? That would be remarkable in itself. 'And they planned a private dinner? My God.'

They reached the restaurant, which was filled with other Englishmen, as well as soldiers and their ladies. There were few Belgians, probably because the hour was later than their typical dinner hour.

They ordered mussels and frites and fat sausages and large glasses of beer. They started out talking only about the food and it seemed to Marc that Tess finally relaxed around him.

'Did your sisters come to London for the Season?' Marc asked when they'd exhausted comments about the food and the surroundings.

Her expression stiffened. 'Yes, they came.'

He frowned. 'What is it, Tess? Did something happen with your sisters?'

She put her fork down and looked him in the eye. 'My marriage seems to have put some distance between us. Lorene feels I wasted her sacrifice. And I think Genna is angry because I let society dictate that I should marry. I did not tell them what Tinmore was prepared to do to them if I'd not married you.'

'And you probably could not explain why I left so abruptly,' he added.

'Who could explain why you left after the wedding

night?' Her voice was bitter. 'How could anyone understand that?'

His insides twisting in pain, he leaned towards her. 'I did not leave to be away from your bed.'

She glanced around, as if to see if anyone heard him. 'Do not speak of it.'

He glanced down at his plate, spearing a piece of sausage, knowing he was not telling her the complete truth. He had run from her bed, had he not? He'd simply not intended to be forced to run all the way to France.

He looked up again. 'I am sorry I hurt you, Tess.'

Her face filled with colour and she lifted her beer to her lips, taking a long sip. His words hung in the air a long time.

The word *ball* drifted over from a nearby table.

He took that opportunity to change to a safer subject. 'The duchess's ball is a topic of conversation, I see.'

As he hoped, she accepted the turn in conversation. 'Amelie is very excited.'

They talked about the ball and the decorations they'd seen transforming that large room into a ballroom. Soon their meal had ended.

When they left the restaurant, Marc asked, 'Shall we walk back through the park?'

Many gentlemen and their ladies were strolling through the park. Lovers, Marc thought. Those in uniform would soon be marching into battle. Tomorrow he hoped to learn more of when that battle might occur. He hoped he learned soon enough for Tess and his family to leave Brussels.

They reached the hotel and walked up the stairs to her room.

'Thank you for dinner,' she said.

On the landing, she stopped and turned to him. 'Tell

me something, Marc. Can men make love to women without loving them?'

He felt he was about to tread through brambles. 'They can.'

She nodded, looking as if she'd found a final piece to a puzzle.

She started up the stairs again and reached the hallway.

'That is the easy part,' he said. 'Making love without love. Very little is at stake—at least for the man. Love makes the whole thing more dangerous.'

'Because it can lead to death? Like with your brother and your friend?' she asked.

'Yes.'

They reached her door.

'And can women make love without love?' she asked, taking the key from her reticule.

All this talk about lovemaking—did she not realise it was all he could think of as he walked her to her room?

'They can,' he responded. 'Although for women I suspect lovemaking is dangerous whether they feel love or not.'

'Why would you say that?' she asked.

'They risk having a child.'

'A child…' Her voice trailed off.

'Do you want a child, Tess?' he asked, suddenly seeing in his mind's eye a little girl with auburn hair and hazel eyes, a little girl who would not suffer the loss of everyone dear to her.

She coloured again. 'Of course I do.'

She started to enter her room, but he blocked her way with his arm.

'We could make love, then, if you wish it.' Was he insane to even suggest this? He might drive her away again.

She turned pale. 'No. No. I—I cannot. Not after—'

He lightly touched a finger to her lips. 'Never mind. I can wait.'

Desire for her was now pulsing through him. He wanted her so much he was inches from lifting her into his arms and carrying her to her bed.

He kept himself in check.

She put the key in the lock and opened the door.

'Goodnight, Tess,' he murmured, backing away.

She disappeared into the room and the door closed.

'Patience,' he told himself aloud. At least she was talking to him now. At least she agreed to spend time with him. Time might not heal the wounds he'd inflicted, but it might help them come to some sort of truce.

He started down the hallway.

The sound of a door opening reached his ears.

'Marc?' she called.

He turned at her voice speaking his name.

She stood in her doorway. 'Stop by the hotel clerk and ask for a message to be sent to Nancy?'

'My pleasure,' he responded. 'What is the message?'

'That I will not be needing her tonight.'

He nodded, glad she'd given him something to do for her. He turned and continued down the hallway.

'Marc?' she called to him again.

He turned.

'Then come back to me.'

Marc hurried down to the clerk and arranged for the message to be delivered to Nancy. It was all he could do not to run back to Tess. He forced himself not to bound up the steps and race down the hallway to her room.

But he walked as fast as he could.

When she opened the door to him he took her in his arms and indulged in the kiss he'd feared she would repulse. His wife buried her fingers in his hair. Her lips parted and he felt her tongue touch his.

Joy filled him.

But she pulled away. 'I—I want to see how it will be, knowing you cannot love me. I want to see what love-making will be, knowing that.'

What did she mean knowing he could not love her? He did love her! That was what had driven him from her bed that first night.

But he would do this her way. She'd earned that right after what he'd put her through.

'Whatever you desire, Tess.' He took her in his arms again for another kiss.

It seemed as if her body came alive to him.

'Let me undress you,' he rasped when they broke the kiss.

'Like in the cabin?' she murmured.

He held her against him, loving the feel of her body pressing against his. 'Not like the cabin.'

He released her and untied the laces of her dress, letting it slip to the floor. He removed her corset next, this time unlacing it instead of cutting her out of it.

He stepped back, then, and peeled off his coat and waistcoat. He tore off his neckcloth. She pulled his shirt from his trousers and reached her hands beneath it to lift it over his head.

It suddenly seemed urgent that they rid themselves of the rest of their clothing. She pulled pins from her hair while he kicked off his shoes and stockings. As her hair tumbled over her shoulders, she took off her shift. He came to her again for another embrace, savouring the feel of his bare skin against her breasts. He lifted her into his arms and carried her to the bed.

He wanted to touch every inch of her, to assure himself she was real and that she was really warm and eager under his hands. He peeled off her stockings, the last barrier between them.

She reached for him. 'I am like my mother,' she said, her voice like sandpaper. 'I want this.'

Her words took him aback, but this was no time for a discussion.

Maybe she was like her mother in this regard. Maybe she was a woman blessed with the ability to enjoy sensuality. He would savour that.

He ought to be gentle, careful, slow. He ought to treat her reverently, but she urged him on, pressing her fingers against his buttocks.

He kissed her roughly and plunged inside her, his body taking over, needing to move inside her, needing to climb to the peak with her as if this were a race to be won.

She kept up with him, her breath coming in gasps, her hips rising to meet each thrust.

'Hurry,' she groaned. 'Hurry.'

He could not help but hurry. He moved faster and faster until she cried out and writhed beneath him. He felt her release inside her and his own pleasure exploded in return.

The power of his physical response to her astounded him.

This is love, Tess, he wanted to tell her. *This is me loving you.*

He suddenly understood what had driven his parents to marry, what had caused his brother to race to Gretna Green. He understood the desolation Charles must have felt when the woman he loved spurned him. To lose Tess would be devastating.

But he would not lose her, because he had no intention of ever letting her go.

She moved out of his grasp, though, but only to slide on top of him.

'Make love to me again,' she said.

Marc lost count of how many times they made love. It was as if they both needed to make up for lost time. He had no illusions about her forgiving him. He was still a long way from earning her trust, but this was a glorious start.

Sharing such pleasure together made for a very good foundation.

Unless this new war wore it away again, which it could do if it lasted ten more years. He could only be pulled from her so many times before there would be no rebuilding between them.

But for the moment he savoured holding her in his arms as dawn peeked in the windows. She looked peaceful and beautiful in sleep.

He heard a soft knock at the door. Surely it was too early for Nancy? He tried to ignore it, but it continued, louder this time.

'Who the devil?' he whispered to himself as he slipped his arm out from under her and untangled his legs from hers.

He grabbed his shirt and put it on as he walked to the door. 'Who is it?' he said as softly as he could.

'Scott' came louder through the door.

He opened it a crack and held a finger to his lips.

'You have to come now,' Scott whispered.

No, Marc protested inside. Not now. Not again. 'Wait. Let me tell her.'

Scott shook his head. 'No time. Now.'

'I have to dress.' Marc closed the door. He quickly put his trousers and stockings on and grabbed the rest of his clothes. He started towards the door, but stopped and returned to the bed. 'Tess. Tess.' He shook her gently.

She opened her eyes and blinked rapidly.

'I must go. No time to explain. I'll be back for the ball.'

He hoped he would be back for the ball, at least.

He kissed her quickly.

'No!' she cried.

But he turned away and crossed the room to the door, leaving before she could say another word.

Chapter Seventeen

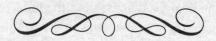

Tess tried to shake herself awake.

Had he been with her? Or had she dreamed it all?

She could still smell his scent on the bed linens and she remembered the feel of him as he drove her to the heights of pleasure.

She also remembered him leaving her.

He said he'd be back, though, had he not? He said he'd be back for the Duchess of Richmond's ball.

Could she believe him?

Nancy came in the room at her usual time, glancing around as if she, too, were looking for Marc. She did not ask any questions, though. Tess could feel her wondering if he had spent the night, why he had gone. Instead she cheerfully got Tess ready to greet the day.

'The lace overdress is coming along very nicely,' she told Tess. 'It should be ready for the ball.'

The ball. Would he come? Or had he run from her again, after making love?

There had been nothing dispassionate about their love-making. On the contrary, they'd both been in the throes of that same sensual madness that he believed led to his parents' misery and to the deaths of his brother and Charles.

Was that why he'd run from her once again?

'Maybe after you eat breakfast, you can try on the over-dress?' Nancy said.

How nice it would be to think of dresses and lace and balls and not that your husband both desired you and re-coiled from being with you.

Everywhere Tess went that day the duchess's ball was talked of. She heard it discussed in the hotel lobby, in the park, certainly whenever she was in the company of Lady Northdon and Amelie.

The invitation list, she'd learned, was quite exclusive, limited to friends of the Richmonds and those other digni-taries, noblemen and army officers who must be included. All the more reason for Tess and the Glenvilles to have been excluded. What sort of influence had Marc, to add their names to the guest list?

Would he come?

Amelie and Lady Northdon insisted Tess accompany them to the shops early in the day for last-minute pur-chases that might be needed for the ball. Amelie bought new gloves. Lady Northdon found an elegant head piece that matched her gown. Tess purchased a lace shawl, but she spent most of her time searching the streets of Brus-sels to see if she could spy Marc.

They'd run into Miss Caldwell while out shopping, but seeing the young woman only reminded her that Marc had wanted to marry Miss Caldwell and not Tess.

When they returned to the hotel from shopping in the afternoon, Tess tried the lace overdress Nancy created. It was lovely and fit perfectly. The girl was in raptures over it, finding finishing touches to complete and new ideas to make it even more lovely. For Nancy's sake Tess pretended to be excited over it.

After she handed the overdress back to Nancy, there was nothing to do but wait for Marc. Her mood dipped near its nadir.

Tess ate an early dinner with Lord and Lady Northdon in their sitting room in the hotel. Captain Fowler, now Amelie's fiancé, was included of course. A place was set for Marc, but the setting was removed when he did not arrive.

While they ate, Tess, not a part of the conversation, became aware of a distant rumble. 'What is that sound?' she finally asked.

They were all silent until the sound repeated.

'*Alors!* It is nothing but thunder!' Lady Northdon waved her hand dismissively and continued talking to Captain Fowler.

A grim-faced Lord Northdon shook his head. 'It is not thunder.'

Tess might have been the only one to hear him. 'Is it cannon fire?' she asked.

He nodded. 'Very distant, though. Likely some testing of guns or something.' But he looked worried.

After dinner, Tess dragged Nancy away from her last-minute sewing to take a walk in the park. Tess did not want the exercise or the air, she wanted to see what was going on in the city.

Or was she looking for Marc?

The atmosphere had entirely altered from the night before when the park had been full of lovers, like her and Marc. Now people whispered together with worried expressions. Uniformed soldiers hurried to and fro.

But she did not find Marc and the cannon fire continued.

She spied Captain Upton, Marc's friend, and stopped him. 'Do you know what is happening, sir?'

He smiled with a reassurance that was not quite genuine. 'There is certainly fighting somewhere. The Prussians, likely, but it is too soon to tell. I am off to see what I can discover.'

She wanted to ask him to come round and tell her what he learned. She wanted to ask him to watch out for her brother, if they must fight a battle. She wanted to ask him if he knew of Marc's whereabouts. Could he have been caught in the fighting like he'd once become caught in that rainstorm in Lincolnshire?

'Captain?' She would ask the only question she could. 'Watch over my brother, if there is a battle.'

He made a crooked smile. 'Your brother is a good soldier. He must watch over me.' He tipped his hat. 'I beg your leave, ma'am.' Upton started off, but stopped a short distance away and turned back to her. 'Never fear, ma'am,' he called. 'The ball will still be held, they say.'

As if a ball mattered when men must fight wars.

Nancy paled. 'Ma'am, is the battle coming here?'

'It is too far away,' Tess told her.

But it was also too close for Tess to be easy.

Nancy finally begged Tess to leave the park and return to the hotel to prepare for the ball. It was to begin at ten o'clock.

Marc had until ten o'clock to show up.

After Nancy helped Tess dress, the lace overdress billowed around her rose ball gown like a cloud over the sky of a setting sun. Nancy had arranged her hair with ribbons of lace that draped over her head like cascading curls. She looked her very best, but what did it matter if Marc did not see her in it?

When it was time, she rode in the carriage with Lord and Lady Northdon to Rue de la Blanchisserie. Amelie and Captain Fowler followed behind in another carriage. The streets were crammed with carriages and cabriolets carrying guests to the ball and it took them longer to reach the house than it had for Marc and Tess to walk the distance the day before.

Once they arrived, there were footmen in livery to escort the guests through the house to the ballroom. Once they entered the ballroom, they followed other guests to be greeted by the duke and duchess. The duke and duchess welcomed them cordially, which, Tess knew, greatly relieved Lady Northdon's nerves.

The room was even more transformed than the previous day. The candlelight gave it a warm glow and made it appear as if it had always been a ballroom instead of a room to display carriages for sale. Great jardinières of flowers were everywhere, producing lovely colour and luscious scent.

'*Mon Dieu!*' exclaimed Lady Northdon, making some heads turn to see who was speaking French. 'It is *magnifique*!'

The guests further decorated the space. Red- and blue-coated officers. Young ladies in white and pink and pale blues and greens. Matrons in richer colours. The dancing had not yet begun, but the musicians played quietly while conversation buzzed.

The atmosphere was one of forced gaiety.

Captain Fowler whisked Amelie away to meet his superior officers. Lord Northdon was summoned by the Duke of Brunswick.

Tess turned to Lady Northdon. 'Shall we find a place to sit?' She struggled to sound cheerful.

Lady Northdon was scanning the crowd. '*Ça alors!* I

thought Marc would come. I did not think he would disappear again.' She waved her hand. '*Bien*. We may sit.'

Mr Scott approached them. 'Mrs Glenville, so good to see you here.'

She presented him to Lady Northdon.

'I know you are largely unknown here,' Mr Scott said to Lady Northdon. 'Let me present you to some of the other guests.'

He escorted them around to several of the guests, choosing mostly the French and Belgian ones for introductions. Countess D'Oultremont and her daughters took a fancy to Lady Northdon's and Tess's gowns and there was much discussion—in French—about their modiste and the latest styles.

Mr Scott, apparently satisfied that he had done enough for them, bowed and walked away. Tess realised she had not asked him if he knew whether Marc would come to the ball. Perhaps Mr Scott would know where Marc had gone and why.

She rose to follow him.

At that moment, though, pipers sounded and men of the Gordon Highlanders, dressed in their kilts, appeared in the doorway. They marched into the room and danced a set of reels to the delight of the guests, especially those who had never seen such a sight. The tapping of their boots and the bellowing of the bagpipes filled the ballroom.

After the Highlanders marched out again, Tess could no longer find Mr Scott in the crowd. Lady Northdon happily resumed talking about dresses with the countess, but Tess continued to scan the room.

She felt tension in the room. With each new set of officers who entered the ballroom, the tension seemed to heighten and the buzzing of the crowd increased. Something besides a gay ball was filling this room and Tess was determined to learn what it was.

'Lady Northdon,' she said in French, 'I am going to take a turn around the ballroom, but remain here where you are comfortable.'

She strolled through the ballroom, not acquainted with anyone, but trying to listen to their conversations. She saw Amelie still looking deliriously happy, holding on to Captain Fowler's arm.

Did the cannon fire she'd heard today have something to do with this sense of trepidation? Was the army finally going to march into France? If so, Edmund—Captain Fowler, too—would be a part of it. And all these men in uniform. The idea made her sick inside.

'Tess.' She heard a voice behind her.

She turned.

Marc!

He was dressed in formal clothes, but looked ashen and fatigued.

'Forgive me for being late,' he said.

The music swelled and the first dance was announced.

Marc extended his hand. 'Come to where I can talk to you.'

He led her back to the anteroom through which the guests entered the ballroom.

'Where have you been?' she asked, worried about his appearance.

'On the road,' he said dismissively, but added quickly, 'I need to tell you. Napoleon has marched into Belgium and his army fought the Prussians today. He is marching towards Brussels.'

'I heard the cannons.' She grasped his arm. 'How do you know this? Who told you?'

'No one told me.' He looked down at her.

'You saw them,' she guessed. He'd left town, but returned to warn them.

'I've just come back from speaking with Colonel De Lancey, Wellington's aide-de-camp. Wellington has ordered the army to march. There will be a battle, Tess, and it will be close to Brussels.'

Three gentlemen passed them and entered the ballroom.

'His Grace, the Duke of Wellington,' they heard announced.

They both walked to the doorway. One of the men who'd passed them had been the Duke of Wellington. He was tall and slender, a vigorous-looking man, much more handsome than the caricatures she'd seen of him.

She turned to Marc. 'You must be mistaken. The Duke would not be here if Napoleon was on the march.'

'He is appearing here to reassure people,' Marc answered.

One of the Duke of Richmond's daughters left her dance partner and hurried over to speak to Wellington.

Marc took Tess's hand. 'Come with me. I must find my father. My sister and mother, too.'

They found a serious-faced Lord Northdon talking to a group of men. Lord Northdon left them abruptly when he saw his son approach.

'You have heard the news?' his father asked him.

Heard the news? Tess thought. Marc saw it with his own eyes.

'I have,' Marc answered. 'This is the time to leave Brussels, Papa. Go to Antwerp, if you can.'

His father nodded. 'I will arrange it.'

Marc went on. 'You should return to the hotel now. Soon the streets will be filled with marching soldiers.'

The music stopped briefly and the distant sound of reveille could be heard.

'I'll get your mother,' Lord Northdon said.

When they found Amelie, she ran up to Marc. 'Is it true?' she cried. 'They are saying that Napoleon is at the gates of Brussels. All the soldiers must go fight!'

'Brussels is safe for now,' Marc assured her. 'But our soldiers are marching tonight.'

She ran back to Captain Fowler. 'Marc says you must leave,' she wailed. 'But I do not want you to go.'

'I must, my love,' Fowler said tenderly. 'It is as I've been trying to tell you. I must leave very soon.'

Amelie flung her arms around his neck and wept into his chest.

'We must get them back to the hotel,' Marc told him.

Fowler nodded and dragged a clinging Amelie along to where her parents waited.

'Should we not say something to the duchess?' Lady Northdon asked.

The Duchess of Richmond looked distraught. She was begging guests to stay, but the room was quickly emptying itself of all the military men. Everywhere there were couples embracing like Amelie and Fowler and saying farewell.

Her brother. Tess had hardly seen him. Now he would be going to war. She must say goodbye to him. She wanted to see him, just in case...

When Marc got his parents and Amelie out the door, Amelie was crying to Captain Fowler, 'I will not let you leave me!'

'My darling.' Captain Fowler embraced her.

Lord Northdon went in search of their carriage.

Fowler kissed Amelie before approaching Lady Northdon. 'May I walk Amelie to the hotel? These may be our last moments together.'

Lady Northdon waved her hand. *'Oui. Allez-vous.'*

Amelie and Fowler disappeared through the crowd.

Lord Northdon returned. 'Where is Amelie?'

'Captain Fowler is taking her back to the hotel,' his wife told him.

Lord Northdon looked worried, but he gestured for them all to follow him to the carriage.

When they reached it, Tess pulled Marc aside. 'I want to find my brother. I must say goodbye to him.'

'Tess, he may already be gone,' Marc told her.

'Or he may not.' She stood her ground. 'Direct me to Rue Sainte Anne. He might be there.'

'Your mother's house?'

'Tell me how to find the street. Please, Marc!'

His father snapped, 'We must hurry!'

Marc walked over to speak to him. His father shook his head, but climbed in the carriage after his wife and it went on its way.

Marc walked back to Tess. 'I will take you to Rue Sainte Anne.'

It was near two in the morning but the streets of Brussels could not have been more filled with activity. Everywhere was the sound of reveille, the pounding of marching boots, the wailing of women and children saying goodbye to loved ones. Tess did not know how she would have made it without Marc holding her hand tightly and pulling her through.

Her mother's house was not a great distance from the Duke of Richmond's. It was, however, more grand. Lamps shone in the windows and the door was opened by a footman almost immediately after they knocked.

'Lady Summerfield's daughter to see Lieutenant Summerfield,' Marc told the man.

The footman ushered them in and quickly closed the door. 'Wait here.'

'He did not ask why we called in the middle of the night,' Tess remarked.

Marc still held her hand. 'This night follows no rules.'

Tess expected her brother to appear. Instead a beautiful woman descended the stairway in her nightdress and robe, her blonde hair down upon her shoulders.

'My dear girl!' the woman cried.

Tess had a memory of her mother coming in the nursery in the mornings dressed just this way. She'd hug and kiss Tess and her sisters and ask them their plans for the day.

'My dear girl! You are here!' She walked directly up to Tess and took her hands, clasping them to her chest. 'Oh! My little girl. You have grown into such a beauty!'

'Mother,' Tess managed, pulling away. 'Where is Edmund?'

'Edmund will be down shortly,' her mother said. She turned to Marc. 'Is this your husband? Edmund told me you were married. Trust my daughter to pick a handsome one.'

Marc bowed. 'I am Marc Glenville, ma'am.'

'It is a pleasure to meet you.' Her smile still charmed. She turned back to Tess. 'And Lorene is married, too, is she not? She is Lady Tinmore now. How unexpected. Such an old man.'

Tess leapt to Lorene's defence. 'It was what she wanted.'

Her mother waved a finger. 'No young woman wants to marry an old man, even if he is a rich one.'

'You are an expert on marriages?' Tess asked, her voice sarcastic.

Her mother's eyes flashed. 'I am an expert on men and on falling in love, my dear, sweet girl.'

Marc stepped forward. 'Lady Summerfield, my wife is very eager to see her brother.'

'Glenville.' Her mother pointed her finger at Marc. 'Now I remember! Your father married a Frenchwoman.'

'Yes, Mama,' Tess said. 'You have likely heard the stories. Where is Edmund? Does he know I am here?'

'He is almost done packing.' She took them both by the arms. 'Come. Let us wait for him in the drawing room. Is it not terrible? Napoleon at our doorstep! Edmund leaving to fight battles! I cannot bear it. We were awakened from our sleep with the news.'

She led Tess to a sofa upholstered in pale green brocade and sat next to her.

The door opened and an elegant gentleman walked in. His hair was now peppered with grey, but Tess recognised him. He was Count von Osten, the man who took her mother away from her.

'Ossie, my love.' Her mother reached out to him. 'Come greet my beautiful daughter Tess and her husband.'

'This is Tess?' The count smiled warmly. 'My gracious, you have grown up to be almost as beautiful as your mother.'

He offered his hand and Tess felt she had no choice but to accept it. Instead of a handshake, he blew a kiss over it.

'I remember you, Count,' Tess said tightly.

Marc stepped in and introduced himself and drew the count aside.

'Where is Edmund?' Tess asked her mother. 'I came to see him.'

Her mother patted her hand and spoke soothingly. 'Do

not worry, pet. He will not leave without saying goodbye. He knows you are here.'

'Some brandy?' Count von Osten offered Marc. 'Sherry, ladies?'

'So thoughtful, Ossie,' her mother cooed. 'Yes, we will have sherry.'

Her mother chattered on as the drinks were poured and handed out. Tess drank hers gratefully. Seeing her mother shook her badly. She felt as if she were nine years old again, so excited to have her mother notice her, so despondent when her mother left.

All Tess wanted to do was see Edmund before he went to battle. Where was he?

Finally the door opened again and Edmund walked in. Tess left her seat and ran over to him. 'I could not let you go to battle without saying goodbye.'

He hugged her. 'Tess. My dear sister.'

She held him tight. 'Stay safe, Edmund. Do not do anything foolish. You must come back to us.'

'Do not worry over me.' He released her. 'I must go.'

He turned to Marc and shook his hand. 'Take care of my sister.'

Marc nodded.

The count clapped him on the back. 'Fight well, Edmund.'

He turned to Tess's mother. She enfolded him in an embrace that made Tess ache with remembered loss. 'My dear boy. I will be so angry with you if you do damage to yourself.'

Edmund laughed. 'Then I have no choice but to return in one piece.'

He came back to Tess, holding her one more time.

When he finally released her, Marc came to her side

and put an arm around her. Edmund gave them all a smile of bravado. 'I am off, then.'

He turned and walked out of the room.

Tess tried to stifle a sob. It helped that Mark's arm was around her.

Mark felt Tess's worry and grief as if it were his own. She might suffer yet another loss, her brother this time. Her brother might be killed in battle the very next day.

'My dear girl,' Lady Summerfield murmured, coming close and patting her cheek. 'You must stay here with us. We will have a room ready for you in an instant. I'll find you a nightdress and anything you need.'

Marc felt Tess bristle. 'Understand, Mother. I came to see Edmund, not to reconcile with you. I do not see how I can reconcile with you. You left us. You forced Lorene to become older than her years. Genna was only six years old. You left us to our father, who resented us.'

Her mother looked wounded. 'My only regret was leaving my children.'

'But you left anyway,' Tess accused.

Her mother seemed to grow older in mere moments. 'Stay here, Tess. Give me time to explain it to you.'

'No. I will go back to the hotel.'

Marc spoke up, 'I must take her back, ma'am. My father will be arranging carriages to take them to Antwerp in the morning.'

'Antwerp!' Lady Summerfield exclaimed.

Marc turned to the count. 'You might plan to leave, too, sir.'

'Leave Brussels?' Count von Osten's eyebrows rose. 'I think not.'

'We will stay,' agreed Lady Summerfield. 'Nothing will come of this, you will see.'

'As you wish.' Mark lifted Tess's lace shawl and wrapped it around her shoulders. 'We need to leave now.'

'We will have our carriage sent around,' Lady Summerfield said.

'No!' Tess instantly replied.

Marc quickly added, 'The streets are too crowded. We will make better time walking.'

Lady Summerfield took Tess's cheeks in her hands and kissed her. 'My darling girl.'

Tess shrank back. 'Goodbye again, Mother.'

They were soon outside and the streets were even more filled than before. Mark grasped Tess's hand again and they threaded their way through.

Reaching a relatively open area, he paused. 'Are you warm enough, Tess?'

'Yes,' she said distractedly.

They finally reached the hotel, which, even so late, was busy with people going to and fro in the lobby. They walked up the stairs and reached the hallway where her room and the rooms of his family were.

Marc stopped her. 'Tess, you must get what rest you can. I suspect my father will be leaving early.'

'For Antwerp,' she said.

'Yes. You will be safe there.'

She nodded, but still seemed in a daze. At the door of her room she removed her key from her reticule. He took the key and placed it in the lock.

He wanted to kiss her, but feared she'd already had enough for one night.

'Goodbye, Tess,' he said. He did not know when he would see her again.

She looked stricken. 'Where are you going?'

'To my hotel.'

She shook her head. 'Do not leave me.'

* * *

Tess opened the door and stepped aside so he would enter first.

'I am too tired to argue with you,' he said as he crossed the threshold.

'Oh, you are here!' Nancy rushed over to her. 'Mr Glenville. You are here, too!'

He nodded to the maid. 'I'll just sit for a moment. Do what you need to do.' He took off his coat and waistcoat and lowered himself into a cushioned chair.

Nancy turned back to Tess. 'Have you heard the news? Of course you have. You have been out. I was so worried about you! The others came back so long ago and you were not with them, but Staines told me that Lord Northdon said I was to pack your things. I just finished. Except for your nightclothes, that is.'

Tess kicked off her shoes. 'Help me out of this gown, would you, Nancy?'

Nancy unpinned the lace overdress and took it off. 'Do you think Napoleon will march into Brussels? The Belgian maids say that is what will happen and that no English-woman's virtue will be safe from his soldiers.'

Surely Wellington would not allow that to happen. 'Napoleon would have to defeat our soldiers first,' Tess said.

Nancy unbuttoned the long row of buttons at the back of the dress. 'Lord Northdon will take us to Antwerp to-morrow where it will be safe, Staines said. We are to be ready at six.'

A mere two hours away.

'Then there is no sense of my dressing to sleep.' Tess stepped out of the ball gown. 'Let me change into a trav-elling dress.'

While Nancy laced up the dress, Tess pulled the pins from her hair and put it in a plait. 'You must pack your things, as well, Nancy. And try to get a little sleep.'

'What about Mr Glenville?' Nancy turned to him.

His eyes were closed and his head rested in his hand.

'I will attend Mr Glenville,' Tess told Nancy. 'Do not worry.'

Nancy curtsied and hurried out of the room.

Tess turned to Marc.

He was sound asleep in the chair.

There was so much she wanted to say to him. Twice he'd left her after making love to her. She wanted to tell him she finally understood that he did not want those intense emotions that rose up between them, the sort of aching emotion that he believed led to his parents' unhappiness and the deaths of his brother and friend.

She also wanted to thank him for returning to warn them about the French advance, for taking her to her brother and helping her endure meeting her mother.

She wanted to tell him she forgave him for abandoning her, because he came back.

She wanted to tell him all of that, but he needed sleep more than her words.

She bent down and grasped his arm. 'Wake up, Marc. You need to walk to the bed.'

His eyes opened and fixed on her. He smiled.

'Come on,' she coaxed. 'Stand up.'

She placed her shoulder under his arm. He stood and allowed her to lead him to the bed. He climbed in it and immediately settled into sleep. She pulled off his shoes and climbed in next to him. She wanted to lie next to her husband.

He rolled over and spooned her next to him. 'Tess,' he murmured.

There would be no passion between them this night. The need for sleep was too great. They would share this bed as they had shared the cot in the cabin. Then and now he made her feel warm and secure and safe.

Chapter Eighteen

Tess closed her eyes just for a moment and must have slept, because the next thing she knew, Nancy was knocking on the door. 'Mrs Glenville! Mrs Glenville. Lord Northdon wants us in the lobby. Are you awake?'

She sat up. 'I am awake.'

'Come now!' Nancy cried. 'Leave your trunk and portmanteau. Staines will see they are brought down.'

'Everything is ready,' Tess answered. 'We will be down in a moment.'

Marc groaned. 'Must we rise now?' He put his arms around her.

She would like nothing more than to remain in his embrace. 'We must hurry. Your father is waiting in the lobby.'

He held her tighter. 'I am not going with you, Tess.'

It was as if the wind had been knocked out of her. 'You are leaving me again?'

He drew away. 'I must.'

She climbed off the bed and thrust his shoes at him. 'No. You must come to Antwerp with us where it will be safe.'

He frowned as he put on his shoes. 'I cannot. I—I must be elsewhere.'

She peered at him. 'You are going to the battle.'

'I am not saying where I am going,' he countered.

'You are going to the battle. You want to be a part of it.' Tess's throat constricted with emotion. She'd heard of men who craved such excitement.

She slipped her feet into her half-boots and tied the laces. She wrapped her plait in a knot and put a bonnet over it. She picked up her shawl and a pair of gloves and felt as if her world was crumbling around her.

'Are you ready?' he asked.

She nodded.

They walked out the door and started down the stairs to the lobby, which was filled with more people than usual, even at its busiest time of day. Tess felt as if she were marching to the gallows.

He stopped her on the landing. 'I dare not take the time to bid goodbye to my family.' He clasped her to him and held her tightly.

'You are leaving me again, Marc,' she cried against him. 'To go to a battle. You are not a soldier. You do not have to go. You could be killed. I'll never forgive you if you leave me again.'

He still held her. 'I must go, Tess.'

'You choose to go. Just like before.'

He released her. *'Au revoir.'*

She covered her mouth with her fist, stifling a sob as he made his way across the lobby. She watched until she could see him no more.

Wiping away tears, Tess walked down to the lobby and searched for Lady Northdon. She finally found her. Amelie stood with her, red-eyed and pale.

'Ma chère,' Lady Northdon said to Tess, 'where is Marc? Your maid said he was with you.'

'He left,' she managed.

'Pfft!' his mother exclaimed. 'He is always leaving! I wanted him to come with us, although he would have had to ride on top of the carriage. John says we will ride in two carriages. One for you, me, Amelie and John.' She used her husband's given name. Twice. 'The servants will ride in the second one.'

Lord Northdon worked his way over to them. 'Staines is collecting the luggage.'

'Marc is not coming with us,' Lady Northdon told him. 'He is disappearing again, Tess says.'

Lord Northdon muttered under his breath. 'Not disappearing. Working.'

Tess heard him.

'Maman, may I sit?' Amelie looked ready to collapse.

Lady Northdon walked her to some chairs and sat with her. They were out of earshot.

Tess turned to Lord Northdon. 'What did you mean by *working*, sir?'

He shook his head. 'I ought not to have spoken.'

She faced him directly. 'What did you mean?'

He leaned down and whispered in her ear, 'Working for the Allies.'

She felt the blood drain from her face. 'Marc told you he worked for the Allies?'

He leaned down again. 'No. He told me nothing, but I am certain of it.'

Her hands shook. 'Will he be in danger?'

'I fear so,' he said. 'I fear he has been in danger more times than we ever knew.'

He'd not left her to hike through the Alps. He'd been called to duty.

The hotel door opened as two carriages rolled up.

Staines ran in from outside. 'These are our carriages, sir,' the footman said.

The streets were nearly empty except for a stray officer here and there who apparently was getting a late start. Peasants with their carts filled with cabbages, green peas, potatoes and other produce rumbled leisurely past the hotel. It seemed a peaceful, normal day.

Lord Northdon nodded. 'Let us get the trunks loaded as quickly as possible.'

While they waited for the luggage to be brought to the carriage, Mr Caldwell and his daughter entered the hotel.

Mr Caldwell carried a portmanteau. 'My lord, there you are. Are you leaving the city?'

'I am taking the ladies to Antwerp,' Lord Northdon answered.

'Might I beg a favour of you, then,' he went on. 'I must remain in Brussels, but might I prevail upon you to take my daughter with you to Antwerp? I would be most grateful to you.'

Lord Northdon looked to his wife. 'I am not certain we have room in the carriage.'

'John,' Lady Northdon said. 'We cannot leave the girl. We must take her.'

'Very well, Caldwell.' Lord Northdon turned to his wife. 'I will sit on the outside.'

Lady Northdon looked aghast. 'You will do no such thing. We will simply squeeze into the seats.'

Miss Caldwell, looking very stressed, gave them a wan smile. 'Are you certain of this?'

'There will be room for Miss Caldwell.' Tess raised her voice. 'I am not going with you. I am staying here.'

'Tess!' Amelie cried. 'You cannot!'

'I will stay.' She thought quickly. 'My—my mother invited me. She is here in Brussels. My brother has been staying with her.' Although Tess had no intention of accepting that invitation.

Lord Northdon faced her, a look of concern on his face. 'It may become dangerous here.'

'Count von Osten will protect us.' She did not explain who the count was and none of them asked.

Lady Northdon peered at her. '*Ma chère*, are you certain?'

Tess answered her in French. '*Oui, madame. Je suis certaine.*'

Nancy spoke up. 'I will stay, too.'

Tess walked over to her and put her arm around the girl. She knew Nancy was afraid. 'You will do no such thing. You must go to Antwerp and help Lady Northdon and Amelie. You may attend Miss Caldwell.'

'But you will be alone!' Nancy cried.

'I will not be alone. I will be with my mother and she has dozens of servants. I will be safe. I promise you.' She turned towards Lord and Lady Northdon. 'I want to be here to see my brother. I will also look for Captain Fowler and send you word of him.'

But most of all she wanted to stay in Brussels for Marc, because it all suddenly made sense. Why he left without any notice. Why he sent no letters. Why he lied about where he'd been. Mr Scott. The Duke of Richmond. Were they involved in this, as well? Marc would come back to Brussels to report to someone, she guessed, if not them.

If he came back.

Marc was no longer running away from her. He was running into danger.

Nancy said a tearful goodbye to Tess before she climbed in her carriage and it pulled away. The first carriage carrying Lord and Lady Northdon, Amelie and Miss Caldwell had already left. Tess returned to the hotel lobby and informed them she would still be their guest. Her trunk and portmanteau would be returned to her room while she ate a quick breakfast in the hotel's dining room. There were a few other guests like herself with worry written all over their faces.

At a table near her were two officers seated with two young women and another man—their brother by the family resemblance. Why had the officers not yet left? she wondered.

'Nothing will happen today,' one said confidently. 'We may be assured of overtaking the regiment at a place called Waterloo where the men are to stop to cook.'

Tess hoped they were right. She hoped no men would die on a battlefield this day.

She ate only a little and returned to her room to sleep, removing only her hat, gloves and shoes and lying down in her clothes where she'd so recently lain with Marc.

She woke to cannonade, louder than the day before. Yesterday's had come from a battle between Napoleon's army and the Prussians. Where was today's cannonade coming from?

She rose and did what she could to neaten her hair. Again donning her bonnet and half-boots, she left the hotel and made her way to the park in hopes of learning some news.

The park was a different place than it had been that first day when she and Amelie saw it for the first time. Gone was the gaiety and sense of anticipation. It was replaced by strained expressions on the few people walking there. The cannons boomed over and over, like a death knell. How many men were fighting at this very moment, how many men were falling injured, how many were falling, never to rise again?

Where was Marc?

'Dear God,' she prayed. 'Keep them safe. Keep Marc, Edmund and Captain Fowler safe.'

She saw the two women and their brother from the hotel. Their soldier companions were no longer with them.

She approached them. 'Pardon me. Do you have any news? Do you know where they are fighting? Do you know anything at all?'

One of the women smiled sympathetically. 'We have talked to many people. Some say the battle is six miles away; some say it is twenty miles away. Someone told us our army won a complete victory. Someone else told us our men were completely cut to pieces. It is all rumour. We do not know anything with certainty.'

Tess thanked her and walked on.

A few minutes later she saw Count Von Osten crossing the park at a brisk pace. There was no way to avoid him.

He recognised her and hurried to her side. 'Tess! We thought you would be on your way to Antwerp.'

'The others went. I decided to stay,' she said.

'Where is your husband?' he asked.

'Gone.' What more could she say? 'I am alone.'

'Alone?' His brows shot up.

'Yes. Alone,' she responded. 'Do you have any news of the battle?'

He looked concerned. 'What? You should not be out walking unescorted. The town is not safe.'

'Do not worry over me. Have you any news?'

'Well,' he finally answered, 'I just spoke with Scovell who was at the battlefield. Our army was attacked when only two of the regiments were at the ready.'

'Which regiments?' she asked.

He looked sympathetic. 'The 92nd and 42nd Highland Regiments; the 28th —Edmund's regiment—and the Royal Scots joined the fighting later.'

Tess's heart shot into her throat at his mention of her brother. 'Is there any word of Edmund?'

'No casualty reports yet, I'm afraid. We know nothing of Edmund.' He frowned. 'The good news is that our boys held their own. There was no victory, but no loss, either, and the entire army will be ready for what comes next.'

It was not over.

Two Belgian men, obviously inebriated, staggered towards them.

'What have we here?' one said in French. 'Come with us, miss. We will show you a better time than that old man.' He grabbed her arm.

That old man, Count Von Osten, flew into action. He rapped the man's fingers with his walking stick, so hard that the man let go. He beat on both men with his stick until they turned and ran.

'Are you all right, my dear?' he asked Tess.

She nodded.

He offered her his arm. 'Come with me. You need protection. I am taking you to your mother's house.'

She was so shaken that she agreed.

'We will go directly to your mother,' he said. 'I will send one of our servants to collect your things from the hotel.'

As they walked, the cannonade continued. 'It is not over,' she said more to herself than to the count.

He made a worried sound. 'Apparently not.'

When they reached the house, the count sounded the knocker, but the door did not open. Instead a voice from inside shouted, 'Who is it?'

'Von Osten,' the count called back.

The door opened a crack and the footman who had greeted them the night before opened the door.

Lady Summerfield spoke from the top of the stairs. 'Is it the count, Jakob?'

Von Osten answered as he entered the hall, 'I have brought you your daughter.'

'My dear girl!' Lady Summerfield rushed down the stairs and threw her arms around Tess. 'You have come back to me!'

Her mother's affection was painful. 'It seems I needed a safe place to stay after all. The rest of the family have gone to Antwerp.'

Lady Summerfield released her. 'Why did you not go to Antwerp, sweet one?'

Tess swallowed. She could not explain about Marc or about how she needed to find him when he returned to Brussels. 'I—I wanted to stay. For Edmund.'

Lady Summerfield pressed the back of her hand against her forehead. 'Oh, Edmund! I have been so worried about him! Did you hear those cannons today? But, come, we will have our best bedchamber prepared for you. Have you eaten?'

Tess shook her head.

'Then we must feed you, as well.' Her mother put an arm around her and walked her into the drawing room. 'And give you a nice, warm bath.'

Tess was pampered as she had never been pampered before. Bathed. Clothed. Fed. It was as if her mother was trying to make up for all the years she'd been absent. Every word, every kindness, only reminded Tess of how it felt to be abandoned by her. She appreciated her mother's efforts, but was not ready to forget how it felt to be abandoned by her.

Her mother kept trying, though.

* * *

The next day in the afternoon, Tess extricated herself from her mother's solicitude and had some relief. She sat on a window seat in her bedchamber overlooking the street, which was still busy with people rushing here and there and carriages rumbling past.

As she sat storm clouds gathered, like harbingers of doom. The heavens opened and rain fell in thick sheets, finally clearing the street. Tess watched the rain and listened to its roar and remembered that rain of only a few months back. This rain was as thick, as loud. She remembered again the sight of the horseman appearing through the grey curtain of rain, the horseman who rescued her and became her husband.

Where was Marc now? Were he and Apollo caught in the downpour, like on that fateful day? She shivered, remembering the cold. For Marc's sake she was grateful the temperatures this day were not so dangerously frigid.

So much had changed since that rainstorm and, Tess suspected, much would change after this one. Armies would clash. One would be the victor and the other, vanquished, but not before many men would die.

She gazed up at the bleak sky. 'Please keep them safe,' she prayed. 'Edmund, Captain Fowler—' Her throat tightened. 'And Marc.'

Chapter Nineteen

Marc was where he was supposed to be, behind the French lines. He'd reached his position in the night, carefully moving past the tents of the French soldiers, acting the part of a Belgian citizen, changing his bearing and expression as he'd also changed into Belgian clothes. No one stopped him, however. No one had come close enough to notice him. He supposed it was due to the rain. Uncomfortable as it was, it acted as a shield.

He discovered a place that seemed deserted, a thicket of trees and shrubs where he and Apollo concealed themselves and waited for dawn.

The night, the rain, all made him think of Tess and remember how they'd been caught in rain this thick. He was chilled to the bone, but nothing like he'd been that February day. He spent a miserable night.

When dawn broke, Marc ate some food he'd carried with him. He walked up the slope through grain as tall as he was, reaching a ridge.

Below him was what looked like the entire French army, waking, like him. Soon popping sounds broke out all over the valley. The men were clearing their muskets of the charges that had lain in them all night.

There was no doubt he was behind the French lines, all right. His task was to keep watch, follow the army if they fell back, report any potentially useful information and create mischief, if he could—anything to help the Allies. He had an excellent vantage point of what he'd learned would be the battlefield, if Napoleon decided to attack. Wellington had chosen the ridge of Mont St Jean, a narrow space for a battle, only two and a half miles, by the look of it. On Marc's right was a farm, La Haye Sainte; on his left, another one, Hougoumont. Wellington had men in each.

Marc glanced around him. He seemed to be alone at this spot. It gave such a view of the field that he expected to see Napoleon himself ride up to use it as his command base, but no one was near. He took out his field glass and looked down at the French army. There was no command post that he could see. His first order of business, then, was to find Napoleon and his generals.

Without getting discovered.

That second morning at her mother's house, Tess waited in her mother's sewing room, waited for the sound of cannon to reach her ears, but none came. She wished it would rain again so the battle could not be fought, but the sky cleared and the sun shone. Out in the street wagons of wounded soldiers rolled by. Count von Osten sent Jakob the footman out to discover where they were from. They were from the first battle at Quatre Bras. Some wore the uniform of the 28th Regiment, but he'd been unable to discover if Edmund had survived Quatre Bras.

Count von Osten had gone out himself to visit the Place Royale in hopes of getting information. Tess's mother, who insisted on keeping her company, seemed determined to talk about anything except the impending battle. She asked incessant questions about the people she'd known in Yardney, about the servants at Summerfield House, about the house itself. Did it have new furnishings? Had her garden been changed? Whatever happened to her portrait that used to hang in the drawing room?

Her mother did not ask how it had been for three little girls to be abandoned by her and left with a bitter man for a father. She did not ask who arranged for their education, who taught them how to be young ladies, who tended their cuts and scrapes and injured feelings. Tess had no opportunity to explain how much those tasks fell to Lorene, who'd still been a child herself.

But her mother was not the only one who avoided questions. Tess did not ask her mother whether she found it easy to leave her children, or why her mother had never written to them or tried to see them or tried to discover how they were faring without her.

It was nearing eleven o'clock in the morning and her mother had been chattering for almost two hours. Tess's mind kept straying to some unknown battlefield where her brother and Captain Fowler would fight. Where would Marc be? Would he be in harm's way?

'Did you know I met the count at Vauxhall Gardens?' her mother asked. 'What a lovely night that was! We slipped away and walked together on the Dark Walk…'

Her mother, of course, had been married at the time and Tess's father had been left wondering who his wife had run off with this time. Tess had heard her father's version of this event many times.

'I know it may be hard for you to understand, but we loved each other. It was love at first sight.' Her mother's tone turned more subdued. 'There was no denying it. We needed to be together.' She glanced aside and smiled, but the smile was not meant for Tess. 'We still do need to be together.'

'Is that so?' Tess managed to keep her voice bland.

Her mother reached over and grasped her hand. 'But you have a love match. You must understand.'

'A love match,' Tess repeated. 'Why do you say so?'

Her mother laughed. 'Why do I say so? Your husband dotes on you. You are very lucky, you know. It makes life so much easier to love your husband and for him to love you.'

Easier? Tess wanted to scream. Realising she loved Marc made nothing easier, not when he might be killed this day.

Boom!

She and her mother both jumped.

Boom!

'The battle has started,' Tess whispered.

Marc found Napoleon's headquarters only a mile from where he had viewed what would be the field of battle. He'd seen the great man himself and his generals in conference at an inn called La Belle Alliance. Oddly Napoleon seemed to have chosen to remain at the inn, but surely his aides could have found the same location Marc had found with its perfect view.

Marc watched the inn for as long as he dared, but, though the generals had ridden off, Napoleon stayed. It was safer to return to the ground where Marc could watch the battle, though he would probably not be of any use to the Allies on the French side of the field.

It would be hard to watch the battle and not be in the thick of the fighting, to witness men dying and not be down there doing his part.

The sun was high in the sky when the French advanced on Hougoumont Farm, the first action of the battle. Marc had been in battle before his brother's injury and he knew he'd witness carnage this day and be helpless to stop any of it. Yet he also knew he could not take his eyes away.

He watched the French attack Hougoumont Farm. The fighting looked hard, but the Allies held on.

French guns pounded into the British line, which remained on the far ridge, mostly out of view. Through his glass Marc could see Wellington on his horse, riding from one end to the other, issuing orders, surveying the battlefield.

No comfortable inn for Wellington.

The French cannons stopped firing but their smoke put a haze over the field. Through it, though, Marc saw the French infantry go on the march, straight for the middle of the British forces. It was a magnificent, terrible sight. Thousands of soldiers, marching in column, like a human battering ram ready to pound down the British door. Their drums beat the Pas de Charge.

Could the British hold?

The French came closer and the Allied guns fired on them. Men fell and were left like litter on the field as the mass moved on.

'The guns are not making a dent,' Marc said aloud.

He had to stay low, lest he be seen, but he wanted to pace, to shout orders.

He wanted to fight.

On the crest of Mont St Jean, the British line fired their muskets, one volley after another, until the French infantry broke into retreat. Marc nearly whooped with joy to see the cavalry giving chase. He put his field glass to his eye again. The Scots Greys were among them, he could tell by their beaver hats.

Amelie's Captain Fowler would get his chance at glory, Marc thought, trying not to envy him.

It took only moments for the glory to turn to devastation. The cavalry had ridden all the way to the French guns, but it was too far. Fresh Cuirassiers cut off their return and Marc witnessed slaughter.

Few Scots Greys made it back to the line and likely Fowler was not among them. Marc memorised the ground where the cavalrymen fell, where he'd search for Fowler.

Later in the afternoon the cavalry charged again, this time riding in full force for the British line of infantry. Surely this was a mistake? The infantry formed squares that held, though the squares became smaller and smaller as men were wounded or killed. But this time the French cavalry suffered great losses, being fired upon from the squares. Through his glass Marc found the 28th holding their own. Tess's brother would be one of the officers on horseback in the middle of a square. It was where Marc would have been, had his brother lived. He and Charles might have fought this battle together—if things had been different.

Marc shook those thoughts from his head. Instead, he analysed the tactics on each side.

The whole of Napoleon's strategy seemed like a mistake. Why attack the centre and not the more vulnerable flanks? Why commit so many men to the siege of Hougoumont? Why attack in column and not in line, which would have given them so much more fire-power? Still, with all these mistakes, Napoleon's forces were close to victory. The Allies were straining to hold on. The field was awash in bodies and blood and evening was approaching.

From Marc's right, another army approached. His heart sank. French reinforcements? If so, Wellington was doomed. He put his glass to his eye once again, but these regiments were still too far away. He kept his eye to the glass as they marched closer and closer.

Marc's spirits soared from the depths to the heights. The Prussians were marching towards the battlefield. They'd arrived to support Wellington!

He swung his glass to the battlefield again. His elation was short-lived. Napoleon sent in the Old Guard, his finest soldiers. They churned across the field towards a very thin British line. The Prussians would be too late by mere minutes.

The drumbeat of the Pas de Charge pounded in Marc's ears. The Guard advanced. Marc could almost taste their triumph as they fired upon the poor line of redcoats.

But just as Marc despaired, thousands of British soldiers rose up as if by magic, all firing round after round into the Guard. Many fell. The others broke and ran.

Marc bounded to his feet and cheered.

The entire French army broke and ran with the Allies at their heels. Marc stuffed his glass in his pocket and hurried to where he'd left Apollo. The fleeing soldiers were running towards him, and if he did not get out of there, he'd soon encounter a multitude of panicked, desperate men.

A more horrid day, Tess could not have imagined. When the sounds of the battle reached Brussels, even her mother's determination to talk of other things failed. They sat, silent and worried, while the booms of the cannons went on and on. Count von Osten went out every couple of hours in search of information, but nothing reliable came his way. Each time he returned to the house, he said he'd heard both that all was lost or that Wellington was victorious, but neither report could be believed. At one point, a whole regiment of Belgian soldiers rode through the city, declaring the battle lost, but messengers from the battle-field did not confirm that, and the cannons kept firing, indicating nothing was finished.

It was near nightfall when the guns finally went silent and von Osten left once again. It was midnight before he returned. He burst into the sitting room where Tess had endured the entire day in her mother's company.

'My darling!' he cried. 'Tess!'

They both rose to their feet.

'He has done it! Wellington has done it! The French are in full retreat and the Prussians are chasing them all the way back to France!'

'How wonderful.' Tess's mother flew into his arms and he swung her around in a joyous display.

'Are you certain?' Tess asked cautiously.

He'd come home so many other times saying first one thing, then another.

He smiled at her. 'I was at the Place Royale when the dispatch came in. There is no doubt!'

Tess sank back in her chair, suddenly exhausted. 'Thank God.'

'Ossie,' her mother said, 'we must celebrate. Drink a toast to our fine soldiers. Let us bring out the champagne and gather the servants to be given some, as well. Champagne! It is perfect for toasting a victory over Napoleon!'

He ran out of the room and returned a few minutes later with a bottle of champagne and three glasses. 'There is celebration in the servants' quarter, never fear. This bottle is for us.'

Tess's mother stood up and took two of the glasses from him. He'd filled them to the brim with the bubbly wine.

She handed one glass to Tess. 'Be more cheerful, my darling girl! We have won.'

Tess accepted the glass, spilling a little over her fin-

gers. 'I will be more easy when I know Edmund is safe.'
And Captain Fowler.

And Marc.

Where had he been during the battle? Had he been in
danger? Was he safe now?

The count's expression sobered. 'There were many ca-
sualties, they said.'

Some of the exultation evaporated.

The count put his hand on Tess's shoulder. 'Do not
worry. Tomorrow I will take the carriage to the battlefield and see what word I can find of our dear Edmund.'

'May I come with you?' she asked.

'To a battlefield?' He looked upon her kindly. 'I think
not.'

Marc changed back into his own clothes before riding
to where the soldiers were bivouacked for the night just
steps from where they'd fought the most desperate battle
he could imagine. It had not been possible to follow Napoleon in his retreat. The vanquished emperor was swallowed by the desperate men clogging every road, running
over the countryside, all trying to reach the safety of home.
Darkness was falling fast, making it even more difficult.
Besides, with no more army, where would Napoleon go
except Paris?

Marc instead would search among the survivors for
Tess's brother and Amelie's fiancé. Exhausted men sat
around small campfires, haunted expressions on their
faces. The battlefield was in their view, but it was now a
macabre sight of bodies that appeared no more than grey
mounds in the darkness. The stench of blood and death
was inescapable and the cries of wounded and dying men
and horses pierced the air.

No one dared come to their aid. The looters, the most

ruthless and heartless of men—and women—moved among the bodies, stripping them of clothes, pulling out their teeth, taking anything that might bring money. Looters would think nothing of killing anyone who tried to stop them. But every cry that reached Marc's ears hit him like a sabre thrust. Were they Edmund's cries he must ignore? Or Fowler's?

If Marc found them among the survivors, he would not have to search among the dead and dying when dawn broke. He started with the 28th. Edmund's chances of making it through were a lot greater than Fowler's.

And Marc did not want Tess to suffer yet another loss.

It took him hours but he finally found Edmund.

Among the wounded.

Edmund lay on the ground outside a house where one of the army's surgeons was occupied with amputating limbs. Edmund's uniform was stained with blood.

'Glenville?' he mumbled hazily as Marc knelt next to him. 'What the devil are you doing here?'

'Tess would want me to be here,' Marc told him.

The day after the battle was even more stressful for Tess, if that were possible. The count went out early, but returned almost immediately because the roads were too crowded with the wounded pouring in to Brussels, some in wagons, some on foot. He left again, this time to return to the Place Royale to see what names were on the lists of killed and wounded. Tess went out herself, then, much against her mother's wishes. She walked to the main road over which scores of wounded soldiers travelled and asked any soldiers from the 28th Regiment if they knew what had happened to her brother.

The sight of countless men so terribly injured was heart

wrenching. Some of the injuries were so terrible that she did not see how the men were still alive. She suspected they would not survive long. Where would they all go?

She spied another wagon with men wearing the red coat with yellow facing and the stovepipe shako that identified them as being in the 28th. She ran alongside. 'Excuse me, gentlemen, do you know Lieutenant Edmund Summerfield?'

One man answered, 'We know him.'

She did not mince words. 'Is he alive?'

Two of the men shook their heads. 'Don't know, ma'am.'

'I saw him fall,' said a third. 'Didn't see him rise again.'

'Dead?' She stopped.

The wagon rolled on.

A bitter taste filled her mouth. She ought to continue, ought to search for Captain Fowler, but her vision blurred with tears.

She wiped her tears away with the back of her glove. This was no time to weaken, when these men had endured so much worse than she could imagine. She could still do her duty to Amelie and find Captain Fowler, no matter that she'd lost her dear brother.

And, possibly, Marc. How could she search for Marc? She did not know where he was or if he would return.

But she knew someone she could ask.

She turned around, trying to get her bearings. Using the towers of the cathedral to guide her direction, she started to walk to the Rue de la Blanchisserie, to the home of a duke and duke's secretary, who undoubtedly would know more about Marc's whereabouts than anyone else.

She tried to cross the street.

Two wagons rumbled by. A crowd of wounded men staggered behind them. In the midst of the crowd was a lone horse carrying two men on its back. The crowd parted for a moment and Tess could see that a man not in uniform led the horse.

It was Marc! The man leading the horse was Marc!

She ran into the street, trying to reach him, blocked by the poor wounded soldiers.

'Marc!' she cried when she came close enough. 'Marc!'

He glanced up and stopped.

She ran towards him and threw herself in his arms. 'You are safe! You are safe!'

He hugged her close while men flowed past them. 'Tess. Tess. You were supposed to be in Antwerp.'

She clung to him. 'No. I stayed. I feared you would not come back.'

The sea of men washed around them, but it was a while before he broke the embrace.

'I found them,' he said.

She did not know what he meant at first, but he turned to the two men on the horse. On Apollo. One man held the other, a man wrapped in a blanket.

'Captain Fowler.' He looked like death itself.

The other man said, 'Hello, Tess.'

She looked up at him. 'Edmund.' It was like seeing a ghost.

She ran to him but could only hold his leg. 'Edmund.'

He flinched. 'My leg, Tess. It is injured.'

She jumped away.

'Bring them to my mother's house,' she said.

Chapter Twenty

Marc could not believe Tess walked next to him through the streets of Brussels, or that she stayed in her mother's house.

When they reached it, her mother took immediate charge. She directed rooms to be made ready for Edmund and Captain Fowler. Water was heated; food prepared. The men were bathed, fed and given clean bedclothes as well as clean bed linens. Their wounds were dressed. She'd sent for her physician and surgeon, but neither came. Too many wounded to be cared for in Brussels; too few surgeons and physicians.

Edmund suffered a ball through the shoulder, a sabre cut to his torso and another through his leg. He was feverish, but there was every chance he would recover completely. Captain Fowler, whose wounds were many, hovered near death and was insensible. Tess's mother did what she could for both of them.

Marc had to leave Tess again that afternoon, this time to call upon Mr Scott and the Duke of Richmond to make his report. Afterwards he collected his portmanteau from his hotel. Wherever he went there were wounded men.

They were on the roads, still walking from the battlefield or riding in wagons. They sat in the pavement or in the parks. They hung out of open windows.

How many more would die before daybreak? A vision of the battlefield, of the dead and dying, came back to him, sickening him all over again. He'd forced himself to walk through it to search for Captain Fowler and he'd carried Fowler back.

He felt sick anew.

That night he dreamed of the battlefield again, again seeing the faces of the dead and dying. He woke with a start.

The battlefield vanished and there was only Tess lying next to him. He held her closer and buried his face in her hair to erase the memory.

She turned to face him. 'Something woke you.'

'A bad dream,' he murmured. 'It is gone now.'

She nestled in his arms. 'I cannot believe you are here next to me.' Her soft breath warmed his skin. 'I thought you would not come back.'

'From the battle?' Waiting, not knowing what was happening must have been its own sort of hell.

'Not the battle,' she responded. 'Although I was afraid of that, too. I meant I thought you would not come back this afternoon. I thought you might be sent away again.'

'Sent away?' He sat up.

She sat, as well. 'You went to see Mr Scott, did you not? To make a report?' She met his eye. 'A report on the battle, I suppose.'

She was not supposed to know this. How could she know? 'Do not make guesses like that, Tess. Making up guesses like that could—could be dangerous.'

'Do not fear.' She touched his face. 'I have said nothing to anyone.'

'That is because you know nothing, Tess.' He tried to be emphatic.

No one knew what would happen next. Was Napoleon vanquished? Or would he and his army rise to fight another day? Marc was not yet free of his duties and it still could be lethal for his clandestine life to be revealed.

She smiled. 'Your father guessed. He guessed you were not simply running off; you were off doing a job.' She held the covers over her nakedness and looked down at him. 'It all suddenly made sense why you left and why you made up the story about the Alps.' She sighed. 'And here I thought you left me because of the lovemaking.'

'Because of the lovemaking?' Leaving her bed had been wrenching.

'You explained it to me,' she went on. 'You thought making love to me would bring us unhappiness, like your parents, or death, like your brother and your friend.'

'That is correct, Tess,' he admitted. 'I did not know of any man who felt so powerfully for a woman who did not experience disaster.'

'It pains me to say it, but I believe the count and my mother have not experienced disaster,' she repeated. 'I mean, my mother hurt me terribly by running off with him, but look at them. They are still besotted with each other. They are happy.' She spoke sadly of their happiness.

'They might have managed together, but they left children without a mother,' he said.

She nodded.

He sat behind her and held her tight. 'I thought I lost you, Tess. I thought you would never forgive me for leaving you again.'

She twisted around to look into his face. 'You were only doing your duty.'

He held her face in his hands and kissed her, a long, lingering kiss, and felt the passion flare between them again.

'I love you, Tess,' he said.

She rested her forehead against his and smiled. 'I have my love match after all.'

Epilogue

February 1816—Lincolnshire, England

Marc had insisted upon bringing Tess back to Lincolnshire after they'd spent Christmas with his family in the country house. Lord Tinmore was hosting another house party to which they'd been invited and Marc had convinced Tess they must accept. It was a chance to see Lorene and Genna and Edmund, so Tess acquiesced.

They'd left Brussels as soon as Edmund and Captain Fowler were well enough to make the journey. Edmund healed well. Fowler returned to his parents and, his health still poor, had broken his engagement with Amelie. Amelie had become depressed and her parents had taken her to the country house to recuperate.

Marc and Tess had the house on Grosvenor Street to themselves. For all the turmoil of their meeting and marrying, the life they'd settled into was quietly wonderful. No longer did Marc disappear now that Napoleon had been exiled to St Helena. He and Tess spent much of their time together.

Spending Christmas with his parents at the country house had been their first trip together. This was their second.

Marc had suggested they make the trip on horseback—
he, riding Apollo, she, riding her Christmas gift from him,
a sweet mare she'd named Artemis. Somehow they'd taken
a wrong turn. Instead of familiar roads, they wandered
places that she could not recall ever having seen.

'I cannot believe you got us lost,' she complained.

'*I* got us lost,' he countered. 'You are from here. You
should know where we are.'

She glanced around at the fields on each side of her. 'I
have no idea where we are. We could be in the Alps, for
all I know.'

'The Alps? Very amusing, Tess.' He looked up at the
sky. 'Well, we had better find Yardney or Tinmore Hall
or some place soon, because it looks like it might rain.'

'Wonderful. We are going to be caught in the rain
again,' she said sarcastically. 'I cannot believe our luck.'

He grinned at her. 'I, too, cannot believe our luck.'

The roads turned this way and that and became narrower and narrower.

'Marc, I am starting to worry. What if we do not find
our way?' She remembered how it felt to be lost and caught
in the rain. At least this time she would not be alone.

Apollo pulled ahead of her a little distance and Marc
turned down an even narrower path.

'Marc!' she called to him. 'This cannot lead anywhere.'

He did not heed her.

The path led to a small cabin with a small stable next to it.

Tess laughed with joy and cantered up to ride next to
him. 'It is our cabin!'

He grinned. 'I've arranged for us to spend the night.'

They settled the horses and walked to the cabin door.

Marc put a key in the lock. 'I have the real key this
time.'

She blinked. 'How did we get in last time?'

'My skeleton keys.'

He opened the door and she stepped forward to enter.

He stopped her. 'Last time I carried you.'

He scooped her up in his arms and carried her over the threshold.

She gasped at what she saw. The table was set with bread and cheese and biscuits and tarts. There was a tin of tea and bottles of wine. A fire already burned in the fireplace and their chairs and the cot were arranged the way they'd left them.

'I cannot imagine how you arranged this!' she cried.

He put her down and enfolded her in an embrace. 'My luckiest day was when I found you in the rain and we wound up here. I wanted to celebrate it.'

At that moment lightning flashed, thunder rumbled and rain pattered the roof.

Marc swung Tess around as they both laughed in delight.

They stopped and stared into each other's eyes.

Tess touched his face. 'It was my luckiest day, too.'

He leaned down and took possession of her lips as the sound of the rain filled their ears.

* * * * *

BOUND BY ONE
SCANDALOUS NIGHT

To the memory of my uncle, Edward Gelen, with his shock of white hair and infectious laugh.

Chapter One

Early hours of June 16th, 1815—Brussels, Belgium

Brussels was in chaos.

Bugles blared in the streets, their sounds echoing off the huge buildings of the Grand Place, repeating, over and over the call to arms. All officers and soldiers must report for duty!

For battle.

Wellington had learned that Napoleon and his army crossed into Belgium and were marching towards Brussels. Wellington's soldiers needed to mobilise quickly to stop him.

Lieutenant Edmund Summerfield of the 28th Regiment of Foot wound his way through townspeople of all shapes and sizes and well-dressed gentlemen and ladies still waiting for carriages to bring them back from the Duchess of Richmond's ball. Everywhere men were shouting, women wailing, children crying. Soldiers in uniforms of all colours rushed to and fro. British and Hanoverians in red, Belgian and Dutch in dark blue, British light cavalry in light blue, Rifles in dark green, Highlanders in plaid kilts. The array of colours mimicked a carnival, but the mood was tense, a tinderbox that with one spark could turn to riot.

Edmund forced himself to remain calm. He shifted his bag from one shoulder to the other and wished his head were clearer. He'd spent the evening in a tavern, drinking and playing cards with fellow officers too low in rank and importance to be invited to the Duchess's ball. The bugle's repeated call, still resounding through the tension-filled air, had sobered him greatly.

He pushed his way to the curb of the rue du Marais. Horses, wagons, carriages, men and women dashing on foot, blocked his way. Through the kaleidoscope of colour he spied a vision in white across the street, an angel amidst the tumult. While he watched, a man in labourer's clothing grabbed her around the waist. She beat on the man's arms with her fists and kicked his legs, but this man, rough and wild-eyed, dragged her with him.

Edmund bounded into the busy street, heedless of the traffic, narrowly missing being run down. He made it to the other side and chased after the man abducting the woman. Her shimmering white gown made it easy not to lose sight of her. The man ducked into an alley between two buildings. Edmund reached the space a moment after.

'Let me go!' the woman cried. Her blonde hair, a mass of curls, came free of its bindings and fell around her shoulders.

The man pinned her against the wall and took the fabric of her dress in his fist.

'*Vous l'aimerez, chérie,*' the man growled.

'No!' cried Edmund. He pushed his bag like a battering ram at the man's head.

The man staggered and loosened his grip.

Edmund dropped his bag and slammed his fist into the man's jaw, sending him sprawling to the cobbles. 'Be off with you! *Allez! Vite!*'

The man scrambled to his feet and disappeared into the dark recesses of the alley.

Edmund turned to the woman. 'Did he hurt you? *Vous a-t-il blessé?*'

She looked up and the light from a street lamp illuminated her face.

He knew her!

'Miss Glenville!'

She was Amelie Glenville. Her brother, Marc Glenville, was married to his half-sister Tess.

Her eyes, wide with shock, looked past him.

'Miss Glenville?' He touched her chin and made her look at him. 'Do you remember me? I am Tess's brother, Edmund. We met at your parents' breakfast two days ago.'

Her face crumbled. 'Edmund!' She fell into his arms. The beautiful Amelie Glenville fell into his arms. Who would believe this?

When Amelie entered the room that morning, for one heady moment he'd been caught in the spell of her unspoiled beauty. Fair of face. Skin as smooth as cream. Cheeks tinged with pink. Eyes as azure as the sea. Hair, a mass of golden curls, sparkling in the light as if spun from gold. Lips lush and ripe for kissing. Innocent. Alluring.

And smiling at him during their introduction.

The next moment, though, he had been introduced to her fiancé, a most correct young man, a Scots Greys cavalry captain and son of an earl. Reality set in and Edmund had instantly dropped her from his mind. Even if he wanted to court some young woman—which he did not—a viscount's daughter like Amelie Glenville would never do for a bastard like him.

And here she was embracing him.

'What are you doing here?' he asked her. 'Why are you alone?' She'd obviously been to the Duchess of Richmond's ball. Her white gown must have been lovely before it had been so roughly handled.

She drew away and tried to sort out her clothing. 'Captain Fowler left me here.'

The fiancé? 'Left you? Why?'

She huffed. 'We had words.'

'He left you because of a quarrel?' No gentleman, under any circumstance, would desert a lady on a city street in the middle of the night, especially not on a night like this. 'What about?'

'It does not matter,' she snapped.

She sounded more angry than alarmed, at least. That was fortunate. Did she even realise what had almost happened to her?

'And I have no idea how to walk back to the hotel,' she continued in a peeved tone. 'Could you direct me?'

Good heavens! The man had abandoned her without her knowing the way back? 'I think I had better escort you.'

She rubbed her arms.

He shrugged out of his coat. 'Here, put this around you.'

'Might we go back now?' Her voice wobbled a bit. 'It is the Hotel de Flandre.'

She'd be better off staying angry. 'I remember what hotel it was.'

He picked up his bag and offered her his arm, which she readily accepted and held with an anxious grip.

They stepped from the relative quiet of the alley back into the cacophony of the street.

'Hold on tight,' he cautioned, and she squeezed his arm as people bumped against them, the soldiers hurrying to battle, the others to somewhere safe.

What on earth had possessed Fowler to abandon her on such a night? This was not an afternoon stroll through Mayfair. It was after one o'clock in the morning, and the soldiers on these streets would soon be facing battle; the townspeople, possible occupation by the French. She'd already discovered what could happen to a beautiful, unescorted woman when emotions were so high.

She was lovely enough to tempt any man. Even him.

But he must not turn his thoughts in that direction.

'Do you not have to go to your regiment?' she asked as a company of Belgian cavalry rode by, the horses' hooves drumming on the stones of the street.

He did need to reach his regiment as soon as possible, but why stress her with that knowledge? 'I am more in fear of what my sister and your brother would do to me if I left you alone on the street. My sister would draw and quarter me. Your brother would probably do worse.'

'Why would they ever know, unless you told them?' she retorted peevishly. 'I have no intention of speaking a word of this night to anyone.'

So much for trying to use levity to counteract this nightmarish episode.

'Then blame my conscience,' he said. 'I would think very ill of myself if I abandoned you.'

'Unlike some gentlemen,' she muttered.

'There will be plenty of time for me to reach the battle.' He hoped. 'I doubt Napoleon will disturb his sleep.'

Fine words, but who knew how close Napoleon was to Brussels? Edmund had heard varying accounts. One thing was certain, though. Men would fight soon. And die.

He concentrated on getting her through the crowd without further mishap. The streets cleared a bit when they reached the Cathedral of Saint Michael and Saint Gudula. It rose majestically into the night sky, its yellow stone glowing against the black sky. Men would be stopping at that Gothic church for a few prayers before battle, Edmund would wager. It could not hurt to pray a little.

Pray not to die.

Edmund shook his head. *Don't think such thoughts*, he

told himself, but he'd seen too many battles on the Peninsula, seen too many good men die while he survived. Soldiers always talked of having only a finite number of battles in which to remain unscathed before it was their time to die.

Miss Glenville swiped her gloved fingers across her eyes. Was she weeping? If only he could have prevented this ghastly night from happening to her. She was too lovely and unspoiled to have been so roughly treated. To think what that ruffian had in mind to do to her made him tighten his hand into a fist.

He needed to distract both of them from their thoughts. 'So what did happen with Captain…Captain Whatshisname?' He only pretended to forget.

'Fowler.' She spoke the name as if it were a term of contempt.

'Captain Fowler.'

'We quarrelled and he walked away and left me.' She turned her head away.

The scoundrel. 'What sort of quarrel would make a man abandon you?'

The doors of the cathedral opened, revealing the glow of candlelight inside. A man in uniform emerged, head bent. Edmund hoped the man's prayers would be answered.

He turned again to Miss Glenville. 'Tell me what you and Captain Fowler quarrelled about.'

She swiped at her eyes again. 'I certainly will not.'

He persisted. 'Is that what is making you weep?' He feared it was the other man's mistreatment of her.

'I am not weeping!' she cried. 'I am angry.'

Anger was better. Good for her.

Better for him, too. He was caring too much, caring about never seeing a beauty such as Amelie Glenville again if he lay dead on the battlefield.

'It is really none of your business, you know,' she snapped.

'No doubt,' he persisted. Ungentlemanly of him, but it distracted him from morbid thoughts. 'But you say you will not speak of this, say to your brother or my sister. You should talk about it with someone, since it is plaguing you so. I am unlikely to say anything to anyone.'

After all he might soon be dead.

'Why would I talk to you?' she responded in an arrogant tone.

He'd almost forgotten. He'd been talking with her as if she'd consider him her equal. 'Yes, wise not to tell the likes of me.'

'The likes of you?' She sounded puzzled.

Need he explain? 'Surely the scandalous details of my birth were whispered into your delicate ears.'

'What has that to do with it?' she asked, then smiled wryly. 'But you are correct about the details of your birth being whispered in my ear.'

He gave her a smug look.

'Your sister told me more about you,' she went on.

He laughed. 'What did she tell you? That I was a horrid boy who teased her and played pranks on her?'

'Did you?' She glanced at him but quickly glanced away.

This was better. Who would guess that he'd think talking about himself was desirable? It kept them both from more painful thoughts, though. 'Tess could not have informed you of my wayward activities in the army. My sisters know nothing of that. Their ears are delicate, too, you see.'

She batted her eyes at him. 'Wayward activities? Are you some sort of rake? I have been warned against rakes.'

'Oh, be warned, then,' he joked. 'I am a shameless rake.'

'Are you?' Her voice lowered almost to a whisper.

Had he gone too far in this bantering? Had he reminded her of the ruffian who'd accosted her? 'You are quite safe with me, Miss Glenville.'

She glanced at him again, and her good humour fled. She turned away. 'Yes. Safe.'

If only he really were a rake, he thought. He would steal a taste of her lips and take the memory with him into battle.

They walked in silence until they reached the Parc de Bruxelles, its main paths lit by lamps. The *parc* looked almost as busy as it did in the daytime, but now other couples were not leisurely strolling on the paths. They were either hurrying into the shadows or clinging to each other.

'Shall we cross through the park?' he asked. 'It will be safe enough tonight. Or would you prefer we walk around it?'

'We may cross the park,' she responded.

She was still lost in her own thoughts. Edmund wanted her to talk to him again. Seeing so many sweethearts clinging to each other affected him. How many would be torn apart for ever? He supposed they were trying to grab one more moment of feeling alive. Perhaps that was what she and Fowler quarrelled about. Perhaps Fowler asked her for more than she could respectably provide. Soldiers leaving for battle often wanted one last coupling with a woman.

As they walked through the park, he heard faint sounds of lovemaking coming from behind the shrubbery. Surely she had noticed, too. Surely she could hear the sounds.

'I have a suspicion that your Captain Fowler might have asked for liberties,' he tried to explain. It did not excuse Fowler's abandoning her, but maybe it would help explain his behaviour toward her. 'Men often want a woman before battle.'

She stopped. 'You think he propositioned me?'

Now he was not so certain. 'That was my guess, yes.'

* * *

Amelie kept walking. He really could not be more wrong. Fowler had not propositioned her. But he had left her.

'He put you in danger by leaving you,' the lieutenant went on. 'That was unforgivable.'

Could he not talk of something else? Anything else?

Was it possible to grow older in an instant? Because that was how it felt to Amelie. One moment she was young and in love; the next…

'Unforgivable,' she repeated. But his leaving was only part of his unforgivable behaviour.

Not that it mattered to Fowler.

They continued across the park, heading to the gate on the other side. As they reached it, another couple entered, a plainly dressed young woman and a tall, red-coated infantryman.

The young woman halted. 'Miss Glenville?'

Amelie stared at her. 'Sally?' She glanced back to Edmund. 'My maid,' she explained.

'Oh, miss!' the maid cried. 'Are you back from the ball? There is to be a battle, and your father wants to leave early in the morning for Antwerp. I have packed for you. Must I come to you now? I—I hoped for a little while longer.' Her words came out in a rush.

Next to Sally a young infantryman stood at attention, eyeing Amelie and Edmund warily. But when he gazed at Sally his countenance turned soft and worshipful. Amelie envied her so acutely the pain was physical.

She glanced from the maid to the infantryman and back. 'Of course, you must have as long as you like, Sally. In fact, I do not need you at all tonight. I will manage quite well without you.'

The maid grasped Miss Glenville's hand in both of hers. 'Oh, thank you, miss! Thank you so much.'

The maid pulled on the infantryman's arm. The young man bowed quickly to Edmund, and the couple disappeared into the park.

'He is, I believe, an old friend of Sally's,' she said, as if she owed Edmund an explanation. 'Amazing that they met here in Brussels with all the soldiers here, but, then, your sister and I met my brother in this park the first hour we arrived. And a friend of yours with him, as I recall. And a friend from London, as well.' Now she was babbling.

'Such lucky happenstance,' he remarked.

Not as lucky as she had been that Edmund had happened to be across the street when that horrible creature attacked her. She could still feel the man's hands gripping her, smell his unwashed skin—

She buried her nose in Edmund's red coat. Its scent—his scent—banished the memory.

'You were very kind to your maid,' he said.

She shrugged. 'How could I refuse her? It was her one chance, perhaps.'

It was a chance she would never have. When Fowler first paid her court, she had woven joyous dreams of living happily ever after in her very own fairy story, but she learned that real life was not a fairy tale. It was more often filled with lies, deception, painful words and grave disappointments.

At least Sally might be able to capture a few moments of joy. Amelie hoped the girl would have many such happy moments.

Amelie would not.

'I commend your liberal attitude,' Edmund said.

She was startled. She'd been lost in her own miseries. He grinned.

She blinked and really looked at him for the first time this night.

He was taller than Fowler. More muscular, easy to see

now that he was without his coat. The hair beneath his shako was as dark as night, his thick brows the same hue. His lips were finely formed as if some master sculptor had created them; his chin, strong and shadowed by what was probably a day's growth of beard that made him appear more like the rake he claimed to be. His smile robbed her of breath.

When she'd met him two days ago, she'd immediately felt taken with him. He'd appeared so handsome in his regimentals, the bright sunlight from the windows making his red coat even more vibrant, his smile even more dazzling. He'd looked then like a fine man, a strong soldier, a brother Tess could be proud of. Even with her head full of Captain Fowler as it had been, she'd thought how nice it would be to know Edmund Summerfield better and how sad it was that his birth made him even less acceptable to society than her own family.

What did birth matter, though? Fowler's was as respectable as one could be, but he'd behaved abominably, walking away without a second glance, leaving her utterly alone just because—

Edmund's smile faded. 'Your Captain Fowler must not have appreciated you.'

Tears stung her eyes. 'No, he did not. Not at all.'

To her surprise, he put his arms around her. She knew he meant only to be comforting, but, his strong arms wrapped around her, his muscular body flush with hers, other emotions were stirred. It gave her a hint as to what she so desired, what she could never have. She knew that now.

She did not pull away from him. This might be the only time a man's arms held her.

Edmund released her and they resumed walking.

'So what was it that caused the words between you and

Captain Fowler?' he persisted. 'If it was not him propositioning you.'

'I do not wish to say,' she responded. 'Not to you.'

She felt him bristle. 'I forgot. One must not confide in a bastard.'

'It is not because you are a bastard,' she shot back. 'It is because you are a man.'

He nodded, and an amused look came into his eyes for a moment but vanished as quickly. He lowered his voice. 'That is precisely why you should talk to me. I am a man. I may be able to explain the actions of another man, perhaps explain the actions of both of the men who hurt you tonight. It may ease your mind.'

She felt the tears threaten again. 'Nothing will ease my mind.'

They reached the entrance of the hotel just as a throng of Belgians, obviously full of drink, filled the pavement, blocking their way. One of the men seized Amelie's arm, jabbering in French, and tried to pull her away from Edmund. His uniform coat fell off her shoulders and her heart raced in fright.

It was happening again.

But Edmund grabbed the man's clothing and shook him. The man lost his grip on Amelie. Edmund lifted him off the ground and thrust him into the crowd, knocking several other men down. They jumped back to their feet and came after Edmund, who took hold of Amelie, picked up his coat and charged into the hotel in one swift movement.

The men did not follow them into the hotel.

'There,' he said. 'You'll be safe in here.'

She was beginning to wonder if she would ever feel safe again. Napoleon could be knocking at the door by morning. Men in the street seemed to feel entitled to do as they pleased, and even men who had once professed love could speak words that wounded more grievously than a sword.

'Will—will you escort me to my room?' she asked.

He put an arm around her, but, again, it was meant only in sympathy. 'Directly to your room, and I will see you safe inside.'

Chapter Two

Under ordinary circumstances it would be scandalous for Edmund to walk a young, unmarried woman up hotel stairs in the wee hours of the morning, but this night no one would pay them any heed. Even if someone noticed them, it would not change what he must do. He must escort her all the way to her room. She'd had two brushes with danger and that was quite enough. He would see her to safety or be damned.

'Do you object to me calling you Edmund?' she asked as they climbed the stairs. 'It is how Tess refers to you, so I think of you as Edmund.'

To hear her speak his name felt intimate to him. They'd spent mere minutes together, not more than an hour, certainly, but, somehow, it seemed right that she call him by his Christian name.

Besides, all this hour he'd been thinking of her as Amelie.

He smiled again. 'I do not object, but that means I must call you Amelie, you know.'

'Would that be so hard to do?' she countered, somewhat uncertainly, he thought.

He pretended to need to think about it. 'I suppose I could manage it. We are somewhat related, one could say. By marriage.'

They reached the upper floor where her hotel room was located.

'Since we are now so familiar, *Amelie*,' he emphasised *Amelie*, 'there is no reason not to tell me why you and Captain Fowler quarrelled.'

'Would you stop pressing me on the subject?' she snapped. 'I have no intention of telling you. It is very private.'

'But we are somewhat related.' He added, *'Amelie.'*

She lifted a finger to her lips, and he fell silent. They were near her parents' rooms, where he'd breakfasted with her two days before.

She knocked softly. 'Maman, Papa, I am back.'

Footsteps could be heard from behind the door. She gestured for him to stay out of sight.

Her mother opened the door a crack. *'Dieu merci!* I was worried.'

'No need to have worried, Maman,' she said.

Of course, she'd only been abandoned once and nearly abducted twice!

'We are leaving Brussels,' her mother said. 'Your father has arranged for carriages to take us to Antwerp very early. Your maid will wake you at five.'

'I will be ready.' The door opened wider, and she leaned in for her mother to kiss her on the cheek. She kissed her back. 'Try to sleep, Maman.'

She waited a moment after the door closed, then indicated to Edmund to follow her again.

When they reached her hotel-room door, he extended his hand for her to give him the key. He unlocked the door, opened it and stepped aside for her to enter.

She hesitated, though. 'Will you check the room for me?' she asked in a nervous voice. 'I am a little afraid to enter it alone.'

He crossed the doorjamb. A fire was lit in the fireplace,

but the room was dark and full of shadows. He found a taper on the mantel and used it to light the lamps. The room brightened a bit.

He carried one of the lamps with him throughout the room, not believing there was anyone hidden and ready to jump out and attack her, but wanting to reassure her of that fact.

'There is nothing to fear here,' he told her. He placed the lamp on a table and placed the key into her hand. 'Lock the door after I leave.'

She took the key and stared at it for a moment before looking back up at him. 'Must you go to your regiment immediately?'

It would be a two-hour ride, at least. 'I have time,' he said.

Her shoulders relaxed in relief. 'May I offer refreshment?'

'Do not go to any trouble.'

'It is no trouble.' She pulled off her gloves, and he noticed her hands shook. 'I think Sally hides a bottle of sherry in here. Shall I pour you some?'

He'd prefer brandy. 'Sherry? Why not?'

She found the bottle and two glasses. 'Please sit, Edmund.' She poured his glass and one for herself, a large one, which she gulped down.

He waited for her to sit first. She lowered herself into a chair and poured herself another glass.

She was still distressed from the night's events, he thought, and Edmund wondered how he'd be able to leave her until she was comfortable again. Why he should feel this responsibility foxed him. She was once merely a pretty face—a beautiful face—to him. Now, perhaps because he'd rescued her, she'd become someone whose welfare mattered to him.

He watched her gulp down the second glass of sherry.

'You should talk about what happened to you tonight.' He spoke in a low voice. 'The sherry won't be enough.'

She quickly put down the glass. 'I suspect there is not enough time. You must leave for your regiment.'

His brows rose. 'A moment ago you were anxious for me to stay; now you want me to leave? Which is it, Amelie?'

Her glance darted to the door before focusing on her lap. 'I do not want to be alone right now.'

'Then talk to me,' he persisted.

She looked up at him and snapped, 'Why are you so sure talking will help me?'

'I have three sisters.'

The challenge left her eyes, so that must have been explanation enough.

'The—the attacks from those horrid men.' The distaste showed on her face. 'It was frightening, but what more can I say except that?'

'Then talk about what is most unsettling you,' he said.

'I am certain you do not have enough time for that!' She huffed.

He raised his brows and spoke with humour. 'Is it so long of a story?'

Her glance darted back to him. She smiled.

He pinched the stem of his glass.

By Jove, she was temptation itself when she smiled.

Was it possible that talking could calm her? Amelie doubted it very strongly, but, if he left, she would be alone—and likely alone for the rest of her life. Why not tell him?

Courage was necessary. Her trust in men had been shredded this night, and Edmund Summerfield was certainly a man.

'You will not tell anyone? No matter what?' she asked.

He looked directly into her eyes, his expression serious. 'Upon my honour.'

His words resonated inside her. From her brother she knew men did not say such words lightly. At least, *honourable* men did not.

Edmund delayed his duty to his regiment to bring her safely off the streets of Brussels. There was honour in that.

She was stalling and he was waiting patiently, no longer pressuring her to speak, no longer using humour to cajole her.

But to speak it aloud meant facing it, did it not? Facing what she had done. Facing the truth she had learned in return. Opening her bleak future to herself.

He sipped his sherry.

She tossed him a defiant look and poured herself a third glass, but this time she did not gulp it down.

She took a breath and took the risk. 'You know, of course, that Captain Fowler and I had just become betrothed—'

He nodded.

She could not sit still and speak of this. She stood and paced in front of him. 'My brother procured invitations to the Duchess of Richmond's ball, you know, my first ball given by a duchess. I was in raptures about it. Captain Fowler was my escort. I thought nothing could be better, especially when Wellington himself arrived! Wellington! At the same ball.'

Even though Amelie's father was a viscount, it did not mean they were invited everywhere. Because of her mother. Not only was her mother French, her mother was also a commoner and, after the Revolution, her family had become active in the Terror, beheading friends and relatives of the British aristocrats.

Consequently Amelie and her parents were barely tolerated by the *ton*. It was only because of Edmund's sister, the one who'd married an elderly earl, that she'd been invited anywhere last Season. That was how she met Captain Fowler. She thought he had not minded about her scandalous family. At least he'd told her so.

Edmund broke into her reverie. 'The ball ended early, I heard.'

She collected herself. 'Yes. I was much affected when Wellington announced that Napoleon was marching towards Brussels. I—I knew it meant Captain Fowler would ride into battle. I knew it meant I might never see him again. I begged my parents to allow him to walk me back to the hotel instead of riding in their carriage. I wanted to be alone with him.'

She glanced at Edmund, who continued to watch her from his chair with eyes that merely waited for more but showed nothing of what he thought.

She turned away from his gaze. 'You thought he propositioned me. You thought he might have taken advantage, saying, *give me something to remember you by*, or something like that.'

'Men think about last chances when they know they will go into battle,' he said in a quiet voice.

She swung back to him. 'Not only men! I thought of last chances, too! I begged the captain to come to this room and make love to me.'

His brows rose.

'Are you shocked?' she asked.

'Surprised. Not shocked.' He lifted his glass to his lips.

Her voice turned shrill. 'Does that make me wanton? Does that bring shame on me, on my family? Is it so very bad that I spoke those words to him? That—that I wanted… the lovemaking?'

He placed his glass on the side table and rose, coming to her and holding her by the shoulders. 'This is what the quarrel was about?'

She nodded.

He guided her back to her chair and sat her down.

Tears pricked her eyes, but she refused to let them fall. 'He said that no respectable woman would ever think such a thing. That I was wanton. Shameful. That I was no better than Haymarket ware. That I must have more of my mother's common French blood in me than he had supposed.'

She burned with anger all over again. True, her mother was the daughter of French merchants who had worked to guillotine aristocrats, but her mother had no part in that. Her mother was the dearest creature in creation. Amelie tried to slap Fowler across the face for speaking of her so.

It had enraged him.

Her throat tightened with the memory. 'Fowler said he was finished with me and that he was certain some man on the street would pay me for what I was offering.' He'd said more, as well.

'Damned prig.' Edmund said.

She looked up into his face. 'Is it not I who deserves censure?'

She was not well bred, obviously, she thought to herself. Otherwise she would not have made such a proposition to Fowler. Or maybe she'd merely been a silly romantic, who believed love conquers all. *Amor vincit omnia.* She'd learned the phrase in Latin.

He reached over and put his hand on her chin and made her look at him. 'What you felt was the most natural thing in the world.'

She averted her gaze. 'Other young women like me do not say such things to men.'

Perhaps it was her mother's blood that made her crave a man's touch. Even Edmund's hand heightened her senses.

Edmund shook his head. 'Do you not suppose other young ladies at the ball said the same to the men leaving them?'

'The captain said not.'

He leaned back. 'The captain is a fool.'

She reached for her glass of sherry again and drank the remainder.

He pointed to the glass. 'What else are you not telling me?'

She was feeling a bit giddy. 'Nothing.' Except what was hardest to face. She picked up the bottle. 'There is just a little more left. You may have it.' She refilled his glass and tried to summon her courage to continue speaking.

'Fowler broke the betrothal,' she finally said.

'Fortunate for you,' he countered.

She bristled. 'Fortunate? Fortunate?' She jumped to her feet and strode over to the window. 'It is easy for you to say such a thing, but it shows your complete lack of understanding!'

'Enlighten me, then,' he said.

She could not even listen to him. Her voice rose. 'Do you know what he said to me?'

'Tell me.'

'He said he had made a terrible mistake asking me to marry him, that he'd done so only because of my dowry.' She'd never guessed that fact. 'He said his parents were against me, but he'd learned that too late. He'd thought himself trapped, he said.'

'Heed me, Amelie.' His voice turned low and firm. 'You are exceedingly lucky not to have married him.'

She knew that now. The thing was, she'd thought Fowler loved her. She'd been convinced of it. She'd seen nothing in him to suggest he was not head over ears in love with her.

'He threatened me,' she went on. 'He said that if I told anyone that he broke the betrothal, he would spread the news about what a wanton hoyden I was.'

Edmund's countenance darkened. 'The blackguard!'

His outrage surprised her. And warmed her.

But he still did not comprehend. She'd been fooled.

So easily fooled. That was the most distressing part. One moment she'd believed Fowler blissfully in love with her; the next he had abandoned her on the dangerous streets of Brussels.

Amelie leaned her head against the cool pane of the window. 'What is the use to talk about this? It does not change anything.'

'What would you change?' he asked. 'Surely you do not want him now.'

'No.' The sadness crept in to her voice. 'I do not want *him*.'

Again he did not understand. The moment she realised she had been utterly misled by Fowler, she also realised she could never trust any man. How could she know if a man truly loved her? She could never marry without knowing.

'But—you see—' she tried to explain. 'It is unlikely now I shall ever marry.'

He rose and walked over to lean against the wall next to the window. 'You are spouting nonsense.'

She lifted her chin. It was not nonsense. 'I must face the reality of my situation. I am too scandalous—my family is too scandalous. Who would wish to marry me? Except, perhaps, for my dowry. If I can be fooled so easily, how would I ever know if what a man wanted was me or simply my dowry?'

'Ah, I see.' Edmund nodded. 'Fowler wanted your money.'

'I do not want a man who only wants my money!'

'Of course you do not,' he said soothingly.

She swung away from him. 'Oh, stop it!'

'Stop what?' He sounded surprised.

'Stop speaking platitudes.' She huffed. 'I knew talking to you would do nothing for me!'

He seemed to ignore her outburst. 'Did you not have several suitors before Fowler?'

'I did not!' Only Fowler.

He'd been the perfect suitor, she'd thought. The man she'd dreamed of finding, she'd thought. So respectable. The younger son of an earl. In a fashionable cavalry regiment. She'd fancied herself so in love with him, when his regiment was sent to Brussels, she convinced her parents to follow him here. He'd seemed happy she'd come. Their betrothal made her parents happy. Made her happy.

Edmund took a step closer. 'Forget Fowler. Do not let what happened with him decide the rest of your life. You will find a man worthy of you.'

'Worthy of me,' she repeated sarcastically. 'I shudder at the thought. What sort of man is worthy of a hoydenish ninnyhammer with a family who is accepted nowhere?'

He touched her chin again and made her look into his eyes. 'I see only a beautiful woman with pretty manners, who, I suspect, thinks more deeply than anyone gives her credit for.'

He was so close to her now she could see the individual hairs on the stubble of his beard. She felt her face flush, but she was unsure if it was because he was so close or because of his words. 'Now who is talking nonsense?'

He stepped back and crossed his arms over his chest. 'Be truthful, Amelie. You know you are beautiful, do you not?'

She used to think so. At least her family said so. Her maid said so. And men on the street sometimes looked at her, but Fowler had also said she was beautiful. Was that another lie? 'How do I know if being told I was beautiful was simply empty flattery?'

He leaned close again. 'I have no reason to flatter you, and I say you are beautiful.'

This time it felt as if all her skin had blushed.

She dared to meet his eye. 'Do you truly think so?'

He came even closer, so close his lips were an inch from hers. She felt his breath on her face and the heat of his body.

'I truly think so,' he murmured.

Chapter Three

Edmund stepped back.

Heavens! What was he about? He'd nearly kissed her, and now she looked bewildered.

'Forgive me,' he said.

'For what?' she whispered.

'For coming too close.'

Her brow creased in confusion. 'I thought you were going to kiss me.'

He could not meet her eye. 'That would be pretty shabby of me.'

She turned back towards the window. 'I suppose it is something you would not want to do.'

Should not do, was more the piece.

'That was one thing Fowler must have been honest about,' she spoke more to the windowpane than to Edmund. 'He never kissed me. Except on the cheek like my brother might do.'

Edmund had not felt like kissing her like a brother.

'He obviously did not want to.' She released a long sigh. 'No man has wanted to kiss me.'

'It is more likely that they wanted to, but refrained,' he said.

She whirled around. 'And you? Did you want to, but refrained?'

'I am really not a rake, Amelie.' Although he'd nearly behaved like one.

She turned away again. 'I wish you were.'

He was uncertain he heard her correctly.

She glanced over her shoulder. 'Are you shocked at that? I did proposition a man tonight, after all.'

He'd tried to treat her like his little half-sister Genna instead of the alluring creature she was at this moment. He'd promised her she was safe with him.

She laughed drily. 'I would certainly hate to think that the only men who wished to kiss me were those ruffians in the street who tried to have their way with me.'

'They would have done more than kiss you, Amelie,' he said. 'If you yearn for love, they were not offering it.'

She turned back to him. 'Do you know what distresses me the most about never marrying?'

'You must not give up on marriage.' How could any man fail to see the merit in her?

She whirled around again, halting his speech. 'It distresses me that I will never know a man's kisses. I'll never know the lovemaking that passes between men and women. Husband and wife.'

'You will,' he said.

The lamplight reflected in her eyes, filling them with fire. 'Will you kiss me, Edmund?'

Every muscle and sinew in his body yearned for him to taste her lips. 'No, Amelie. It would not be wise.'

Her eyes filled with tears, making them look even bigger. 'I suppose it would be distasteful to kiss me, would it not?'

'No, Amelie, it would not be distasteful.' It was a struggle not to crush his mouth against hers.

'Then you are repelled because I am so wanton in the

asking.' Her voice strained, as if she was trying to stifle a sob. 'Like Fowler.'

He moved closer to her. 'I am anything but repelled by you, but I am not the man for you. You must wait—'

'For whom?' she cried. 'Why can you not be the man who first kisses me? You've been my friend this night.'

'A friend, but not your equal,' he tried to explain. 'Remember, I am nothing but a bastard and you are the daughter of a viscount.'

'And what does that signify? You are the son of a baronet and I am the daughter of a French commoner,' she countered. 'Why is any of that an impediment to a kiss?'

'My sister is married to your brother.' He was grasping at straws.

She gave him a speaking look. 'You are not kissing your sister and I am not kissing my brother.'

How could he convince her? He must not cross that line with her, and he was very close to doing so. Something had changed as they'd talked. She'd somehow become important to him.

She turned back to the window. 'Listen to me.' Her voice filled with pain. 'I'm standing here begging you to kiss me. How pathetic a creature I am! No wonder Fowler wanted to rid himself of me.'

Her pain pierced through him like the sabres he'd soon be facing.

He put a hand on her shoulder and turned her around to him. He cupped her cheeks in his palms and tilted her head to him. Leaning down so his lips merely hovered over hers, he asked again, 'Are you very certain you want a kiss?'

'Yes,' she rasped.

'It may not be wise, but I will comply.' He closed the short distance between them.

A satisfied sound escaped her mouth. She wrapped her arms around his neck.

Her lips parted and his tongue touched hers. Her lips were soft and warm, and her mouth tasted of sherry.

It was as if a spark had touched off a firestorm. Desire flashed through him, engulfed him. He pressed his body against hers.

Her fingers dug into his hair and she ground herself against him. He was powerfully aroused. Imagine her believing herself unlovable. She was everything a man could desire. She'd affected him as no other woman.

But she was not for him.

She deserved what she'd thought she had in Fowler. A respectable aristocrat who loved her, not a bastard taking advantage of her vulnerability.

The rumblings of heavy wagons and the clap of horses' hooves reached her window. A reminder. Where he must go. Who he was—a lowly lieutenant from an infantry regiment, without name or fortune. This would change some day, he vowed. He'd earn his fortune, some day, somehow, but he was still a bastard and not for her.

He released her and eased her away.

'What?' She looked dazed.

He tried to smile. 'There now. You have been kissed, but if we do not stop, we may commit a more serious indiscretion.' Being alone with her in her hotel room, kissing her, was indiscreet enough. 'Besides, Napoleon beckons. I need to go.'

She nodded. 'You must go fight a battle. I do understand.' She backed away from him. 'Thank you for saving me. Thank you for—for the kiss.'

His grin came naturally. 'It was my pleasure.'

She smiled in return and their gazes held.

'Best I take my leave.' He crossed the room and retrieved his coat. She followed him and helped him put it on. Standing behind him, she put her arms around him and rested her cheek against his back. 'I do not want you to leave me.'

He did not want to leave her either, but his resolve was weakening by each moment he stayed.

He turned around, still in her embrace. 'Will you be all right?'

She looked up at him, her jaw firmly set. 'I shall have to be.'

The lamplight made her skin glow, and the tumble of curls around her face shone like a halo. He tried to commit her face to memory, a memory to soothe him on the battlefield, a reminder of who and what he fought for. If he survived—*if* he survived—who knew if he would ever see her again? Could he bear that?

She rose on tiptoe and placed her lips on his, unschooled and tentative.

Desire slammed into him again. He put his fingers into her hair and held her in the kiss, savouring it like a man feasting on his last meal. Her soft curves pressed against him once more. Good God. He was on fire, wanting all of her, craving to ease the need that threatened to consume him. He picked her up, and she curled her legs and arms around him. Without heed of what he was doing, he carried her to the bed, prominent in the room, even though he'd not allowed his gaze to stray in its direction.

'Yes,' she murmured against his lips. 'Yes.'

Amelie knew what Edmund wanted. She was not so green a girl not to know what could transpire between a man and a woman, why young ladies like herself were carefully chaperoned. What difference did it make now, if she were chaperoned or not? She was not destined for marriage or respectability. Fowler had taught her that.

But ever since she'd met Fowler and fancied herself in love with him, she'd felt that urge to couple with him.

She'd savoured every touch of his hand. She'd felt frustration when his lips touched her cheek and not her mouth. She'd realised that she was a woman who wanted the bedding part of marriage. She'd thought she wanted it so much with Fowler that she dared to ask him to make love to her before he went to battle, lest he be killed and she never know his embrace.

Of course, that all died in an instant when he rebuffed her.

The thing was, the urge for lovemaking was even stronger with Edmund. Why not indulge it? She was unlikely to have another chance.

He sat her on the bed and captured her mouth again. She savoured the delight of it. To touch her tongue to his was so incredibly intimate, and it sent sensation shooting through her. It was as if her body had come alive for the first time.

His hand slipped to the sensitive skin of her neck and moved down to cup her breast.

Oh, my! How could a touch in one part of one's body be felt so acutely in another? His hand on her breast ignited sensation in her most womanly place. It made her want more, much more. It made her want him to touch her skin all over and even to touch that—that most private of places.

She must be wanton. There was no other explanation. What was she to do with these feelings for the rest of her life? The least she could do was indulge them this one time. There could be no unwanted consequences the first time, she'd heard the maids say. When else could she do this without anyone knowing?

Edmund would not tell. And, even if he did, who would believe him? No one knew they were together. No one would ever know.

But Edmund suddenly broke off the kiss. 'Amelie, we cannot do this. I won't do this.'

She was bereft. And a little wild. To have those sensations aroused and so abruptly denied was like dousing a raging fire with a bucket of water.

Except this did nothing to extinguish the flames inside her.

She pushed him away and leapt from the bed. 'Then stop! And be gone! And do not tease me so. Do not pretend you want me and then just stop! You are worse than Fowler! At least he told me right away he did not want me!' Her emotions were running away with her mouth, and she could not stop herself. 'Does no man want me? Not even when I offer myself? What is wrong with me? Am I really as detestable as Fowler said? Not even as desirable as Haymarket ware—'

He seized her by the shoulders. 'I did not say I did not want you!'

She pressed herself against him again, putting her arms around him. 'Then make love to me, Edmund. This may be my only chance. I want to know love at least once. Show me, please. Please!'

How was he to resist her?

He kissed her again, a long and tender kiss that showed all the yearning he could no longer disguise. He wanted her with every fibre of his being. He wanted this one last moment of beauty and joy before facing cannon fire, blood and death.

When his lips left hers and tasted of her neck and shoulders, she sighed. 'Yes. That is glorious. Yes.'

His hand slipped beneath the neckline of her poor battered dress, now ripped and dirty from the violence of the street. He savoured her smooth skin and the feel of her nipple as his palm scraped against it.

She writhed with his touch and twisted around, presenting her back to him. 'Unbutton my dress. Please, Edmund.'

Somehow his fingers undid at least a dozen tiny buttons. As soon as they were free, she pulled her dress over her head. He took off his boots and coat.

She presented her back to him again. 'My stays.'

He untied the laces of her corset, loosened them and pulled her corset down so she could step out of it. He stripped off his trousers and drawers and added them to the puddle of clothing on the floor. He lifted her onto the bed and, as he climbed after her, she pulled off her shift.

She was naked and as beautiful as any goddess could possibly be. Her breasts were full, high and firm; their nipples dark rose. Her waist was narrow, but her hips a pleasing balance. Was she perfection? What had he done to deserve such a gift? Perhaps it meant he would meet his end. If so, he was thankful for her.

'Do—do I please you?' she asked, her voice small.

He allowed his gaze to luxuriate over her. 'Very much.'

She smiled and gazed upon him. His chest bore more than a few scars, gifts from the Battle of Albuhera, but she did not seem to notice. Her eyes widened as she gazed farther down, but, then, she would not have seen a man fully aroused before.

Edmund could have taken her quickly and roughly and eased the almost painful desire coursing through him, but his mind still functioned well enough to remember she was a virgin. He had no wish to hurt her. He wanted to show her pleasure. He wanted to show her all the delights of lovemaking, to show her she was meant to have pleasure from it. Most of all he wanted to reassure her that she was worthy of love.

He settled beside her and kissed her again, on the lips, on the tender skin beneath her ear, on the long column of her throat. He caressed her breast and relished the feel of it beneath his fingers. He scraped her nipple with his palm, and she moaned in response. He explored her with his hands and lips, and she writhed beneath his touch.

Her skin was as soft as rose petals beneath his rough hand. He fancied she was like some special flower, pampered into blooming in a hothouse, protected from all harshness. A lonely flower, apparently, and one who wished only for someone to love her. He was not the man for her, though, not a low-ranking, baseborn son of a failed father with no name and no one to recommend him.

He could but try to show her what love could be between a man and a woman. He could show her the delight and the satisfaction.

'I am going to touch you,' he warned. 'So I won't hurt you.'

He slid his hand down her body.

'Yes, yes, touch me,' she whispered, placing her hand on his and guiding it to the moist place between her legs.

He eased his fingers inside her and gently stroked and stretched her. The feel of her aroused him further, but still he held back to make certain she was ready for him.

'Just do it,' she cried. 'I want you to.'

He could not hold back now. He rose over her and entered her, moving as slowly as he could manage, when all his body wished to do was to rush to the climax.

Amelie marvelled at the sensations he created in her. To feel him joined to her was glorious, but each stroke left her urgent with need. This was beyond her expectations, yet her whole body seemed to be screaming, *More! More!*

She was glad it was Edmund showing her these delights. He was kind and strong and…skilled. Even she, with no experience at all, could tell he knew exactly how to please her. Fowler had left her and Edmund had not. She felt safe in Edmund's arms in a way she could never be in Fowler's.

The pleasure Edmund had already given her had been remarkable, but she knew there was more. She needed more. She needed to rush to some destination, though she did not know what it was. The closer they came to it, the faster they ran. She wanted—needed—to reach this place, but, at the same time, she did not want these sensations to end. It was like riding in a racing carriage, powerless to stop, but giddy with excitement, even so.

He moved faster and she moved with him, seeking more.

Suddenly the sensations exploded inside her, flooding her with waves and waves of pleasure, over and above all she'd experienced so far. He thrust one more time and tensed inside her. Was he spilling his seed? It must be so.

He relaxed on top of her, covering her with his body and his weight. How had she suddenly turned to butter, melting beneath him, with no will to move?

He rolled to her side, breathing hard, an arm flung over his face.

'I—I did not know it could feel like that,' she murmured.

He turned to face her. 'It doesn't always.'

She furrowed her brow. 'Did I disappoint you?'

He reached over and toyed with a lock of her hair. 'No, Amelie. You did not disappoint. Anything but.'

She released a breath. 'Good, because it did not disappoint me either. It was quite the most wonderful thing I have ever experienced. I shall remember it always.'

His expression softened, then turned sad. 'A memory,' he murmured. 'A fine memory.'

She smiled. 'Yes. And I thank you, Edmund. You have given me more than I knew to desire.'

He turned his head away, and it felt as though he'd run a far distance from her.

Amelie rose on to her elbow. 'What is wrong, Edmund?' *Why leave me now?* she wanted to add.

He sat up and the lamp illuminated his bare chest criss-crossed with scars. He'd soon be in battle again, she remembered.

'It was not well done of me,' he said.

She blinked in surprise. 'Not well done?' Nothing could have been better.

He looked down on her. 'Do not let this stop you from seeking a proper marriage, Amelie. No matter what people say, men cannot tell who is a virgin and who is not. This need not spoil your future.'

She sat up. 'I told you. There will be no marriage for me. This was my only chance—to—to feel that.' Only now, how was she to bear that she would never feel such sensations again?

'You will find a man worthy of you, I am certain,' he said. 'Do not let this one night stop you.'

She did not care about the rest of her life, only of this moment with him. She was glad he'd been the one to show her such delight. She could not imagine making love to any other man. How had she ever believed she'd want this with Fowler?

She did not wish to argue with Edmund about it though, not when he was bound for battle. 'I am glad I shared this with you, Edmund. Truly I am.'

He seemed to wince in pain with her words. He rubbed his face and glanced around the room before meeting her eye again.

'Do you know how to take care of yourself?' he asked.

She had no idea what he meant. 'Of course.'

He relaxed. 'Good.'

She peered at him. 'Are you regretting this, Edmund?' She did not want him to regret it. She wanted it to be a lovely memory for both of them.

He stared into her eyes. 'I am not regretting it for me.'

She flushed with happiness. 'Then might we do it again? Just one more time before you must leave?' And face Napoleon's army.

One more time could not hurt, could it? It would still be like the first time, would it not? No consequences?

He pulled her down on top of him for a kiss that sent the sensation surging through her again and sent any doubts about consequences scattering in the wind.

Edmund felt no reluctance in making love to Amelie this second time. His guilt belonged solely to the first event, did it not? At least he told himself so. Told himself to savour this unexpected opportunity to experience again the pleasure of her body, the sweetness of her spirit.

Whoever finally won her love would be fortunate indeed.

But to Hades with that man, tonight she belonged to him and this sweet memory of her would always be his alone. When he left here, he'd go to where his horse was stabled. He'd ride hard to where his regiment was billeted and then, when dawn came, they would march toward Napoleon's army.

To battle.

Edmund had cheated death many a time before. If this was the time luck would fail him, at least he'd die knowing this lovely creature had wanted him.

Had loved him.

He pressed into memory the feel of her skin under his hands, the luxury of her breasts, the taste of her kiss. He rejoiced in her unschooled but sensuous response under his touch. When he entered her again, she felt familiar, as if they'd belonged together for an eternity.

It was a gratifying illusion when the eternity of death was a distinct possibility.

Each moment of lovemaking drove the thought of death from his mind. To Edmund, Amelie represented life. With each stroke his resolve grew. He would live. He must live.

Life was full of possibilities.

His spirits soared as she moved with him, building their need, anticipating their release. He rode the passion to its culmination and, just as if they'd had an eternity to attune themselves to each other, they reached the heights together.

Edmund burst with joy. This was life! He would live for this!

When he lay in languor with Amelie in his arms, they did not speak. He simply enjoyed the comfort of lying next to her, the warmth of her body warming him. Her breathing turned soft and even. She slept the deep satisfied sleep of a woman well loved.

He slipped out of the bed and dressed as quickly and as quietly as he could. It must be nearing three in the morning. He'd need the rest of the night to ride to his regiment. He folded her clothing and searched the room for paper and pen, finding both on a small writing table in the corner.

Dear Amelie,
I shall remember this night with great fondness and gratitude. I hope you remember it without regret. Do not lose heart. Do not let one night or one man take away your dreams. You possess everything any man could desire. One day you will make some lucky gentleman a wonderful wife.
Best regards always,
E.

He folded the paper and placed it next to her on the bed. Then he moved quietly around the room extinguishing the lamps.

All except one candle. By the light of that candle, he took one last look at her. One last image to burn in his memory.

He picked up his bag, blew out the candle and walked out the door.

Chapter Four

Three months later, September 1815—London

'Edmund? Edmund Summerfield?'

Edmund, just stepping out of Horse Guards onto the parade, turned.

Marc Glenville quickened his step to catch up to him. 'I thought that was you.' He extended his hand to shake. 'How are you, Edmund? What a surprise to see you in London.'

Edmund was surprised as well. It was September. He thought everyone would be in the country hunting birds, not in London. He'd not written to any of his sisters that he would be in England, because he expected to return to Brussels in a week or two, and he assumed they would not be in town. Who could have thought he would run into his half-sister Tess's husband?

Amelie's brother.

He accepted the handshake. 'I arrived a few days ago.'

He'd come into town to settle his affairs in person. He'd planned to write to his sisters from Brussels after he returned. Better to inform them by letter afterwards than tell them ahead of time what he intended to do.

'Tess will be delighted you are here,' Glenville said. 'Where are you headed?'

'Back to my hotel.'

'Are you staying at Stephen's Hotel?' Glenville asked.

It was a good guess. Stephen's Hotel catered to army officers and, even though Edmund was not in uniform, Glenville would assume he would stay there.

He nodded. 'I am.'

Glenville clapped him on the shoulder. 'Come have a drink with me first. It is but a short walk to Brooks's.'

Edmund could think of no excuse. 'A drink would be welcome.'

As they started to cross the parade, Glenville gestured to Edmund's leg. 'How is your injury?'

'Mostly healed.'

A French sabre had sliced into Edmund's leg at Waterloo. He still limped a bit when he first rose in the morning, and it still pained him at night. He'd helped Marc carry a grievously wounded Fowler back from the battlefield, despite his own injury. Fowler, the supposed fiancé who had abandoned Amelie on the streets of Brussels—although Edmund had said nothing to Glenville about that. Fowler had been wounded in the ill-fated Scots Greys' cavalry charge. Would Glenville have brought Fowler back to Brussels if he'd known how reprehensibly he'd treated Amelie? Edmund did not regret saving Fowler, though. Even a cad like him did not deserve to die on that battlefield. Too many of them died undiscovered, and none of them deserved that fate.

How strange was fate? Edmund's life had become entwined with Glenville when he married Edmund's sister. Had Glenville not met Edmund, he might have walked by Edmund at Waterloo and not asked him to help bring Fowler back to Brussels. Care of Edmund's leg might have been delayed. The wound might have festered. He might have lost his leg. Or his life. Many of the wounded died for lack of immediate care.

Fate also entwined him with Fowler, a man he'd preferred to have known nothing of. But he would not for all the world have missed his brief time of knowing Amelie. What if he'd never met her? What would have happened to her if he'd not noticed her on the streets of Brussels that night, had not been there to save her from that brute who'd meant to molest her? What if he'd not walked her back to the hotel, not made love to her?

How the memory of that night had sustained him! During the hard fighting at Quatre Bras. All during the rain-drenched night after that battle. During tense moments of inaction at Waterloo.

After his injury.

Knowing that Amelie, with all her warmth, beauty and passion, was still in the world had been and still was a comfort. Spending those precious hours with her had been like touching light. He'd become more resolved than ever to make something of his life, to succeed where his father had failed, to prove to his departed mother that her sacrifices had not been for naught.

How had Amelie fared? What memories did she hold about that night? Regret? Shame? He fervently hoped not.

Of course, he could simply ask Glenville how Amelie was.

'How is Tess?' he asked instead.

Glenville's expression turned soft. 'Tess is wonderful.'

Edmund nodded in approval. Tess deserved such a man to love her.

'And your family?' he went on.

'My parents are getting along very well.' Glenville spoke this with some surprise.

'And your sister?' He tried to keep his tone even.

'Amelie?' Glenville rubbed his forehead. 'Amelie has had it rougher than the rest of us. Fowler, you know.'

Edmund was surprised. 'Fowler died, didn't he?' That should have been the end of it for her.

When last Edmund saw Fowler, he'd been barely clinging to life—but still alive. Glenville and Tess had taken him back to England to his parents. Edmund had stayed in Brussels to be cared for by Lady Summerfield, his half-sisters' mother, and her lover, Count von Osten. Even though that lady had run away from Edmund's father and abandoned her children years before, Edmund had searched for and found her. He'd stayed with her and the count in Brussels both before the battle and after.

'Fowler lived,' Glenville said. 'But there is no thought of marriage between him and Amelie now. His parents said he was in no condition to marry and that it was best to break the engagement. Amelie never speaks of it, but there is no doubt she's been changed by all this.'

Was the change due to Fowler? Or was Edmund responsible? It had been nearly three months since that night together. He'd hoped she'd rebounded from both.

He and Glenville continued walking past Carlton House, the grand residence of the Prince Regent.

Glenville suddenly halted. 'I have a better notion than going for a drink! Come to dinner tonight. My parents are at the country estate, but that will give you and Tess more of a visit. We have no plans for the evening. I will go home directly and send word to you at your hotel if by some chance we must withdraw the invitation, but I can think of no reason you should not be very welcome.'

If Glenville's parents were in the country, Amelie would be with them. There was really no reason not to see Tess now that she knew he was in town. He could tell her in person what he'd planned to write in a letter.

Besides, he missed her. And Genna and Lorene.

Might they be in London, too?

'Dinner. Name the hour and I will be there.'

'Come at seven,' Glenville said. 'We are at my parents' on Grosvenor Street. Third house from the corner adjacent to the square.'

Edmund had not spent much time in London and none in the fine houses around Grosvenor Square, but he knew where Grosvenor intersected with Bond Street. 'I will find it.'

Glenville smiled. 'Excellent! Tess will be happy to have a nice long visit with you.'

At a little past seven, Edmund sounded the knocker at the third town house adjacent to Grosvenor Square.

A footman opened the door, and Edmund gave him his name. 'This way, sir.'

Edmund followed him to the door of the drawing room, where he was announced. As Edmund stepped into the room, Tess was already on her feet, rushing towards him.

'Edmund!' She flung herself into his arms for a hug. 'What a nice surprise.' She immediately pulled away to look at him. 'How is your leg? Marc said it was healed. Is it? Does it pain you still?'

He smiled at her, surprised how pleased he was to see her. 'My leg is healed. Nothing to worry over, I assure you.' He gazed at her sparkling hazel eyes, her shining chestnut hair. 'You look even more beautiful than in Brussels, Tess.'

She blushed. 'I am happy. That is the reason.'

Her husband approached. 'How good you could come on such short notice. I am delighted we will have the evening together.'

Glenville and Tess stepped aside.

From a chair near the fireplace, another woman stood. 'Hello, Edmund.'

Amelie! He caught himself before he spoke her name

aloud, bowing instead. 'Miss Glenville. Good to see you again.'

A memory of holding her in his arms, feeling her soft skin against his palms, her lips against his, slammed into him. He'd missed her, although why he should miss a woman he'd only spent a few hours with would make no sense to anyone.

Except to him. Those hours together had had an impact that would never leave him. She was the inspiration for him to dare to make himself a success.

She looked as beautiful as ever, but thinner. Paler.

'You must call me Amelie.' Even her voice seemed altered. Softer. Tenser. She made an attempt at a smile.

Tess pulled him towards the sofa, near Amelie. 'Come. Sit. Marc will pour you a glass of claret. You must tell me why you are in London and why you did not write to us that you were coming.' She gave him a scolding look.

He glanced at Amelie, who sat again, before turning to Tess. 'I assumed you would be in the country.' He assumed they all would be in the country.

'Marc had some work to finish,' Tess said. 'And Amelie came for a visit.'

Marc poured the wine and handed a glass to him and one to Tess. 'That was why I was at Horse Guards.'

Edmund tore his eyes away from Amelie. 'Work brought you to Horse Guards?' What sort of work at Horse Guards did a viscount's heir perform?

Glenville smiled. 'Indeed.' But he did not explain.

It appeared Edmund and Amelie were not the only ones to keep secrets.

'But why did you come to London, Edmund?' Tess asked again.

He took a sip of his wine and took one more glance at Amelie before facing Tess. 'I sold my commission.'

Her eyes widened. 'You are no longer in the army?'

'I sold out.' He gestured to his clothes. 'That is why I am not in uniform.' He met Tess's gaze, but wondered if Amelie even attended to his words. 'Napoleon is defeated. The war is over. Without the war, there is no future for me in the army. Regiments will disband, I fear. There will be fewer and fewer opportunities to advance.'

And who would promote a bastard when there were plenty of aristocratic sons wanting the higher ranks? When fighting in Spain, he'd been passed over for field promotions. Captaincies had been given to men with fewer skills and less seniority.

'But what will you do?' Tess asked.

He could not resist a glance at Amelie, who sat primly, eyes lowered, hands folded in her lap. 'I plan to return to Brussels.'

'Brussels? With Mama?' Tess's voice rose.

Tess and her sisters had not known their mother was in Brussels, let alone that Edmund had corresponded with her for several years and stayed with her when his regiment was sent to the area. Because of Edmund, Tess and Lady Summerfield had forged a reconciliation, albeit an ambivalent one. Unlike Edmund, Tess had not forgiven her mother for abandoning them.

But this was not the time to discuss Lady Summerfield.

'There are fortunes to be made on the Continent, now that the war is over,' he said instead. And Count von Osten had a talent for finding them.

'You sound like Papa,' Tess accused.

Their late father had always chased an easy fortune, finding instead only debts and failure. When his half-sister Lorene sent him money to purchase a captaincy, Edmund had been surprised there had been any money left to inherit. While Edmund recuperated in Brussels, he used that money, not to purchase an advancement in the army, but to make the very sort of investment his father might have made. Except, unlike his father, Edmund made good profits from taking the risk. Now that he'd sold his lieutenancy, he had even more money to invest.

'I'll do well enough, Tess,' he assured her. 'Besides, I only have me to worry over.' Not a wife, three daughters and a bastard son, like their father.

'No more talk of money,' her husband said cheerfully.

'Then tell me of Lorene and Genna,' Edmund said, glad to change the subject. 'Are they in London, too?'

Their sister Lorene had married a very old man, a reclusive earl who lived near their village in Lincolnshire. She'd married him for his money, which seemed unlike her. Edmund had never met the man.

'Lord Tinmore has retired to the country.' Glenville's voice rang with contempt. 'He has filled Tinmore Hall with guests who are invited for the bird shooting.'

'Guests?' Edmund said. 'I thought he was an old recluse. Was that not what was said of him when we were growing up?'

'He probably has invited his eligible gentlemen friends in an effort to get Genna married off,' Tess responded. 'He is eager to be rid of her, I think.'

'How old is Genna?' Edmund asked. 'Is she not too young?' His eyes darted to Amelie again. How old was she? he wondered. Had she been too young? He'd not given that a thought that fateful night.

'She is nineteen now.' Tess rolled her eyes. 'Plenty old enough, but she professes to be against marriage. She sometimes vows never to marry, but it is unlikely Tinmore will allow her that choice.'

Edmund was alarmed. 'Surely he will not force her!'

Tess exchanged a look with her husband, who answered, 'I fear Tinmore is capable of almost anything.'

'What of Lorene?' Edmund asked. Could he take care

of both Lorene and Genna if it became necessary? 'Does he treat her ill?'

Tess shook her head. 'He is indulgent of Lorene as far as I can surmise. She wants for nothing, but he wants Lorene all to himself, not shared with her sisters.'

Edmund curled his fingers into a fist. 'You will tell me if he mistreats either of them.'

'We will not let them be mistreated,' Glenville said emphatically.

The butler entered the room to announce that dinner was served. Tess took Glenville's arm. There was nothing for Edmund to do but offer to escort Amelie. Her graceful fingers wrapped around his offered arm.

'How are you, Amelie?' he asked in a lowered voice as they trailed behind Tess and Glenville.

She raised her blue eyes to his for a moment but quickly averted them again. 'I am well enough, I suppose.'

She appeared altered, though, not full of sparkle and happiness like when he first met her in Brussels. She was different than when he'd made love to her, as well. She seemed...worried.

In the dining room she was seated next to him, and he was aware the entire time of her closeness. He found himself wanting to see the expressions on her face to gauge how she was feeling.

There were so many questions he wished to ask her. Was she ill? Was she still affected by Fowler's behaviour in Brussels? Did she ever think of the night they'd spent together? If so, did she remember it as he did? As a transforming experience? Or did she feel regret, remorse, or worst of all, shame? Should he have left her at the hotel door?

He hardly attended to the conversation at the table, hardly knew what he'd said to anyone. He'd talked about his investments, his plans to travel to wherever a fortune could be made. He and Glenville debated what countries that might be and also what the end of the war might mean to the economies of Britain, France and the rest of the Continent. If only he could remember what they concluded. A part of his mind had fixed on Amelie and would not let go.

Amelie made a show of eating, although she mostly pushed food around her plate. She'd not had an appetite of late. Would he notice?

She'd forgotten how handsome he was. Out of uniform in a beautifully tailored coat and trousers that showed his muscular legs, he was an impressive sight.

Was he glad to see her? She could not tell. There was no way to talk to him alone, and she dared not reveal that she knew him a great deal better than Marc or Tess could ever imagine. Perhaps his reticence to even look at her was to help keep their secret. She hoped so. She hoped it was not that he disliked encountering her again.

After dinner he and Marc did not linger over brandy. Instead they all returned to the drawing room for more conversation.

She'd thought she might never see Edmund again, thought he'd return to the army and be sent somewhere far away, but here he was and now she needed to make a decision. To speak to him now, to tell him of her—situation— or to have him find out later, perhaps in a letter from Tess.

It had bothered her greatly that he would find out after the fact and not hear it from her own lips.

He was here now, though. This might be her only chance.

But how to speak to him alone?

She could not think of any excuse to do so. He seemed not to pay her much mind, so would likely miss any hint she could try to send him to let him know she wanted to see him alone, with no one around. Just her and Edmund.

Eventually she excused herself, saying she was going to bed. Instead she put on her cloak and sneaked outside. She'd stand in the chilly September air until he walked out the door.

She waited in the stairs that led from the street to the servants' entrance, hoping none of them opened the door and caught her there. The wind and damp seemed to find their way to her hiding place, making the minutes ticking by move even more slowly. How easy it would be to simply turn around and re-enter the house and tell herself she'd tried. He might stay for hours, might he not? Could she wait so long? Her feet, still in her dinner slippers, felt like ice, and her ungloved fingers trembled as they sought warmth in the recesses of her cloak. How long had it been? She tried to listen for the chiming of clocks, but all she could hear was the wind, an occasional carriage rumbling by or the chattering of her teeth.

Finally she heard the front door open, and she emerged from her hiding place, stepping into the light cast by the rush lamps.

He turned at the sound of her footsteps. 'Amelie! What are you doing out here?'

'I—I wanted to see you alone,' she managed.

He took hold of her arm and walked her back into the darkness. 'Tell me truthfully, Amelie. How do you fare? Your brother said you were not doing well. Are you ill?'

'I'm not ill,' she said.

'Do not tell me you are still affected by Fowler.'

She almost laughed. 'Certainly not.'

'Then is it what transpired between us?' He sounded distressed. 'If so, I am so sincerely sorry—'

'It is not that,' she broke in. 'At least not precisely.'

'You must not allow that night to change you. You are still beautiful. More beautiful, in fact. There is no reason you cannot marry—'

She cut him off again. 'There is a reason, Edmund! A very important reason. That is why I contrived to see you alone. There is something I must tell you.'

'What is it?' His voice was tense. She could not clearly see his face.

Her heart pounded painfully in her chest. She took a deep breath and said words she'd never until this moment spoken aloud.

'I am going to have a baby.'

Chapter Five

The air was knocked out of Edmund's chest.

A baby.

He knew efforts to prevent a baby were anything but reliable, but he'd ignored that. He'd allowed his passion to overtake him.

'You might wish to ask if the child is yours,' she said stiffly. 'I assure you it is. And I am certain I am carrying a child. I have not had my courses since—since that night. I am sick every morning, fatigued all day, and I feel… altered. No one knows. Of course, they will discover it soon enough.'

'A baby,' he whispered.

She lifted her chin. 'Do not fear. No one knows of our meeting that night, and I will say nothing. You will be safe from blame. I am perfectly aware I was the cause of this.'

'No.' He knew who was to blame.

She took a breath. 'Well. There it is. That is why I wanted to see you alone.'

She turned to leave, but he seized her arm. 'Do not tell me such a thing and then leave.'

'There is no more to say,' she told him. 'I ask nothing of you.'

'Nothing of me?' he repeated. She wanted him to have no part of it?

Her eyes flashed. 'I'll not get rid of it, if that is what you are about to say.'

He still gripped her arm. 'I was not about to say that.' He was about to ask her why she wanted him to have no part in a child they created together, why she did not see what they must do, even if she disliked it.

'I do not yet know what I will do,' she went on. 'Perhaps my parents will send me to France. I have relatives there. I've never met them, but perhaps they will be accommodating.'

He released her and paced in front of her, talking more to himself than to her. 'You would give the baby away? Or pay someone to care for it?' She preferred that?

She shrugged. 'I do not *want* to do either of those things, but I cannot imagine my parents allowing me to keep the child. Think of the scandal I would bring on them.'

He came closer. 'There will be scandal, no matter what.' But he knew the right thing to do.

'You need not worry about that,' she said.

He need not worry? He'd been born to scandal. He never worried about what people thought of him.

Except for one person. He cared what Amelie thought of him, and it seemed she wanted nothing to do with him.

He was so close to her now his body flared in response to her, betraying him as it had that night in Brussels. He again remembered how it felt to lie next to her, how it felt to be inside her.

It wounded him that she did not want him to take responsibility for the child, but what did that matter? She must see there could be no other way.

He began pacing again. 'I can provide for the child.'

'Money is no issue,' she said. 'I have an inheritance, and my father can easily pay.'

'I am not speaking of money.' He was speaking of what must be done.

She cleared her throat. 'I have no more to say. I—I thought it my duty to tell you. I truly ask nothing of you—'

Before he could protest, before he could tell her what he thought they must do, no matter how distasteful to her, she turned and rushed down the servants' stairs and into the house.

She left him standing on the pavement. Alone.

Amelie closed the door and ran up the servant's staircase to her bedchamber, fighting tears.

There. She told him. She'd done her duty to him and assured him she would not use the child against him. No one would ever know it was Edmund's child; no one but her. At least she could console herself that he would be free to live his life, to build his fortune, to have his adventure, like he'd spoken of at dinner with so much energy and passion. She would do nothing to stop him, nothing to spoil his happiness.

She tore off her cloak and flung herself on her bed.

If only he had not looked so handsome. If only he had yelled at her for being so foolish as to allow a baby to be conceived. If only he had not roused in her those wanton feelings. Goodness! Merely having his hands gripping her arms made her recall how those hands felt against her naked flesh. Even in her predicament, she'd yearned to couple with him again, to feel that intense ecstasy that he created in her.

Well-bred young ladies did not feel such things. Well-bred ladies did not get themselves with child. They married for social advantage for their families and procreated to beget heirs, not because they craved a man's touch and the thrill he could create. This was her downfall, certainly. If she had not been so wanton, she would not be in this fix, but she was determined she would not ruin his life along with her own.

It was some consolation that she'd assured him of that fact.

Edmund returned to the Grosvenor Street town house at ten the next morning. As he announced himself to the footman attending the door, Glenville walked down the stairs.

'Edmund!' Glenville was, of course, surprised to see him. 'You are back so soon. To what do we owe this pleasure?'

Edmund had come to call upon Amelie, but to say so now would only cause Glenville to ask questions. He might as well provide the answers first.

'A moment of your time?' he asked.

'Certainly,' Glenville said, still sounding puzzled. 'Come to the library. Would you like some refreshment?'

'No,' Edmund handed his hat and gloves to the footman. 'Just a word with you.'

Glenville gestured for Edmund to follow him. The library was behind the drawing room, in the back of the house. If the drawing room was designed to impress and entertain, the library was intended for comfort and solitude. It was lined with books and filled with comfortable chairs.

Glenville lowered himself into one of them. 'Please have a seat.'

Edmund remained standing and debated how to start.

Might as well charge ahead. 'I came to ask for something which, no doubt, you will be unprepared to hear.'

Glenville's brows rose.

'Actually, it is not something I think you can grant, but I owe you the courtesy of hearing it from me.'

'And this is?' Glenville asked.

'I would like to pay my addresses to your sister.'

Glenville's eyes widened. 'Pay addresses?'

'Court her,' Edmund went on. 'Marry her.'

Glenville shook his head in bewilderment. 'But you do not know her!'

Edmund knew her better than Glenville could guess, but he could not explain. He'd promised to never speak of that night to anyone.

'It is true we have not been in each other's company—' he began.

Glenville cut him off. 'Not above twice! Once in Brussels and last night.'

Three times, actually. 'I would still like to speak to her.'

Glenville stood again and walked over to a far corner of the room. He turned. 'Do not get me wrong, Edmund. I think you are a fine man. I am proud to be connected to you by marriage, but I do not think this will work.' He paused. 'Your suit is—is just not...' His voice faded.

'Not acceptable because I am a bastard?' Edmund finished for him.

Glenville lifted his hands. 'That is of no consequence to me, but I cannot see my father giving his permission.'

'I will have to speak to him, of course,' Edmund said. 'But first I would like to speak to your sister.'

Glenville frowned. 'Are you thinking she will accept you, because her betrothal to Fowler fell apart? She is still young. My parents will expect other suitors.'

Better than he, a bastard with uncertain prospects, though perhaps not once the pregnancy was discovered. 'I am well aware that she might deserve a better suitor than me.'

Glenville shook his head. 'I still cannot wrap my mind around this. What makes you think she will accept you? She spoke hardly two words to you last night.' He frowned and peered suspiciously at Edmund. 'Are you experiencing financial difficulties? Because Tess and I would be glad to help you—'

Edmund straightened. 'I am not after her dowry! Believe me, money does not enter in this at all.'

Glenville sputtered. 'This is hardly making any sense!'

'What is your objection to me speaking to her?' Edmund pressed on. Even a decent gentleman, like Glenville, could not help but wish for a better man than Edmund for his sister's husband, apparently. Edmund was disappointed, but not surprised. 'I am perfectly willing to withdraw if she should refuse me.'

Glenville's expression, however, seemed filled with kindness. 'I do not object to you speaking to Amelie, Edmund. I do not object to you at all. I am merely taken aback.'

'That is all I ask,' Edmund said. 'To speak to her.'

'By all means. And I wish you well.' Glenville walked to the door. 'Wait here. I will send her to you.'

He left the room, and Edmund pressed his fingers against his temple. No one would think this viscount's daughter should marry a mere bastard. Even Edmund did not think himself worthy of her. Her marriage to him would cause talk. More talk when a baby was born too soon, but this was the respectable solution, the honourable choice.

A few minutes passed before the door opened again.

Amelie walked in. 'Edmund?' She looked surprised and less than happy to see him. 'What are you doing? My brother said you wanted to speak to me.'

She also looked unwell.

'Are you ill?' he asked, taking a step towards her.

She halted him with her hand. 'Mornings are bad for me. Tell me what you are about, though. My brother looked uncertain. You did not say anything to him about—about—?'

About Brussels? 'Never,' he responded. 'I gave my word.'

'Well, my guess is that my brother is going to pound me with questions after you leave. Why would you wish to speak to me? Marc and Tess are going to want to know. When the truth comes out about—about me, this might make them think you were involved.'

'I *was* involved,' he said. 'I *am* involved. Stop talking and listen to me.'

She clamped her mouth shut and crossed her arms over her chest.

'You ran off last night before I could make plain to you what we must do—'

Her eyes flickered, but she did not move.

'There is only one solution, Amelie. We must think of what is best for the child, not for you or me.' He was not coming to the point. He took a breath. 'We should marry. Marry me, Amelie.'

'Marry?' She looked shocked.

He hurried on. 'The baby will have my name instead of no name. He or she must never know the scandal of being a bastard or of growing up not knowing who his parents really were. The child will be able to grow up respectably.'

'You cannot truly wish to marry me!' she cried.

He'd never dreamed it to be possible. 'You cannot wish to marry me, but our wishes cannot matter in this. We must do this for the baby.'

'For the baby,' she repeated, glancing away.

He strode up to her and placed his hands on her shoulders. 'I know what it is to grow up a bastard. It is an albatross one must carry all one's life. It is the fact against which everything else one does is judged. I do not want that for our child. I cannot allow what I have done to so burden a child.'

'It was *my* doing, Edmund,' she said sadly. 'You should not have to pay the consequences of what I have done.'

'What *we* have done,' he corrected. 'I accept my part

in it.' Indeed, he knew he bore the lion's share of the guilt. 'But the child. He or she should not have to pay the price.'

In so many ways Edmund had been lucky. He'd not been abandoned to the streets of the Rookery. His mother had loved him. His father had acknowledged him and raised him as a gentleman, sent him to school and purchased his commission. But, even so, never, in any situation, had he been allowed to forget he was a bastard.

'What say you, Amelie?' he went on. 'Will you marry me?'

Amelie glanced away, at war with herself.

The idea of it made her immediately feel safe, when before she'd been consumed with fear. To face this problem with Edmund at her side dispelled the fear.

She winced inwardly. How awful of her to think of her baby as a problem. Edmund was right that they should think of the baby, not as a problem, but as a child who would grow into adulthood. What they decided right now would affect the rest of the child's life.

But marrying Edmund would affect *his* life, too. Could she rob him of his future? All his wonderful plans?

She walked over to a chair and lowered herself into it.

She lifted her gaze to him. 'Yes, Edmund, I will marry you.'

A relieved smile crossed his face, and he sat in the chair adjacent to hers. 'We are in agreement, then.'

'What shall we do now?' she said.

'We should marry right away,' he said. 'I will procure a special licence.'

'Yes, right away,' she murmured. 'People will still talk when the baby comes early.'

'But not so much. All is forgiven if we are married.' His tone was subdued.

They were both resigned to a fate neither would have

chosen. They sat in silence together while the mantel clock ticked away.

'Marc and Tess will want to know what we discussed here,' she said finally.

'We will talk to them together,' he said. 'If you desire it.'

'Yes. I do agree.' They might be strangers discussing how to reach a destination.

'What do they know about that night in Brussels?' he asked.

'Why, nothing,' she responded, more energy reaching her voice. 'My family still believes I walked back to the hotel with Captain Fowler.'

'You did not tell them he broke the engagement?'

'There was no reason to,' she explained. 'Especially when he was injured. When his parents wrote that he had to withdraw from the betrothal because of his injuries, it was easy to accept it and say nothing.'

'You were not sorry?' Now his voice showed some emotion.

'Not at all.' She'd be pleased never to face Fowler again. Ever. 'Although I was sorry he was so grievously hurt in the battle.'

'Your brother thought I was daft to ask to court you,' he said with some humour.

'You told him you wished to court me? He did not say so.' No wonder Marc had acted so strangely. She could not help but laugh. 'He must think we are strangers!'

He smiled and her heart seemed to flip in her chest. When Marc told her Edmund was here, Amelie resolved not to think of how handsome he was, nor how skilfully and kindly he'd made love to her, but both thoughts came rushing back.

She felt the colour rise in her face and suddenly she felt awkward with him. 'Perhaps we should speak to Marc now.'

'Certainly.' He stood and offered his hand.

She put her hand in his, relishing the strength of his grip and the masculine roughness of his skin, as she'd relished touching his body that night in Brussels.

That scandalous night that had changed both their lives.

They walked out of the library and into the hall, where Staines stood in attendance. 'Mr and Mrs Glenville wish for you to go to them,' he said.

'Where are they?' she asked.

'The drawing room.'

As they walked to the drawing room door, Amelie glanced at Edmund. 'Are you certain of this?'

'Very certain,' Edmund replied.

She nodded and Edmund opened the door. Marc and Tess immediately looked up and left their seats.

Tess walked up to Edmund and gave him a hug. 'What are you about, Edmund?' she asked at the same time.

'Did Marc tell you why Edmund wished to see me?' Amelie asked her.

Tess nodded. 'Marc said… Well, it is nonsensical.'

'I have accepted him,' Amelie said. 'We will marry as soon as possible.'

'What?' Marc's voice grew louder.

'You do not know each other!' Tess cried.

Marc gripped Amelie's arms. 'Amelie, do not be so hasty—'

Edmund broke in. 'I realise I am not the husband you would choose for her.'

'I already told you it is not that,' Marc insisted. 'It is that you have no real acquaintance and—and our father is not likely to approve.'

Amelie's spirits dropped. 'I had forgotten. Papa must approve who I marry until I come of age.'

'I had not considered this,' Edmund said. 'How old are you?'

'Edmund, you do not even know how old she is!' Tess cried. 'You know nothing of each other!'

'I am nineteen,' Amelie answered.

'Good God,' murmured Edmund, but as if to himself. 'Nineteen. Same age as Genna.'

Marc looked from Edmund to Amelie. 'Why do you not wait? What is the haste about marrying? You need time to know each other. And if you wait until you are twenty-one, it will not matter if Papa approves or not.'

Amelie glanced at Edmund. He raised his brows.

'We do not have the luxury of time,' Amelie said.

Edmund looked at her.

She met his eye. 'I might as well tell them.'

'Tell us what?' Tess asked.

'They will know soon enough,' Amelie went on.

'Know what?' Tess's voice turned impatient.

Amelie took a fortifying breath. 'We cannot wait, because—'

'Are you certain of this?' Edmund asked her.

She nodded.

'Certain of what?' Tess's voice grew shriller.

Amelie faced both her brother and sister-in-law. 'I am certain we need to marry quickly, because I am carrying Edmund's child.'

Her statement was met by a stunned silence.

'No,' Marc said in a low voice.

'Edmund's child?' Tess shook her head at Edmund. 'It cannot be. This is all a hum. You have not been together.'

Edmund spoke quietly. 'We were together, Tess. Obviously. The night of the Duchess of Richmond's ball.'

'No,' she insisted. 'Amelie left the ball with Captain Fowler.' She swung towards Amelie. 'Is this Fowler's baby?'

'No!' Amelie and Edmund cried in unison.

Amelie's face flushed. 'Fowler abandoned me that night,

Tess. He left me alone on the streets of Brussels. I do not know what I would have done if your brother had not found me and escorted me back to the hotel.'

'I dare say you would have been better off!' Glenville's nostrils flared as he turned towards Edmund. 'You seduced my sister?'

Amelie stepped in front of Edmund. 'He did not seduce me. It was my doing. All of it.'

Edmund pulled her back. 'Do not try to put a better face on it, Amelie. I seduced you.'

'No! Edmund!' Tess cried again. 'You would not do such a thing to an innocent girl. You would not!'

It pained Amelie to see Edmund lowered in Tess's eyes.

'I *did* do it, Tess,' Edmund said. 'I *am* responsible.'

Amelie broke in. 'No. The fault is mine.'

But no one listened to her.

'I do not know how he convinced you,' her brother growled. 'But he took advantage, of that I am certain.'

No. *She* had taken advantage!

Edmund looked Marc directly in the eye. 'I accept my responsibility and my duty. For your sister's sake, I will do the honourable thing.'

Marc's eyes flashed. 'Honourable. There is nothing honourable in what you have done. This will cause our family more scandal.'

'I cannot change what happened,' Edmund said. 'But I can do what is right now.'

Marc swung to Amelie. 'You still need Papa's approval, you know. He will never give it.'

'He will give permission,' Tess said dispiritedly. 'What other choice will he have? There will be a baby.'

'I will speak to your father in person,' Edmund said. 'I will explain.'

Marc shook his head. 'He will not believe you. He'll toss you out. Your story is too far-fetched.'

'But it is true!' Amelie cried.

'It sounds like a cock-and-bull story,' Marc said, 'even if it is true. Papa will never believe Edmund if he travels there alone with that tale.'

'I do not believe it!' cried Tess. 'Not of Edmund.'

Edmund gave Tess a quelling look but glanced back at Marc. 'Then come with me. He will believe you.'

'Go with you?' Marc still looked as if he'd rather accompany a pen of swine.

Why couldn't her brother be on her side about this?

'He will believe you.' Edmund repeated, keeping his gaze steady.

Amelie interrupted. 'Neither of you have to go. I will write Papa a letter.'

Edmund turned to her and gently touched her arm. 'No letter, Amelie. I must face your father. It is the only way.'

It was good of Edmund to offer, but Amelie was certain he would be treated very ill.

Marc's shoulders fell. 'Edmund is right. This is not news for our parents to read in a letter. Papa is more likely to approve if Edmund tells him like a man.'

It pained Amelie that she'd caused her brother to be so angry at Edmund. Before this Marc had held him in high regard.

Her brother straightened. 'It is but a six-hour ride. We can be at Northdon House before nightfall if we leave soon.'

'I should accompany you,' Amelie said.

'No!' Edmund cried.

'Absolutely not!' her brother added.

At least they agreed on that idea.

'Not in your condition,' Tess added. 'You must take care, or you will endanger your health.'

Six hours on horseback could not be good for the baby.

Edmund turned back to Glenville. 'I can ride the way

I am dressed, and I do not need a change of clothing, but I need to hire a horse.'

Marc started for the door. 'I'll send Staines to the stables to tell them to saddle my horse and to hire one for you.'

Tess followed him. 'I will tell Cook to pack you some food.'

Amelie and Edmund were alone in the room. Her insides were churning, not only from the morning sickness, but also from the stress of this encounter. The stress of everything.

She turned to Edmund. 'My brother blames you. My father will blame you, too. It is I who should tell him what really happened.'

He looked down on her. 'What really happened was I took advantage of you. Let it go at that, Amelie. That night in Brussels I should have seen you safely to the hotel and left you there. That fact cannot be disputed. I must accept their anger just as I must accept that our marrying is what we must do.'

'But it is my fault,' she said in a small voice.

He touched her arm and attempted a smile. 'I have faced men in battle lunging at me with swords and shooting pistols. I've had cannon balls miss me by inches. Facing your father will not be so difficult nor so dangerous.'

She was not so certain.

She placed her palm on her abdomen to quiet her roiling stomach. 'Marrying me changes things for you. I am so dreadfully sorry.'

His gaze seemed to harden. 'We simply do what we must, Amelie. That is how we manage. One task at a time. The first task is your father's permission.'

Chapter Six

It took no more than an hour before Edmund and Glenville were on the road to Hertfordshire, where the Northdon country estate was located. Glenville rode a few paces ahead of Edmund, clearly having no wish to converse with him. Glenville's displeasure was palpable, and Edmund could not blame him. Edmund would react the same—worse, in fact—if a near stranger had violated any of his sisters.

Edmund let Glenville decide when to stop and rest the horses, when they should quicken the pace and when they should slow. Why quibble about such trifles? They rode past crumbling Roman ruins and pretty villages with houses all in a line next to the road. They passed through busy market towns and quiet villages where the few people in the street took notice and eyed them with curiosity.

Edmund had too much time to think, and that was not a pleasant circumstance. *Turn off your thoughts*, he told himself. *Numb your mind as you used to on long marches in Spain.*

The sun was very low in the sky when they rode through a pretty village that time appeared to have forgotten. The houses and shops looked as if the War of the Roses had been fought the day before. Edmund knew they must be close. The village was called Northdon.

Soon he spied a large Palladian house in the distance, its white stone gleaming in the waning light. Northdon House, no doubt. At its grand wrought-iron gate, Glenville dismounted and opened it.

As they approached the house, Glenville said, 'Let me do the talking.'

'No.' This time Edmund must be in charge. 'I tell him.'

'Let me do the talking up to that point, then,' Glenville said anxiously.

Glenville's presence was greeted with happy excitement. Both his parents ran to greet him. There were hugs and kisses and exclamations of pleasure showered on him before Lord and Lady Northdon even seemed to notice Edmund, who was greeted with greater reserve but kind civility.

They all retired to a drawing room.

As soon as Lord and Lady Northdon were seated, Edmund faced them. 'We have come because I have a very important matter to discuss.'

Lady Northdon looked worried, Lord Northdon apprehensive.

Edmund took a breath. 'I will not mince words. Your daughter and I must marry. She is carrying my child.'

'*Mon Dieu!*' Lady Northdon cried.

Lord Northdon's face grew red with rage. 'You did what to my daughter?' he said after.

'She carries my child,' Edmund repeated.

'You ruddy bastard!' Northdon charged at him.

Glenville held him back.

Edmund stood his ground. 'I accept your anger, sir. I understand it. But what is important now is for us to marry quickly and avoid as much scandal as possible. To accomplish that we need your permission.'

'No!' Northdon cried, his son still holding his arm. Northdon shrugged him off but faced him. 'Amelie does not wish this, does she, Marc?'

'It is what she wants,' Glenville answered.

'It cannot be!' his father cried.

'Ma pauvre fille,' whispered Lady Northdon. 'Is she in good health?'

Edmund answered her. 'She is sick in the mornings and greatly fatigued.'

'You know this?' Glenville looked surprised.

Edmund turned to him. 'She told me.' He faced Lord Northdon again. 'Do we have your permission?'

'I would rather kill you,' Northdon snapped.

'Then your daughter will have an illegitimate child.' Edmund kept his voice as even as possible. He was used to people hating him because of his birth. This was not much different. 'I wish to prevent that.'

'You have to give permission, Papa,' Glenville said. 'It will be best for Amelie.'

'Marriage to this—this bastard cannot be what is best for her.' Northdon spat out the word *bastard*.

'He is the child's father,' Glenville pressed. 'You must allow them to marry.'

'Give your permission, John!' Lady Northdon became more agitated. 'Remember Lucien! I will not lose my daughter the way we lost Lucien.'

Who was Lucien?

Lord Northdon's shoulders slumped, and he suddenly looked old and feeble, which he was certainly not. 'Yes, Ines,' he said in a weak voice. 'Not like Lucien.'

A pall came over the room, as thick as smoke.

When Lord Northdon finally raised his head, his eyes were filled with pain. 'Please get him out of my sight before I change my mind and kill him.'

'Come.' Lady Northdon took Edmund by the arm. 'You must be hungry.'

Lady Northdon was still a beautiful woman, although her features, so like Amelie's, were pinched with stress and unhappiness. The crisp sunny September day had been rendered bleak—by Edmund. If only he could simply remount that horse and ride far away from all of them.

But that would not safeguard his future son or daughter.

Lady Northdon led him to a smaller drawing room, one with many windows and furnished with a table and chairs. The breakfast room, Edmund thought.

'I will have Cook prepare some food. Someone will bring it in a moment. Please enjoy your repast and wait for me here. I will come back for you.'

It seemed expedient to agree. 'As you wish it, *madame*.'

A few minutes later, a servant brought him a tray.

He ate the warm bread and cold meat, downed a cup of tea and waited. Finally Lady Northdon returned carrying a letter.

He stood.

'It is the permission. Signed and sealed.' She handed him the folded paper.

'*Merci, madame*.' He took the letter and slipped it into a pocket inside his coat.

She looked up at him. 'Treat my daughter well, *s'il vous plaît*.'

He met her eyes. 'You have my promise.'

She held his gaze for a moment before gesturing for him to follow her back to the hall. He assumed he was taking his leave. At least he was not leaving the house through the tradesmen's door.

On the way he asked, 'Who is Lucien?'

She paused and turned towards him. 'My son. My first son.' Her words were strained.

'Why was he spoken of today?' he persisted.

She averted her gaze. 'He was killed in a carriage accident on his way to Gretna Green.'

'I see.' Gretna Green. The village in Scotland that was close to the border and a frequent destination for hasty, unlicensed weddings. He did not ask Lady Northdon to explain further. He had no desire to cause her more pain. She'd been an ally, albeit a reluctant one. He was grateful to her for it.

She turned and continued to walk to the hall. 'Say nothing of your situation to anyone,' she said, as if they'd not just spoken of her dead son. 'We wish no one to know, not even the servants. Let them guess, if they must, but no one must know.'

'I give my word.' He never intended to speak of the reason of his marriage. Scandal was best dealt with by a closed mouth.

They reached the hall, where a footman handed him his hat and gloves. The man crossed the hall to the door ready to open it and, Edmund supposed, eject this unwanted visitor.

'Your horse will be ready for you outside,' Lady Northdon said.

He bowed to her and spoke quietly. 'Thank you for the refreshment. You did not have to be so kind.'

She shrugged. 'I am French. We expect these things to happen, no?'

He smiled inwardly. She sounded like Amelie.

Lady Northdon went on. 'Lord Northdon and I will travel to London as soon as we can arrange it. In two or three days, I expect.'

He reached out his hand. 'I will keep my promises, *madame*.'

She hesitated before accepting his handshake. *'Bon voyage, monsieur.'*

Edmund walked out the door to his waiting horse. He'd

ride to the village and take lodging in an inn there before heading back to London in the morning. After a wash up and a change of clothing, his first stop in London would be Doctors' Commons and the office of the Archbishop of Canterbury.

For the special licence.

That evening Amelie had no desire to eat, but she sat in the dining room with her sister-in-law, pushing at her food and trying to force some of it into her mouth. She and Tess had avoided each other all day. Amelie loved and esteemed Tess as if she were the sister she'd always dreamed of having. Now, though, she'd surely lost Tess's good opinion. She'd known it ever since Edmund's unexpected arrival and his quick departure with Marc.

Where were they at this moment? she wondered. Surely they'd seen her father by now. How had her father reacted? Had he given his approval?

The question consumed her mind and had done so all day.

Never had Amelie dreamed marriage would be a possibility, a way to salvage some respectability for the family after her impulsive night with Edmund. He'd rescued her again, just as he had on the streets of Brussels. Just as his lovemaking had rescued her sense of self-worth after Fowler had dashed it to the pavement.

What if her father refused his permission for the marriage, though? Would they elope to Gretna Green?

Gretna Green. The name always made her think of Lucien. Of how he died and of how her mother and father had shouted at each other afterwards.

They'd only so recently reconciled, in Brussels where Amelie's vision of her own marital happiness had been shattered. What if her problem made them fight each other again?

Her problem. Her *baby*, she meant. Babies were supposed to be happy events, were they not? How awful that hers had become a problem to get through. She glanced down at her plate, but instead saw in her arms a baby swaddled in soft blankets and Edmund smiling down at the tiny being. Her heart thrilled for a brief moment.

Was this what other women felt when they knew they were carrying a child? Was it possible or merely more of her fanciful thinking?

She glanced up at Tess, who picked at her food just as much as Amelie had. What were Tess's thoughts? Amelie dared not ask, not with the footman in the room serving the meal. Perhaps Tess was quiet because she did not want to speak with her. Perhaps Tess had a disgust of her behaviour, like Fowler had been disgusted of her. Perhaps Marc despised her as well, her brother, whom she loved with all her heart.

Tears pricked her eyes. She blinked them away.

Enough of this self-pity. She'd been bold with Edmund in Brussels, and, if nothing else, being bold had exhilarated her. She could confront Tess. Find out where she stood with her.

'I have an idea,' she spoke into the silence of the large dining room. 'Let us take our tea in Maman's sitting room. It will be so much more comfortable than the drawing room.' Where the silence would bounce off the walls.

Tess looked up. 'If you like.'

Amelie turned to the footman. 'Staines, would you bring the tea to us there?'

'Yes, miss.' He took her plate.

'And dessert, too?' She glanced over at Tess. 'Shall we have our dessert there, too?'

Tess nodded.

They left the table and walked in silence to the sitting room. Amelie busied herself lighting the candles so there was no need to talk. Staines and another footman soon brought the tea tray and the small cakes Cook had baked for dessert.

When they left, Amelie gathered her courage. 'Speak plainly to me, Tess. I fear what you must think of me.'

Tess looked at her with surprise. 'Of you? I am so angry at my brother, I cannot think of anything else. How could he do that to you? Seduce you like that. Ruin your life?'

'It was not Edmund's doing. It was mine.' Amelie took a sip of her tea. 'I wish you and Marc would understand that.'

'Nonsense.' Tess gave her a reproving look. 'We do not hold you at all responsible. You did not know what you were about, but Edmund did.'

This was too difficult to believe. Was all the blame to be borne on Edmund's shoulders?

'You must think ill of me, though.' Amelie tried again.

Tess leaned over and put a comforting hand on Amelie's. 'Not at all. I am worried for you, though. You do not look at all well. We must devise a way for you to see a physician without anyone finding out why.'

'I am a little sick to my stomach and very fatigued,' Amelie admitted. 'And I have not been able to speak a word of it. Why my maid does not question it, I cannot tell, although Sally seems very distracted these days. I do not know what is wrong with her.'

'Well, it is good that she has not guessed,' Tess responded. 'I have no doubt the servants will discover the truth, but perhaps they will keep the family's confidence. By the time you show, you should be married and perhaps no one will bother to count the months.'

No one had much bothered with her before all this. Perhaps they would not think about her and Edmund at all.

Amelie picked up one of the cakes and tried taking a little bite.

Tess went on talking. 'I did write to my sisters. They must know what Edmund has done.'

'Oh, Tess. Did you have to do that?' Now his other two sisters would be angry at him. Why could Tess not have let them think Edmund *wanted* to marry her?

'Of course they must know,' Tess said, although she sounded uncertain now. 'They are my sisters.'

Tess's older sister Lorene had married a very old man. Married him for his money, people said. Amelie had met Lord Tinmore once. He was as intimidating as he was ancient. Tess's younger sister Genna was Amelie's age. Amelie and Tess had attended some entertainments in their company. Unlike Amelie, Genna seemed to enter any party with confidence, as if she did not care a fig about whether anyone spoke to her or danced with her. She never wanted for partners.

So, in addition to everything else, Amelie would probably ruin Edmund's relationships with his sisters. He would despise her even more for it, would he not?

After leaving Doctors' Commons, Edmund walked directly to Grosvenor Street to see Amelie. Staines, the same footman who'd attended the door before, gave him entry and bade him wait in the drawing room while he went to find Amelie. This room was becoming familiar. Its arrangement of chairs, tables and sofa. The porcelain figurines on the mantelpiece. The portraits of Lord and Lady Northdon hanging on the walls.

At least the portraits were not red-faced with anger at him, nor aching with remembered pain because of him.

Amelie entered the room. She was still pale, making her blue eyes seem even larger and her hair more golden. She stole his breath.

'Edmund? You are back so soon? Is Marc with you?'

He was not about to tell her that he had been sent away alone.

'He stayed behind.' And Edmund had no idea when Glenville would return.

She merely stared at him, eyes wide in the unasked question.

'Your father gave his permission,' Edmund assured her.

She released a relieved breath, but her brow then creased in worry. 'Was it very bad for you?'

His cheek flexed. 'Not intolerable. Your mother was kind.'

Her expression softened. 'Did I not tell you she was the dearest creature?'

No use telling her of the pain his presence caused, nor the memories he had provoked. 'She was all that.'

She bit her lip. 'Are you still resolved on the matter? Because I would not fault you for withdrawing your proposal.'

It was the very thing that nagged at him—the impulse to simply vanish. 'Is that what you wish me to do?'

'I could not blame you for it,' she said. 'I have made everything miserable for you and you seem to accept it in a way I cannot.'

He raised his brows. 'So it is not what you wish?'

She did not meet his eye. 'It is the best solution. The right thing.'

Which was not precisely saying it was what she wanted. Well, it was not what he wanted either, was it?

She took a breath. 'Forgive me. You must be very fatigued. Please do sit, Edmund.'

He shook his head. 'I will not stay. I merely came to tell you that I have applied for the licence. It will take a few days. The archbishop's clerk said they must write to my parish.' More time for him to change his mind. 'But I will call upon you as soon as it is ready.'

A line formed between her eyes. 'You are welcome to call before that.'

Not by anyone else in the household, he'd wager. 'I am not so certain of that.'

'What do you mean?'

He should not have spoken. 'Your parents are returning to London. I do not think they welcome me.'

'I see.' She looked confused, however.

He took a step towards the door. 'I might as well take my leave.'

'No!' Amelie cried. 'Do not go.'

He turned, surprised she would wish him to stay.

She averted her gaze but spoke in a low, quiet voice. 'Do not leave me, Edmund. I have no one to talk to about this!'

It had not occurred to him that Amelie would want him to stay. Would she not resent the sight of him like everyone else in her family? The truth was, his emotions were still in turmoil, and this room simply could not contain them.

He stared at Amelie. 'Would you like a walk in the park?'

She smiled. 'I would!'

Soon they were strolling through Grosvenor Gate onto one of the footpaths that crossed Hyde Park. It was late afternoon, but the weather was fine. It was actually a fine day for a walk in the park and, to Edmund's surprise, the tension inside him calmed.

Because he walked with Amelie.

Much like that night in Brussels, it seemed as if they'd known each other a lifetime.

Edmund broke their silence. 'You know I fully support you talking to me.'

'What?' She looked puzzled.

'You said you wished to talk to me. You know I believe you should tell me everything.'

'Oh!' Understanding dawned on her face. 'Like the night in Brussels.' She smiled. 'You made me tell you about Fowler.'

Her smile made her even more beautiful.

'I did not make you,' he said. 'I encouraged you.'

'Encouraged me, then,' she responded.

'So talk to me now.' She was not alone, he wanted to assure her. Now, as inexplicable and as fraught with tension as it was, they belonged together.

She hesitated a moment, then her words came out in a rush. 'I—I want you to know how grateful I am that you will marry me.'

He did not deserve her gratitude, not when he'd created her problems. 'I am not certain gratitude is what you ought to be feeling.'

'No one else will believe it is my fault and that is so unfair to you. I know it is my fault.' Her voice was firm.

'Let us not return to that topic, Amelie. It does not concern me that I am held to blame.' He accepted his blame. 'What else is on your mind?' Something he could change, he hoped.

She did not speak for several steps. 'I also feel so ashamed. I only thought of myself. You thought of the baby.'

'Your situation was different than mine. It cannot compare.' He could leave and resume his life with very little consequence. She could never do that.

'I want so badly to think of the baby the way you do.' She sighed.

At times the idea of the baby struck him like a cannonball in the chest. A little life made from that sensuous night they had shared, a little person who would truly belong to him, the line of the triangle that joined him to Amelie for ever.

Because he was a bastard, his connections to family were always fractured in some way. His mother was not married to his father. His sisters were only half-sisters. But he, Amelie and the baby made a family. A proper family.

The emotions around that were too acute to be discussed.

'Perhaps if we made plans, it would help.' So much easier to talk of practicalities.

'Plans?' she asked.

'Such as where to live.'

'Oh.' She fell silent again. 'I have not thought beyond—beyond anything.'

'I had planned to return to Brussels.' Although he'd intended to remain in Brussels only a short time. He'd toyed with the prospect of seeking his fortune in the Colonies or in the new United States of America, but he would not take Amelie into such uncertainty. 'We could live quite well in Brussels.'

He felt her body stiffen. 'I must go where you wish, Edmund. I do understand that.'

But she did not want to go to Brussels. 'Speak the truth to me, Amelie.'

She took several steps before speaking in a low voice. 'I—I had hoped to remain near my mother. With the baby—'

He'd forgotten. She was so young. He must not take her from everything and everyone she loved and needed.

'Would you prefer to stay in London?' He could continue managing his investments from here in London.

'Oh, yes!' But her voice lost its excitement. 'Our town house is so small, though. There is hardly enough room for Marc and Tess.'

Edmund had no intention of living in the Northdon town house. 'We would lease rooms of our own.'

'Could we?' She smiled. 'That would be perfect!'

It would suffice.

The Serpentine came into view. They walked towards it.

The rippling water of the Serpentine, the green grass and trees added to the ease of talking together. Edmund was glad of it.

Or was it being in Amelie's company that soothed him?

She pulled on his arm. 'Look, Edmund.' They walked closer.

A nanny and two very small children, a boy and a girl, stood at the edge of the water throwing pieces of bread to a gaggle of geese who swam towards the easy food. Edmund did not know how to gauge the ages, but both looked barely out of leading strings.

The little girl threw a piece of crust and squealed with delight when the geese fought over it.

The boy pulled away from the nanny and toddled towards the grass and pulled out a clump. He held it in his little fist until he reached the water and threw it in. Half the geese swam for it, but they quickly lost interest.

The nanny dashed over to the child and brushed his hands clean.

'Is that what we will have, Edmund?' Amelie asked in wonder. 'A sweet creature like those darling children?'

The little boy turned back to grab more grass; the nanny followed.

'No. No more grass,' she admonished.

At that same moment, the little girl reached for the ducks and lost her footing.

Edmund dashed over and scooped up the child before she fell in the water.

'Oh, my goodness!' cried the nanny as she rushed over.

'No harm done,' Edmund said.

The child, oblivious of her close call, merely squirmed around and wrapped her pudgy arms around Edmund's neck.

The little girl's skin felt smooth as finest silk, and she smelled like sweetness and innocence.

Edmund glanced at Amelie.

She wore a look of wonder that perfectly mirrored his own emotions.

Soon he would be holding his own child, *their* child, a child he and Amelie created together.

His heart soared with joy.

Chapter Seven

Two days after Edmund returned to London, Marc Glenville sent word that Lord and Lady Northdon had also arrived. No invitation to the house had been included, however. That rebuff stung, like so many of the slights he'd endured his whole life. Were they trying to keep him from Amelie? If so, it was wrong. He and Amelie needed the time together. He called upon her every day.

They went out each day and visited the sights of London, places he'd never had the opportunity to see—the Tower, Westminster Abbey, the Egyptian Hall. They were easy in each other's company. That was an encouraging sign.

Her family remained an impediment. Her father avoided encountering him when he called and if her mother appeared, she acted civilly, but nothing more. Amelie avoided speaking of them.

Today Edmund would not see Amelie. Instead he would use the day to discharge several errands that needed doing. First and foremost was to check on the special licence. It had been seven days since his first visit to the office of the Archbishop of Canterbury, and he presumed they would have received the necessary information from Lincolnshire by now.

He went to Doctors' Commons first thing.

'The information has not yet arrived,' the Archbishop's clerk said in a snooty tone.

The clerk knew of Edmund's father and knew Edmund was the bastard son. No doubt that had played a major factor in the delay.

'What is the delay?' Edmund demanded.

'I am certain I cannot say,' the clerk responded. 'Come back tomorrow. Or the next day.'

No doubt the man would make no effort to discover why.

This was ridiculous.

Edmund left the office and went immediately to Bow Street. He hired a man to travel to Lincolnshire to procure the necessary documents. He ought to have done so in the first place.

From there he stopped at the Exchange to meet with the stockbroker he and Count von Osten used. The investments Edmund made had the potential of rather quick profit. He aimed to grow his funds enough in order to leave Amelie's dowry entirely untouched, and he was well on his way to achieving his goal. His guiding principle in investing was to think of what his father would have done and do the opposite. So far that strategy had worked exceedingly well.

After the Exchange he walked back to his hotel. When he entered and turned to the stairway to climb to his room, the hall servant called to him. 'Lieutenant Summerfield!'

Edmund had given up explaining that he was no longer Lieutenant Summerfield.

'There is a gentleman to see you,' the servant said. 'He awaits you in the parlour.'

The parlour was off the hall and was a place where one could receive visitors or simply sit comfortably to read or write letters. Who would call upon him except Lord North-don or Glenville? He did not relish receiving either of them.

Edmund thanked the servant, crossed the hall again and opened the parlour door.

An elderly man sat in a chair facing the door. He did not rise at Edmund's entrance but raised his brows, 'Summerfield?'

'Yes,' Edmund said uncertainly.

'I am Lord Tinmore.'

Tinmore? His sister Lorene's husband.

'Has something happened to Lorene?' Edmund asked. Why else would this man call upon him?

'My wife is in excellent health.' Tinmore acted as if Edmund's question had been an impertinence.

'I am glad to hear it,' Edmund replied, more puzzled than ever.

Tinmore flushed. 'I'll have no sarcasm, young man!'

How the devil could he have offended Lord Tinmore? He'd never seen the man before this moment.

Edmund glared. 'Are you in a position to dictate to me, sir?'

'I most certainly am!' Tinmore cried.

This was madness. Edmund attempted to stifle the animosity this man had instantly aroused in him. 'You have an advantage over me, sir.' Edmund struggled for a civil tone. 'You know why you have called upon me, and I haven't the slightest notion.'

Tinmore pursed his lips. 'A clever man might guess.'

'There you have it.' Edmund lifted his arms. 'I am not clever.'

Tinmore pointed to a chair adjacent to the throne-like one upon which he sat. 'Sit.'

Edmund had met men like Tinmore in the army. Colonels or generals, typically, consumed by their own importance. Defiance was the only way to earn their respect.

'I'll stand,' he said.

Tinmore flinched as if surprised his order had not been instantly obeyed. 'Very well, I will get to the point.'

At last, Edmund thought.

'My wife tells me you have left the army and that you have got a respectable young woman with child, Glenville's sister.'

How the devil did he know?

Tess.

Tess always told Lorene everything, even when they'd been little girls. Why did Lorene tell Tinmore, though?

Edmund straightened. 'You have not yet told me why you have called, sir.'

'Did you think I would not react to this? Leaving the army. Debauching an innocent. What have you to say for yourself?'

This was the outside of enough. Edmund took a step closer and spoke in his most menacing voice. 'I fail to see why my actions are any affair of yours.'

'Of course it is my affair!' Tinmore shot back. 'I provided you money for your captaincy, not for you to sell out and sully the reputation of the family.'

Edmund felt the blood drain from his face. 'You provided the money?'

'It was at my wife's request.' Tinmore's expression turned smug.

Lorene implied that the money had been from their late father's estate. Edmund had used these funds for his investments in Brussels, investments that had yielded immediate returns. That money had been the seed from which he would grow his fortune.

'I certainly did not provide the money for you to leave the army,' Tinmore went on. 'Now look at you, about to bring scandal to the family—'

Edmund held up a stilling hand. 'Your money will be

returned. With interest. If you would be so kind, please furnish me with the name of your man of business and I shall see it done.'

'Because of you, Lady Tinmore and I have returned to London—'

Edmund interrupted him again. 'Then I will see you receive my bank draft at your town house.' He bowed. 'That ends your involvement in my affairs. Good day, sir.'

Edmund turned and walked to the door.

'Come back here!' Tinmore called to his retreating back. 'I am not finished with you.'

Edmund was finished with him, though.

Edmund did not return to his hotel room. Instead he strode out of the hotel again and made his way swiftly to Curzon Street, asking a man on the street to direct him to Lord Tinmore's house. He trusted he could walk more swiftly than Tinmore could return either by carriage or on foot.

Edmund intended to speak with his sister before her husband returned.

He was admitted to the hall and was left waiting there until the footman announced him. Both Lorene and Genna appeared on the stairs and hurried down to greet him.

'Edmund!' Genna cried, flinging herself into his arms. 'I have been pining to see you!'

Lorene was more reserved. 'What a lovely surprise. Shall we sit in the drawing room? I'll order tea.'

'I will not stay long enough for tea,' he said. 'I need only a few minutes of your time.'

'We have a lot to ask you!' Genna said with good humour.

A lot he had no intention of answering.

The Tinmore town house was more opulent than Amelie's family's house on Grosvenor Street. They crossed a large hall to a drawing room twice the size of the North-dons'. Its furnishings were elegant, but slightly outmod-ish, remaining in the neo-classical style of a bygone era, all pale colours, Roman themes and intricate plasterwork.

As soon as they were alone in the room, away from servants, Edmund faced Lorene. 'Did the money you sent for my captaincy come from your husband?' He was too angry to mince words.

She blushed. 'Yes.'

'That and Tess's and my dowries, although he got out of paying Tess's dowry,' Genna added.

He could not focus on that statement at the moment.

'Why did you say it came from our father?' he de-manded.

'I did not say so precisely,' Lorene prevaricated. 'I said I found some money that belonged to you. I did not say that it came from Lord Tinmore.'

'It is why she married him,' Genna broke in.

'Genna!' Lorene cried.

Genna tossed her a glance. 'Well, it is. You married him because our father left us no money for dowries. You did it so we would not have to become governesses or la-dies' companions.'

Edmund swung back to Lorene. 'Were things so bad?'

Lorene, more petite and fine-boned than Genna or Tess, glared at her sister. 'It was the best decision I could make, and I think it is churlish of you to be annoyed about it!'

Edmund took her by her shoulders and turned her to-wards him. 'Why did you not tell me?' he asked in a softer voice.

She raised her eyes to him. 'What could you have done, Edmund? You could not have supported us on a lieuten-ant's pay. It barely supported you.'

If he had not devised ways to make money elsewhere, he'd have been hard-pressed to even keep his horse.

'I will return the money to Lord Tinmore,' he continued. 'So this need not be between us any more.' Nor between Lorene and her husband. Tinmore could not hold it
over her head as he'd held it over Edmund's.

'Can you afford to return it?' Lorene looked sceptical.

'Yes, I can afford it.'

'Of course he can,' Genna commented. 'Miss Glenville's dowry should be a large one.'

It was Edmund's turn to glare at Genna.

'What about that, Edmund?' Lorene asked in a scolding
tone. 'Tess wrote us about Miss Glenville. I cannot believe
you could be so shabby. She was such a pretty girl. Look
what you have done to her.'

Amelie was still pretty. Beautiful, in fact.

But he was not about to discuss this with Lorene and
Genna. 'We are to marry, yes, but her dowry has nothing
to do with my repaying Tinmore.' He kept his tone even.
'That is all I wish to say about it.'

'I just hope there is not too much talk,' Lorene said.

'Yes, how awful for the Summerfields to be the topic of
gossip and scandal,' Genna said with sarcasm.

Edmund heard a carriage outside. Luckily it did not
stop but reminded him that he intended to leave before
Tinmore returned.

'I must go,' he said.

'When will we see you again?' Genna asked.

'I do not know,' he admitted. 'Soon, perhaps.'

'I hope so.' Lorene added, 'We should talk about this
marriage, Edmund.'

Not if he had any choice in the matter. 'I will see you
are kept informed.'

'I'll walk you out.' Genna stepped forward and clutched
his arm.

Lorene followed them into the hall, where Edmund

collected his hat and gloves. Genna walked out the door with him.

'How do you and Lorene fare here?' he asked Genna as soon as they were outside.

'Under Tinmore, do you mean?' She released a breath. 'He delights in ordering everyone about, that is for certain.'

'Does he mistreat you?' If so, the man would answer to Edmund.

'Not mistreatment, not really,' she said. 'Lorene never complains about doing his bidding, and I hardly ever do as he says. I am certainly not going to marry someone just because he wishes to be rid of me as soon as possible.'

Genna. Always obstinate.

He placed a kiss on her forehead. 'You will tell me if you need me.'

She waved a dismissive hand. 'I am able to take care of myself.'

He smiled at her. 'Then tell me if Lorene needs me.'

'That I will do.'

A carriage appeared at the end of the street.

'That is Lord Tinmore's carriage,' Genna said. 'I prefer to go in before he sees me.'

He squeezed her hand. She hurried into the house, and he walked in the opposite direction of the approaching carriage. He, too, preferred that Tinmore not see him.

Amelie rested on a chair in her bedchamber, her feet on a stool. She'd managed some tea and toast. Nonsensically, on the days she'd spent in Edmund's company, the morning sickness had been barely noticeable.

Her maid, Sally, entered the room, carrying some freshly laundered, folded clothing. Sally walked slowly as if every step was an effort.

'Are you feeling unwell?' Amelie asked her.

'Just a little weary, miss,' she replied.

Poor Sally. The young soldier she'd spent time with that night in Brussels had not survived the battle. It had been very hard for her.

'Well, rest today,' Amelie told her. 'I do not require much of you.'

'Thank you, miss.'

There was a knock at her door, and Sally answered it.

Staines, the footman, appeared in the doorway. 'Miss Summerfield asks to see you, miss.'

'Miss Summerfield?' Why would Tess's sister call upon her?

Perhaps Tess was out.

Amelie did not have the energy to go down to the drawing room. 'Ask if she minds coming up here and show her up.'

'Very good, miss,' Staines said.

'And send up some tea?'

He nodded.

'Do you need me, miss?' Sally asked.

Amelie gave her a reassuring smile. 'Not at all. Tell anyone who questions you that I ordered you to rest. '

'Thank you, miss.'

Sally slipped out of Miss Glenville's room and wearily climbed the stairs to the small attic room she shared with Mrs Glenville's maid. She took off her shoes, sat down on her cot and buried her head in her hands.

What was she to do?

She touched her belly. There was no question now. She had Calvin's baby inside her. All that was left of him. His body had lain among the dead on the Waterloo battlefield. She could not bear to think of it.

He hadn't meant to abandon her. That night before he left for the battle he promised to marry her, but now he was gone.

What was she to do?

Lady Northdon would sack her, she was certain. The only family she had left was her sister, and she was in service, too, not in any position to help. Calvin had a cousin somewhere, but why would Calvin's cousin take her in, even if he believed that she carried Calvin's child?

She lay her head on her pillow and tried to slow her racing heart. Sometimes she could not even breathe she was in such a panic about what would happen to her and her baby. Would she be forced to take the baby to the Foundling Hospital? To abandon all that was left of Calvin? How could she bear to do that? But how could she live with the baby? She would lose her position here, and who would hire a ladies' maid with a bastard child?

Staines knocked on Amelie's door and announced Miss Summerfield.

'Hello, Miss Glenville!' Miss Summerfield breezed in, taking off her hat as she walked in the room. 'I am so delighted you are at home.'

'Did you want to see Tess? Is she out?' Amelie assumed that Tess was Miss Summerfield's first choice to visit.

'No!' she said cheerfully. 'I came to see you!' She lowered herself into a nearby chair.

By appearance Amelie and Miss Summerfield could be sisters, both blonde haired and blue-eyed. Genna was a bit taller and her figure more lithesome, but they looked more like each other than Miss Summerfield looked like her sisters. Amelie and Tess had accompanied her and Lady Tinmore to some society entertainments last Season, but Amelie still felt as though she hardly knew her.

'How are you?' Miss Summerfield gave her a significant look.

She *knew*. Tess said she'd written to her sisters. Must

Amelie talk about it to this young woman? She was nearly a stranger. 'I am well, thank you. And you?'

'Come now! None of that. You know I know my brother has got you with child. I cannot believe it of him, but there it is.' She took a breath. 'I came to let you know that I am an ally. I presumed you might need a friend at such a time.'

Once Amelie would have melted with gratitude at such an invitation for friendship, but her trust was hard-won now. Even Tess could not be entirely trusted.

She proceeded cautiously. 'That is very kind of you, Miss Summerfield.'

The young woman smiled. 'Oh, call me Genna. We are so connected now through brothers and sisters that we might as well be sisters ourselves. Shall I call you Amelie?'

'If you like.'

Throughout most of Amelie's growing up, including the very unhappy year she spent at school, others her age had stayed away from her. She was certain it was because of the stories about her mother—a commoner with family in France active in the Terror. Amelie's mother and father thought she did not know of this, but there had been other girls only too eager to inform her precisely who her French relations were and where their names had appeared in old French newspapers.

Only last spring, in her first Season, had Amelie thought she'd begun to make friends. When Fowler began courting her, she was certain she'd finally been accepted for herself.

How foolish she'd been.

The tea came and Miss Summerfield busied herself with the pouring of it. She handed Amelie a cup of tea and a biscuit. Amelie's stomach roiled at the smell of the tea at first, but the sensation passed. She was grateful. She did not desire to vomit all over Edmund's youngest sister.

What errands kept Edmund away today? she wondered.

Spending time with him these last few days had made her feel almost happy.

'So.' Genna took her first sip. 'What are the wedding plans? Edmund has told us nothing about it.'

Amelie glanced up at her. 'You saw Edmund?'

Genna nodded. 'He called upon us this morning. Upon Lorene and me. Not Lord Tinmore.' She spoke that man's name with the same disdain as Tess and Marc always did. 'But he would not tell us a thing. He came only to talk about money, the money Lord Tinmore gave him that he says he will give back.' She took another sip of tea. 'In any event, he did not stay long enough to tell us *anything*. I would love to help you with the wedding, you know. I could help you choose your bride clothes.'

'Bride clothes?' Amelie had not even thought of bride clothes. 'I am sure I have some gown that will suit.'

'Oh, no! You must have something new. A beautiful dress to be married in! Otherwise, people will think you do not care very much about marrying.'

Amelie certainly wanted to minimise the gossip that would occur. Even so, purchasing a bride dress seemed very unimportant. Even her mother, who prided herself on being *au courant* in fashion, had not mentioned a dress. Who would know, after all? It was not likely anyone outside the family would attend the wedding.

'Does not Tess have a maid who designs gowns?' Genna asked. 'Why not let her make you a bride dress?'

'Nancy is now apprenticed to my mother's modiste, Madame LeClaire,' Amelie said.

'Well, we should go there and have them make you a pretty dress!' Genna clapped her hands together. 'Shall we go tomorrow morning?'

Edmund would be checking on the special licence then, he'd told her, but she did not want to provide even that much information to Genna.

Amelie remembered Tess's wedding, how Tess and Marc had gazed at each other, how beautiful Tess had appeared in the gown Nancy made for her. Amelie could not hope to receive a loving glance from Edmund, but she could at least try to look her best.

'We can go to Madame LeClaire's tomorrow,' Amelie said.

'Excellent!' Genna jumped to her feet and gave Amelie a quick hug. 'I am so delighted! I think someone in my family must treat you well, since my brother certainly did not.'

'It was not your brother's doing,' Amelie said.

Genna's eyes grew wide. 'Do you mean he is not the father?'

'No. No.' She meant only to defend him. *She* was to blame. 'Edmund is the father, but it is not his fault about all this. It is mine.'

Genna gave her the same look of scepticism that Tess had given her when she attempted to accept the blame for what had happened between her and Edmund. 'I am certain Edmund knew precisely what he was doing.'

Amelie sighed.

Something seemed to catch Genna's eye and she rose to look out the window. 'Oh, no.'

'What is it?'

'What is he doing here?' Genna asked, but spoke to herself.

'Who?' Amelie asked.

'Lord Tinmore.'

Chapter Eight

Edmund opened the sealed note that had been delivered to him early the next morning.

An invitation.

To dine at the home of Lord and Lady Northdon, Amelie's parents.

He blew out a breath. What had precipitated this?

He supposed he owed them a visit to apprise them of the status of the special licence, although he would have told Amelie today when he saw her.

He would attend, of course, even though Amelie's was the only company he did not dread.

He'd send a message accepting the invitation and then go to his bank to arrange his repayment to Tinmore.

He wrote out his response and walked down to the hall to find a servant to arrange for its delivery.

'Another message arrived for you,' the man said.

Edmund opened it.

It was from Amelie, saying she would not be at home if he planned to call. Instead she would be at the dressmakers with his sister Genna.

With Genna?

That evening Edmund started out early because waiting in his hotel room seemed a waste of time. He strolled down

Bond Street, gazing in the shop windows and stopped in front of Trelegon & Co., Jewellers.

Why not?

He entered the shop.

'May I be of assistance, sir?' the clerk asked.

'I am in need of a gift,' Edmund said. 'And a wedding ring.'

He left the shop twenty minutes later, now late for the dinner on Grosvenor Street. At least the package in his pocket made the delay worth it.

He was admitted to the Northdon town house and announced by the butler, who had been attending the hall. He entered the drawing room, ready to make his apology for being late.

Instead he stopped in his tracks.

He'd not been told there would be guests.

Lord Tinmore, Lorene and Genna were there, seated with Lord and Lady Northdon, Glenville, Tess and Amelie.

'Well this is a surprise,' he said without enthusiasm. He turned his gaze on Amelie, who was the only one in the room who did not look as if a snake had just slithered into the gathering.

'How are you, Amelie?' he asked.

'I am well, Edmund.'

But she was paler than the last time he'd seen her, when they'd walked through Bullock's Egyptian Hall, gazing at the curiosities Captain Cook brought back from the South Seas and the displays of African beasts.

Lord Tinmore waved his hand as if ordering Edmund to approach him. 'I am certain you will agree that a family meeting was in order,'

Edmund stood his ground. 'I do not agree at all, but I see that is what has been manipulated.'

Tinmore was behind this. Lord Northdon would certainly not have desired a *family meeting*.

Amelie rose from her chair and walked over to a table with a wine decanter and glasses. 'Shall I pour you some claret?'

'Please,' he responded.

'What is the news of the special licence?' Lord Northdon demanded as if Edmund had wilfully withheld that information.

Edmund answered as civilly as he could muster. 'I checked at Doctors' Commons today, but there has been no word from my home parish as yet.'

'And you simply left it at that?' Tinmore sniffed. 'A gentleman must be a man of action if he is worth any salt at all.'

Amelie deserved to hear about the licence, and, Edmund supposed, her parents had a right to know, but it was none of Lord Tinmore's affair.

Edmund took a sip of his claret before facing Tinmore. 'I am not quite certain where to locate the insult in your words, sir. Are you accusing me of not being a gentleman? Or of not being a man of action? Or, perhaps, you merely wish to make the point that I am not worth my salt.'

'Impertinent puppy,' Lord Tinmore grumbled.

Edmund ignored him and spoke to Amelie as if only she were in the room. 'I hired a man to go to my old parish to see about the delay.'

A tense silence came over the room. Edmund did not care if his resentment of Tinmore was the cause. Except on Amelie's behalf. She did not deserve this *family meeting*.

Luckily the butler came to announce dinner.

Amelie expelled a relieved breath when Matheson announced dinner. How much ruder could these people be to Edmund? Her own family and his?

No one had even greeted him.

Her mother and Lord Tinmore led the procession to the dining room.

What a disagreeable man Lord Tinmore was. He offered his arm to her mother without even looking at her. He'd not spoken more than two words to her. Her father escorted Lady Tinmore and Marc, Tess.

Edmund glanced at both Amelie and Genna and offered them each an arm. 'Ladies?'

As they walked to the dining room, Genna spoke to Edmund in a low voice. 'Don't antagonise Tinmore. Let him think he's ordering you around but then do whatever you like.'

'Is that what you do, Genna?' Edmund responded.

'Yes. It is,' she admitted.

Amelie disagreed. She'd thought it rather admirable that Edmund had stood up to such a formidable man.

In the dining room, her mother had deviated slightly from the standard tradition of seating everyone by precedence. She'd placed Lord Tinmore at her father's right and Lady Tinmore at his left. Unfortunately Amelie was seated on the other side of Lord Tinmore. Edmund sat across from her between Lady Tinmore and Tess. Genna and Marc were on the same side of the table as Amelie.

The deadly silence was broken by Lady Tinmore admiring the table setting. This led to a general discussion by the ladies of what was the latest fashion in dinner service.

When the soup was served, Lord Tinmore took a loud sip that seemed to echo though the room. He conversed with her father exclusively, except for an occasional remark to his wife. Edmund attended to his food and nothing else.

Amelie could not help looking at him. She could make the excuse that he was seated across from her, so she had little choice but to look at him, but to her he seemed the only important person in the room. Though he did not show any discomfort for it, she thought it shabby that he was not included in the conversation.

Of course, she was not talking either.

Genna finally turned to her. 'What did you think of Nancy's idea for a bride dress?'

The two young women had spent the morning with fashion prints and fabric swatches. Tess's former maid, now dressmaker, had taken over the design of the dress.

'It was lovely, but I fear it would take too much time,' Amelie replied.

'Did Madame LeClaire approve of the design?' Amelie's mother asked.

Madame LeClaire made all of Amelie's mother's gowns. In some ways she was the closest thing to a friend her mother possessed. They'd known each other as young girls in France.

'She was impressed,' Genna answered. 'Nancy is so very talented. She designed the dresses Lorene and I are wearing tonight.'

Marc asked questions about the apprenticeship agreement between Nancy and Madame LeClaire. More women were coming to Madame LeClaire's for Nancy's designs.

'Has the business grown?' he asked.

'Madame is thinking of expanding to the house next door. They've hired new seamstresses and they are running out of space,' Genna replied.

Lord Tinmore raised his voice. 'What is all this talk about dresses?'

Tess replied, 'Amelie and Genna visited Lady Northdon's modiste. We were discussing her business.'

Tinmore's brows rose, and his tone turned indignant. 'You were discussing *trade*?'

Amelie shot a glance to her mother, who had been the daughter of a tradesman, a linen draper, one of the trades that supplied dressmakers. Her mother's lips thinned, but she sat up straighter and lifted her chin. Amelie glanced to her father next. His eyes flashed with anger.

Lady Tinmore tried to smooth over the moment. 'Tess's maid recently became a partner to Lady Northdon's modiste.'

Tinmore swung back to his wife. 'Talking about servants? Not proper dinner conversation, my dear.'

The room fell silent as the tension banked.

Edmund took a sip of wine and set down his glass.

'Well, it is a family party,' he said, ever so casually. 'Why should the family not discuss what interests them? Besides, to ladies, dressmaking is not simply a trade; it is a collection of other people whose lives they care about. Servants. Dressmakers. Seamstresses.'

Amelie gaped at him. It struck her. *Struck her.* Like a lightning bolt from the sky, like an arrow piercing her heart.

Edmund was unlike any man she'd ever known. He was strong. And kind. And stepped up to whatever situation was placed before him.

No other man at the table confronted Lord Tinmore when he'd spoken so cruelly. Only Edmund. Edmund had defended all of the women at the table. Especially Amelie's mother. Tinmore's insult had been intended to hurt her, Amelie was convinced.

Her heart beat faster. It was hard to breathe. Even harder to look at him now.

But harder to look away.

Lord Tinmore sputtered. 'You dare to instruct the rest of us?'

Edmund looked from one sister to another and smiled. 'I come by my expertise honestly...by having grown up with three very excellent teachers!'

He was glorious!

Amelie glanced around the table. Did they not all think

Edmund was magnificent? Their expressions looked strained.

Finally her brother spoke. 'Shall we drop this topic of conversation?'

Lady Tinmore turned to Amelie's mother. 'These potatoes are delicious. They are cooked with rosemary, are they not? You have such a fine cook.'

Amelie's mother was not so ready to pretend those words had not been spoken. She answered in a tight voice, 'Thank you.'

Amelie stared at Edmund, who had returned to his food. He glanced up and caught her looking at him but cast his gaze back to his plate.

Amelie's father quickly signalled for the final course, the dessert. At least dessert gave them all more food to discuss. Tinmore surveyed the room and then again confined his conversation to her father, as if secure that everyone else was conversing properly. Her father's response to Tinmore, though, had turned more dutiful than cordial.

When dessert was finished, Tinmore tapped his knife against his wine glass. The crystal rang like a bell. Everyone glanced at him in surprise.

What now? Amelie thought.

Tinmore raised his voice. 'Before the ladies retire to the drawing room, we should discuss the wedding that has been foisted upon us.'

'No!' Edmund spoke slowly and emphatically. 'We will not discuss the wedding.'

Tinmore was undaunted. 'We must discuss how to limit the inevitable scandal. I want none of this shabby affair to reflect negatively on my wife.'

Lady Tinmore blanched. 'My lord!'

Amelie cleared her throat and made her voice strong. 'You have no right to call it a shabby affair!'

'Yes,' her father added in a milder, more tentative tone. 'We have the matter in hand. No need to discuss it.'

Tinmore leaned back. 'Well, as long as you give me your assurance that my wife's name will be kept out of the gossip...'

How could anyone assure him of what other people might do?

He nodded officiously. 'The ladies may retire, then.'

The others exchanged glances. Tinmore was a guest, not the host or hostess of this party. Amelie and the others looked to her father. All except Edmund.

Her father nodded.

The ladies rose to leave the room. As they were walking out the door, Amelie turned to see Edmund stand, as well.

'I must take my leave,' he said.

'You will do nothing of the sort!' Tinmore said.

Edmund glanced towards Amelie's father. 'I will call upon you tomorrow, sir, if that is agreeable.'

Her father nodded.

The dining room was across the hall from the drawing room, but the other ladies, who'd heard Edmund, hung about in the hall. Amelie stood just outside the dining room door.

Edmund walked out, one of the footmen behind him. The footman closed the dining-room door and waited to attend him.

Edmund spoke to him. 'Would you bring my hat and gloves, please?'

The footman bowed and went to do his bidding.

Lady Tinmore came up to Edmund. 'Why are you being so difficult?'

'Me, difficult? Your husband was insulting, rude and meddling, and I was not inclined to stand for it.' Edmund responded. 'Tinmore is nothing to me. I paid back his money. He has no say in what I do.'

What money? Amelie wondered.

He turned to her mother. 'I would like a few moments alone with Amelie, ma'am.'

Her mother nodded.

'We can go to the library,' Amelie said, her heart beating faster. She would be alone with him.

It was behind the drawing room and still had a lamp burning and a fire lit.

Edmund remained near the doorway. 'I should not remain very long.'

Amelie stood near him, near enough to inhale his scent, which had now become familiar to her. 'You wished to speak with me?' What she wanted to say was that he was magnificent! That she was so very grateful to him for defending her mother. That she was proud to be marrying such a man.

But she said none of that.

He reached into his pocket and pulled out a small velvet box. 'I've been remiss. You should have a gift. A betrothal gift. Forgive me for not thinking of it sooner.'

He handed her the box. She opened it and found a gold ring with a lovely sapphire surrounded by tiny pearls. Her hand shook. 'It is lovely, Edmund.'

He took the ring from the box and put it on her finger. 'Good. It fits. I was assured by the jeweller that it could be made the proper size if it did not.'

She lifted her eyes to his. 'Thank you.'

His gaze softened. 'I should leave. I will call upon your father tomorrow.'

'My father?' It seemed he'd been avoiding her father all week. Of course, she could not blame him. Her father was being impossibly churlish.

'Your father has a right to speak about the wedding with me.' His voice turned hard. 'Tinmore does not.'

Now. Now she could tell him how thrilled she'd been by his defiance of that detestable man.

'I will walk out with you,' she said instead.

When they reached the hall, the footman gave Edmund his things. Edmund turned to Amelie and took her hand. 'Goodnight,' he said, squeezing her fingers.

Before she could think of how to say goodbye to him, he'd walked out the door.

Edmund hurried away from Grosvenor Street and the unpleasantness he'd just endured. Curse Tinmore. And curse his father for losing his fortune and leaving his sisters in such a desperate condition. Lorene was correct. Edmund could not have helped them, not when he was still in the army, but now he could. He was determined to make his fortune by any means offered him.

Except he never, ever considered that he'd make his fortune by marrying a wealthy viscount's daughter.

He did not want Lord Northdon's money. He'd stand on his own. It was all he'd ever wanted. To make his way in the world, no matter his disreputable birth. He thought he'd achieve his fortune in Brussels or some other part of the world, but he could manage it in London.

He made his way to Covent Garden, a place he felt more at home than Mayfair. He found his way to Rose Street and walked in to the Coopers Arms tavern.

The Coopers Arms was dark, crowded and noisy, filled with workmen, clerks, soldiers in uniform and the occasional gentleman. Plenty of brightly dressed women adorned the place, no doubt women of the town hoping to lure a man above the stairs. The clinking of glass, the smell of hops and gin and sweat enveloped him as he made his way through the room, looking for a table where he could drink in private.

'Summerfield!' A red-coated officer called his name.

Edmund looked closer. 'Upton?' Upton had served with him at Waterloo. In fact, it had been Upton who'd told him Tess had been in Brussels.

'Come! Sit with me!' Upton was at a small table alone.

Edmund joined him. 'What the devil are you doing in London? Is not the regiment still in Paris?'

Upton signalled the tavern maid to come to the table. 'They are. I had to come home.'

The maid approached. Upton lifted his tankard. 'More ale.' He turned to Edmund. 'You?'

'Ale,' he told the woman.

Upton continued. 'M'father died.'

'I am sorry to hear it,' Edmund said.

Upton sounded as if he'd had plenty of ale already. 'M'brother is such a loose screw, m'mother wants me to stay. Must sell out. Do not want to.' He peered at Edmund. 'Where is your uniform?'

'I sold out.' Edmund said. 'Without the war, the army offers no opportunities.'

'You sold out?'

'I did.'

'I'll be damned.' Upton waved a finger, which finally pointed to Edmund's leg. 'How's the injury?'

'Healed.'

'Good.' Upton drained his tankard.

Edmund had been drinking with Upton and others that last night in Brussels. Perhaps he'd consumed too much ale that night. What if he hadn't…?

The maid brought the ale, and Edmund drank thirstily. It tasted better than the wine at Lord Northdon's dinner.

Upton raised his tankard. 'Here's to the 28th!'

Edmund tapped his tankard against Upton's. 'To the 28th.'

'What'll you do now?' Upton asked. 'Now that our days of glory are at an end?'

Edmund leaned closer to his friend. 'I'm going to be married.'

'Married?' Upton's voice rose. 'Noooo. Not you. What of all that talk about seeking your fortune?'

Edmund stared into his drink. 'I'll still find my fortune.'

'I thought you would stay in the army or go to India or something,' Upton said.

Edmund shrugged and took another sip.

'Who are you marrying, then?' Upton asked.

There was no reason not to say. 'Miss Glenville, Lord Northdon's daughter.'

'Northdon?' Upton's brow creased in thought. 'Oh, I know Northdon. Married to the Jacobin commoner.'

It was an unkind way to refer to Lady Northdon.

'Met his son in Brussels.' Upton's eyes widened, as though something had struck his mind. 'Hey. Your sister is married to him. Told you about her. Where she was.' He poured a great deal of the contents of his tankard into his mouth, then gaped at Edmund. 'Do not say you are marrying that beauty! That golden-haired angel?'

'Miss Glenville. Yes.' He did not know what else to say about her.

'I'll be damned. That beauty?' Upton shook his head. 'I'll wager she has money, too. Big dowry. How the devil did you manage that?'

Yes, he should be thought lucky. Beauty and wealth were to be desired in a wife, were they not? But what about Amelie?

He certainly was nothing a woman desired in a husband.

The next morning, before calling upon Lord Northdon, the man Edmund hired to travel to his home parish found him at his hotel.

The man handed him a packet. 'Here it is.'

Edmund was stunned. 'You've only had two days.'

'I was lucky with the mail coaches,' the man said.

Lucky? He must have spent most of the two days in coaches.

He pointed to the packet. 'It is all there, the vicar said. He also sent his best wishes.'

The vicar at Yardney had always been kind to him. In a pitying manner.

Edmund lifted his hand. 'Wait a moment.' He went into the bedchamber and came out with an extra guinea. He placed it in the man's palm. 'You did well. I am grateful.'

The man grinned. 'Thank you, sir. If you ever need another service—'

'I will seek you out,' Edmund said. 'And I will recommend you.'

After the man left, Edmund brought the packet directly to Doctors' Commons and the office of the Archbishop. He handed it to the clerk, who pursed his lips as he unsealed it.

'That is the information you require, is it not?' Edmund demanded.

The man lifted his chin so that he looked at Edmund through spectacles worn low on his nose. 'It appears to be so.'

'The Archbishop is here today, is he not?'

'He is,' the clerk admitted.

Edmund folded his arms across his chest. 'Then I will wait here until you hand me the special licence.'

Not an hour went by before the clerk placed the required document in Edmund's hands.

Edmund walked from the Archbishop's office to Grosvenor Street to call upon Amelie's father. He was escorted to the library, where Lord Northdon and his son appeared to be waiting for him with their typical expressions of displeasure.

'Good morning.' Edmund bowed.

He'd be polite even if they would not.

Lord Northdon nodded to him. 'First let me tell you that I found Lord Tinmore's manners most offensive last evening.'

That might have been the most civil statement Amelie's father had ever spoken to him.

He went on. 'Had I known he would act in such a reprehensible way, I would not have agreed to the dinner.'

'Had I known Tinmore had engineered the encounter, I would have declined your invitation,' Edmund said. 'Even at the risk of offending you, sir.'

Glenville spoke up. 'I have no fondness for the man.'

'Yes, he is most unpleasant,' Lord Northdon agreed. 'But I must work with him in Lords, so I must watch my tongue.'

'I have no such restraints.' Edmund paused a moment before continuing. 'But be clear about this. Tinmore is no relation of mine. He is married to my sister, but that does not make him my relation.' Edmund would change that if he could. 'Tinmore has no part—no say—in my marriage to Amelie or in anything I do.'

He thought Glenville gave him an approving look. It was fleeting, however.

'That is another thing.' Lord Northdon went on without any apparent acknowledgement of Edmund's words. 'Why is the special licence taking so long? I think we might all agree that the sooner you marry the better.' Northdon glanced away. 'Not that I wish for this marriage. Tinmore suggested we send Amelie away for a year and foster the child out to someone, but she would not hear of it.'

Tinmore thought he could decide what was to be done with the baby? That was the outside of enough.

Edmund glared at Lord Northdon. 'The baby is mine and will have my name.'

'Well, that is what Amelie wishes, so it must be.' Lord Northdon sighed.

'It is for the best that Amelie and Edmund marry, Papa,' Glenville said. 'You know that.'

Support from Amelie's brother?

'Enough discussion.' Edmund pulled the paper from his pocket. 'I have the licence. The wedding can take place today, if a clergyman can be found to perform it.'

'We know someone who might officiate.' Glenville looked relieved. 'The clergyman who married Tess and me.'

Edmund nodded. 'I want the wedding to be as Amelie wishes.'

'It will be,' Glenville said. 'I will make certain you are informed of all the details.'

'There should be nothing required of you except to show up,' Northdon said, his tone dismissive.

'What of the marriage-settlement papers, sir?' Edmund asked.

Northdon's face turned red with anger. 'Yes. I comprehend you would be very interested in the marriage settlement.'

'I am,' Edmund said, trying not to display his own anger. 'I want them drawn up so Amelie retains control of her dowry, not I.'

Northdon's mouth opened in surprise. 'What?'

'I can support Amelie and our child,' Edmund said. 'I know what people will say of my marrying her, but I want you to know I am not marrying her for her money. I want Amelie to know that, as well.'

'I do not believe you,' Northdon said.

'Have the papers drawn up the way I wish, and I will sign them.'

There was nothing more to say. Edmund turned and strode from the room.

Chapter Nine

Two days later, Amelie woke feeling sicker than ever. She thought the morning sickness was easing, but it seemed to have returned threefold. And on her wedding day, as well. At least beginning her day by vomiting saved her from any fanciful illusions. She was marrying for one reason only. She was pregnant and there was no other choice.

Amelie had once had romantic dreams of a wedding day. Not grand romantic dreams. She'd never expected anything more than the small family wedding Marc and Tess had, but she'd dreamed about the beauty of the words spoken in the ceremony. She'd dreamed about happiness, her family's happiness about her marriage, the happiness she would feel in her heart and see in the eyes of her groom.

Instead, her family acted as if this were her funeral, and she could not even keep toast and tea in her stomach.

What would she see in Edmund's eyes? She feared that would be the worst of all.

Sally was little help in the preparations. Amelie worried about her, but Sally evaded her concern.

Nancy, Tess's former maid, now dressmaker, came to help with the gown and Amelie's hair.

'I am so sorry we could not complete the gown we planned,' Nancy said.

'It does not matter,' Amelie said.

This dress was one Nancy altered from a very plain pale blue silk Amelie had in her wardrobe. Nancy had quickly embellished the gown with an overdress of white net and with white lace at the sleeves and the hem.

'I am pleased with this dress,' Amelie told her.

At least the dress was light as air, making it easy for her to move. This day also saw a return of her fatigue. Moving was an effort, when all her body wished to do was sleep.

There was a knock on the door and Tess entered. 'How are you faring?'

Tess tried to be cheerful, but her eyes looked strained. Tess blamed herself for Amelie's situation, because Tess had introduced her brother to her. Amelie could not convince Tess that the real blame was solely Amelie's.

She could not convince anyone of that. Except herself.

'We are doing splendidly,' Nancy answered in seeming good cheer, although how she could miss the morose mood in the house was beyond Amelie.

A moment later, Amelie's mother walked in. 'All is in order downstairs,' she reported, although Amelie had not given those preparations a thought.

'Is my brother here yet?' Tess asked worriedly.

'Not yet.' Her mother pressed her lips together.

Amelie stared down at her sapphire ring. The blue gem caught sunlight from the window and glowed with blue light.

Edmund would come, she knew. Edmund was honourable that way.

Edmund made his way up Bond Street, as busy as usual with people entering and leaving shops, hurrying to appointments or simply sauntering leisurely on the pavement. This was no ordinary day for him, though, his wedding day.

This would be the day he and Amelie would forge their

own life together separate from her parents, her brother and his sisters.

A family of his own.

He'd endure the Northdons' animosity towards him for a family of his own. He'd even put up with his sisters' disappointment in him. He and Amelie—and the baby—had a chance for happiness.

He arrived at the Northdon town house and was admitted by the footman he now could address by name. 'Good morning, Staines.'

'Good morning, sir,' Staines replied, his expression neutral.

What did Staines know about him? Edmund wondered. Surely the servants knew that Amelie's family was not happy about this marriage. He'd bet they knew all about his birth. For Amelie's sake, he hoped they did not know about her pregnancy. He hoped she'd be spared that scandal.

Tess walked down the stairs as he entered the hall.

'There you are!' Her face was pinched. 'I was beginning to worry.'

He was still in her black books, obviously. 'Did you think I would not show up?'

She gave him a frank look. 'I wondered.'

There was another knock on the door.

'Am I late?' It was Genna. 'I rushed all the way here.'

Edmund had not expected her. 'You were invited, then?'

Genna grinned. 'I would have come even if I had not been invited.'

Edmund kissed her on the cheek.

'Do not worry.' Genna handed her shawl and gloves to Staines. 'Lord Tinmore will not attend. That means Lorene won't come, though.'

'I am sorry about Lorene. Not about Tinmore.' Lord Tinmore was the last person he wished to witness his marriage.

Tess crossed the hall and gave her sister a hug. 'How pretty you look.'

Genna opened her arms and displayed her dress. 'It is one of Nancy's designs.'

'Come,' Tess said. 'We should go to the drawing room.'

Edmund was glad to walk into that room with his sisters. They might still be angry at him, but they supported him.

As they crossed the threshold, Tess called out, 'Edmund is here.'

The room had been rearranged for the ceremony, furniture moved out of the way to provide a sort of aisle leading to where the clergyman stood and where, presumably, he was to stand. Glenville and Lord Northdon were conversing with the clergyman.

Glenville approached Edmund and extended his hand. 'Good morning, Edmund.'

At least Glenville was being cordial.

Edmund accepted the handshake. 'Glenville.'

Glenville turned to Genna. 'Good to see you, Genna.'

She returned a wan smile. 'I would not wish to be anywhere else.'

He glanced back at the clergyman. 'I'll introduce you, Edmund.'

Glenville presented him to Reverend Cane. 'Reverend Cane performed the ceremony for Tess and me.'

'And I am happy to be here again.' Reverend Cane smiled. He had a kind face and looked Edmund directly in the eye.

'Thank you for being available.' Edmund glanced at Lord Northdon, who stood next to the reverend. 'Good morning, sir,'

'Morning.' Northdon looked at Edmund as if he were the wolf at the sheep's door.

Edmund wished he could convince Northdon he intended to be a good husband to Amelie. He hoped she would not regret marrying him.

Lady Northdon entered the room. Her worried look disappeared when she caught sight of Edmund, but she certainly did not break into a smile. 'Good. You are here. Amelie is ready.' She turned to Tess. '*Chérie*, would you tell Staines to ask the servants to come in and let Amelie know we may proceed?'

'Of course.' Tess hurried out of the room.

Lady Northdon greeted Genna and chatted with her.

A few minutes later the servants filed in and stood against the walls. It seemed to Edmund that no one expected a joyous occasion.

And then the door opened and Amelie appeared.

Edmund was reminded of that night in Brussels when she had appeared ethereal, an angel in the midst of chaos. She was even more beautiful today, with a gown that seemed to shimmer around her. Her hair was loosely dressed with a crown of fresh flowers. She resembled a mythical woodland creature.

Even better, she walked tall, head held high.

Well done, Amelie, he thought.

Where were the flowers?

When the door to the drawing room opened, Amelie saw how few there were. Her mother had filled the room with flowers when Marc and Tess were married. Today there were but two big vases on two of the tables.

The gloomy mood of the room threatened to suffocate her. She took a deep breath and looked up.

Edmund gazed at her, not with the frown visible on the faces of her family and his sisters, not with the carefully neutral expressions of the servants, but with an admiring gleam.

It was enough.

She straightened her spine and walked towards him, keeping her eyes on only him.

When she came to stand beside him, he reached over and took her hand. His skin was warm and comforting, and she knew then that she was not alone. She did not know what their future held, but at this moment they were together.

Reverend Cane smiled at her and looked from her to Edmund and back again. 'Ready?' he mouthed.

She and Edmund nodded.

'Dearly beloved,' he began. 'We are gathered together here in the sight of God, and in the face of this congregation, to join together this Man and this Woman in holy Matrimony....'

That one reckless act now bound them together. That and the baby growing inside her, the baby created that night. With Edmund's hand holding hers, though, she could not regret any of it.

Reverend Cane continued. He spoke the words as if it were only Amelie and Edmund in the room, as if the words had been created just for them and not over decades and decades of nuptials.

He turned to Edmund. 'Wilt thou have this Woman to thy wedded Wife, to live together after God's ordinance in the holy estate of Matrimony? Wilt thou love her, comfort her, honour and keep her in sickness and in health; and, forsaking all other, keep thee only unto her, so long as ye both shall live?'

Edmund looked into Amelie's eyes. 'I will.'

Of course he would say yes. He was honourable and kind.

The reverend directed his gaze at Amelie. It would be her turn to decide.

'Wilt thou have this Man to thy wedded Husband, to live together after God's ordinance in the holy estate of

Matrimony? Wilt thou obey him and serve him, love, honour and keep him in sickness and in health; and, forsaking all other, keep thee only unto him, so long as ye both shall live?'

She answered, 'I will.'

A wave of nausea swept over her, and she lost the words that Edmund repeated when making his vows. She heard nothing past, 'I, Edward, take thee, Amelie…'

She fought through the sensation, knowing her vows came next, and she was able to repeat them in a clear but trembling voice.

When she had finished, Edmund reached into his pocket and handed the reverend a ring. Reverend Cane gave it back to him, having him say, 'With this ring I thee wed, and with all my worldly goods I thee endow…'

Edmund placed the ring on her finger. It was a gold band with a circle of blue sapphires all around it. She glanced up at him. It was beautiful. Something special. A worldly good that he'd taken some trouble to purchase for her.

Reverend Cane said more prayers and then placed their right hands together. 'Those that God hath joined together, let no man put asunder.'

At the end, the clergyman lowered his voice and spoke with more intensity. 'I pronounce that they be Man and Wife together.'

He finished with the blessing in the same manner, as if he were instructing them that they would be able to manage a marriage together.

And then it was over.

She was married. Her reputation would be rescued. With any luck, no one would guess that the baby was conceived before this date.

She glanced up at Edmund. He took her hand again and smiled at her.

* * *

After the ceremony, there was cake and punch for the servants, just as there had been at Marc and Tess's wedding. There were congratulations from servants Amelie had known her entire life. She introduced the servants to Edmund. He spoke to each one of them in a personal way, not annoyed like some people become when they must interact with their inferiors. Another thing about him that pleased her. Many of these people were very dear to her.

Still, there was a restraint that had not been in this room when the previous wedding took place. The servants, no doubt, had caught the mood from her parents.

Her maid, Sally, was the last to come shake her hand. 'Best wishes, miss.' Sally almost choked on the words, and her eyes filled with tears.

'Thank you, Sally.' Amelie almost burst into tears herself, although she did not know why either of them should be weeping. 'Allow me to present you to my husband, Mr Summerfield.'

Sally looked at him quizzically. 'How do, sir.' She curtsied.

Did she remember him from Brussels?

Edmund offered Sally his hand to shake. 'You've made Miss Glenville look very beautiful today.'

He thought her beautiful? Amelie turned warm inside.

'Wasn't me, sir. T'was Nancy.' Sally walked away.

'You met Nancy,' Amelie reminded him. 'She made my gown. She used to be Tess's maid.'

'I remember,' he said, standing very close to her. He smiled. 'But I forgot to call you Mrs Summerfield.'

She felt her face flush at his nearness. 'I forgot, too.'

The servants left the room and returned to their duties. Marc, Tess and Genna walked up to them.

'It was a lovely ceremony,' Tess said. Surely Tess noticed that there had only been a perfunctory attempt at making the room look like a celebration.

'Let me see your ring,' Genna asked.

Amelie lifted her hand, and the sapphires glittered on her finger.

'I've never seen such a wedding band!' Genna exclaimed. 'Well done, Edmund. Did Tess help you pick it out?'

'Not at all.' Tess gazed at the ring and then at Edmund. 'It matches the other ring you gave her.'

Genna asked to see the other ring, which Amelie wore on the other hand. 'I didn't know you gave Amelie a ring.'

'It was a betrothal present,' Amelie said.

Marc sidled over to Amelie and kissed her on the cheek. 'You make a beautiful bride.'

'Maman has said nothing.' She spoke so only he could hear. 'You know how she scrutinises what everyone is wearing. I think she might have preferred I dress in black bombazine.'

'She wished for something very different for you,' he said.

She lifted her chin. 'I think Edmund has done all that is admirable.'

'Not all.' Marc frowned, and she knew he referred to their encounter in Brussels. 'But I own he has behaved well since.'

Their butler announced that the breakfast was served, and they all went to the dining room. Much effort was made for all to appear as it should be—happy—but Amelie assumed that was for the benefit of Reverend Cane. When it came time for the reverend to leave, Genna said she would go as well and the goodbyes were said in the hall.

Genna gave Amelie a brief hug. 'I am happy to have another sister,' she said. She presented her cheek for Edmund to kiss. 'Behave yourself, Edmund, or answer to me.'

If Edmund resented this, he gave no indication. He kissed her cheek and said, 'You have nothing to fear, Genna.'

Reverend Cane came up to Amelie and Edmund and took both their hands in his. 'I wish you both joy.' He leaned towards them with a conspiratorial air. 'And, remember, joy is something you make yourselves. I've no doubt the two of you are very capable of it.'

When the guests had left, Edmund turned to Amelie. 'There has been no discussion of where this wedding night should take place.'

Amelie had certainly not thought that far. Apparently her family had not seen fit to discuss the matter with Edmund either.

Amelie's parents and Tess and Marc stared at him as if surprised he was still there.

He seemed to ignore them. 'I have a choice for you,' he said to Amelie. 'We may stay here, if that was your and your parents' intention. I have also engaged a hotel room at the Clarendon Hotel for us and one for your maid, if you would like her to come.'

'Of course you may stay here, Summerfield,' her father snapped. 'Where else would you stay?'

Her mother looked distressed. 'We assumed you would stay with us.'

Amelie was out of patience with them. They'd barely been civil to Edmund and they'd treated this occasion as if it were her funeral instead of her wedding.

'I choose the hotel,' she said.

Amelie hurried up to her bedchamber to find Sally and have her pack a bag.

'You may also come to the hotel, Sally,' she told the girl. 'Mr Summerfield has procured a room for you, as well. Would you like to come?'

'If you wish it,' she said without enthusiasm, as she folded a nightdress and a dress to wear the next day.

'It will be a little adventure for you.' Amelie tried to cheer her up. 'Or, at least, a nice respite alone.' Amelie was less sure of what the night would mean to her.

Her mother knocked on her door and entered the room. 'How *stupide* of us not to plan for this night.'

She and Amelie's father had barely planned for the wedding ceremony, but Amelie did not say that. 'It is of no consequence, Maman.'

'We have so little room,' her mother went on. 'There is only a small bedchamber on the floor with Marc and Tess's rooms. That is not ideal.'

Maybe Edmund would stay in her room. 'I will explain the situation to him, Maman.'

Her mother sighed. 'Perhaps you should come to the country with your father and me. Your papa needs to return to the estate.'

'We shall see, Maman.' She did not have the heart to tell her mother they would stay in London.

Amelie sat at her dressing table and unpinned the garland of flowers she wore in her hair. The blooms were drooping, but she was trying not to let her spirits droop, as well. Her mother's unhappiness and Sally's glumness threatened her own mood.

After packing her bag, Sally helped her change out of her wedding dress.

'You've become so thin,' her mother said when she was only in her corset and shift.

'I've had the nausea, you know,' Amelie said.

Her mother inclined her head to Sally, a warning not to speak aloud about the scandalous family secret.

'I am better now,' she said, although that morning had been one of her worst.

Sally helped her into a blue sprigged-muslin day dress while her mother watched.

Her mother went into her wardrobe and chose a shawl and bonnet. 'These will look *très jolie* with that dress.'

Once dressed, Amelie sent Sally to pack her own bag. She was alone with her mother. 'Do not worry about me, Maman. I will be safe for one night in a hotel.'

Her mother glanced away. 'You were not safe from him in the hotel in Brussels.'

'He did not attack me, Maman,' Amelie said. 'And he has done all that was right about it since. Edmund has not hesitated. Not once.'

Her mother nodded. 'I was so certain you would marry that nice young man, Captain Fowler.'

She shuddered. No matter what, she was glad she had not married Fowler. 'That does not bear thinking of.'

Her mother crossed the room and put an arm around her. 'I only wanted your happiness, *ma fille*. I believed you would make the respectable marriage. Not like your father and me.'

Amelie turned and embraced her mother. 'Papa was always lucky to have married you, Maman.'

'We did not always feel it to be so,' her mother admitted.

For most of Amelie's life, her parents had quarrelled or had simply not spoken to each other, but they'd reconciled in Brussels, their love coming together as hers fell apart.

Amelie put on a brave smile. 'Perhaps some day we will say I was lucky to have married Edmund.'

Her mother's expression turned sceptical.

Chapter Ten

Edmund and Amelie did not speak much in the coach he'd arranged to carry them to the hotel. Amelie's maid rode with them, but that was not the only reason, Edmund suspected. Did either of them know what to say to each other? He certainly did not know what to say to her.

Instead he spoke to the maid. 'You will have a dinner prepared by a French chef, Sally. You will like that.'

'Yes, sir,' she said without enthusiasm.

He glanced at Amelie, who raised her brows and shook her head.

Edmund held Amelie's gaze. 'We will have the dinner in our room.'

She seemed to force a smile. 'That will be pleasant.'

Deuce take it. Now he had two women he could not please, not even with French cooks and fine hotels.

He glanced out the carriage window and wondered how it would be to escape. Jump out and run down the road. He could probably manage to be back in Brussels within days and from there could easily disappear.

He glanced back at Amelie. Abandon her? Abandon his family? He would never do that.

Although he worried about how it would be for her if her family and his continued their resentment and anger at him. How could they not? He remained cognisant of what she would be required to give up for him. They would be even more on the fringes of society than her family had been. In fact, they would be completely outside of it. Their child would have his name but would never belong in the world her family planned for her.

The carriage drew up to the hotel's entrance, and soon they were settled into their room. Sally unpacked Amelie's bag and left for her own room.

Edmund arranged for refreshment so they had something to converse about. Was the wine to her liking? Did she enjoy the cheese and blackberry tarts?

She dutifully nibbled at the food and agreed that the wine was perfect and the cheese and tarts the best she'd ever tasted.

Edmund was exploding inside. They could not go on like this. There had been more ease between them in Brussels when they did not know each other at all.

He faced her from across a small table in the sitting room adjacent to the bedchamber. 'We should speak plainly to each other, Amelie.'

She looked up at him uncertainly. 'Speak plainly? About…?'

'About how we are to go about,' he said. 'About how we are going to manage.'

She met his gaze. 'I do not know how to answer you.'

His frustration grew. 'Well, for one thing, where will we live until we find rooms to let?'

She glanced away. 'Am I foolish for admitting that I have not thought of this? I could only think of marrying as quickly as we could.'

'Let us talk about this now,' he persisted.

She shrugged. 'I suppose we could stay with my parents. I am certain they will return to Northdon House soon, and then there will be more room.'

In his mind's eye he saw the caged lion in the King's menagerie at the Tower, pacing back and forth behind bars, its eyes flashing. That's how it would feel if he were forced to stay in the same house with her father even for a few days.

His feelings must have shown on his face, because she glanced away. 'I realise it would be difficult for you to stay with my parents, though.'

He set his jaw. 'It would not be for long.'

She reached across the table and touched his hand. 'What alternative is there?'

Her touch aroused him. What was he to do with that sensation? What was he to do about the physical side of marriage? Would she wish to make love? After all, making love had created this undesired situation for her. At the moment she was grateful to him, but how long would it be before she resented him as much as her parents did?

He pulled his hand away. 'This hotel?' Why even speak it?

She stared at her hand before wrapping her arms across her chest. 'If you wish it,' she said stiffly.

'Just say what you want!'

She flinched and looked wounded.

'I spoke too sharply. Forgive me.' He instantly softened his tone. 'I want you to be honest with me. Do you wish to stay in your parents' town house or do you wish to stay in the hotel?'

Amelie met his gaze. 'You would prefer the hotel, would you not? My parents treat you so shabbily.'

'I am quite used to shabby treatment, Amelie,' he said. 'I asked what you want.'

She averted her face. 'I want to please you, Edmund. I realise you are merely being kind. We may stay in the hotel.'

'I am not merely being kind,' he responded. 'Your needs are more important than mine.'

'Why? Was not marrying me the ultimate kindness, Edmund? Even though I have trapped you—'

He shook his head. 'Do not keep saying you trapped me.'

She was feeling obstinate. 'It is true, though.'

'I made a choice,' he said. 'You chose marriage, as well.'

But it was a choice he could not have wanted. He'd made it because of the baby, and she'd accepted for the same reason—that and it prevented more scandal befalling her family. Why could he not simply acknowledge the truth—that she was responsible?

She stood and paced in front of him. 'I wish we were visiting the Tower or a museum. It was easier to talk, then.'

He looked uncertain. 'We could visit the Tower if you wish.'

'No!' she cried. 'I do not want to visit the Tower.'

'What do you want, Amelie?' he persisted. 'I am waiting for you to tell me.'

She took a breath.

Could she dare tell him?

She mustered her courage. 'I—I want a marriage like Marc and Tess's. And my parents'. I know I cannot have that, because you do not love me. How could you? But maybe if we came to know each other better, we—maybe we would like each other.'

His mouth slowly stretched into a smile. 'I already like you, Amelie.'

Her face flushed and she stopped pacing. 'But you do not know me, not after a few outings and—and—' And one scandalous night.

His eyes shone with humour. 'Are you saying you have some dark secret? If so, this might be the time to tell me.'

She liked that he was teasing her. It reminded her of Brussels when he had cajoled her into confiding in him.

Brussels.

Did he not remember? Brussels had revealed her dark secret, the one he alone knew. Did he know she possessed it still?

Ever since their hands touched, thoughts of that night, of lovemaking, were rushing through her brain. If he knew how easily wanton thoughts possessed her, would he rise from his chair and stride out the door? Would he abandon her as she'd been abandoned on the streets of Brussels?

She stopped herself.

It had not been Edmund who'd abandoned her. Edmund rescued her. He stayed by her side. He made love to her.

She sat again and finished her glass of wine.

He poured her another. 'So is there a dark secret?'

If he wanted honesty, she would dare to give it to him. 'I want a marriage where we—we share the same bed.'

His eyes darkened. 'That is the secret?'

Her heart beat faster. 'Does it offend you?'

His features softened. 'Offend me?' He took her hand in his. 'I would very much enjoy sharing your bed, Amelie. I remember Brussels with great delight.'

Her skin tingled. 'You—you do not think me wicked to say that I *want* it?'

His hand tightened around hers. 'Not wicked. What we did in Brussels was not wicked. It was wrong. Wrong because we did not consider the consequences.'

She lowered her lashes. 'I considered the consequences, but I thought a woman could not get with child the first time.'

He scowled. 'Who told you that?'

Her face grew hot. 'I overheard the maids talking.'

His brows lifted. 'They were wrong.'

She laughed. 'I have since surmised that.' Her mood quickly sobered. 'I should have known better.'

He glanced away. 'I knew better. I knew the risks and I ignored them.'

She tightened her fingers around his hand. 'Hush, Edmund. No one else will listen to me, but you and I must agree that I was responsible. I was the one who wanted the lovemaking.'

He stroked her hand again. 'I wanted it, too.'

The sensations inside her grew, like a wild vine winding into every part of her.

'I want it now.' She looked at him expectantly. 'Do you?'

'Of course I do.' His brow furrowed. 'If it is safe for you and the baby.'

'It is safe.' She spoke with surety, but she really had no idea if it was safe. She merely knew she wanted it to be.

He released her hand and poured more wine for each of them. She drank hers quickly, handing her glass to him for more. He poured again, but already her head began to swim and a languor came over her limbs. At least the nausea had stopped. It had eased after she'd spoken her wedding vows.

The hands of the clock on the mantel were nearing six o'clock. A long time before bedtime. 'When must we eat dinner?'

'Eight o'clock. It will be brought up to us.'

Two hours.

'Can one make love in the afternoon?' She blinked. 'Or is that too wanton?'

He grinned. 'It is our wedding day, Amelie. Let us be as wanton as we like. Shall I call your maid for you?'

She recoiled in horror. 'No! No. I can manage without her.' Otherwise Sally would guess precisely what she would be doing. Perhaps Edmund would not censure her profligate nature, but her maid might.

'Very well.' He rose from his chair and came to her side. 'We have managed before, have we not?' He extended his hand.

She took his hand and let him help her stand. The edges of her vision blurred, softening the reds, blues and greens in the room into a pleasant sort of rainbow. He led her to the bedchamber, and her legs gave the illusion of floating. Once inside the room he closed the door, and the space immediately became more intimate. She turned her back to him and waited while he unlaced her dress. She pulled off her sleeves, and the garment slipped to the floor. He unlaced her corset, and she stepped out of both pieces of clothing and turned to Edmund dressed only in her shift.

He gazed at her as he kicked off his shoes, removed his coat and unbuttoned his waistcoat. She reached up and started pulling pins from her hair, combing it with her fingers until it fell upon her shoulders.

His gaze had feasted on her nakedness in Brussels, and she flushed with anticipation at seeing the admiration in his eyes again. She removed her stockings and her shift and stood before him. His gaze swept over her before capturing her own. He, dressed now only in his shirt and trousers, stepped closer to her, put his hand behind her head and drew her into a kiss.

His mouth was warm and sent flames darting through her. A moan came from the back of her throat. She wrapped her arms around his neck and pressed herself against him as their lips parted and his moist tongue, tasting of wine, touched hers.

She longed to feel his skin against hers. Still kissing him, she reached down and unbuttoned the fall of his trousers. A sharp shard of need pierced her. She felt his arousal and her need intensified.

She'd yearned for a repeat of the delights of his love-making in Brussels, but what she was feeling now, merely at the beginning, was unexpectedly intense. She needed him inside her so the intensity could be appeased.

She reached under his shirt and moved her hands over his firm chest. Her fingers felt the scars she'd glimpsed before. He pulled off his shirt and backed away from her to remove his trousers and stockings. She forced herself to wait for him to make the next move, although her need screamed for him to hurry. His naked body, illuminated by the waning sun shining through the window curtains, seemed beautiful to her, even though scarred. On his leg one long jagged scar remained pink.

His Waterloo injury. She'd forgotten he'd been injured. He seemed so vital. So strong. She knelt and traced her finger down the long jagged scar. She glanced up at him, wanting to say something—to tell him she was sorry he'd had to suffer it, to say how glad she was he'd not lost his leg—but that seemed a selfish thought.

He seized her hand and pulled her up. 'It is an ugly scar, but the wound is healed.'

Surely it would not be so pink if it had completely healed. Did it still pain him?

'My scars repulse you.' Pain flickered through his eyes.

'No!' She threw her arms around him. 'No. Do not think it.' She wanted to recapture that moment of closeness between them. 'I merely wondered how it happened.'

'I will tell you.' He reached for her. 'But not now.'

His touch ignited her need. 'After?'

'Perhaps.' He lifted her in his arms as if she were a mere feather and carried her to the bed. The bedcovers had already been folded back for sleeping.

Or for making love.

She lay on her back and eagerly awaited him rising over her. His legs straddled hers, and he leaned down to kiss her once more. She put her arms around him and arched her back to him as his hand caressed her breasts and made need shoot through her like a sabre thrust. She could not wait. She opened her legs and tried to press him to her. He groaned and gently pushed himself inside her.

Her need would have been happier if he'd thrust himself inside her, but she tried to hold back her sense of urgency and follow his lead. He stroked slowly, carefully, but she was beyond care. She wanted him to rush her to her climax, to the release she knew she would feel.

But he set a slow, easy pace, and she writhed in passion beneath him, until, more suddenly than she expected, her release came in wave after wave of pleasure, pleasure so acute it was almost painful.

His thrusts accelerated and soon he, too, reached his climax, spilling his seed inside her, the seed that had created a child that night in Brussels.

He relaxed next to her and held her close, as he had in Brussels. The familiarity of it was a comfort. Would it always feel so comfortable? Would they be able to make a marriage out of this?

She hoped so.

'That was lovely, Edmund,' she murmured as she snuggled next to him. 'Might we do that again?'

Edmund gladly complied with her request to make love a second time. They could build on this pleasure they gave each other, this physical connection that now bound them with the baby inside her. He might never deserve her, but perhaps he could make her happy. He would certainly try.

He entered her intent on again giving her delight, of showing her that all would be well. They would make a good life together.

Need, not rational thought, drove him. Her desire pushed him harder. This coupling was not gentle, not worshipful, but rough and wild and dictated by a carnality neither one of them seemed able to control.

She cried out in her release, and a moment later he groaned with the spilling of his seed. They shuddered together, suspended in time and in the moment. No thought, no censure, no self-blame. Only pleasure in each other.

Afterwards they did not speak. He held her against him and felt truly calm for the first time since seeing her in London. He sensed her ease as well. He simply relished the comfort of her next to him and let time float by. There was hope for them, for the family they were creating.

The clock struck eight.

Blast. 'They will be delivering dinner soon.' He rose on one elbow. 'I must dress. You stay here if you like.'

She sat. 'I will get up.'

He donned his shirt and trousers in time for the knock on the door. He closed the bedchamber door and walked out to their sitting room. Opening the door, he instructed the two servants to place the trays on the table.

'Wait a moment.' He went to the writing table and jotted a quick note to Amelie's maid that they would not need her until morning. He folded it and handed it to one of the men. 'Would you deliver this to the maid's room two doors down?'

'Very good, sir.' The servant bowed.

Edmund tipped them both and closed the door behind them.

Amelie stood in the bedchamber doorway, covered by a silk wrapper. 'I am famished.'

They shared a leisurely dinner, talking together. He told her about growing up with Tess and his sisters, how they escaped from their governess's lessons and explored the far reaches of their father's property, about swimming in the cool pool formed by the stream that ran through the property, climbing trees in the woods, racing each other to the folly.

She shared a lonelier childhood but said the only person lonelier had been her mother, with whom she had spent many hours, listening to her tales of her childhood in France or learning needlework from her mother's instruction.

He did not talk of the bad times. Of losing his mother when he was nine. Of watching her die giving birth and of being quickly whisked away from the only house he'd known to the mansion of a father who, until that time, had barely noticed him. His growing up at Summerfield House had been privileged, but no one, not even the servants, governesses or tutors ever let him forget he was the illegitimate son.

He did tell Amelie about Lady Summerfield, who, even though she had been his father's wife and ought to have despised him, had been the one person besides his sisters who'd treated him as if he mattered. Years after she abandoned the family, he began a correspondence with her and lived with her before the Waterloo battle and recuperated there afterwards.

When he and Amelie returned to bed, they made love again, this time more leisurely, like two people who had all the time in the world to be together.

She fell asleep almost immediately afterwards. He gazed at her lying next to him, looking much like he imagined she must have looked as a little girl. The wonder of it, he would be sharing her bed for the rest of their lives.

With that thought, he drifted contentedly off to sleep.

A pain, horrible and intense, woke Amelie. She cried out.

Edmund woke. 'What is it?'

She sat up. 'Something is wrong. In here.' She pressed her belly. Another pain hit, and she cried out again and hugged her knees.

He bounded out of bed and began dressing. 'I'll get help. Send for a doctor.'

'No. No doctor,' she pleaded. 'I want to go home. Take me home, Edmund. I want my mother!' Another pain in her belly, worse than any she'd ever had during her courses, shook her. 'M-my mother will know what to do.'

He continued to pull on his clothes. 'Are you certain? A carriage ride might not be good—'

She cut him off. 'I do not care. I want to go home.'

'Yes. Right away.' He headed for the door, still putting on his coat. 'I'll send Sally to you.'

He rushed out and she was alone.

Something was wrong with the baby! Something terrible. She knew it.

Another pain hit and she hugged her legs tighter. When it passed she got herself out of the bed and put on her shift.

The door opened and Sally rushed in. 'Miss! What is wrong?'

'It hurts! I am afraid I'll lose it.' She shook.

'Lose what, miss?' Sally asked.

'My baby,' Amelie whispered. 'My baby.'

'Baby?' The girl's eyes grew wide.

Amelie had forgotten that she'd kept the baby a secret from Sally, who had never questioned why she threw up most mornings.

Sally recovered quickly. 'Mr Summerfield is getting a carriage. Let me get you dressed.'

Sally helped her step into her corset, which she laced very loosely. Next she helped her into her dress.

'I am bleeding, too,' Amelie said, more to herself than to Sally.

Sally laced her into her dress and wrapped her in a shawl.

Edmund rushed in as Sally was packing the clothes she'd so recently unpacked. 'Leave the bags, Sally. We'll get them later. There should be a coach downstairs by the time we get there.'

He picked up Amelie and carried her down the stairs and out the door to a waiting hackney coach.

Chapter Eleven

They soon reached Grosvenor Street and Edmund jumped out of the coach to sound the knocker. Someone should be awake. If not, he'd bang at the door until they roused.

Matheson, the butler, dressed in a banyan, opened the door.

'What is this?' he cried, then saw it was Edmund.

'Quick,' Edmund said. 'Miss Glenville is ill.' He forgot she was Mrs Summerfield now.

'What should I do?' Matheson asked.

'Pay the coachman.' He handed Matheson a purse of coins. 'I'll carry her inside.'

With Sally's help, he gathered Amelie into his arms again and carried her through the door.

The butler and Sally were right behind him.

'Wake Lady Northdon,' Edmund ordered. 'And my sister. Tell them Amelie is here and needs them.'

'I'll find Mrs Glenville,' Sally said, bounding up the stairs.

By the time he'd carried Amelie to her bedchamber, Lady Northdon rushed in behind him. 'What has happened?'

Edmund laid her on the bed.

'I'm having pains, Maman,' Amelie cried. 'In my belly. And I am bleeding.'

'Mon Dieu!' Her mother exclaimed. 'We must send for the physician.'

'I'll attend to it,' Matheson said.

'An *accoucheur*,' Edmund clarified.

The butler's brows rose.

'Rapidement, s'il vous plait!' Amelie's mother lapsed into French.

Matheson hurried off.

Lord Northdon appeared at the doorway. 'My God.' He swung to Edmund. 'What did you do?'

'Papa! It is not because of Edmund!' Amelie cried. 'It is the baby!'

Edmund was not so certain. They'd made love three times. Had that caused the harm?

Her brother and Tess rushed down the stairs to Amelie's room. 'Sally said something is wrong with Amelie's baby.'

Lord Northdon inclined his head to Edmund. 'He's done something. I am certain of it.'

Glenville took his father by the arm. 'Control yourself, Papa. Can you not see how distraught Edmund is? Accusations are not going to help. Let us stay out of the way.'

'Oui,' his mother said. 'We must get her undressed. Tess, come help.' She turned to Edmund. 'You go, too. We will take care of her.'

'I am staying,' Edmund said.

'Come with us,' Glenville said.

'Yes,' Tess agreed. 'Go with Marc and his father. We will keep you informed.'

'I am staying,' he said.

'This is no place for a man,' Tess said.

'It is my place,' he countered.

'Amelie will not wish you to stay,' Lady Northdon insisted.

'He—can—stay,' Amelie managed, talking through another pain.

Sally dared to speak up, although she usually did not when Lord or Lady Northdon was around. 'Mrs Bayliss might be able to help her. She knows of such things. Shall I wake her, ma'am?'

'*Oui! Oui!* Bring Mrs Bayliss,' Lady Northdon said.

Sally heard Mrs Bayliss, the housekeeper, say she used to accompany her mother, a midwife, on her calls. She'd seen dozens of births before she was even fifteen years old, she'd said. One of the other maids also told Sally that midwives knew how to get rid of babies before anyone knew of their existence, but Sally could not bring herself to ask Mrs Bayliss about that.

She hurried below stairs, where Mrs Bayliss and Mr Matheson had their rooms.

She knocked on Mrs Bayliss's door. 'Wake up, Mrs Bayliss! Lady Northdon needs you!'

She heard the housekeeper moving in the room. 'I am coming.' She opened the door, dressed in her nightdress and a wrap. 'For goodness' sake! What is it, Sally? Why does her ladyship need me at this hour?'

Sally took a gulp of air. 'It is Miss Glenville—Mrs Summerfield, I mean—she—she is having a baby, only it is too soon to have the baby!'

Mrs Bayliss gaped. 'She is what?'

'She is having a baby!' Sally repeated. 'Please come and help her.'

'Where is she? Did she not leave with her husband?'

'He brought her back,' Sally explained. 'Oh, please, just go to her.'

The housekeeper retied the sash of her wrapper. 'Yes.

Yes. Indeed.' As they rushed to the stairs, she added, 'Fetch some towels and linens, Sally. Lots of them.'

'Merci, merci!' cried Lady Northdon when Mrs Bayliss appeared.

Thank goodness, thought Edmund, because none of them had a clue what to do to help Amelie.

'Let me see her.' The housekeeper went straight to Amelie's bed. 'What are you feeling, miss?'

'Pain,' answered Amelie. 'In my belly. And my back. It feels wrong! Something is wrong!'

'Let me touch you.' Mrs Bayliss put her hand on Amelie's abdomen. 'You are not far along?'

'A little over three months.' A day before Waterloo.

Sally came in, carrying several towels. She handed them to Mrs Bayliss and helped her place them under Amelie.

Afterwards Mrs Bayliss told Sally to bring some tea for Amelie. Sally nodded and left the room.

'What is wrong with her?' Tess asked.

'A miscarriage, likely,' Mrs Bayliss said quietly.

'What is to be done?' Tess wrung her hands.

Mrs Bayliss patted Tess's hands. 'Nothing but waiting and hoping, dear.'

The women stood around Amelie's bed, but Edmund waited in a corner of the room, fighting memories of another room, another woman surrounded in just such a way.

His mother. Dying. Her baby born dead.

Not again, he prayed as time ticked by.

Sally brought the tea, but sipping it made Amelie throw it up again.

Edmund had seen men pierced through with bayonets. Shot in the chest from musket fire. He'd seen cannon balls take off a man's head, but, somehow, watching Amelie seize up with pain, over and over, seemed more difficult to endure.

'The pain. It is worse.' she moaned.

She sat up and clutched her abdomen, keening in agony, a sound that only brought back his mother's cries from so many years ago. Amelie lay back down again, gripping her mother's hand, her arm trembling.

'Oh, dear. There it is,' said Mrs Bayliss, her voice sorrowful.

'Non. Je prie, non.' Her mother's voice was anguished.

Amelie half sat up again. When she collapsed back on the bed, she did not stir.

Edmund stopped breathing. 'Is she—?'

'She's lost the baby, sir.' Mrs Bayliss quickly pulled the towels from beneath Amelie and folded them into a bundle.

Amelie rose onto her elbows. 'I've lost the baby?'

The baby! But not Amelie. She was alive.

Her voice became more strident. 'I've lost the baby?' She reached for the bundle, which the housekeeper pulled away.

'There is nothing for you to see, miss,' Mrs Bayliss said. She gestured for Sally to follow her. They left the room.

'Maman!' Amelie cried.

Her mother sat on the bed and hugged her daughter, comforting her as if she were a small child.

Tess also put an arm around Amelie, murmuring to her that she would be all right.

She was alive, Edmund said a prayer of thanksgiving for that. But nothing was right. There was no baby. Nothing to connect them together.

No family.

He walked out of the room and leaned against the wall.

From an open door to another bedchamber, he heard Lord Northdon's voice. 'Why the devil could she not have lost the baby yesterday? Now it is too late.'

Was the man glad the baby was gone? Edmund could not bear it. He thought of the little girl in Hyde Park. Now he'd never smell the sweet scent of his own baby. He'd never feel his own baby's chubby arms around his neck. Lord Northdon thought this a good thing?

He closed his eyes and let his grief turn to anger.

He stepped into the doorway. Lord Northdon and Glenville turned to him.

'It is unfortunate that your daughter's miscarriage did not come at a more acceptable time for you, sir.' Edmund bowed and walked away before he could no longer resist the temptation to put his fist into Lord Northdon's face. He continued down the stairs to the hall and stepped out into the chilly night air.

Why had this happened this night? Edmund could think of only one reason. He'd made love to her. Lord Northdon was correct on one score. Edmund was to blame.

A carriage entered the street and stopped in front of the town house. Matheson stepped out, followed by the doctor.

The butler only gave him a fleeting glance before leading the doctor into the house and taking the physician's greatcoat and hat.

'Come with me,' Matheson said to the doctor. 'I will take you to Lady Northdon and her daughter.'

Edmund went below stairs in search of Mrs Bayliss to let her know the *accoucheur* had arrived.

He found her in the kitchen with one of the maids.

'Carry on, Kitty,' Mrs Bayliss said. 'Add one cup for the doctor and I will be down shortly to bring the tea upstairs.' She glanced at Edmund. 'I expect you'd rather have brandy.'

'You have the right of it,' he said.

She touched his arm, a look of sympathy on her face. 'These things happen sometimes, sir.' She dried her hands on the apron she'd donned and bustled off to Amelie's room.

Edmund walked slower. When he reached the floor

where Amelie's bedchamber was located, her father, the doctor and Mrs Bayliss were all deep in conversation.

'You are confident she expelled all the tissue?' he heard the doctor ask.

'Oh, yes, sir,' Mrs Bayliss assured him. 'I've seen many of these untimely deliveries. I know what to expect.'

'I'll just look in on her, then,' the doctor said.

'This way.' Mrs Bayliss knocked on the door and opened it. 'The *accoucheur*, Dr Croft.'

Edmund followed the man in to the room. The *accoucheur* turned to him with haughty eyebrows raised. 'You cannot march in here, sir. Who are you?'

Edmund glared at him. 'The lady's husband.'

Lady Northdon and Tess were still at Amelie's bedside. Amelie appeared to take no notice of the doctor's entrance. Or Edmund's.

'This is Dr Croft to see you, Amelie,' her mother said gently. 'He will want to examine you.'

Dr Croft examined Amelie without her seeming to care.

'All looks well,' he said. 'But contact me immediately if she develops a fever.'

While the doctor spoke to Lady Northdon and Tess, Edmund kept his eyes on Amelie, who now lay on clean linens and wore a clean nightdress. Her gaze drifted over to him and paused for a moment before she turned her head away.

'Let us go to the drawing room to talk about this,' Lady Northdon said. 'Will you bring refreshment, Mrs Bayliss?'

'Yes, m'lady,' the housekeeper said.

Lady Northdon looked at Tess. 'You will stay with her?' She did not address Edmund.

'Of course I will.' Tess rearranged Amelie's bedcovers. She kissed her on the head. 'Close your eyes and try to sleep, Amelie.'

As soon as the room had cleared, Tess glanced over at Edmund. 'How unforeseen,' she commented.

He nodded. 'My father-in-law reckons it happened a day too late.'

'Did he say that?' She sounded surprised.

He wondered if Tess felt the same. He wondered if she blamed him, too.

There was merit in what Lord Northdon had said, after all. But if it had happened one day earlier and Amelie then had refused to marry him, Edmund would feel no relief.

A knock sounded on the door and Tess answered it. Tess took a small tray from whoever it was and carried it over to Edmund. 'I gather you ordered this?'

A decanter of brandy and two glasses. He said a silent thank you to Mrs Bayliss.

'You should sit, Edmund,' Tess said.

There was a chair right next to him. He lowered himself in it and poured the brandy into a glass. 'May I offer you some?' He lifted the glass to her.

She took it from his hand and drank the whole. 'Thank you.' She peered down at him as he poured more brandy into the glass. 'How are you faring, Edmund?'

'Me?' He lifted his face to hers. 'This did not happen to me. It happened to Amelie.'

She returned a sceptical look. 'Still it must affect you.'

It was eviscerating him, but he could not speak of it.

She walked back to Amelie and sat in a chair beside the bed. Edmund drank his brandy in his dark corner.

When the glass was empty again, he spoke. 'Would you do me a service, Tess?'

'If I am able,' she responded.

'Leave Amelie to me.'

She whirled around and looked about to protest.

'I will sit with her. I promise to alert you or her mother if she has any difficulty at all, but I want to be the one to sit with her.'

'Oh, Edmund.' Tess sighed. 'Do you think that is wise? I am perfectly happy to sit by her side all night, if need be.'

'I am her husband,' he said more firmly. 'I need to be with her.'

She smiled at him—a little sadly. 'Yes, of course! I am unused to this change. It has not yet been a whole day.'

He returned her gaze. 'And yet so much has happened...'

Amelie opened her eyes to daylight. It took her a moment to realise she was in her room and a moment longer to remember what had happened. She squeezed her eyes shut again and rolled over, curling up in the bed and trying not to feel the emptiness inside.

Now that there was no baby.

She heard a rustling and opened her eyes again, resting her head on one arm.

In a chair near her bed sat Edmund, legs stretched out before him, his coat and waistcoat open, his shirt half out of his trousers. His face was shadowed with a dark beard but seemed pinched with worry. He shifted in the chair again, then stilled. Watching the rhythmic rise and fall of his chest and listening to the soft hum of his breathing was comforting.

Had he been at her side all night? He certainly looked as if he'd spent the night in a chair, but why had her mother not found him a bed?

She remembered that her mother and Tess had stood at her side during her awful ordeal. She also remembered Edmund standing in the corner, refusing to leave.

Blinking against tears that threatened to sting her eyes, she gazed at him. Much easier to think of him than the pain and the loss.

Had it been her fault? She'd wanted the lovemaking. Had that caused her baby to die?

He shifted again, startling her.

Did he blame her? She'd told him there was no harm in making love, but she did not really know.

He suddenly took a deep breath, and his eyes opened into narrow slits. They widened and he sat up straight in the chair. 'Amelie. How are you feeling?'

How was she feeling?

Numb. Best she stay numb. To feel anything seemed too risky.

'I am better,' she finally said.

He leaned towards her, 'What can I do for you? Do you need anything?'

She shook her head. 'Would my mother not give you a bed?'

'I did not ask for one.'

She remembered the commotion she'd caused. How he carried her inside and set the house into an uproar. 'I've caused everyone so much trouble.'

He pushed his chair closer to her. 'Not so very much.'

'I lost the baby.' Her voice cracked. 'I am so sorry.'

'It happened,' he said carefully. 'We simply go on from here.'

But how? she thought.

'We could not have foreseen this, Amelie.'

'Yes, but…' She could not finish her thought. It had been the wedding that had caused it. Or rather, her desire for the marital bed. Did he comprehend? It would not have happened if they had not married—if they'd not made love.

She moved in the bed and became aware she was bleeding still. It frightened her. She did not know how to tell Edmund about it, either. Such a womanly thing. But urgent.

She sat up. 'Could I trouble you to send Sally to me?'

'Right away.' He stood and put his clothing in order. He still looked exhausted, though.

'And then you must get some rest,' she said. 'I am in no distress.' She hoped.

His expression turned puzzled. 'I am rested enough.'

'I really do not need you to stay here, Edmund.' She needed him to leave, actually.

His brows knitted again as they had in sleep. 'If you would rather I not be here, I will attend to other matters. I will collect our bags from the hotel.'

'You could send Staines for the bags. You need not go yourself.' She wanted him to rest—and for Sally to come and change the linens folded beneath her. 'My mother will have a bed fixed for you.'

'No need. I am well able to return to the hotel. I have other matters to see to today, as well.' He walked to the door. 'I'll send for Sally. Rest, Amelie.'

He walked out of the room without a second glance.

Amelie sat up and hugged her knees. She'd forgotten to tell him something important. She'd forgotten to thank him for not leaving her alone.

She lay back down in the bed and let her misery envelop her.

Chapter Twelve

Edmund found a servant to summon Sally. He also left word that he had gone out. He returned to the Clarendon Hotel and arranged to have Amelie's and Sally's luggage sent back to them. He carried his bag to the Stephen's Hotel, where he still had his rooms.

He stripped off his coat and waistcoat, kicked off his shoes and flopped down on the bed. He was in no condition to stay at the Northdon town house and risk encountering Lord Northdon, not with his emotions in such a volatile state. Best he rest here.

He did not need to witness everyone else holding him to blame. No one knew that better than he did. Besides, no one desired his presence there. Everyone wished the marriage had been scheduled for today rather than yesterday. Even Amelie seemed impatient to be rid of him this morning.

He'd battled being unwanted his whole life. Certainly his mother's life would have been happier—and longer—had he not been born. His father had only wanted a legitimate heir, not a bastard son. No schoolmaster, tutor, governess or servant wanted to deal with him. His superiors in the army had preferred junior officers with proper family connections.

Still, his sisters and Lady Summerfield accepted him, even though his sisters were now angry at him. What would Lady Summerfield say if she knew what had happened, why he'd had to marry Amelie? The selfish risk he'd taken with the baby's life? How he'd lost it all?

She'd probably tell him to buck up and stop feeling sorry for himself. Lady Summerfield always chose to be happy.

He'd thought happiness had been in his grasp, too, but now there was no baby and he was not at all certain Amelie wanted him.

He rubbed his face. He'd had to live with things he'd done on the battlefield; he supposed he'd have to learn to live with this, as well.

The baby he'd almost held. The family they'd almost created.

He slept until nearly the dinner hour. Dragging himself out of bed, he dressed in a clean shirt and brushed his coat until it looked presentable again. He'd look the proper gentleman and act the proper gentleman. Let no one push him too far, though. His emotions, while under control, were very raw.

He kept his room at the Stephen, though. Lord and Lady Northdon had never offered him a room at the town house.

He walked outside into a grey, drizzling evening that perfectly matched his mood. When he reached the house and sounded the knocker, he wondered what would happen if he asked for a key so he could come and go as he pleased.

Staines answered the door. 'Evening, sir.'

As he handed Staines his coat and hat, he asked, 'Anything I should know about, Staines?'

Lines appeared on the footman's forehead. 'It is quieter, sir. No more harm to Miss Glenville—I mean Mrs Summerfield—that I know of. She's been resting, I hear.'

'Good. I am glad.' Very glad. 'I'll go up and see her.'

Staines's brows rose. 'Should I announce your arrival?'

Edmund smiled. 'No one knows quite what to do with me, do they? I do not know myself. Do tell the family I am here, though. They will want to know.'

Staines's mouth twitched, and his eyes indicated some empathy.

Edmund climbed the stairs to Amelie's room. He knocked softly, not wishing to wake her if she was sleeping.

The door was opened by Tess. Instead of letting him in, she stepped out in the hall.

'Where have you been?' she said in a scolding tone.

He glared at her. 'I am not likely to tell you when you talk to me that way. How is Amelie? She is not worse, is she?'

'No.' She looked chastened. 'She's slept most of the day, and she is weak, but no worse, the poor dear.' Her disapproving look returned. 'She asked about you, but no one knew what to tell her.'

'I told her I was going out. I did not know when I would return.' His voice turned acerbic. 'I doubt anyone else here desired my presence.'

'Edmund, you must understand,' Tess cried. 'You seduced their daughter!'

'It is not only that, Tess, and you know it.' He looked her in the eye. 'Tell me. How might they have reacted if it had been Captain Fowler instead of me?' There would have been celebration, he'd stake his life on it.

Tess's face showed that she saw his point.

He shrugged. 'All that matters now is that Amelie gets well.' He reached for the latch on the door. 'I want to see her.'

'She is sleeping. The doctor told us to give her laudanum.'

'Laudanum?' he asked. 'Is she in pain?'

Tess shook her head. 'It is just to help her sleep. Just for today, he said.'

He nodded. 'I will not awaken her. But I want to see her.'

He lifted the latch and slipped quietly into the room.

The curtains were drawn and only one lamp was lit. He could see her on the bed, but only as a shadow.

The shadow stirred. 'Who is there?'

He stepped closer. 'It is Edmund.'

'Edmund.' She sat up against the pillows. 'You came back.'

He walked to the side of her bed. 'Of course I came back. I only left to do some errands.' And to sleep.

'I thought you would never come back.' Her voice slurred. 'I thought you ran away to Belgium.'

He wiped a stray hair from her forehead. 'Why would you think that?'

'Oh…' She blinked as if keeping her eyes open was difficult. 'Because of the baby.'

Had she wanted him to leave? He could not tell.

'No, I am here, as I said I would be.' He rested his hand on her bed.

She placed her hand over it, and her lids fluttered closed. 'Your hand feels very nice.'

'How are you faring, Amelie?' he asked.

'Oh…' Her eyes opened again briefly. 'I am so very sad. But the bleeding stopped so that makes me grateful.

'Bleeding?' His voice rose in anxiety.

She nodded. 'Mrs Bayliss said it is all right to bleed. I much prefer her to the doctor.' She added, 'Sally helped me, though.'

'I am glad.' She was not making much sense. Perhaps he could contrive to speak to Mrs Bayliss, discover whether bleeding was serious or not.

She started drifting off to sleep.

'I'll leave you now. Sleep well,' he murmured.

Her eyes flew open. 'Do not leave! Do not go to Brussels.'

He clasped her hand. 'I am not leaving. For Brussels or anywhere else.'

'Not leaving…' She started drifting off again.

'I will look in on you tomorrow,' he said.

She nodded, but her eyes were closed and he was uncertain if she knew what he was saying.

He left the room and found Tess waiting in the hall.

'Lord and Lady Northdon know you are here,' she said. 'They told me they would be pleased for you to stay to dinner.'

Pleased? He doubted it. 'Do they mean it, Tess, or am I expected to refuse?'

'Of course they mean it!' she said a little too forcefully. 'I am going to stay with Amelie, but you go on. They will probably be gathering in the drawing room by now.'

Tess would not be present? Luck would have it that way, wouldn't it? Tess was the closest thing he had to a right flank.

'I'll head down.' He started for the stairs but stopped and turned back to her. 'Oh, Tess?'

'Yes?' She was about to enter Amelie's room.

'Thank you for helping to care for Amelie.'

Her brows rose. 'Oh, my goodness. You really care for her, don't you?'

He gave her a direct look. 'I do indeed.'

When he reached the hall, Staines said, 'They are waiting for you in the drawing room, sir.'

He made a wry smile. 'Thank you.'

He crossed the hall to the drawing-room door, hesitated a moment and straightened his spine, promising himself to remain civil and gentlemanly, no matter what.

He entered the room.

Lord and Lady Northdon were seated together on the sofa, their heads close together in conversation. Glenville had his back to the door and looked to be pouring a glass of wine.

'Good evening,' Edmund said.

They all glanced his way. Wariness in Glenville's expression. Anxiety in Lady Northdon's. Lord Northdon looked upon him with raw antipathy.

Lord Northdon spoke first. 'Where have you been all day?'

Glenville crossed the room, shook his hand and handed him a glass of wine. 'Good evening, Edmund.' He was trying to be cordial, at least.

Edmund was grateful.

Edmund turned to Lady Northdon and bowed. 'I hope you were able to get some rest, *madame.*'

'*Oui,* a little,' she said.

Glenville gestured for him to sit, and he took a chair not too close to Amelie's parents. He took a sip of wine.

'Sir,' he said to Lord Northdon. 'I did not immediately answer your question. I returned to my hotel and slept most of the day.'

'Your hotel?' Lady Northdon exclaimed.

'I kept my room there.' He did not explain he'd kept it because they'd never invited him into this house. 'It is best I stay there until Amelie recovers. Less trouble for you.'

'We can make up a room for you,' Lady Northdon said.

'Your offer is appreciated, *madame*, but it might be better if I am not underfoot.'

'Humph!' Lord Northdon shot him a contemptuous glance. 'You simply abandon my daughter after all she has been through? All you caused?'

Edmund bristled and fought to hold his tongue. And his fists.

'Papa,' Glenville broke in. 'You need to give Edmund a chance. We all do.'

Maybe Edmund did have one more ally besides Tess.

He leaned towards Lord Northdon. 'I sat with your daughter all last night, sir, and I just went up to see her before this. I will not abandon her.' She could send him away, but he'd never abandon her.

Lord Northdon averted his head and drank his glass of wine.

Edmund understood to a point. Lord Northdon wanted to know him only as the bastard son of a baronet who'd defiled his daughter, not the man he was. Too many people in Edmund's life had been like that.

He shrugged inwardly. He could only control his own behaviour, not how others reacted to him.

'Amelie seemed comfortable,' he said, seeking a normal conversation. 'Although she was not entirely making sense. That was the laudanum, though, I'm certain.'

'Hmmph.' Lord Northdon took a sip of his wine. 'You are certain. Are you an expert on laudanum now?'

Edmund faced him. 'Not an expert, but I had some experience with laudanum when I was injured in Spain.'

'You were injured in Spain?' Glenville asked.

'At Albuhera,' he responded.

Lord Northdon finished his wine and turned away.

The butler came then to announce dinner.

Dinner was a strained affair, but Edmund tried to make pleasant conversation with people who wished he had never existed.

No one mentioned the baby.

After dinner Edmund excused himself to return to Amelie's room, but before going there, he used the servants' stairs to go below in search of Mrs Bayliss.

She was in the servants' hall, talking to two of the maids.

'Mrs Bayliss,' he called to her from the doorway. 'Might I have a word with you?'

'Mr Summerfield, sir.' She stood and walked towards him. 'Of course. What may I do for you?'

He liked this housekeeper. She was both efficient and kind. 'I had a question. Miss Glenville—Mrs Summerfield, I mean—said she'd had bleeding. Is that something serious?'

The cook patted his hand. 'Not at all. It is like her monthly, you know. Nothing to worry over. Merely her body coming back to normal.'

'I thank you, ma'am.' He hesitated before speaking again. 'May I ask how you come by this knowledge? It seems considerable.'

'My mother was a midwife, sir, and I went with her many a time soon as I was old enough to follow her directions. I would have followed in her footsteps, but she died young and I went into service instead.'

Another person whose plans in life had been abruptly altered. 'I am very grateful you were here when we needed you.'

She blushed. 'Thank you, sir.'

He started to leave but turned back to her. 'Ma'am, I wonder if you might beg a favour from the servants. Ask them not to speak of these events? I wish to protect my wife's reputation and that of the family. They have all suffered enough from gossip.'

'We have already agreed upon it, sir,' she told him, her expression firm. 'We are devoted to the family.'

He extended his hand to her, and she placed hers in his. 'If ever I can be of assistance to any of you, let me know.'

She curtsied. 'Thank you, sir.'

He walked back to the stairs, acknowledging the curious stares of the kitchen maids and other servants he passed.

When he reached Amelie's room, he knocked and waited for Tess to come out.

'She's still sleeping,' Tess said.

'Has she eaten?' he asked.

Tess frowned. 'Nothing to speak of. We were able to convince her to take some broth, but that is all.'

She had to eat.

'Have you eaten?' he thought to ask.

'No,' Tess responded. 'I feared I would wake her.'

He waved a hand. 'Go. Have dinner. I will sit with her.'

'Are you staying here tonight?' she asked.

'In the room with Amelie, you mean?' He had not planned to. 'Yes. I'll stay with her.' He wanted to, he realised.

'You do not have to stay in her room, you know,' Tess said. 'We can have a bedchamber ready for you.'

They'd obviously not gone to that trouble yet. 'No need. All my belongings are at Stephen's Hotel. I'll return there in the morning.'

'You will not move in here?' she asked, clearly disapproving.

He gave her a direct look. 'Tess. I have yet to be invited to stay.'

'Of course you are welcome to stay!' she protested.

'I am not welcome,' he said. 'I dare say they wish I had left the day before yesterday.'

She put her hands on her hips and leaned forward. 'You must stop this, Edmund. For better or for worse, you are connected to this family, and you must learn to get along with them.'

He bent his head and nodded. 'I will try. I am trying.'

She touched his arm. 'Good! We should all try to make something good of this, right?'

He shrugged. 'If something good can come from losing a child.'

'It is awful, I know.' She gripped his arm and shook it. 'Marc and I had to overcome a great deal to make something good of our marriage. You can, too.'

He was puzzled. 'What did you and Marc have to overcome?'

She released him. 'Some day I will tell you. Not now. I am famished, and I intend to take your direction and find something to eat.'

She walked away, and he opened Amelie's door and entered the room, where curtains were drawn and only one lamp was lit.

She stirred and he halted, watching her, but she did not wake. He lowered himself into the chair and drew a hand through his hair.

How could they make something good of this? It seemed impossible.

Chapter Thirteen

When Amelie woke the next morning, it was like swimming through a dark, murky sea into the light. Even her room was bright with sunlight. She remembered strange dreams and a feeling like floating in water, bobbing along like a fish caught in a current too strong to swim against. Her head ached and she felt a little dizzy, but at least the objects in the room remained still and did not alter their appearance.

Was she alone? Any time she woke before, when the room was dark, someone was sitting with her. Or at least she thought she'd been awake. She rolled over to see.

Edmund was with her. Sleeping on the chair as he had done the night before. She'd thought he'd left her! That is what her muddled mind and frantic dreams had told her. Yet here he was.

She checked herself. Her bleeding was not so alarming now. Mrs Bayliss said it was normal, and even the *accoucheur* told her to expect bleeding for a week or so. She need not stay in bed. She longed to be out of it, longed to be anywhere but this room, this bed, with the memories of what had happened here.

No reason why she could not rise now, put on a wrapper and sit by the window. She glanced over at Edmund, still sleeping, and moved as quietly as she could. Her legs seemed weak, and her head spun as she tried to stand. Steadying herself on the bed, she reached the trunk upon which her wrapper was folded. She sat on the trunk to put it on and then slowly rose and moved as if she were Madame Saqui, the Vauxhall Gardens tightrope walker.

She was surprisingly weak for just being in bed a day. Perhaps that was what happens when… No, she did not want to think of why she felt this way. She only wished to look outside at the street and reassure herself that carriages still rolled by, that trees and grass still grew. Her world seemed so changed, why not all of it?

She stood at the glass and discovered the same street, the same row of houses as always. A cat crossed the road and that small thing felt even more reassuring.

'Amelie?'

She turned. Edmund had risen from the chair, his hair mussed and his face again in need of a shave.

He walked over to her. 'Are you feeling better?'

She nodded. 'Merely a little weak.'

'Hungry?' he asked.

Food seemed so utterly unimportant, but his mention of it made her stomach growl. 'Yes. I suppose I am.'

He buttoned his waistcoat. 'I will have some food sent up to you. Shall I summon Sally, as well?

Her heart started to race. 'Are you leaving?'

'I should,' he said. 'But I will be back. I'll come in the afternoon and look in on you.'

She could only stare at him. He smiled, but whether it was in reassurance or apology, she could not tell. Perhaps it was pity.

He walked out the door, and she was helpless to stop him.

There was nothing in his leaving to make her bereft, she told herself, yet her throat tightened and tears pricked her eyes. She willed them away. Why should he stay? His reason to stay existed no more.

She should be happy he had stayed with her these past two nights. She'd rather he'd lain next to her.

There she went again, thinking shameless thoughts. Such thoughts had led to—to all that had happened.

Why had he spent the night in her room? She could not figure it. He stayed and he left. He seemed kind, but it felt as though a wall stood between them.

A wall erected because—because of what she had lost.

There was a knock on her door, and Sally peeked her head in. 'Mr Summerfield said you might want me, miss—ma'am, I mean.'

Amelie smiled at the girl. 'Good morning, Sally. Yes. I think I would like to get dressed, but before you help me, would you tell Cook that I will not need a plate of food sent up to my room? I would like to eat in the dining room.'

She did not wish to sit alone with her memories in this room.

Amelie held on to the banister but managed the stairs fairly well. The more she walked, the steadier she felt. Staines was in the hallway, and he opened the door to the dining room for her.

Marc and Tess were seated at the table.

'Amelie!' Tess cried.

Marc jumped to his feet to assist her to a chair. 'What are you doing out of bed?' he asked. 'Where is Edmund?'

'Edmund left.' She did not like the frowns that appeared on both their faces. 'He had several errands.'

'You must be feeling better.' Tess forced a smile. 'But are you certain you should be up and about?'

Amelie stared past them. 'I could not stay in that room.'

'Well, now you are here,' her brother broke in. 'Shall I fix a plate for you?'

'Thank you.' She was not certain she could balance a plate of food and walk at the same time. 'Some toasted bread and jam would be lovely.'

He cut pieces of bread and put them in the toasting rack and set it near the fire.

Tess poured her a cup of tea. 'Tell us how you are feeling.'

Unhappy, confused, aching. *Grieving.*

'Almost back to my old self,' she said instead. 'I do feel a little weak, though. Almost as though I had too much wine to drink.'

Tess handed her the cup of tea. 'The doctor gave you laudanum to help you sleep yesterday.'

Marc turned her toast. 'Do not exert yourself today,' he said.

'I promise,' she responded. 'But I would love to sit in the library, unless Papa needs it to work.'

Marc brought her the toast, a dish of butter and one of raspberry jam. 'I do not know his plans.' He paused and glanced at Tess again. 'I must go out, but Tess may be able to keep you company.'

She actually preferred to be alone. 'That would be lovely, but unnecessary. I do not need anyone with me all the time. I am sufficiently recovered.'

The only person she wished to have as company was Edmund. Until she saw him, talked to him, she did not even know what tomorrow would bring.

After Edmund returned to the hotel and shaved and changed clothes, he sat down to read his correspondence.

Anything to distract him.

A letter from Count von Osten detailed some possible investment opportunities Edmund could explore. He ought to look into it today. He needed to stay occupied.

He should write to the Count and Lady Summerfield.

Inform them of his marriage, but then he would have to tell them about—the other. He was not ready to write those words.

He rose from his chair and picked up his hat and gloves. In the hall he told the servant where he was going, just in case he was needed. In case anything happened to Amelie.

He walked briskly to Threadneedle Street and the office of his stockbroker. When he finished with the man, though, his malaise returned. He wandered through the Exchange, watching its vendors energetically sell their varied wares.

Perhaps he should buy Amelie a gift?

What a paltry idea. As if a mere gift could compensate.

'Summerfield!' a voice behind him shouted. 'I would speak with you now.'

He turned.

A few feet away, Lord Tinmore leaned on his cane, a footman in attendance. Other gentlemen in the area stared curiously. If he cut the man, likely the tongues of the *ton* would start to wag. Better he not add to the inevitable gossip.

He strode over to Tinmore. 'Sir?'

Tinmore's eyes glinted with triumph. At having one of his orders followed, probably.

'What is your business here?' Tinmore demanded.

Could this man be any more insufferable? Edmund leaned down to him and spoke in as mild a tone as he could muster. 'I will not answer that question, sir.' He bowed. 'I hope you are well, sir. How is my sister, your wife?'

'Hmmph,' the man uttered. 'She is in excellent health, of course. If you must know, I kept her from that patched-up affair of a wedding of yours.'

As Genna had told him. 'It saddened me not to have her there.'

Tinmore grimaced. 'I would not have her distressed.'

'It was not a distressing event.' Edmund did not need this. His temper was worn thin as it was.

'And now the whole reason for it is gone. Ha! How is that?' Tinmore's expression turned smug.

Edmund felt the blood drain from his face. Tess! Could she not keep her mouth shut? He closed his eyes and fought for control. When he opened them again, he glared directly into Tinmore's face. 'You have crossed a line, sir. Our conversation is finished.'

He turned away.

'It would be a shame for that whole mucked-up story to leak out, would it not?' Tinmore called after him.

Edmund swung back. 'What is your meaning?'

Triumph returned to Tinmore's eyes. 'I am greatly desirous that my wife and her unmarried sister have as little contact with you as possible. I would not be so unkind as to forbid it of them, but...' He grinned, revealing yellowing teeth.

'You damned blackguard,' Edmund said just loud enough for Tinmore to hear. 'You are blackmailing me.'

'That is it.' Tinmore's smile merely widened. 'I want you gone. Leave or somehow the whole story of your sordid mess will become known to everyone.'

Tinmore hobbled away, signalling his footman to come with him.

That cursed reprobate! Threatening to expose Amelie's secret. Edmund stood frozen with rage.

'What did he want?'

Was he to have no peace this day? Edmund swung around. It was Glenville who'd spoken.

Edmund evaded Glenville's question. 'To be as unpleasant as possible.'

Glenville frowned. 'He threatened you, didn't he?'

Edmund's brows rose. 'Why should he threaten me?'

'Because he's a damned autocrat who enjoys manipulating people.' Glenville snapped.

Edmund regarded him closely. 'And how do you know this?'

His brother-in-law's eyes flashed with anger. 'He once threatened me.'

Indeed? 'Well, he is still up to the same old tricks.'

Glenville did not press him to say more. 'Where are you bound now?' was all he asked.

Edmund's eyes narrowed. 'Why?'

'Because I would like to talk to you,' Glenville responded mildly.

'You came looking for me,' Edmund realised.

'Yes,' Glenville admitted. 'The servant at the hotel said you would be at the Exchange.'

His anxiety rose. 'Amelie! Is she ill again?'

'No. No.' Glenville made a placating gesture. 'She is much improved, as a matter of fact.'

Edmund's shoulders relaxed.

'I merely desired to talk with you away from the house,' Glenville explained.

Away from his parents? Tess? Or from Amelie?

'Very well.' Edmund was eager to be done with it.

They found a nearby tavern and sat in a secluded booth. The tavern maid brought them two tankards of ale.

Glenville took a sip of his. 'One thing I miss about Brussels is the beer, but this will do for now.'

Edmund was in no mood for friendly chitchat. 'What did you want to speak to me about?'

'I want to apologise for my parents. And for myself. We have not made any of this easy for you.' Glenville sounded sincere.

'I understand it,' Edmund said.

'You are welcome to stay at the town house,' he went

on. 'My mother and father are remiss at not making that clear to you.'

He appreciated the gesture, but Glenville was mistaken. He'd be tolerated, perhaps, but not welcome. 'It is better I remain at the hotel, at least until Amelie is recovered and we can leave.'

'Leave?' Glenville's brows rose. 'Where will you go?'

'I am not certain,' Edmund responded. 'But after this encounter with Tinmore, we'll not stay in London.' And risk having what Amelie would wish kept secret become the latest on dit in town.

Amelie curled up in one of the comfortable chairs in the library, using her shawl to help keep her warm. She really did not have the energy or concentration to read or do needlework, so she merely watched the glow of the coals in the fireplace.

Staines came to the doorway. 'Miss Summerfield to see you, ma'am.'

Ma'am. She could not get used to being ma'am instead of miss, but, then, there was not much around that would remind her she was married. She glanced down at her hands. Her rings. Her lovely rings.

'Ma'am?' Staines asked again.

'Yes.' She tried to focus her mind. 'Show her in.'

Genna breezed in. 'Amelie! How are you?' She came over to her and bussed her on the cheek. 'How terrible for you.'

She knew? 'Tess told you what happened?'

'Of course she did,' Genna said.

Amelie slumped in her chair. Why had Tess spoken so soon?

'I am very well now,' Amelie said. 'No one need be concerned about me.'

'Well, I am.' Genna lifted her chin. 'What an ordeal and the night after your wedding.'

She wished Genna would go away. 'It is over.'

'Did you regret it had not happened before the wedding?' Genna's voice was without malice and entirely sympathetic.

Still, the question jarred Amelie. It also jarred her that she did not know the answer. 'Have you asked your brother that question?'

'Goodness, no!' Genna laughed. 'He'd chew my head off if I did and would never answer me. I am half-surprised that you have not told me to go to the devil, but, then, you are much too nice.'

Was that a compliment or an insult? Amelie was unsure.

'It is what everyone is thinking, you know,' Genna went on. 'How much better it would have been and all that.'

Amelie bristled. 'Is that what you think?'

Genna sobered. 'I think all of this must be very hard for you, Amelie, and I wish my brother would have thought of what might happen before he indulged in an indiscretion.'

Edmund was not to blame for any of it. Not even the loss—

'I indulged in the indiscretion, too,' Amelie said.

Genna considered this. 'Yes, I suppose you did. How easy it must have been to be carried away by emotion that night of all nights. I confess I have never felt such emotion towards a man. They all seem like fortune hunters to me. Not that the fortune Tinmore has settled on me is all that great. It does seem the most important thing to them, though.'

It had been for Fowler. 'At least that did not matter to Tess and Marc. They are a love match.' It certainly hadn't mattered to her parents either.

'Tess and Marc?' Genna sounded surprised. 'I admit they seem to be devoted to each other now, but—' She peered at Amelie. 'Do you not know the circumstances of their marriage?'

'They met in Lincolnshire,' she said lamely.

'Yes,' Genna agreed. 'They met in a storm. He rescued her and they took refuge in a cabin overnight. Tinmore found out about it and forced them to marry or he threatened to cause a big scandal.' She glanced away. 'If I had been Tess, I would have called his bluff, though. Or let the scandal happen.'

Marc and Tess had been forced to marry? That explained why Marc had left her after the wedding. Why had no one ever told her? 'It worked out for them, though. They seem besotted now.'

'Amazing, isn't it?' Genna said. 'But they are the exception, do you not think? What other married persons do you know who truly care about each other?'

Her mother and father, although throughout most of her life they'd been at loggerheads with each other. Somehow they had reconciled in Brussels.

The clock on the mantel chimed, and Genna stood. 'I must go. Heaven forbid I arrive home after Tinmore and need to explain where I've been!'

Amelie started to rise, but Genna gestured for her to remain sitting.

She walked over to Amelie's chair and clasped her hand. 'You continue to recover, do you hear? I will see myself out.'

Like a whirlwind zipping through a meadow, she was gone.

Amelie's mind was spinning with what Genna had left in her wake. The idea that Edmund might wish she'd had the miscarriage a day earlier. That Marc and Tess had been forced to marry. That she could trust no one to tell her the truth.

Chapter Fourteen

Edmund and Glenville talked of other things on the walk back to Mayfair. Glenville asked about his investments. Edmund told him, even though he suspected his sister's husband worried that he'd lose everything the way their father had.

When they reached Bond Street, Glenville asked, 'Will you come home with me?'

'I'll come after I change for dinner.' He'd promised Amelie he would return.

'Good,' Glenville said.

They reached the entrance of Stephen's Hotel.

Glenville extended his hand. 'I'll leave you here, then.'

Edmund accepted the handshake.

'I am glad I had an opportunity to talk with you,' Glenville said.

Edmund was still not certain of this man. Was he friend or foe?

'I will see you shortly,' he said.

Edmund arrived at the Northdon town house within an hour. Again he sounded the knocker like the outsider the family felt him to be.

Staines opened the door and greeted him with less surprise than the day before.

He handed Staines his hat and gloves. 'Is Mrs Summerfield in her room?'

'The library, sir,' Staines responded.

'Ah,' Edmund remarked. 'She must be feeling better.'

'I believe so, sir,' Staines said.

Edmund went to the library and knocked on the door before entering. He could not see her, and the light was low in the room. 'Amelie?'

She peeked out from a large chair facing the fireplace. 'I am here, Edmund.'

He crossed the room to her.

'Please have a seat.' She, too, spoke as if he were a visitor.

He longed to touch her, to enfold her in his arms and tell her how sorry he was, but her reserve held him back. Instead he lowered himself into a chair flanking hers. 'I am pleased to see you up.'

'I do not like staying in my bedchamber.' She shuddered. 'My mother or Tess comes in to check on me. They seem to believe I cannot be left alone too long.'

'Likely they worry about you.' He worried about her. Her sadness enveloped her like a shroud.

'Your sister Genna called,' she went on, although her conversation seemed forced. 'Out of curiosity, I suspect. Or because Lord Tinmore would not want her to come.'

Either sounded like Genna. 'Tess would have told her what—what happened.'

'Yes.' She glanced away. 'Genna asked me if I had wished it had happened the day before instead.'

'Genna asked you that?' He blew out a breath. 'Damned impertinence!'

Amelie lifted one shoulder. 'She merely said what everyone is thinking.'

Was Amelie wishing that, too, wishing she had waited one more day before marrying? That assumed the baby would be lost anyway and not because he'd made love to her.

'It suits no purpose to think about what might have been.' Of the baby who never quite was.

The door opened and Amelie's mother entered. 'How are you? I have brought tea.' She saw Edmund and stopped. '*Pardon*. I did not know you were here.'

Edmund rose and bowed. 'Good afternoon, *madame*. I hope you are well.' He stepped over to her. 'Let me take the tray off your hands.' He placed the tray on a nearby table.

'*Merci,*' she said, glancing away.

'Maman,' Amelie said. 'Why have you not arranged for Edmund to stay? Surely a room could be provided for him.'

'*Bien sûr*, he may stay. He stays the night in your room, no?' she snapped.

He broke in. 'Until you are fully recovered, it may be best for me to keep my room at Stephen's Hotel.'

'Is that what you want?' Amelie asked him.

What did *wanting* have to do with it? Nothing happened as he wanted.

Lady Northdon answered for him. 'I think it is best.' She gave Amelie a significant look. 'Your father. *Tu comprends?*'

'I agree,' Edmund said. 'Your father will be more comfortable if I am not underfoot.'

Lady Northdon nodded approvingly. '*Là*, I will leave you to your conversation. Amelie, you can pour the tea, no?'

'I will pour, Maman.'

'And do not dress for dinner, *ma chère*. It is only family.' She leaned down to give Amelie a kiss on the cheek and hurried out the door.

Amelie carefully rose from her chair and moved unsteadily to the tea table. 'How do you take your tea, Edmund?

'A little milk.' Lawd. They did not even know how the other took tea.

He reached for the cup so she would not have to hand it to him. She balanced her own with difficulty as she walked back to her chair.

'You are still weak,' he said.

She shrugged. 'A little.'

He sat. 'You should stay in this house until you are completely well.'

'And then?' There was no expression in her voice.

'Then we should leave London.'

She looked puzzled. 'But we decided—'

He did not have the heart to tell her of Tinmore's threat. It was too cruel and she was too vulnerable.

He searched for what to say. 'Until the gossipers forget all about us.'

Her blue eyes turned sad. 'But the reason for the gossip is gone now.'

He felt the pang of that loss, too, like a rapier thrust into his heart.

'Still…' What could he say?

She eyed him suspiciously. 'There is something you are not telling me.'

He glanced away.

Edmund was hiding things from her, too. She turned away from him, wishing he would leave.

Fearing he would leave and never return.

Finally he made a frustrated sound. 'Forgive me. You should know this. I fear it will hurt you, but you should know this.'

Was he leaving, then?

His eyes were pained. 'Tinmore sought me out today. He threatened to reveal everything. About our marriage. About the—the baby—'

She turned back to him. 'Why would he do such a thing?'

'Because he wants me far away from my sister. His wife.'

She shook her head. 'No, it is because you stood up to him.'

He made a disparaging laugh. 'And all I accomplished was to hurt you.'

Did he think a little gossip hurt? She might have once agreed, but now she knew what real pain felt like.

He gazed at her again. 'I do not wish to trap you with me, if you do not wish it. I could go away. You could stay with your parents. Go with them to the country.'

She gaped at him. 'Do you wish to leave me?'

He left his chair and knelt at hers. He touched her hand, but it only reminded her of how the feel of his skin against hers had once ignited her senses. Everything seemed dead inside now.

'I know our—our loss changes things,' he said. 'We are married, though. I will not leave you unless that is what you desire.'

She pulled her hand away and curled up in the chair, covering herself with her shawl. 'Then let us go far away. Together. Where we know nobody.'

She closed her eyes, needing to be alone. His was the only company she could bear, but, at the moment, she could not even stand to be with herself.

She heard him rise.

'When it is time for dinner, shall I come for you, Amelie?'

She nodded.

As soon as she heard the door close behind her, she instantly regretted not asking him to stay with her. Where would he go? To the drawing room where her father would snap at him and her mother look upon him with disappointment?

Getting away. Going far away. The idea grew inside her. New scenery. Unfamiliar walls in some strange house. People who never knew her before. It all sounded lovely.

A place without reminders.

When Edmund came for her and escorted her to dinner, they did not speak. At the dinner table he sat across the table next to Tess. It was easier to look at him than the rest of them. Her father still seemed ready to explode at any moment. Her mother's lovely face was etched with worry. Tess's was all sympathy.

Why could they not at least pretend everything was normal?

Amelie had no appetite. She stirred the soup with her spoon.

'You must eat, *chérie*,' her mother chided.

She did not want to cause more worry. 'Yes, Maman.'

She made herself lift the spoon to her mouth but tasted nothing.

At least her mother's worry lines eased a bit.

Maybe that was the trick. Maybe if she pretended everything was as it should be, her family would follow suit.

'The soup is very nice.' She forced a smile and put another spoonful in her mouth.

Her mother, father and Tess smiled back. Her brother, seated next to her, gave her a playful tap on the arm.

When the main course was served, she made herself eat a little of everything.

'I believe I was hungry,' she said to murmurs of approval.

Yes, pretending would work.

'I think my health will return in a day or so,' she said.

Her mother frowned. 'Do not rush so, *chérie.*'

She girded herself. 'Edmund and I will wish to leave as soon as possible.'

'Leave!' her mother, father, and Tess all cried in unison.

'Non,' her mother said. 'There is no hurry. You must rest. '

'Give yourself time,' Tess added.

Her father glared at Edmund. 'What is this about leaving?'

Edmund put down his knife and fork. 'We talked today about living away from here for a while.'

'Then you must come to the country with us,' her mother said. 'There is plenty of room at Northdon House.'

'Not Northdon House, Maman,' Amelie said. 'Some place new that I never saw before.'

Her father turned to Edmund. 'This is your idea, no doubt.'

'It is,' Edmund agreed.

'It is not a bad idea,' Marc said. 'By the time they return, no one will pay them any mind. We'll all be spared the sort of mean-spirited gossip we've suffered in the past.'

'I will miss you,' Tess said. 'I'll miss you both.'

Amelie took a breath. This was going well. She could almost believe she cared about where she lived or what she did.

She looked at Edmund. 'I was thinking we should go to the Lake District. Wordsworth says it is beautiful there.' They had all read the poet's *Guide to the Lakes*.

He gazed at her, his expression soft and...hopeful. 'Would you truly like to go to the Lake District, Amelie?'

Could he tell she was pretending?

'Yes,' she replied as emphatically as her pretence would allow. 'It will be a lovely adventure, and everyone says the air is like a tonic.'

He smiled at her, a tentative smile. 'Then that is where we shall go.'

Marc slammed a hand down on the table. 'Middlerock!'

'Middlerock?' Her father's brows knitted.

Marc addressed Edmund. 'Middlerock is one of Father's properties. A sheep farm in Cumberland.' He turned to his father. 'You have not travelled there for years. Would it not be advantageous for Edmund to see how it is faring?'

Her father frowned. 'True, I have not travelled there for years, but my man of business keeps tabs on it.'

'Do you not say it is wise to make an appearance at your properties?' Marc persisted. 'Have I not heard you say you should visit Middlerock?'

'Cumberland is so far away,' her mother murmured.

'It is very remote.' Her father seized on that idea. 'And it is a bit rustic for Amelie. More like a hunting lodge than a comfortable house.'

'I would like rustic.' Amelie made herself sound enthusiastic. 'I want a complete change of scenery.'

Her father's stern expression wavered.

'You must be comfortable with this, sir,' Edmund told him.

'Bah!' Her father waved a hand. 'What do you know of sheep farming?'

Edmund cocked his head. 'We had sheep on my father's estate. I was often my father's companion when he visited the estate manager and the farm workers. I learned a great deal about running a farm.'

'Please, Papa,' Amelie said.

Her father loved her, she knew. He had difficulty denying her anything. Her pretending was working rather well. She almost believed she wanted this.

'One thing, though,' Edmund said. 'You must give me complete authority to act on your behalf. I will not go there unless I can be useful to you.'

Her father reached for his wine glass and drank its contents. He shot a glance at Amelie before staring down at his plate. 'Very well. I'll give you permission to act in my stead.'

'Fully?' Edmund asked.

'Well, I would not like it if you sold the place or lost it in a card game or something,' her father snapped.

The corners of Edmund's mouth twitched as if he were suppressing a smile. 'I give my word I will do neither of those things.'

'We can go to my solicitor tomorrow and draw up the papers.' Her father's shoulders slumped.

'Mon Dieu,' her mother muttered.

Amelie's hand trembled. She was suddenly weak with fatigue. It took too much effort to keep up her façade.

She stood. 'Forgive me. I am very tired. I must retire.'

Her mother rose as well and darted to her side. *'Ma chère pauvre*! I will take you to your room *tout de suite*!'

Amelie drew away from her. 'Edmund will take me, Maman.'

Edmund was already on his feet. He walked around the table to her. 'Can you walk, Amelie?' he asked her gently.

She nodded.

He wrapped his arm around her, and she leaned against him. His scent, his warmth enveloped her. She wished she'd let her mother help her upstairs. Her mother would not make her think of what it had been like to lie with him.

And what happened as a result.

When they reached the stairs, she took hold of the banister. 'I can manage.'

He remained next to her, though, and he offered her his arm when they started down the corridor to her room.

'Are you in any pain?' he asked her.

She shook her head. Not the physical kind anyway. 'I am tired. I did too much.'

'Promise you will rest tomorrow?' His voice was filled with concern.

She planned to pretend to be all better if she could. 'I will.'

As they neared the door she shrank back. 'I hate this room.'

He hugged her next to him, but she pulled away. His kindness was hard to bear when he should be furious with her.

'I—I feel I pushed you into this idea of the Lake District,' she said. 'I should have spoken to you privately.'

'It is an excellent idea, Amelie,' he said. 'If you desire it, it is where we will go.'

She leaned against the wall. 'Are you certain?'

He stood close but did not touch her. 'It meets our needs. If that changes we will go elsewhere.'

'What I need, I cannot have.' She gazed up at him, her sadness nearly choking her.

He nodded.

She pushed away from the wall and braced herself before reaching for the door handle. She turned back to him. 'Goodnight, Edmund.'

'Goodnight,' he murmured.

She opened the door and quickly entered.

Edmund stared at the closed door for a few moments before turning back towards the stairs. He still did not move. Instead he pressed his forehead against the wall where Amelie had leaned and fancied he could still feel her warmth.

It was a good idea to take her away, away from wagging tongues, away from families, away from the memories.

This farm, though, sounded like the furthest thing from the power and energy of Brussels or the excitement of foreign lands that Edmund had once wanted. But he wanted to please Amelie, to make up to her what he'd caused them to lose. If a sheep farm in Cumberland pleased her, then that was where he wanted to go.

If they could be alone, away from all this, perhaps they might find a way to reconcile themselves to this forced marriage, even though the reason for marrying was lost.

He pushed away from the wall and walked down the corridor to the stairs. He descended slowly, reluctant to rejoin her parents, who so clearly did not welcome him into their home.

Amelie only woke a few times during the night to toss and turn with memories and grief. When morning came, she felt stronger.

Perhaps it would not take as much effort to pretend to be recovered as it had the evening before.

Sally came into the room, carrying fresh linens and looking pale and unhappy. 'You are awake, ma'am.'

What was troubling the girl? Whatever it was, Amelie's grief so consumed her she had nothing of herself to give to her unhappy maid.

'Will you wish to dress this morning?' Sally asked.

Amelie sat up in the bed. 'Yes, please. I am going to try to have a normal day.' As if she could ever have a normal day again.

Sally helped her out of her nightdress and set out her clothing while Amelie washed herself. She helped Amelie into her dress before she sat down to the dressing table and began to brush the tangles out of her hair.

'They say below stairs that you will be leaving soon,' Sally said.

The servants knew already. They knew everything now.

'That is so,' Amelie responded. 'Mr Summerfield and I will be moving to the Lake District.'

In the mirror she saw Sally's face contort in distress.

The girl turned her face away, but when she again resumed brushing Amelie's hair, tears rolled down her cheeks.

It made it almost impossible for Amelie to keep her tears at bay. 'Do not worry. I will tell Maman to keep you on. You will not be without employment.'

'I am not so certain.' Sally's words came haltingly.

Amelie turned around to face her. 'Tell me what troubles you.'

Sally shook her head. 'I cannot tell you after all that's happened to you!'

Tears stung Amelie's eyes. 'Of course you can tell me. I am nearly all better.'

'I am in such a fix.' Sally dropped the brush and sobbed.

Amelie left the chair and guided Sally over to sit with her on the bed. She held Sally's hands. 'What is this fix?'

Sally blinked her tears away. 'Do you know the soldier you saw me with before Waterloo? Calvin Jones?'

The poor young man who was killed in the battle. 'Of course, I remember.'

'Do you remember he was to marry me as soon as he could get leave?' Sally's voice trembled.

'Yes.'

'I—I—that night—it did not seem so bad—you must know—but what can I do now—?' she sputtered.

Amelie trembled. She knew what Sally was about to say. 'Tell me.'

Sally faced Amelie, her eyes red from crying. 'I am going to have a baby.'

A baby.

The words caused an ache deep in Amelie's belly. It felt as if a dozen swords were slashing her. She couldn't breathe. She closed her eyes, pushed the pain away as hard as she could.

She put her arms around Sally, who began to sob against her chest.

'There. There.' Amelie comforted the girl. 'We will make this right. I will help you.'

'I—I thought I should get rid of it, but I didn't know how,' Sally wailed.

Amelie hugged her tighter. 'No, you mustn't try to get rid of it. Never think that.'

Sally leaned against Amelie's heart. 'I don't want to take my baby to the Foundling Hospital!'

'Not that either. We will fix this. I promise.'

Sally pulled away to stare at her. 'Truthfully?'

Amelie's heart pounded. 'You will come with me to the Lake District. I will not leave you.'

She could not save her own baby, but she would save Sally's.

Chapter Fifteen

Four days later they were on the road to the Lake District, beginning a journey that would take at least three days to complete. Lord Northdon provided the carriage so that the trip would be as comfortable as possible for Amelie. Lord and Lady Northdon rode with them the first day to their country house, where they spent the first night.

Lady Northdon had arranged separate bedchambers for them, and Edmund was rarely alone with Amelie more than a few minutes at a time. When they continued the journey, the bulk of which covered the Great North Road, it was no more private. Amelie's maid rode with them and spent the night in Amelie's bedchamber.

Edmund could not ascertain how Amelie felt about anything on the journey. She seemed more concerned with her maid's comfort than her own, and everything on the journey was acceptable to her. The food at the inns, the rooms for the night, the times they rose, the times they retired. Agreeable as she was, she seemed to keep herself at a distance from him.

He could not blame her, though. Before that fateful night in Brussels, she had been the cosseted daughter of an aristocrat. Now she was the wife of a reckless bastard who was taking her far away to live on a sheep farm.

* * *

On the last day they turned off the main road onto smaller and smaller ones that wound over and around hills covered in green grass and dotted with sheep. Majestic mountains rose in the distance, tinged with the reds and yellows of autumn. The air seemed crisper and cleaner than it even had been in the countryside near Northdon House. The lakes they glimpsed shimmered with water as blue as—

As blue as Amelie's eyes.

'This country is unlike what you are used to, is it not?' he asked.

'It is lovely,' she said politely.

Was she seeing it? Or merely staring into space? Her maid seemed to be taking it in.

Compared to the wilder hills and mountains of Spain, this land seemed comfortably tidy. He'd relish long walks on hills like these.

Would Amelie?

They passed through the tiny village of Middlerock, where the people on the street stopped to stare at their carriage. The farm could not be far.

About a mile from the village the carriage passed through a wrought-iron gate and made its way along a woodland drive. A white stucco house, gleaming in the afternoon sun, came into view. It was definitely small compared to the very grand Northdon House, and it looked as if it had been constructed without any notion of symmetry. Additions grew like appendages off each side of the house, one side earning three distinct sections, the other side merely one.

'There it is. What do you think of it?' Edmund asked Amelie.

An expression of dismay flitted across her face, but she quickly schooled her features. 'It should do.'

The house had five bedrooms, Lord Northdon told him. Edmund wished it had only one. Perhaps he would not feel so distant from her if he could hold her in his arms all night.

The carriage reached the unimposing entrance, a single door under a small portico with only two thin and unembellished columns. It came to a full stop before the door opened and four people emerged. Two older women, an older man and another woman of uncertain age. All were plainly dressed, and the women wore white caps.

'Our servants, I believe,' he said to Amelie.

She peered out the window. 'Oh, I did not think,' she murmured. 'I must run the house.'

'Does that worry you?' He'd take it over if she did not feel up to the task.

She darted a glance at him as if surprised he'd heard her. 'No,' she said in that annoyingly bland tone. 'I'll manage.'

The older man met the carriage as it stopped. He pulled down the steps and opened the door. One of the coachmen jumped down from the box and held the horses' heads.

Edmund disembarked first so he could help Amelie and Sally out of the carriage.

He leaned down to Amelie's ear. 'Shall we greet our servants?'

He turned to the older man who'd attended the carriage. 'I am Mr Summerfield,' Edmund said. 'And this is my wife, Mrs Summerfield, Lord Northdon's daughter. You were expecting us, I believe.'

'We were, sir,' the older man said. 'I am Lloyd, your butler.' He stepped back to where the women were waiting. 'This is Mrs Wood, the housekeeper. Mrs Stagg, the cook. And Jobson, the maid.'

It seemed too thin a staff to run a household, Edmund thought.

Amelie smiled at the servants. 'A pleasure to meet you.'

She turned to Sally, who had gathered their belongings from the carriage. 'Let me present my lady's maid, Sally— Mrs Brown, I mean.'

Edmund's brows rose. How had Sally become *Mrs Brown*?

'You will help her settle in?' Amelie asked.

The housekeeper nodded. 'We'll see to it.' She opened the door and led them inside.

They entered a small hall with a slate floor and a rather handsome arched-mahogany staircase and banister.

Mrs Wood pointed to the right. 'That is the drawing room. The dining room is on the other side of the hall. Both have been prepared for you. We do not have the whole house in order yet, I fear. The bedchambers are ready, however.'

'Show us to our bedchambers first,' Edmund told her.

'And then perhaps you would like some tea?'

He glanced to see if Amelie would answer, but she seemed to preoccupy herself with gazing at the wainscotted wall.

'Tea would be most welcome,' he said.

They climbed the mahogany stairs to the first floor, where two adjoining bedchambers had been made ready for them. The rooms were adequately, if not finely, furnished.

Amelie and Sally disappeared into one bedchamber. Edmund thanked the housekeeper and entered the other.

After a few minutes, Lloyd and the coachman carried in Edmund's trunk. After they left, Edmund changed his shirt and brushed the dirt of the road off his coat and trousers. He tested the bed. Comfortable enough, but would be much more so if shared with Amelie.

He waited, giving Amelie a sufficient amount of time to change her clothes, remembering when he'd helped her

with the task and wishing they had that measure of closeness now.

What must he do now to help her recover? To make
amends?

He walked to the connecting door. His hand remained
suspended in the air before he finally knocked.

'Come in,' he heard her say.

He opened the door but stayed in the doorway.

Her gaze rose from where she sat on the bed. 'Sally has
gone to see her room.'

He tried a smile. '*Mrs Brown*, you mean?'

She averted her face. 'I will explain that to you later.
Not now, if you please.'

'Whenever you wish,' he said mildly. He glanced around
the room, which was as serviceably furnished as his own.
'Will this room do, Amelie?'

She looked at it as if seeing it for the first time. 'Yes.
It is fine.'

It was so difficult to talk with her.

'I've endured much worse,' he said for something to
say. 'Like a leaking tent on a cold and rainy night in the
Pyrenees. But you are used to finer things.'

Her expression turned fleetingly sad. 'I do not need
finer things.'

The word *need* hung in the air. She meant that she
needed her baby, he supposed. The loss seemed so much
more important than physical discomfort, he could agree.

He stepped into the room. 'Shall we see about the tea?'

Mrs Wood brought a tea tray with biscuits as soon as
they entered the drawing room. Amelie poured the tea and
handed Edmund a cup.

Poor man! she thought, so concerned with her comfort
and trying so hard to make things right for her. Her efforts
at responding in kind fell short.

The long, idle hours in the carriage had been a horror for her. Too much time to think and so difficult to pretend she was well when tears were ever ready to fall.

She did not want this—to be weak and weeping. She wanted to be strong. To convince Edmund—and herself—that she was recovered.

She took a sip of tea and a bite of biscuit and discovered her appetite had returned. She could taste the flavours and feel the hunger for more. She finished the biscuit, took another and glanced around the room.

She liked this house, she decided. It was rustic and sparsely furnished and reminded her of nothing she knew.

The drawing room had tolerably comfortable chairs and sofas, tables, lamps, a fireplace. A carpet on the floor. Everything had been dusted, polished and brushed clean.

She thought of something positive she could say to Edmund, who leaned against the mantel drinking his tea.

'They did a fine job cleaning this room, did they not?' It occurred to her she must tell the housekeeper so.

He looked surprised she'd spoken. 'It is clean.' There was the tiniest bit of sarcasm in his voice.

It almost made her smile.

'I wonder if the room once had more adornment,' she went on.

'Perhaps we will be able to discover if it had,' he responded encouragingly.

Her sadness crept back. What did it matter whether there were porcelain figurines or vases of flowers or colourful paintings on the walls?

The clock chimed the quarter-hour.

Edmund gestured to it. 'At least there is a clock.'

It was the plainest clock she'd ever seen. A plain white face with black numerals encased in an oak box.

'Is the time correct, I wonder?' she asked. If so they had

hours to go before it would be time for dinner, after which she could beg fatigue and retire to her room.

He reached in his pocket and pulled out his timepiece. 'Three twenty. Close enough.'

What was she to do with so much time?

Edmund adjusted the hands of the clock and turned away from the mantel to place his cup on the tea tray. 'Shall we explore the house?'

It was an excellent idea, a good distraction, a way to pass the time. Plus she needed to walk after days of being cramped in the carriage.

Across the hall where Mrs Wood had indicated, they found the dining room and behind it a corridor which they guessed led to the kitchen. The back of the house revealed a library, tucked behind the drawing room, and another sitting room, this one bright with a wall composed almost entirely of windows. It was perfect for a breakfast room, Amelie thought.

They entered the library and examined the books on its shelves, the titles mostly referring to agriculture and sheep farming.

'I suppose I shall have to read some of these,' Edmund said. 'Something to look forward to.'

If there were novels tucked between such titles, Amelie did not discover them.

Off the sitting room was a surprise—a conservatory, empty of plants, but with large glass doors leading to the back garden and walls completely made of windows.

'Someone once must have cared for this house,' Amelie said. 'To build this.'

'We can grow things here,' he said encouragingly.

She tried to imagine the room filled with greenery, fragrant with flowers, filled with life. It was now a desolate, abandoned place, too much like the interior of herself, the place she was trying to keep hidden.

She wished she could respond to his efforts to cheer her. He alone knew her secrets. He alone knew she was the cause of...everything. It once had drawn her closer to him; now she'd effectively destroyed his every ambition. How could running a sheep farm compare to travelling the world and seeking a fortune?

Edmund opened a door. 'Let us go outside.'

He opened the door, and they stepped out on a terrace that had weeds growing between its flagstones.

'Oh, my!' she exclaimed, forgetting her misery.

In front of her was a great expanse of green lawn with a view of mountains turning blue in the late afternoon light, moors wild with heather, lush forest and a peek of pastures dotted white with sheep.

'It is beautiful,' she whispered.

Off to the right were the farm buildings built of ancient stone and slate roofs. A man wearing a flat wool cap stood near the buildings, elbows akimbo. Spying them, he began to approach. When he came close enough, Edmund walked forward to meet him.

'You must be Summerfield,' the man said, offering his hand. 'I am Reid, the farm steward.'

Edmund accepted the handshake and acknowledged the introduction. He turned to Amelie. 'Let me present you to my wife, Mrs Summerfield, Lord Northdon's daughter.'

'Ma'am.' He tipped his hat.

She nodded. 'This land is beautiful, Mr Reid. How lucky you are to wake to this every day.'

His brows knitted for a moment. 'It is sometimes cruel, as well,' he commented. He turned to Edmund. 'I meant to give you time to settle in before calling.'

'Kind of you,' Edmund responded. 'I am eager to speak with you. When might it be convenient?'

Reid looked wary. 'I keep early hours. Up at dawn. I'm out in the pastures shortly after.'

'I am used to early hours,' Edmund replied.

Reid's expression turned sceptical.

Amelie spoke up, 'My husband was an officer in the army, sir. That is why he is used to early hours.' Reid should know Edmund was more than the husband of Lord Northdon's daughter.

Reid looked no more interested. 'I see.'

The conservatory door opened, and Sally hurried out, coming up to them out of breath. 'Mrs Wood sent me to find you.' She noticed Mr Reid and stepped back.

Reid gazed at Sally in return, and his countenance softened.

Sally pulled her gaze back to Amelie. 'Mrs Wood said I was to ask if you would mind keeping country hours here and having dinner in half an hour.'

'Of course. We will be happy to.' Amelie turned to Mr Reid. 'Sally, this is Mr Reid, the steward.'

'Miss.' He tipped his hat to Sally.

'*Mrs Brown*, I should say,' Amelie corrected. 'Mrs Brown is a widow. She is my lady's maid.'

'Ma'am,' he corrected.

Sally blushed but did not speak to him.

Edmund broke in. 'I will meet you at the farm building at six in the morning. Will that do?'

'I will look for you.' Reid nodded to both Amelie and Sally. 'Good evening to you.'

'Good evening, Mr Reid,' Amelie said.

After their dinner, which consisted of mutton stew, bread, cheese and stilted conversation, Amelie could not feign exhaustion and retire for the night. It was too early. Instead she and Edmund returned to the drawing room.

Austere as the room was, a wood fire crackling in the fireplace gave it a welcoming warmth. The hissing and popping of the burning wood took Amelie back to the last year's yule log. A lifetime ago, it seemed. Before she'd met Fowler, before she travelled to Brussels, before the scandalous night she spent with Edmund, before the baby...

Tears stung her eyes, but she blinked them away. She glanced over to see if Edmund had noticed, but he was bent forward, rubbing his injured leg.

'Does your leg pain you?' she asked.

He looked up at her. 'A bit tonight. I think the carriage ride did it no favours.'

She'd been too self-absorbed to think of *his* comfort during the journey.

He straightened again. 'It has been a long day.'

Every day seemed long to Amelie. This evening seemed long, too, as they continued to strain for things to talk about. Amelie knew what preoccupied her, but what was Edmund thinking? How could he not be wishing he'd never met her?

'Mr Reid seemed taken with Sally,' he remarked.

'Sally is a pretty young woman,' Amelie's voice had a churlish tone, she feared.

'She is,' Edmund agreed.

They lapsed into silence again, until she remembered she owed him an explanation.

This would not be easy. 'I promised I would explain about calling Sally Mrs Brown.'

He merely raised his brows and waited for her to continue.

She took a breath. 'That night in Brussels.' She did not have to explain what night she meant. 'Do you remember that we encountered Sally in the *parc*?'

'With her soldier. I remember.' His voice was deep and smooth, and she seemed to feel it as well as hear.

'He died in the battle,' she said.

His expression turned bleak, and he averted his gaze. Remembering that day, she supposed.

She went on quickly. 'Sally is going to have his baby.' Like us, she wanted to say. Only what might have been.

'A baby,' he repeated, his voice low.

'No one knows her here, so we are calling her a widow. She is, really, in many ways, because he was going to marry her.' At least Amelie hoped Sally had not been deceived the way she had been. If so, better she never know. 'She will not be disgraced this way.'

'I see.' He frowned. 'But what of when we return to London?'

'I shall worry about that later.' They could concoct another story, if necessary. 'Her baby will have every chance in life. I am resolved in that.' To make up for her own lost child. 'I will see to it.'

He turned silent, staring into the fire.

She bit her lip. 'You do not approve?'

He glanced back at her. 'I approve. I very much approve.'

She released a relieved breath. 'You will allow our deception?'

'It is not for me to allow or forbid it, Amelie. I support it, though, and am willing to help.' He reached over and touched her hand. 'This is good of you, Amelie.'

His touch warmed her, just as it had done on their wedding day. She pulled her hand away. 'I—I believe I shall go upstairs and retire for the night. I—I am much fatigued.'

He nodded, but his eyes were pained. 'I will go, too. Since I am to rise before dawn.'

Edmund carried a candle to light their way as they walked up the winding staircase to their rooms. Amelie did not take his arm out of fear that desire would ignite if she touched him. How awful that would be, showing she wanted him only days after—

He walked her to the door of her bedchamber, their little candle making a cocoon of light around them. In the darkness the house seemed eerie and strange, full of shadows and creaking floorboards.

He put his hand on the latch of her door. 'Do I say good-night to you here, Amelie?'

She could not look at him. 'I—I am very weary.'

He turned the latch and opened the door. 'Sleep well,' he murmured.

She darted a glance to him. She wanted to tell him to knock on the connecting door after Sally readied her for bed, but she couldn't.

'Goodnight,' she said, a little too shrill.

She hurried into the room and shut the door behind her.

Sally was in the room waiting for her.

'I—I believe I'll go to bed early,' she told her.

'Very good, ma'am.'

Sally helped her change into her nightdress, after which she sat at a small dressing table while Sally pulled the pins from her hair and brushed out the tangles.

'How has this day been for you?' Amelie asked her.

'The others have been kind to me,' Sally answered. 'They've been very busy but helpful.'

'Did you get enough to eat?'

'Oh, yes, ma'am,' Sally assured her. 'As much stew as I could want.'

Amelie was glad to hear it. Sally must eat well and stay healthy for the baby's sake.

'And your room,' she asked. 'Is it comfortable?'

'It is very comfortable, ma'am.' She plaited Amelie's hair. 'It is on the second floor. A small room next to the stairway. Very plain, but all I need. Even a chair and table. I have never had a room of my own before.'

'I am glad you like it.' Amelie was determined that Sally have every possible comfort.

Sally tied the plait with a ribbon and Amelie stood.

'Will it be all right if I stay up a little?' Sally asked. 'I am not sleepy.'

'Of course,' Amelie resisted asking the source of her sleeplessness. Sally would not like it, and it would cause too many questions among the other servants if Amelie hovered over her the way she wanted to.

'You have my permission to make use of the library, although it looked thin of anything that might appeal to you.'

'I might look for a book,' Sally said.

When she left, Amelie blew out the one remaining candle. She climbed into bed and curled up under the covers and tried not to think.

Sally went to her room on the second floor. Not only did she have a room of her own, she also was the only one on this floor. The other servants had rooms on the same wing as the kitchen. This room even had a window that looked out on the garden in the back.

She pulled the chair up to the window and sat gazing at the garden, bathed in moonlight. It was such a lovely night, like the ones in Brussels when she had slipped out of the hotel to meet Calvin.

Poor Calvin. She'd known him since they were children in Hampstead. Even then they'd meet at night, sneaking out to explore the Heath. Her happiest times had been at night, with Calvin. She missed the nights; she missed Calvin, terribly.

Her solitary room suddenly no longer seemed spacious. It seemed suffocating. She grabbed her shawl and lit a candle and walked as quietly as she could down the stairs and to the conservatory, where she knew she could easily reach the outside without anyone knowing. She carefully opened the door and made certain it would not lock behind her.

Leaving the candle in the conservatory, she stepped out onto the lawn and gazed at the wild expanse in front of her.

The mountains surrounded her, black shapes against the cloudy grey sky. She'd never seen mountains before. She wished Calvin were here to see them with her.

Would he mind that his baby would be born in this wild place? Miss Glenville—Mrs Summerfield, she meant— said she'd be protected from scandal here where no one knew her, but what would happen to her and her baby later? What would Mr Summerfield do? Mr Summerfield knew she wasn't a Mrs. Sally remembered him from Brussels. He'd been with Miss Glenville that night, not Captain Fowler, the man Miss Glenville had been betrothed to. It had taken a while for Sally to remember him.

Mr Summerfield was a kind man, though, Sally thought. And an honourable one. He had married Miss Glenville to give their baby his name.

Sally had always assumed any baby she had would have Calvin's name. This baby would not have a father's name, merely her family name, but, for his whole life, she would have to lie to him, making up a marriage that never happened and a father who wasn't Calvin.

'Hoo doo, ma'am?' A man's voice made her jump.

She swung around. It was the man she had met earlier, the steward. 'Mr Reid. You startled me!'

'Is anything amiss?' he asked.

She was embarrassed to be caught like this. 'Nothing. I—I felt like some fresh air, is all.'

He stood beside her and gazed out over the mountains. 'I like coming out here on nights like this, as though there was naught but me and the mountains.'

She smiled sheepishly. 'I have spoiled it for you, then.'

His gaze was warm. 'Nae. It is nice to meet someone who appreciates the night.'

His accent was unlike any she'd heard. She had to concentrate to understand him.

'It is peaceful,' she said, even though the night had not brought her peace.

'You've not been here long, but what do you think of it?' He glanced out at the mountains.

'I've never seen the like,' she said. 'It is all hills and trees.'

'And where are you from?' he asked.

'London.' she asked. 'It is mostly buildings and streets except for the park.'

'I've never seen the like of that.' He gazed at her again.

His was a nice face. Tan from the sun but pleasant to look at. Not tall and thin, like Calvin, but shorter and thicker as if there was much power packed inside him.

She suddenly felt bashful. 'I—I should go inside.'

'Mebby we will meet out here again some night,' he said.

'Perhaps.'

'Goodnight, then, lass.' He tipped his hat.

'Goodnight.' She turned around and ran back in the house.

Chapter Sixteen

Edmund woke to a cry.

Amelie's voice came through the connecting door. 'No! No! No!'

He bounded out of bed and donned the banyan he'd pulled out of his trunk before going to bed.

'No!' she cried again. 'My baby.'

He opened the connecting door and ran to her side. She thrashed in the bed.

'Amelie,' he called, holding her still.

Her eyes opened but did not focus. 'I lost the baby, Edmund.'

She was still asleep, he realised.

She reached for him. 'I lost the baby. I cannot find her anywhere.'

If she woke, she would remember the dream and suffer the loss all over again. If she slept there was a chance she would forget the nightmare.

He climbed onto the bed, and she clung to him. 'Find my baby, Edmund!'

'Sleep, Amelie. I'll find the baby. Sleep.' His throat turned raw. This was too much like that awful night. Her crying out in her bed. Her distress.

Their loss.

'Very tired,' she murmured.

'Yes. Sleep.' He laid her back against the pillows and leaned down to kiss her forehead.

Her unfocused eyes opened again. 'Do not leave me.'

Of course he did not want to leave her. Every night he'd spent apart from her had been difficult, especially when she was a mere door, a mere wall, away. Edmund was used to being alone, even among officers in his regiment, schoolmates, sometimes even among the people at Summerfield House. With Amelie, though, so distant, emotionally if not physically, he felt acute loneliness. He hadn't felt such loneliness since—

Since watching his mother die.

He crawled into bed with her and spooned her against him. She relaxed and slipped deeper into sleep. It took longer for Edmund.

When he woke, Amelie was still next to him, soft and warm and tempting him to let Mr Reid and the farm go to the devil so he could hold her longer.

But he was uncertain if she would like finding him next to her. He waited a moment, savouring the scent of her and the soft sounds of her breathing, before carefully moving away from her the way he'd done on that night in Brussels when he'd thought he was merely leaving her with a pleasant memory, a memory that had helped sustain him during the battle and when he lay injured.

Too much had happened since that time.

His bare feet hit the floor, and his skin felt the room's chill. The fire had nearly died. He padded quietly over to the fireplace and put on two more logs so the room would be warm when she woke. Out the window the mountains were haloed in a faint glow.

Dawn was near.

He grabbed his banyan and walked silently to the connecting door and quietly lifted the latch.

She stirred behind him and he froze.

He turned to see if he'd woken her, but she became still again. Her hair had come loose of its plait and tumbled over her shoulders. Her face was relaxed, as untroubled as a child's. He caught his breath at the sight. If only he could keep her untroubled for all her days.

He opened the door and slipped out of the room.

He'd left his trunk in disarray from searching for his banyan the night before and now he disturbed its contents even more, looking for clean drawers and a shirt.

He pulled on his drawers first, then shaved quickly and put on his shirt and a pair of buckskin pantaloons.

The connecting door opened.

He swerved around.

Amelie stood in the doorway. 'I heard you moving about.'

He buttoned his pantaloons. 'I did not mean to disturb you.' He ransacked the trunk again, looking for a coat and waistcoat fit for touring a farm.

She walked over to him. 'You did not disturb me. I just woke up. I slept well, though.'

Except for her nightmare, but, as he'd hoped, she didn't seem to remember it.

She peered into his trunk, which was a rumpled mess. 'Shall I have Sally unpack for you?'

'If she has time.' He put on his stockings and boots.

She handed him his hat and gloves.

'I have no idea when I will be back.' He pulled on his gloves.

'Do not concern yourself over me,' she said. 'I will find something to do. See about making some of the other rooms ready, perhaps.'

'Do not tire yourself, Amelie.' He was certain she was not as recovered as she pretended.

Her eyes turned sad. 'I must keep busy.'

He understood. Keeping busy was his only means of relief from his thoughts. His regrets.

He smiled at her. 'I suspect I will be busy if I make the meeting with Reid in time. Wish me luck.' He opened the door. 'I shall need it.'

She gazed at him earnestly. 'I wish you a wonderful day.'

His heart pounded at her words as he hurried down the stairs and out the front door.

He walked around the house and towards the farm buildings. One long building off to the side he'd guess to be the stables. He trusted Lord Northdon's coachmen had been given good beds and would be provided with a hearty breakfast before they started back to Hertfordshire.

When he reached the place Reid had designated to meet, Reid was not there. The sky was turning lighter by the minute. Edmund pulled out his timepiece. Five minutes past six. Had Reid not waited for him? He paced back and forth in the yard, both to keep warm and to wake himself up.

Finally Reid emerged from the far end of the last building. He did not walk faster even though he saw Edmund.

'You are here,' Reid said.

'As I said I would be,' Edmund responded.

'Not much happening today,' the man went on. 'The sheep are grazing.'

The night before, Reid had made it sound as if he would be consumed with work. Was he putting Edmund through some kind of test? If so, he had passed the punctuality part.

Edmund ought to be the one to test Reid, to see if Reid did his job properly.

'Show me the farm,' Edmund said firmly. 'I need to see everything. No more delays.'

Reid nodded. 'Let us begin with the buildings. I'll show

you each of them.' He opened the big wooden door to the building they were standing near.

After Edmund left, Amelie stood at the window and watched him cross the lawn to the farm buildings. He looked so impressive, walking briskly, the tails of his coat surging behind him.

She felt better this morning. Not exactly cheerful, but not despondent either. For the first time since her miscarriage she had woken to something besides her morose thoughts. She'd woken to the sounds of Edmund moving about in his room. It had comforted her.

She refused to be idle today. She needed to be busy, so busy she couldn't think. Making the house more comfortable and pleasant was something she could do.

Starting with this room.

She gathered the clothing he'd left strewn around. Picked up his drawers—what an intimate thing, picking up his drawers! A proper wifely task. She remembered him removing them, both in Brussels and—and on their wedding night.

But she should not think of either of those nights.

She set his drawers aside and the shirt he wore the previous day. Both would need to be laundered. She hung the coat he wore on the back of a chair and folded his trousers. Kneeling next to Edmund's trunk, she refolded the clothes he'd tossed around in his rush to get dressed. She held a shirt up to her nose. It had been laundered, but she could still smell his scent on the fabric.

Why did he not have a valet? She must ask him some time.

At the bottom of the trunk she spied a packet of letters tied up with a string. She picked it up.

The writing on the outside was in a feminine hand. Amelie had a sick feeling deep in her stomach. Was there another woman he truly loved? How would she know? Had a woman been the reason he wanted to return to Brussels?

She dropped the packet of letters.

They could just as easily be from his sisters. Or from Tess's mother. He'd lived with Tess's mother in Brussels before the battle, he'd said.

If Amelie untied the string and read the letters she'd know for certain.

No. She would not snoop where she was not wanted. If he had a woman he loved somewhere, she would just have to wait until he told her.

Because he would tell her. Unlike everyone else Amelie knew, Edmund always told her the truth.

She put the letters back exactly as she'd found them and refolded all the clothing in his trunk before going back to her bedchamber. The fire in her fireplace was reduced to a few glowing embers. She put on another log and stood warming her hands when flames began to curl over it.

There was water enough in the ewer to wash herself. It was something she could do while waiting for Sally to come and help her dress. She stripped out of her nightdress and washed herself, shivering as she did so. Her bleeding had stopped, that reminder of what had happened. Mrs Bayliss had told her to wait until after her courses before having relations with her husband again.

But she did not want to think about that.

She donned a shift and covered herself with a wrapper and sat in a chair right by the fire, wondering what Edmund was doing. He wanted to be of some use to her father, she knew. She must do her part, as well. Manage the household.

There was a light knock on the door, and Sally crept in.

Amelie swivelled around in her chair. 'I am up, Sally.'

Sally looked alarmed. 'Sorry, ma'am. I thought you would still be asleep.'

'I woke up.' She did not explain that she had woken up and heard her husband in the next room and had had a sudden desire to see him.

'Would you like me to help you dress?' Sally asked.

Amelie smiled. 'First I would like you to tell me how you are feeling.'

'Ohhh.' The maid drew out the word. 'I suppose I am feeling well enough.'

'And how did you sleep?'

Sally looked abashed. 'It felt strange to be up on that floor all alone.'

'I can imagine.' Amelie had not wanted to be alone either. She stood and walked over to the girl. 'You must tell me if you feel unwell or fatigued. I will not have you work yourself too hard.'

'Yes, ma'am.' Sally sounded as solemn as ever.

'And here I am going to ask you to do more than your duties.'

'What is it, ma'am?'

Amelie suddenly felt guilty for it. 'I wonder if you would unpack Mr Summerfield's trunk for him and put the clothes in the wardrobe in his room.'

'Oh, that will not be hard, ma'am. I will do that.' She spoke with more energy.

'Thank you,' Amelie said with feeling. 'I think today I want my plainest dress. And I wish I had thought to have some caps made. I plan to see all of this house, and I have a feeling dust will be everywhere.'

'Would you like one of my caps, ma'am?' Sally offered.

'How kind of you.' She was sincerely touched. 'I will consider it, but first I'll see how it is without wearing one.'

A clock somewhere in the house struck eight as Amelie descended the stairs. She went directly to the dining room, but it was as she and Edmund had left it after the dessert dishes were removed. Amelie had said nothing to the servants about breakfast, and she ought to have done so.

She walked through the dining room to the door she and Edmund had presumed led to the kitchen. As she walked through the corridor she heard voices and headed towards them.

'The thing is, why did Lord Northdon send them here?' It was Mrs Wood's voice. 'Why now?'

'I am worried about what Mrs Summerfield will expect,' another voice said—Jobson, perhaps. 'I can't do all the cleaning of this whole house. It is too much.'

'And I need help in the kitchen.' That must have been Mrs Stagg.

They were all seated around a kitchen table. Mugs of tea or coffee or chicory sat in front of them as well as slices of bread and cheese.

'Good morning.' Amelie tried for a cheerful tone.

They all scrambled to their feet.

Her whole life she'd watched her mother deal with servants. Her mother did the job so well that their houses had always been harmonious—even when matters between her mother and father had not been.

She stepped into a room that must be the servants' hall. 'I could not help but overhear your conversation. Please do not worry about our being here. We know we create more work for you and that you will need more help. Perhaps you can advise me on exactly how much help you require.'

The three women stared at her wide-eyed.

She smiled. 'I came in search of breakfast. And to speak to you, Mrs Wood. Please meet with me after I eat. Simple fare will suffice, Mrs Stagg.' She gestured to the contents of the table. 'Bread and cheese. Some jam, if there is any. And tea. That will do nicely for me this morning.'

They continued to stare.

'Thank you.' She turned around and left.

* * *

It was near the dinner hour when Edmund finally returned to the house. He walked in the front door and found the hall deserted as it had been that morning. He checked the drawing room just to see if Amelie was there, but it was empty, as well. Something seemed changed about the place, though.

It smelled better.

Maybe that was because he was no longer riding through fields dotted with cattle dung or holding pens filled with sheep. He climbed the stairs, his legs weary, his injured leg aching. He'd spent the day on his feet or on horseback, and his leg was making a justifiable complaint.

When he reached the first floor he called for her. 'Amelie?'

Her bedchamber door opened. 'You are back! I did not know whether to worry or not.'

She almost took his breath away, and he was struck dumb for a few moments. She was dressed in a gown of pale pink silk that shimmered when she moved. Her hair was pulled up to the top of her head and tied with a pink ribbon, but her curls were loose about her head.

He finally found his voice. 'You look fresh.' Not merely fresh. As lovely as a rose in bloom.

She twirled around. 'Do I? Sally dressed me for dinner and made me presentable. Believe me, I was not presentable before.'

Very presentable, he thought. He, on the other hand, was covered with dirt from the fields, the road and the pens of sheep. He looked down at himself. 'I need to clean myself.'

Her smile wavered. 'Of course. I will not trouble you.'

No! He had not meant to upset her. 'You do not trouble me, Amelie. I am eager to hear of your day, but I must get this dirt off first. '

'Knock on my door when you are finished, if you like.'

Her voice had turned more subdued, though. She retreated into her bedchamber.

He opened his door and went inside.

The room had been straightened, he saw immediately. His trunk was gone. Certainly part of what Amelie had done was see that the room was put in proper order.

He hated to bring his soiled clothing in there. He stripped down and washed himself and shaved again.

He found his clothes in drawers and in the wardrobe and chose his whitest linen and his formal coat and waistcoat. When he finished dressing he knocked on the door connecting their two rooms. She opened it, but her demeanour had turned wary, like a butterfly ready to take flight.

He smiled at her. 'I suspect you had something to do with tidying my mess.'

'Yes.' She lowered her lashes. 'Well, Sally, actually. Sally unpacked for you.'

'If I do not see her, thank her for me.' He offered his arm. 'Shall we go downstairs?'

They walked down to the drawing room, where a decanter of wine waited for them.

'Wine?' He needed wine right now. 'Nothing suits me more at the moment.'

She looked pleased.

That was an even better tonic than the wine. 'Shall I pour you a glass?'

'Indeed.' She lowered herself into one of the chairs.

He poured the wine and handed her a glass, placing his weight on his bad leg. Pain shot through it and he winced.

She noticed. 'Is your leg hurting you?'

He could be stoic and deny the pain, but why shouldn't she know? 'It hurts like the devil. I was on my feet or on horseback all the day.'

'Were you? You must be exhausted.' She took a sip of the wine. 'What did you do? I hope you ate something.'

He sat in a chair near hers and stretched out his leg. 'We walked over most of the fells, I think, and rode into the village. We had a mutton pie at the inn there.'

She took another sip. 'Do not be surprised if we are eating mutton again tonight.'

'I am famished enough to eat anything.' He drank some of the wine and lifted his glass to her. 'This is quite... tolerable.'

'It is some my father left,' she said. 'There are about five bottles left, Lloyd said.'

He relaxed as the wine slid comfortingly down his throat. She seemed more at ease with him again.

She sipped from her glass. 'Tell me of your day.'

He told her of walking to the closer fells, riding to the more distant ones, seeing the flock grazing. He told of people he met—the farm workers and people in the village—and how he had the sense that they were concerned about his presence among them.

'The servants here were worried about why we came, as well,' she said.

He gave her a direct gaze. 'We need not tell them why we came.'

She turned away for a moment but took a breath and faced him again. 'So what did you think of everything?'

'The farm appears to be well-run. The workers seem well satisfied.' He finished his wine and poured himself another glass. 'I like Reid, but, of course, he doesn't yet trust me. None of them trusts me.'

She looked at him questioningly. 'Shall I show you what we did today?'

He put down his glass and stood. 'By all means.'

She led him to the sitting room next to the conservatory. Its walls had been scrubbed clean, its carpet beaten, furniture polished, curtains laundered. A great deal of work for one day.

He walked around the room. 'You did well, Amelie.'

She blushed. 'There is much I wish to do in the house. Nothing extravagant like replacing furniture, but I would like to open more of the rooms so it will be more comfortable. I'd like to put plants in the conservatory, and I would love to tidy up the garden.'

She was taking an interest—that gratified him most of all. So was he, actually. For all the exertion of the day, he'd found it stimulating. He was determined to learn everything about the running of the farm.

'I want you to do whatever you wish,' he told her. 'Make this home of ours a pleasant place for us.' It was just the two of them. He tried not to think that there might have been a third. 'I mean it, Amelie. Anything you want.'

'I must keep busy,' she murmured before looking up at him again. 'We need to hire more servants. The house is too big for Jobson to clean and Mrs Stagg needs help in the kitchen.'

'I dare say we need footmen, too,' he added. 'Lloyd seems willing enough, but how much can he do? I am persuaded I do need someone to tend to my clothes, as well.'

'And a gardener?' She looked hopeful. 'I would love to see the garden tended. Do you think my father will mind the expense?' she asked.

He tried not to bristle. 'I am not without means, Amelie. I will pay.'

'Then let us go back to the drawing room and finish our wine, and perhaps we can make a list of how many servants we need.' Her eyes sparkled.

Edmund's heart swelled. Perhaps she would recover. Perhaps they could make this marriage into a good thing for both of them.

Mr Lloyd came to announce dinner—mutton stew again, but Edmund did not care. He and Amelie talked throughout the meal of what they could do for the house and the farm.

Edmund never realised how much he enjoyed having a house that was his to live in. With Amelie. Before Amelie he'd never thought of houses.

There was no fortune to be made at this sheep farm, but the day's work had been gratifying. He looked forward, too, to the hay harvest that Reid said would commence in the next few days. And to the market days in the next few weeks. And the tupping—the breeding of the sheep.

Most of all he looked forward to making Amelie happy, to making up to her all the misery he had caused her. If he could do so, perhaps life could always be as good as it felt at this moment.

Chapter Seventeen

The next morning Amelie's courses came and with it, her grief. Just as she felt a little better, her body taunted her with the reminder that her womb was empty. The bleeding and discomfort were not extreme, but she made it her excuse to stay in bed.

Her despondency had returned, and she did not want anyone to know. She smiled valiantly for Edmund, making him think her withdrawal was merely due to her monthly cycle. She fooled Sally, as well. When alone, though, she burrowed in her bed and mourned once more for what might have been.

After the third day, though, everyone became too busy to worry about her.

It was haymaking time.

'I'll be gone all day, I'm afraid,' Edmund told her that morning. 'Reid says rain is coming and the hay will be ruined if we do not get it in. Everyone must take part. Sally can stay to tend you, but the rest of the servants will be needed to help.' His colour was high with excitement.

'I'll fare well enough.' Amelie made certain to smile. 'Do not concern yourself over me.'

* * *

A short time later Sally brought her some breakfast. 'Do you need me all day, ma'am? Because Mrs Stagg asked if I could help bring food and drink to the fields.'

Again Amelie smiled. 'I do not need you at all. Just take care you do not exert yourself.'

'I will only be walking and carrying.' She sounded eager to go.

'Then you must help.' Sally ought to have some enjoyment. 'I am not ill, after all. I am well able to take care of myself.'

By mid-morning, though, Amelie could no longer stand herself. Everyone was working, and here she was secluding herself and indulging in self-pity. She could help, too, couldn't she? There must be some task she could perform.

She already wore her most ordinary dress, one that was fit for work, but she needed more if she were to help in the fields. She left her room and made her way to the still room, where she found an apron to wear over her dress and an old pair of boots that fit her feet. In a potting shed outdoors, she found gloves for her hands, a scarf to cover her hair and a wide-brimmed hat to shade her face.

There. She was ready.

But she did not know for certain where to find the hay-fields.

She walked past the farm buildings and some tidy cottages until she saw women on a hilly field raking the hay into windrows. If not for the mountains, all green and grey, to frame the scene, it looked much like Northdon Hall at haying time. She strode towards the workers, relishing the exercise after sitting and moping for so long. She filled her lungs with clear, crisp air and trudged up the hill where the women were working.

As she came close, several of the workers gaped at

her as if she were some oddity from a foreign land. She searched for Edmund but could not see him.

One of the women, carrying a rake, walked over to her. 'Do you need help, ma'am?'

'No. Thank you.' Amelie extended her hand. 'I am Mrs Summerfield.'

'Aye, I guessed who you were.' She hesitated before shaking Amelie's hand. 'I am Mrs Peet. Mary Peet.'

'How do you do Mrs Peet.' Amelie shaded her eyes and glanced around. 'Have you seen Mr Summerfield?'

The woman pointed. 'Most of the men are on the other side of the hill, cutting the hay.'

'Oh. I mustn't bother him, then.' Amelie had no reason to disturb him.

'Is there something I can do for you?' Mrs Peet asked.

'No, there is really nothing.'

The other women, who had been watching her, went back to turning the hay. All Amelie had accomplished was interrupting them. She observed them, how they moved down the windrow with their rakes, flipping the cut grass so that it would dry in the sun.

Mrs Peet curtsied. 'Best I get back to work, then.' She started to walk away.

Amelie called her back. 'Might I help?'

Mrs Peet turned and regarded her. 'You?' She lowered her head. 'Beg pardon, ma'am, but what would you do?'

'Well.' She gestured to the windrows. 'Might I help you turn the hay?'

Mrs Peet looked uncertain but finally smiled. 'Come with me. I'll show you how.'

Mrs Peet found another rake and showed Amelie how to turn the grass. The women walked down the rows, turning as they went, then they moved to the next row and worked uphill. Amelie was slow at the task, but the other women offered words of advice and encouragement as they passed.

Amelie learned the names of as many of the women as she could, repeating them in her head so she would not forget.

When she reached the top of the hill, she rested a moment. Her muscles seemed to rejoice in the exercise, even though they were tired. Best of all, there was no time, no space to think. Just work. And who knew she would enjoy such labour? Was this yet another way she was different from respectable ladies?

As she started down the hill, she heard her name called.

Edmund strode towards her. 'What are you doing here?' He was stripped to his shirtsleeves and carrying a scythe.

She lifted her chin. 'I am working.'

His grey eyes sparkled in the sunlight, and his face shone with sweat. Her insides fluttered at the sight of him, even though she was ready to do battle if he ordered her to stop.

He gestured to her rake. 'I see you are working, but is it wise?'

'Everyone else is working.' She held his gaze. 'I am doing my part.'

His brows knitted. 'Do you feel up to it?'

She looked into those sparkling grey eyes. 'I am not ill, Edmund, and I want to do this. I like doing this.'

A slow smile grew on his face. 'I like the work, too, Amelie. But stop if you become fatigued.'

Her shoulders relaxed and her spirits rose. 'I will.'

He gazed at her for a moment longer before climbing to the top of the hill and disappearing over the other side.

The sun was low in the sky when Edmund came off the hill. He walked with Reid.

'Will we finish before the rains?' he asked the steward.

'Another two days like this one an' we will,' Reid answered.

Edmund had turned a corner with Reid. He'd been

working side by side with the man these last few days, especially with the haymaking, and Edmund thought perhaps he had started to earn the steward's respect.

He surveyed the land around him. This was not as prosperous a farm as Summerfield had been and not at all the future he'd planned for himself, but he liked the people and he liked the work.

Ahead of him, some of the farm workers walked back to their cottages side by side with their wives. Edmund envied them.

But he caught sight of Amelie heading back to the house. Beautiful Amelie. Who would have thought a viscount's daughter would be willing to work in the fields?

'I'll bid you good day here, Reid. I'm going to join my wife.' It felt good to say those words.

'She did a fine day's work,' Reid said.

'That she did.' Edmund hurried away.

He caught up with Amelie, and she smiled when she saw him.

Edmund fell in step with her. 'How did you fare today?'

She glanced up at him. 'I am exhausted. Every muscle hurts.' She grinned. 'But I feel good.'

He felt good, too. 'It was fine work, was it not?'

'Does your leg pain you?' she asked.

'A twinge. No more,' he replied. 'Work seems to be helping. Making it stronger.'

When they reached the house they washed, donned clean clothes and ate more of Mrs Stagg's mutton stew.

As they finished the simple meal, Edmund asked, 'Should we have tea in the drawing room?'

Amelie rested her elbow on the table and her chin on her hand. 'To own the truth, all I want is to go to bed.'

Edmund felt the flare of desire at her words, but he knew she had no idea her words were provocative. Besides, even if she were not dog-tired, she was not ready, not when she'd spent the last couple of days withdrawn in grief. He'd been grieved, too, but work had saved him.

'An excellent idea,' he responded. 'I must rise early again tomorrow.'

She straightened in her chair. 'I am rising early, too.'

'Are you?' For her to labour one day was more than anyone expected.

'Of course I am,' she responded in a wounded tone. 'Everyone is working tomorrow, is that not correct?'

He gave her a direct look. 'I am not suggesting you not work, Amelie. I am proud of you for what you've done this day. If you wish to do more, I will be prouder still.'

She quickly averted her gaze. 'Thank you, Edmund,' she murmured.

They walked up the mahogany stairs together, and he saw her to her bedchamber door. How he wished, even fatigued as he was, he could sleep with her in his arms like when she'd cried out from her nightmare.

Instead he placed his lips on her forehead. 'Goodnight, Amelie.'

She leaned into him, and he put his arms around her.

'Sleep well,' he murmured.

When he withdrew his arms, she hurried into her room.

The next two days were filled with work, turning hay, stacking it as high as the workers' cottages and covering the stacks with canvas tarps to keep out the rain.

Amelie did not mind any of it. The work, hard as it was, healed her spirits, and she felt happy for the first time since walking into the Duchess of Richmond's ball.

What a far cry from Middlerock farm that night was!

She liked the women turning hay with her more than she'd liked those society women at the ball. She liked the men who cut the hay with their scythes. She liked working with them and accomplishing such a huge task.

She perceived their stay at this farm with fresh eyes. It no longer seemed like an exile or a withdrawal from life. It seemed like life itself, or what life ought to be.

Amelie felt ready to face the future, no matter what it threw at her.

For Amelie, it was not the end of the haymaking she celebrated; it was her new beginning. Everyone gathered in one of the farm buildings large enough to seat them all. Mrs Stagg and the farm wives prepared a feast and everyone ate together, drank ale together and sang and danced.

It was the best party Amelie had ever attended, better even than the Duchess of Richmond's ball.

She glanced at Edmund, seated at the head of the table, laughing and lifting his tankard to his lips. He looked up and their eyes caught.

Her heart leaped into her throat. Edmund's eyes warmed her more than the large stone fireplace, blazing with firewood.

He rose from his seat and made his way down the long table to where Amelie sat, stopping to acknowledge something said to him, a joke told, some cajolery or simply a handshake. He finally reached her and extended his hand.

She put hers in his, and he pulled her from her seat. 'We're to bed, I think,' he said, and the room erupted in raucous shouts. Amelie felt her face turn red.

Why not, though? she thought. Why not behave as man and wife? Why not seize the pleasure it brought them both?

Sally, who sat with Mr Reid, asked her, 'Shall I come with you?'

Amelie gestured for her to stay. 'No, enjoy yourself. I'll not need you tonight.'

'Ohhhh!' exclaimed one of the women, and laughter broke out among them again. The laughter followed Amelie and Edmund out of the building.

As they walked across the yard to the house, dark clouds swept across the moon.

'Storm clouds?' Amelie stopped to look up at the sky. 'Will it storm tonight, just as Mr Reid said?'

Edmund threaded her arm though his. 'Uncanny of him to predict the rain. I do not know if he realises how much knowledge he holds inside him.'

Their bodies bumped each other as they walked. Amelie liked feeling the strength of Edmund's arm beneath her fingers. She remembered the power of that same arm swinging the scythe in a rhythmic and graceful arc. Or its gentleness when holding her in a naked embrace.

'I don't think I've ever enjoyed days more than these,' she said. 'I shall miss haymaking.'

'You impressed the farm workers.' He smiled down at her. 'One man told me he thought offcomers were all lazy and puffed up, but that you and I proved him wrong.'

'Offcomers?'

'Someone not from here.'

They reached the conservatory door and entered the house, which was nearly pitch-black inside.

'We should have brought a candle,' she said.

Edmund took her hand. 'We'll find our way.'

She could see nothing and it was only his hand that told her he was ahead of her. They climbed the stairs, and at the top, it felt as if the darkness enveloped them and shielded them from anything but each other.

He put his arms around her and kissed her.

The feel of his lips against hers, his tongue touching hers, the heat of his body and the scent of him ignited the passion in her that she'd pushed away. He pulled the scarf from her head and dug his fingers into her curls.

When his lips left hers, she murmured, 'I am healed now, Edmund.' In both body and mind.

He took her hand and opened the door to his bedchamber. Enough moonlight streamed through the windows so she could see his face, a face that now had become so familiar and so dear.

'I have wanted you all these nights,' he said, kissing her again. 'I have missed you.'

Her body flared with sensation, a harbinger of the pleasure that was to come, made even more erotic by the darkness. The room was chilled, but the cold did not trouble her. It refreshed her and made her feel more alive.

'Shall I make a fire?' he asked between kisses that had travelled to her cheek, her neck, her ear.

'We can warm each other,' she murmured.

He stepped back and pulled off his boots and stripped off his coat, a mere shadow now that he was at a distance. She watched him, spellbound by the efficiency of his movements, his masculine grace.

He stood naked before her and extended his hand to her.

She clasped it and let him draw her near.

'Your turn,' he murmured, untying her apron and the laces of her dress.

He pulled the dress over her head, leaving her in her corset, shift and boots. She took his hand again and backed to the bed, climbing on top of it and presenting him with her booted foot. He pulled off her boots and peeled off her stockings. He climbed on the bed with her and unlaced and removed her corset. All that remained was her shift. She did not wait for him but pulled it over her head herself.

The undressing seemed like a ritual. So familiar. So much the same as that night in Brussels. And their wedding night.

So much like the first time…and the last.

A loud hum seemed to come from inside her, unsettling her, and a cloud crossed the moon. The room was plunged in darkness, leaving only the memories swirling through her mind, choking off the brightness of her mood, blocking her happiness. Cutting off the very air she needed to breathe.

Edmund touched her and she started to tremble. He rose over her and her heart pounded. She could not get air into her lungs.

'No! No!' She pushed him away.

He moved to her side and sat looking down at her. 'What is it, Amelie? What happened?'

She wanted to run, to be as far away as her legs could carry her, to somewhere she could breathe.

'I—I do not know,' she managed, still trying to gulp air. This was how she had destroyed their baby. This was how she had ruined his future. Her pleasure only brought pain. 'I cannot do this, Edmund. I cannot.'

Was she never to recover completely? Would she ever find happiness?

She tried to scramble off the bed, but he held her shoulders and sat her in front of him.

'We do not have to make love.' He spoke in a quiet, calm voice. 'But stay with me, Amelie. Sleep with me.'

It was all she could do not to fight him to free herself.

'I can't, Edmund,' she cried. 'I can't.'

He released her, and she bolted off the bed and through the connecting doorway to her own room.

Sally walked across the yard with Mr Reid. The celebration had broken up, and the workers were headed for their cottages. She could have walked back with the other servants, but she lingered, listening to Mr Reid, who told her stories of other hay harvests, one he'd witnessed when he was a mere child when his whole family had worked feverishly in the fields to bring the hay in before the rain, but the rain had come, soaking the results of their labour and nearly ruining his father's small hill farm.

Everything he said seemed interesting to her, and the

way he said it, as well. His strange accent made her pay closer attention, and it seemed as though she heard more that way. Her own thoughts could not interfere.

Walking with him in the dark was different than talking in the building where the banquet was held. She'd met him outside in the dark twice since that first time. She'd told herself she just wanted some night air, but sometimes she wondered if she'd hoped he be there.

'I have enjoyed your company tonight,' he said.

They walked side by side, not touching.

'And I yours,' she admitted.

Not the way she'd enjoyed Calvin's company, though. Calvin had been as familiar as her own image in a mirror, as comfortable as well-worn shoes. Mr Reid had strange ways, strange words for things, and it was exciting to be exposed to new things.

They reached the house, a servant's door off the kitchen wing. As she reached for the door latch he stepped in front of her, blocking her way.

'Wait a moment, lass,' he said.

She drew back.

He shifted from one foot to the other before looking directly at her. 'Since we enjoy each other's company,' he began, 'I was wondering if I could—could court you.'

Her stomach dropped. 'Court me?'

'Aye, you're a widow, I know, and not very long of it.' She'd told him the lie her mistress had devised for her: that her husband had died at Waterloo. 'If it is too soon, I'll wait.'

She panicked. 'You can't—you can't—you do not know—'

'Know what?' he asked.

'You do not know me!' she cried and moved around him to the door, opened it and ran inside.

Chapter Eighteen

The next morning Edmund woke alone in his bed. Rain beat against his window.

It most perfectly matched his mood.

He could not blame Amelie her panic. Sometimes memories came back to him, too, and he had to fight to push them away again.

She'd looked so beautiful the night before, so happy. He'd wanted it to last.

'It is raining,' he said aloud. 'Raining in more ways than one.'

He dressed quickly and grabbed his caped greatcoat, the one that had seen him through the rain-filled night before Waterloo and wet marches through Spain, before walking down to the kitchen to get something to eat.

Mrs Stagg greeted him with a smile. 'I did not expect you up so early on a day like this.'

No sense spreading the gloom he felt inside. He smiled at her. 'Mr Reid was right about the rains, was he not?'

She nodded. 'He's a wise one, he is.' She cut some bread and cheese. 'And you'll be looking for something to eat, I expect.'

'This will do.' He took a piece of bread and a wedge of cheese and started to eat. 'Do you have some oilcloth?

Something I can use to carry the ledger books from Reid's office to the library?'

Her face turned solemn. 'Oilcloth for the ledger books,' she repeated without enthusiasm. 'Wait a moment.'

By the time he finished his bread and cheese, she brought him some folded cloth.

'Will this do?' she asked. 'I also brought some twine.'

'Thank you, Mrs Stagg. This will do nicely.' He took the items from her hands.

He had to keep busy or he'd go mad. As long as he was not idle, he could put one foot in front of the other.

Collecting his hat and donning his greatcoat, he opened the door and paused a moment before dashing out into the rain.

He ran the distance to the farm building where Reid had his office and knocked on the man's door.

'Come in,' he heard Reid say.

'Summerfield!' Reid jumped to his feet. 'I did not expect to see you out in the weather.'

Edmund's greatcoat dripped water on the bare wooden floor.

'I thought it a perfect day to look at the books.' He did not move, confining the puddle to where he stood.

'The books?' Reid frowned.

'The ledger books. Surely you knew I would want to examine them,' Edmund said.

Reid rubbed his face. 'I meant to show you more of the workings of the farm first. The entries might make no sense to you otherwise.'

'I've seen my father's ledgers,' Edmund assured him. 'And I will ask if there is something I do not understand.'

'Very well.'

Reid moved slowly from around his desk to a locked cabinet. He took his time opening the cabinet, where several canvas-bound ledger books were stacked one on top of the other.

'How far back do you wish to go?' Reid asked.

Was that anxiety in his voice?

'When did you start here?'

'Five years back,' Reid answered.

'Then give me six years,' Edmund said.

Reid's brows lowered, but he pulled out six ledgers. 'The ink will run if they get wet.'

Edmund lifted his hand. 'I have an oilskin to wrap them in.'

It seemed as if all Reid's wariness and suspicion of those first days had returned, and Edmund did not know why.

Edmund spread open the oilcloth onto a table, and Reid placed the books on top of it. He wrapped them carefully and tied them with twine so the cloth would not open accidentally.

He glanced over at Reid. 'I do not expect to find anything amiss, Reid. I want you to know that.'

'You won't,' Reid shot back, his tone defiant.

Edmund started for the door. 'Nothing displeases me so far. The farm is run well. You should be proud of your work.'

Reid straightened. 'I am.'

Amelie sat on her bed, gazing out the window at the rain, regretting the night before. She had no idea why she had gone into a panic with Edmund. It had suddenly seemed as if something terrible would happen if she allowed herself to indulge in that pleasure. It had come as a surprise attack.

She'd been dreadful to Edmund. One more thing guaranteed to displease him. The list was growing longer.

She heard a light tap on the door. Not Edmund. Edmund would have rapped with vigour.

'Come in,' she said.

Sally entered, her head bowed, her shoulders slumped. Amelie turned away from her own misery to attend to Sally's. Perhaps she could help Sally, and at least one of them could be happy.

'What is amiss, Sally?' Amelie asked.

'Nothing, ma'am,' the maid responded in mournful tones.

'Has someone been unkind to you?' Of everyone, Sally had had the lightest duties during the haymaking. Had the other servants complained?

'Unkind? No, ma'am.' She sounded as if she might cry. 'Not unkind. Not at all.'

Amelie patted the bed. 'Come sit with me.'

Sally joined her and Amelie put an arm around her. 'Tell me what is amiss, no matter what it is.'

Sally turned away and shifted in her seat, but finally she stared at her feet and spoke. 'It is Mr Reid—'

'Mr Reid?' She'd noticed him talking to Sally. He was not the sort to take advantage of her, was he?

Of course, how was Amelie to know a man's true character if he decided to conceal it? She had once been dreadfully fooled herself.

'He—he walked me back to the house last night...' She paused as if it were difficult to go on.

Amelie blanched. Had she been wrong about Mr Reid? She'd been wrong before. 'What did he do?'

Fat tears rolled down Sally's cheeks. 'He—he asked— he asked—to court me.'

Relief washed through Amelie. 'To court you?' If he was what he seemed to be, he was a fine man with a good position. 'Would that be so disagreeable?'

'No, not disagreeable at all!' Sally cried. 'I like him. I like him, and I feel like it is betraying Calvin, but worse, he doesn't know about the baby. No one does, although I think Mrs Wood suspects. What will he think of me?'

Soon everyone would know.

Amelie kept her voice calm. 'He will think you are a widow left with child.'

Sally turned to stare into her face. 'But that is a lie, is it not? What would he think if he knew the truth of me? He would despise me.'

'Do not tell him.'

'And lie to him all my days?' She looked horrified.

Amelie took her by the shoulders, the way Edmund had done to her the night before. 'Then tell him. If he truly has a regard for you, he will not mind.'

Amelie was not as certain of this advice as she made out to be. What would a man like Fowler do with such a confession? Not every man was like Edmund. Edmund would do the right thing.

She rose from the bed. 'Come. Help me dress. You must think about this and decide what to do.'

Sally slipped off the bed and moved slowly to the wardrobe. 'What do you wish to wear today?'

'A morning dress, I think. I doubt I shall venture outside in weather like this!'

She must find something to do, though, or her thoughts and regrets would plague her all day.

It was afternoon before Edmund saw Amelie. He'd set up a space in the library to look over the ledgers, pushing a long table nearer to the window to take advantage of the light, even though not much light shone through the grey sheen of the rain.

Amelie came in the room carrying a tea tray with sandwiches and biscuits. She looked hesitant. 'I brought you some tea.'

'Amelie!' He stood and took the tray from her hands.

'You should not be serving tea. What happened to Lloyd? Or Jobson?'

She blinked as if she'd been reproached. 'Jobson is helping Mrs Stagg in the kitchen. Mrs Wood and Lloyd are busy with other tasks.'

He had not meant it as criticism.

'I—I thank you.' He placed the tray on the table. 'Now I see the food I am famished.'

'I thought you might be hungry,' she said in a quiet voice.

He hated this reserve between them, but he did not know how to break it. 'Please sit with me and tell me how you are faring today?'

Her eyes flickered with sadness. 'I am well enough,' she said.

He gazed at her, wishing he knew how to speak of the night before, deciding it was best to wait for her to speak of it.

She gestured to the table strewn with ledger books. 'What are you doing?'

'Looking through the farm's records for the last six years.' He closed the open book he'd been examining and stacked the others.

She poured his tea and handed him the plate of food. 'What are you finding?'

He sipped his tea. 'Everything seems in order. The farm is doing well under Reid's care.'

'I am glad to hear it,' she said.

They fell silent again.

Edmund put down his teacup and offered her some of the repast. 'How have you occupied yourself this day?'

She shook her head to the food. 'I spoke with Mrs Wood about hiring more help. She knows of relatives and villagers who could use the work. I'll interview them as soon as the rain stops.'

'Good.' He ate one of the sandwiches. 'And what of this afternoon? Do you have plans?' He'd love to take a walk with her away from the house to one of the beautiful spots on the property, but the rain prevented that.

She fiddled with the cloth of an apron she wore over her dress. 'I am going to look through the attic.'

'The attic?'

She glanced at him but glanced away again. 'The house needs decoration, and Mrs Wood says many of the items that once adorned the rooms were brought up to the attic. I thought I might see if we want to use any of it.' Her voice shook a little.

'Sounds like a big task,' he said.

'I must do something,' she whispered.

He stared at her. Why must they always need to get used to each other all over again? 'Shall I help you?'

Her eyes widened. 'In the attic?'

'Yes,' he said quietly. 'We can explore it together.'

She looked wary again, but she nodded. 'I will be glad for the assistance.'

He finished his tea and picked up two of the library's lamps to take with them, handing one to her. They left for the attic, up a steep flight of stairs above the second floor.

He opened the door and entered first before turning and offering her his hand to assist her into the space, which smelled of dust and old wood. They stood and surveyed the vast expanse, their lamps revealing a jumble of wooden boxes, chests and furniture, some shrouded in dust covers.

She placed her lamp on a box and wrapped a scarf around her hair. 'I do not know where to begin.'

This was more than a day's work. 'Shall we walk through and see what we can see?'

She picked up her lamp again. 'I'll go this way.'

She turned to the right, and the implication was that

he should turn left. Not the togetherness for which he'd yearned, but at least they were in the same space.

He threaded his way through some boxes and trunks, obviously put wherever there was space, with no effort at organisation. It was impossible to tell if a box was placed there yesterday or a century ago. He ran his finger across one of the trunks. Except perhaps by the thickness of the dust. He squeezed around a tall chest of drawers, behind which was a dust cover thrown over several small pieces of furniture. He placed the lamp on the chest of drawers and pulled off the dust cover.

'My God,' he exclaimed.

Before him was a baby's cradle, a rocking chair and a hobbyhorse, all arranged as if they were in a nursery instead of a dusty attic.

He felt as if he'd been punched in the chest.

He could see it! Could see the nursery. The baby lying in the cradle on soft white linens. He could see Amelie bending over the cradle. And himself, beaming with pride.

Just as quickly that vision disappeared and was replaced by another—his mother being covered by a white sheet. The baby wrapped in white, being carried away, the way their baby had been carried away. An empty cradle. An empty rocking chair.

'My God,' he cried again. His throat constricted, and he fell to his knees, the unreleased sobs painfully constricting his chest.

Amelie was at his side. 'What is it, Edmund?'

He pointed to the nursery scene and shook his head.

'Oh!' she cried.

She knelt beside him and put her arms around him.

'The baby.' His voice came out in a rasp.

'I am so sorry, Edmund.' She clung to him. 'I am so sorry. It is my fault, all my fault.'

He pulled away. 'No, the fault is mine. I planned that wedding night. I wanted it. I was not gentle with you.'

She hugged him again. 'No, I told you it would be safe to make love, but I did not know.'

They held on to each other, while he battled to rein in his emotions. To no avail. They seemed to be spilling out all over the room.

'Edmund.' She drew away and stared at him. 'Did you want the baby?'

He nodded. 'A family. I wanted a family. The baby made it so.'

'I never knew.' She rose and pulled over two wooden chairs stored nearby. 'Come sit.'

They sat next to each other, the cradle, rocking chair and hobbyhorse a tableau in front of them. Edmund took a deep breath. How could three pieces of furniture spark such a flood of emotion?

'I thought you merely wanted to do the right thing,' she said. 'I thought you, like everyone else, wished I'd had the miscarriage a day before the wedding so we wouldn't have had to marry.' She wiped her eyes with her apron.

'I should not have made love to you in Brussels.' The release of his pent-up feelings untangled a truth for him. 'But I never regretted it. My only regret is that our baby did not live. And it tortures me to think the baby might have lived if I had not—'

'No. No. No. Not you. If *I* had not!' she broke in. 'If I had not wanted the lovemaking.' She turned her face away. 'How you can bear to be kind to me? I have ruined your life in every way possible. You have every right to wish me dead.'

He turned his chair to hers and took her hands in his. 'Never say that, Amelie! When you were in such pain, I feared I would watch you die.' He closed his eyes and saw it all again. 'I watched my mother die. They carried away

her baby, too. My brother who never lived. Seeing this—'
he gestured to the nursery furniture '—it brought it back.'

'You saw your mother die?' Her eyes grew wide. 'In
childbirth?'

He nodded.

She left her chair and held him again. He pulled her
into his lap as his grief washed through him and they
trembled together.

'Mr Summerfield!' a faint voice called. 'Mr Summerfield! Where are you? Come quickly!'

He groaned. 'It sounds like Lloyd.'

Amelie moved off his lap. 'Let us forget the attic today.'
She picked up his lamp. 'Go on. I'll get the lamps and
close the door.'

He hurried and found Lloyd on the first floor, still calling his name.

'What is it, Lloyd?' Edmund felt raw inside, but he was
back in control of himself.

He hoped.

'A leak in the pantry,' the old man told him. 'I need help
moving the stores to a dry place.'

'Yes. Let us go quickly.'

Amelie extinguished one of the lamps and carried them
both out of the attic, returning them to the library. She
went back to her bedchamber to wash her hands of the attic's dust. It all repeated in her mind. Edmund wanted the
baby. He'd wanted a family. He thought the miscarriage
was his fault, but it was hers.

He did not deserve to suffer guilt when she was the one
at fault. If she could only convince him.

As she washed the dust from her hands, her arms, her
face, Sally entered the room.

'Oh, beg pardon, ma'am,' Sally said. 'I did not think
you were in here.'

'No reason to apologise,' Amelie said.

Sally carried freshly laundered clothing, which she started putting away.

Amelie curled up on a chair by the window.

'Did Mr Lloyd find Mr Summerfield?' Sally asked. 'He needed his help.'

'Yes. He is with Mr Lloyd now. We were in the attic.' She lay her head on her knees.

'The attic?'

'To see what was up there.' Her voice cracked.

Sally closed the wardrobe. 'Beg pardon, ma'am. Is something wrong? You look so sad.'

She could not help herself. 'Oh, Sally! We—we talked about losing the baby. About how guilty we feel about it!'

'Guilty?' Sally sounded surprised. 'Why would you feel guilty?'

'If—if I had been more careful—' She would not say more. 'That is why I insist you be careful.'

Sally looked puzzled. 'I do not understand. Mrs Bayliss told me the baby was not growing right. She said the baby had no chance of being born.'

Amelie straightened in the chair. 'What?'

'Mrs Bayliss said it happens sometimes. I asked her, because I was afraid it would happen to my baby. She said sometimes the baby does not grow right from the start and the mother's body lets it go, but if I passed three months, I could be pretty sure my baby was growing right.'

Amelie rose from the chair and faced Sally. 'My baby did not grow right?'

Sally nodded. 'Mrs Bailey said it could never have lived.'

Amelie released a pent-up breath. 'It was not our fault?'

'She said there was nothing anyone could do about it. It just happens sometimes. No one knows why.'

Amelie rushed to the door. 'I have to find Edmund!'

She hurried out of the room and down the stairs to the kitchen, where Mrs Stagg was stirring something in a large bowl.

'Mrs Summerfield!' the cook said in surprise.

Amelie needed to speak to Edmund right away. 'Where is my husband?'

Mrs Stagg pointed to a hallway and Amelie entered it. She heard voices and followed the sound. Mrs Wood emerged from the doorway of one room and soon Edmund and Lloyd appeared.

'Edmund!' Amelie cried.

All three looked at her.

'I must talk with you.' Amelie tried to temper her emotions. 'Come talk with me now.'

Edmund blanched. 'What has happened?'

'Nothing has happened,' she assured him. 'I need to speak with you, that is all.'

'Beg pardon, Mr Summerfield,' Mrs Wood broke in. 'We need to move quickly. The damp.'

Amelie took a step back. 'I can wait.'

Mrs Wood rubbed her hands. 'If you've a mind to help us, it will go faster.'

'Oh!' She moved towards them. 'Of course.'

She and Mrs Wood carried the small items while Edmund and Lloyd tackled large barrels or canvas bags. Amelie's heart pounded.

When all the foodstuffs were secure in a dry room, Amelie seized Edmund's arm and hurried him away.

As soon as they were out of earshot of the servants, he stopped her. 'What is it, Amelie? What has happened?'

Those were almost the exact words he'd spoken after she'd panicked during their lovemaking. 'Let us go to your room.'

No one would interrupt them there. She took his hand and quickly climbed the stairs.

Once inside his room, she turned to him.

His face was grim. 'We are here. Tell me now.'

Her words came out in a rush. 'It was not our fault. Not yours and not mine. Sally told me. Mrs Bayliss said our baby was not growing right and could not have lived no matter what.'

He stared at her.

She took his hand. 'There was nothing we could have done. Don't you see? Nothing we did caused it.'

His voice turned low. 'Say it again. More slowly.'

She took a breath. 'Mrs Bayliss told Sally that the miscarriage happened because our baby was not growing right and could not have lived, no matter what. She said it happens sometimes and no one knows why.'

'We did not cause it?' he asked cautiously.

She shook her head.

He put his arms around her and held her tight.

'It was not your fault,' she murmured. 'It was not my fault.' She rested her head against his chest and felt his heart beat fast.

He held her shoulders and gently moved her away from him. He gazed down at her, his grey eyes filled with relief. 'I feel scraped raw. But this is good news. You must never reproach yourself again, Amelie.'

She touched his cheek. 'You must not either. You have done everything right.'

He glanced away, but she turned his head back to look at her. He was close, so very close. She rose on her tiptoes and reached for his lips. He dipped his head down and closed the distance.

His lips ignited the passion that had panicked her the night before. It would not do so again, she had no fear. Her carnal desire had not destroyed her baby. She was a married woman and free to couple with her husband.

He murmured against her lips, 'We have made love in the afternoon before, Amelie. Shall we do so again?'

A mere hour ago she would have berated herself for wanting the pleasures of the flesh so much she could not wait for night, but that had been when she thought she'd hurt her baby. Now what harm could it do?

She nodded.

This time the ritual of undressing seemed a veneration. She gloried in seeing him naked and felt humbled by the look on his face when he gazed at her. He lifted her onto the bed as if she were some precious idol. When he lay next to her, she ran her fingers over his finely sculptured muscles, reverently fingering his scars and wanting to weep for all he'd endured in battle. She touched the male part of him, now as hard as his muscles.

He groaned and laid her on her back while he rose above her. 'I cannot wait.'

She nodded. 'I cannot wait either.'

Still, he entered her slowly and gently, and the sensation intensified the acute passion already wafting through her. They were joined to each other, made one flesh. She understood those words now, understood that this was the marriage. They'd been one flesh since Brussels. He said he never regretted it. She didn't either, and she did not regret now that they were together in this rustic place and had worked in the fields like ordinary people.

As he moved inside her, her thoughts blew away like leaves in the wind. But he remained. Nothing existed but Edmund, moving inside her, intensifying her need. Promising pleasure.

She clung to him, digging her fingers into his buttocks, pressing him against her, as he moved faster and faster, rushing her towards what she now needed more than air to breathe.

He burst inside her, and she felt his seed spilling into

her. A hairsbreadth of a moment later her own climax came, a glorious paroxysm of joy pulsating within her and wafting through her entire body.

His muscles relaxed first, then hers became like jelly. He slid onto the bed beside her, holding her close. 'I feared we would never have this again.'

It had been her fear, too. 'I thought what—what happened was a punishment for my wanting this so much.'

A part of her wondered again if that made her different from other women in her circles. Perhaps it made her different from even the women she'd worked beside these last few days.

'I like it very much, too,' he said, his voice rough and arousing.

What did it matter? If Edmund liked it and she liked it, what did it matter?

'We have the whole afternoon, do we not?' She ran her fingers through his lovely dark brown hair. 'We must occupy ourselves in some way.'

He rose over her again. 'That we must.'

Chapter Nineteen

Edmund did not mind the two more rainy days that kept them inside and free to enjoy the togetherness of their days and nights. They returned to the attic and found several items to bring down to the rooms below. They discovered paintings for the walls, portraits of unknown men and women, presumably one-time tenants of the house, landscapes, mostly scenes from the Lake District, and still-life paintings with grapes and cheeses and dead fowl.

The days were an idyll, each moment together helping them become used to each other and comfortable in each other's presence.

Their nights were a delight.

When the rains were done, though, Edmund worked with Reid on the farm. One day when they were off to the sheep market in Keswick, Edmund suggested Amelie and Sally come along to shop and to see the town that Thomas Gray had described as 'the Vale of Elysium in all its verdure', where famous poets such as Coleridge and Wordsworth had lived.

The streets of the town were filled with well-dressed ladies and gentlemen who'd come to see the Vale of Elysium. After Wordsworth's *Guide to the Lakes* was published the area became a fashionable place to visit. The war had also contributed. When Napoleon had been amassing his empire, travel to the Continent had been impossible.

Keswick was also a market town where farmers came to do the business of buying and selling livestock. Today sheep were up at auction, and Reid had chosen which ewes and tups he wished to sell and knew the ones he wanted to buy. The farmers showed their sheep in turn, and the others examined the sheep's feet, teeth, their wool and ears. Edmund shadowed Reid, listening and learning.

He learned the qualities Reid looked for to improve their stock and which rams and ewes they'd bred were prized by others. He also gained new respect for the steward.

When they were done, they met Amelie and Sally at an inn for an early dinner.

'What did you buy?' he asked, gesturing to her stack of parcels.

'Some cloth. Some soap. Other—' Something caught her eye and she broke off. 'My goodness.'

He looked to see.

An older gentleman and lady entered the room with a younger man who leaned heavily on a cane.

'Fowler.'

The man who was once Captain Fowler and had once made Amelie's face light up in joy was every bit as dashing as he had been in uniform, even though his civilian clothes showed him to be much thinner. He also had the vacant eye of someone struggling simply to take a step. He and the two people Edmund supposed were his parents were walking directly towards their table. Amelie had frozen, a look of distress on her face.

Fowler, though, walked right up to her. 'Forgive me, ma'am, but did I once know you?'

Edmund stood. 'You knew my wife as Miss Glenville.

I am Lieutenant Summerfield.' He used his army rank without thinking.

'How are you, Captain?' Amelie said, although it was obvious he was not well. She turned to his parents. 'Lord and Lady Ellister?'

They nodded, but their expressions were less than pleased.

She continued. 'I never had the opportunity of meeting you.'

'We know who you are,' Lady Ellister snapped. 'We read of your marriage.'

Fowler still peered at Amelie. 'My memory is not what it ought to be.' He looked apologetic. 'I was wounded in the head. When did I know you, then?'

'In—in Brussels,' she said.

'Ah, that explains it.' Fowler still had his charming smile. 'I remember nothing of Brussels.'

Amelie glanced at Edmund before again turning to Fowler's parents. 'It was my brother who found your son on the battlefield at Waterloo. My husband helped bring him back to Brussels.'

Fowler, obviously, did not remember. 'Did you help rescue me, sir?' he asked Edmund.

'Yes,' Edmund replied.

Fowler hooked his cane over his arm and extended his hand. Edmund accepted the handshake.

'Thank you, sir,' Fowler said. 'Are you taking a holiday as well, enjoying the scenery and the fresh mountain air?'

'We live here now,' Edmund said.

Fowler's brows rose. 'Do you?' He looked at Amelie again. 'Why do I think of London when I see you?'

'I do not know,' she answered.

He smiled again. 'A faulty memory means a great deal of frustration, I assure you.'

'Come, my son,' his father demanded. 'We need to find a table.'

Fowler shook Edmund's hand a second time. 'I hope we meet again.' He turned to Amelie and smiled. 'Ma'am.'

His parents hurried him on.

'He recovered. He seems to be what I thought he was,' Amelie murmured as they were out of earshot.

At this moment, if it were not for his cane, he made the perfect picture of what sort of husband she ought to have married.

Her brows knitted. 'His parents do dislike me, though, do they not?'

'Disagreeable people,' he admitted. He supposed they would have heard of him, as well. The bastard son of Sir Hollis Summerfield.

Reid leaned over to him. 'Who was that, laddo?'

Sally's eyes were wide. She knew who he was.

'A gentleman my wife once knew,' Edmund told him.

'It was a long time ago,' Amelie said.

It had not been more than four months, but it did feel like a lifetime ago.

'Were you at Waterloo, then?' Reid asked.

'Yes.' It was easier to talk of Waterloo. 'I was in the 28th.'

'My brother fought there,' Reid said. 'In the Connaught Rangers. He made it through.'

'I am glad of it,' Edmund said.

Amelie became quiet and seemed miles away.

The encounter with Fowler put a pall over the meal that had begun so cheerfully.

By night back at the house, Amelie still felt affected by the encounter with Fowler. As Sally helped her get ready for bed, all she could do was think of that night. Of what had happened. Of how completely he'd deceived her.

Was Edmund remembering that night, too, and how Fowler's deeds had set in motion all that had happened to them since?

Seeing Fowler reminded her once more that she was not like other society misses. She heard his voice again, telling her she was wanton, shameful, no better than Haymarket ware.

How totally deceived she'd been. Even today he had seemed so sweet and gentle. If she'd met him for the first time today, she'd have been equally deceived.

'It was a surprise seeing Captain Fowler again, was it not?' Sally said, pulling the brush through her hair.

'Yes. It was.' Amelie was not inclined to elaborate.

But Sally looked puzzled and about to burst with questions. 'May I ask you something?'

'Of course,' Amelie said, although she did not want to talk of this.

'Why were you with Mr Summerfield that night in Brussels instead of Captain Fowler? I remember seeing you with Mr Summerfield in his uniform and all, but it was Captain Fowler who went with you to the ball.'

This was an impertinent question for a lady's maid to ask her mistress, but it had been Amelie who had encouraged a closer relationship between them.

'I will tell you.' Amelie met her eyes through the mirror. 'Captain Fowler walked me home from the ball, but we quarrelled and he left me on the street alone. Lieutenant Summerfield rescued me from a ruffian who tried to accost me, and he walked me safely back to the hotel.'

Sally's eyes grew starry. 'And that is where you fell in love with him?'

Yes. It was probably then, although she had not realised it. He'd been the finest man she'd ever met from the moment he saved her on the street.

She did love him. It hurt how much she loved him, because she still felt uncertain about him. He'd told her he did not regret marrying her, but was that the truth?

She'd been fooled before.

Sally stood waiting for her answer.

'Yes, I believe that was when I fell in love with him,' she told her.

'So it is easy to fall in love very fast, do you think?' Sally asked.

The subject had turned to Sally, apparently. 'I do not know about it being easy, but I suppose I am proof that it can happen.'

'Even if you thought you were in love with another man,' Sally went on.

Yes, even so. 'It happened to me.'

Sally put her hair in a plait and stood back, wiping tears from her eyes. 'But it won't work the other way around, will it? He won't love me, not with another man's baby in me and me lying about being married!'

Amelie rose, ready to put her arms around Sally and comfort her, but Sally backed away.

'Is there anything more you need from me, ma'am?' Sally asked, wiping her face with her apron.

'No, but—'

'I'll bid you good-night then.' Sally rushed out the door.

Amelie sat back in the chair.

Had she been wrong to convince Sally to lie about being married? It seemed she was as capable of deceiving as she was of being deceived.

And now she had to face Edmund. The encounter with Fowler had affected him, too, she could tell. It had created a distance between them, when these past few days and nights had been so happy. Would he want her tonight? There was only one way to know. She must walk to the connecting door and ask.

And face the fact that he might say no.

* * *

Edmund stripped down to his shirt and drawers. Somehow, tonight, he did not want to be naked, even though the thin cloth could not be any sort of armour.

He flopped into a chair and waited for Amelie, then wondered what he would do if she did appear.

Her bedchamber door closed and footsteps hurried down the hall. Sally had left. If Amelie was to come it would be soon.

He waited. He rose and paced and took a step towards the door, when it opened.

He loved the way she looked at night in her white nightgown draping her curves and tantalising his senses. He'd undo her plait and free her curls with his fingers. Then the picture would be complete. He'd kiss her and carry her to the bed.

But she remained in the doorway. 'Do you want me tonight?'

She'd not asked before. 'Why? Do you not want to come in?'

'I want to know if you want me.' She spoke louder.

Did she want him to say no? 'Only if you want to be here.'

'That is not my question!' she cried. 'You never say! You never tell me what you want.'

'I do tell you,' he protested. He did tell her, didn't he? 'But it should be as you wish it, not me.'

'Why can I not know?' Her voice turned shrill. 'Why hide the truth from me?'

Now she was being unfair. 'I never lie to you.'

'No, you never lie, but you never really tell me, do you?'

'Tell you what?' Did he want her to hear that he felt she deserved a better man than him? That she deserved a man like Fowler. Or rather how Fowler appeared to be. Gentle. Refined. Devoid of scandal?

'I asked you if you wanted me to share your bed tonight. Tell me if you want that.' She placed her hands on her hips.

'Only if you want it.' How much clearer could he be? Would it not be contemptible of him to require her to bed him if she did not desire it?

She made a frustrated sound.

'What is this all about, Amelie?' he demanded. 'Why tonight must I be put to this test? Is it because you saw Fowler?'

'Yes!' she cried. 'Because he reminded me that I can never know if you—or anyone—is telling me the truth!'

He softened his voice. 'Have I given you any reason to doubt what I say to you?'

She glanced away.

He extended his hand to her. 'Come to bed, Amelie. We will just sleep. It has been a long day.'

She hesitated but finally took his hand. He did not kiss her, nor did he gather her in his arms. When they reached the bed he did lift her onto it and climbed in next to her, spooning her against him as they'd spent their other nights here. One difference was he still wore his shirt and drawers.

Sally was too restless to retire to her little room on the second floor. She wanted the fresh air in her lungs. She wanted to gaze up at the stars and wrap herself in the darkness of the night. She grabbed her shawl and a candle and walked downstairs and outside through the conservatory door.

She ran to the middle of the lawn and lay down on the grass to gaze up at the stars, still in their place. She searched for the groups of stars she and Calvin used to find. Lyra and Perseus. Pegasus and Andromeda.

'What do you see up there?'

She sat up. His voice startled her, but it did not surprise her that he also was outside at night.

'I am watching the stars,' she said.

He lay down on the grass beside her. 'Do you know the names of the stars?'

'I do.' She pointed. 'There is Perseus, holding the head of the Medusa. See the square? That is Pegasus.'

She glanced over at him, but he was not looking at the sky. He was looking at her.

She felt blood rush to her face. 'You should not look at me like that.'

'Why not?' he asked. 'Ye're prettier than stars.'

She sat up. 'Please don't.'

He sat up, too. 'Don't what?'

'Do not talk like that!'

His face turned serious. 'Why do you repel my attentions, Mrs Brown? Are they so objectionable to you?'

'Mrs Brown.' She felt as though those words were sin itself.

His brow creased. 'Do you object to my calling you Mrs Brown?'

She could not hold the lie inside any longer. 'I am not *Mrs* Brown!'

He continued to stare at her. 'Who are you, then?'

She wrapped her shawl around her tighter. 'I am *Miss* Brown. Miss Sally Brown and I've never been married.'

'Why say you are Mrs and a widow, then?' he asked, but his voice was low and even.

'Oh, Mr Reid!' she cried. 'Can you not guess?

He kept his gaze on her but finally shook his head.

She rose to her feet. Dropping her shawl, she pressed the cloth of her skirt against her belly. 'Can you see now? It is starting to show. I am going to have a baby and I am not married.'

He stood, too.

She turned away from him. 'It was Mrs Summerfield's idea to tell everyone I am Mrs Brown. A widow. But I cannot like lying to—to you.'

'Can you tell me about it?' He spoke calmly.

'About the father, you mean?' She swiped at her tears. 'It was in Brussels. He was going to marry me, but he was killed in the battle.'

He said nothing.

'I do not want you to think that I—I did what I did with just anyone! I knew him a long time. We grew up together in Hampstead.'

'Then it is a sad thing he was killed,' he said. 'I am sorry for it.'

'I do not know what will happen to me!' she cried. 'What will happen to my baby? Mrs Summerfield says not to worry, but I do. Surely I can't pretend to be a widow for ever! And what will happen to my child if someone finds out! Will he be shunned? We both will be shunned.'

'It cannot be as bad as all that if Mrs Summerfield will help you,' he said.

'I do not know how. I cannot keep working as a lady's maid if I have a baby, can I? Whoever heard of such a thing?' She took several deep breaths to keep from falling apart entirely.

He picked up her shawl and wrapped it around her. 'You should go inside now. But do not worry. Your secret is safe with me. I will not tell anyone.'

He was being very kind, and it endeared him to her even more than before.

But he was still sending her away.

The next morning the wall that had risen between Edmund and Amelie was still intact. In the next few days they went through the motions of rising, conversing with each other, talking over the events of the day, as if that cocoon of closeness still bound them.

Curse Fowler, Edmund thought. *Why did he have to show up again?* Their marriage was built on shaky ground to begin with. Why did he have to put cracks in the fragile foundation they had been building, day by day? Night by night? Now, again, it seemed in danger of crumbling.

Their days were busy, though, so busy that the only time they spent together was at the dinner meal and afterward. They made love, but almost sadly, as if they were both remembering a giddy pleasure of the past that could be no more.

Edmund rose early and tried not to wake Amelie.

As he was picking up his boots to leave as quietly as possible, she spoke. 'Are you off, then?'

'Yes.' He and Reid were bound for another market day in another town. 'What do you do today?'

'I am going to visit the tenants' and farm workers' homes,' she said. 'I think I ought to, don't you?'

He walked back to her and leaned down to kiss her on the forehead. She seemed to stiffen at his touch. 'I think it will be a good thing to do.'

'I'll ask what they need. See if anything is amiss.'

'I have heard no complaints through Reid, but perhaps the wives will tell you more.' It was an inventory he'd not yet had time to do. He was glad she'd taken the interest.

'My father will expect some sort of report about the tenants and workers, will he not?' she said.

'It is likely.' He kissed her again, still savouring her lips. 'I'll be late, I suspect.'

She nodded.

He left feeling as if he were being crushed by grey clouds.

Chapter Twenty

The sheep auction kept Edmund too busy to think much about Amelie. Today there would not only be sales, but also a show to offer prizes for best sheep. Edmund was beginning to understand what made certain sheep better than others. Some of it was pure theatre—keeping the best sheep out of sight until the judging, then trying to get them in the best position to be seen. Some of it was personal opinion and some the fashion of the moment.

The show was meant to generate excitement for the sales to follow, as well as to show what the judges believed were the highest standards and how well or ill the other sheep met them. The sheep were walked into the judging ring by their breeders, who each tried to get their animal to stand out from the others, by their proud stance or, as Reid was skilful in doing, by getting the sheep on the highest ground so as to be the most visible.

The ribbons won and the prize money awarded were incidental to the showing off of the stock. When the sales began in the afternoon, excitement reached a fevered pitch. All the breeders wanted to buy the best at the lowest price and to sell their best at the highest.

This market scene had become familiar enough to Edmund that he could pay attention to more of the details.

The prices bandied around began to stick in his head, and he began to know the probable worth of the ewes and tups by their appearance.

He carefully watched Reid's dealings with the other sheep farmers and paid particular attention to the amounts Reid spent and how much he earned. The transactions were quickly made, but Edmund was able to take them all in, unlike those first market days when it had all been a blur.

He stood next to Reid as he sold a ewe. Edmund heard the price and saw the money change hands. The transaction was quick, but Edmund saw Reid record it in his pocket book, only he put in a smaller amount. He glimpsed the receipt that Reid gave the other breeder, and it was for that same smaller amount.

'Did you write down the wrong amount?' he asked Reid.

Reid's eyes flashed at him, but he soon seemed to recover. 'Don't be daft,' Reid said. 'You misheard, is all.'

On a purchase, Edmund watched closely. Reid listed the amount he spent as more than he and the man agreed upon. The receipt the man wrote was for the larger amount, even though that was not the amount they'd spoken about.

This time he did not question Reid, but he caught him in similar irregularities throughout the afternoon. It looked to him that Reid made more than he documented and paid less than he documented. Where was the extra money going? In Reid's pocket?

He did not want to believe this. He liked the man and had come to trust in his honesty.

Before he left the market, Edmund spoke with several of the breeders, asking them how the costs of the sheep had changed in the last year. He was lucky that, to the man, they could tell him what they paid for sheep and how much they'd sold them for a year ago. He memorised the amounts.

They rode back on the Cumbrian heavy horses that all the farmers owned in this part of England.

'How would you say the sales went today?' Edmund asked Reid.

'I'd say very well. It's been a good year for the farm,' Reid spoke with pride in his voice.

'How did the prices compare to last year's?' Edmund asked. 'What prices were you seeing last year?'

Reid hesitated before answering much more tentatively than the other breeders had done, but Edmund noted what he'd said.

He could still be wrong. He prayed he was.

When they reached the farm, it was dark. Edmund bid Reid good-night and went into the house.

One of the new footmen was attending the hall. 'Evening, sir. How was the sale?'

Everyone had an interest in the sale of sheep. Their livelihoods depended upon it, if only indirectly.

He handed the man his hat and gloves. 'It went well. Mr Reid was pleased at any rate.' He removed his coat. 'Would you brush out my coat, as well?'

'Aye, sir. I will do it and be glad for the work.' He grinned.

These Lakeland servants knew nothing of the decorum of their London counterparts, but it was a difference Edmund found refreshing.

'Thank you.' He added, 'Do you know where Mrs Summerfield is at the moment?'

'I believe she retired to her bedchamber,' the footman answered.

Edmund reached for a taper from a candle box and lit it from one of the lamps. 'I'll be in the library for a little while. I won't need you further, though, if you wish to leave the hall.'

'Thank you, sir!' The man grinned again.

Edmund carried the taper to the library and lit the lamps on the table where the ledger books were stacked. He opened the book from last year and turned the pages until he came to the recordings for the market a year ago.

The figures were roughly what Reid had said. The problem was, they were different from the numbers the other breeders had given him and in a pattern that was becoming sickeningly familiar. Reid recorded the sales low and the purchases high.

Edmund rested his elbows on the table and hung his head in his hands. It looked as if Reid was systematically embezzling from the farm, taking money from Amelie's father, who had given Edmund the right to act in his behalf.

How he must act was now something he dreaded.

He'd misjudged Reid, apparently. He did not misjudge people often, and he hated the idea of being deceived.

He rubbed his face. How would it be if Amelie knew of this? She liked Reid. She hoped Sally would finally allow Reid to court her. She believed Reid to be a good man. Amelie's trust in Edmund was shaky at present. He just could not yet tell her that another man with the appearance of honour had deceived them all.

Not until he confronted Reid.

Edmund finally closed the ledger and lit the taper again before extinguishing the lamps. He left the library and made his way up the stairs to his bedchamber. He could see no light under Amelie's door. Did that mean she was asleep in her own bed? He feared that would be the case. It seemed to him the only connection that still held them together was sharing a bed. Making love.

He opened his door and was not surprised to see a lamp burning. The servants would have left one burning for him, knowing he was coming home late. He blew out the taper and left it on the table inside the door. As he walked into the room, he unbuttoned his waistcoat and untied his neckcloth.

'It is late,' he heard Amelie murmur. 'Did the market last so long?'

'I've been home a while,' he said.

She was in his bed and he was grateful for it. He crossed the room and gave her a kiss. On the lips this time. She accepted it but held back anything in return.

'I've been in the library. I needed to see something in the ledgers,' he explained.

'What did you need to see in the ledgers?'

He could almost hear what she did not say—what did you need that could not wait until morning?

'Last year's figures for this market,' he said.

'Whatever for?'

He wanted to tell her, wanted to pour out his anger and disappointment at being so deceived by Reid. He wanted to say that he still could not believe Reid could do such a thing.

But he didn't. 'I did not want to forget what I was told at the sale. I thought I'd forget if I waited until morning.' This was all true. It was also true that he needed to know right away if his suspicions would be borne out.

'It was that important?' Her tone of voice was disapproving.

He pulled off his boots and trousers. 'It was.'

'Why?'

'So I would not forget.' He walked over to the washbasin, washed his face and hands and brushed his teeth. As he walked back to the bed, he threw off his shirt. He collapsed onto the bed, suddenly exhausted.

Amelie rose on one elbow. 'You are not telling me something.'

That was so. 'Amelie, let us not debate this. I am tired.'

'Very well.' She pulled the covers up to her neck and rolled onto her side, facing away from him, not touching him at all.

Sally waited outside until Mr Reid and his men had placed all the sheep into pens and finished their work while everyone else on the farm was likely asleep. She figured that he would be the last to leave, and she was correct.

He took one long glance back towards the house before turning and starting to walk to his cottage.

She ran to catch up to him. 'Mr Reid!'

He stopped. 'Miss Brown? What are you doing here?'

'I waited for you,' she said, but she halted. 'Unless— unless you do not wish for my company any longer.'

He took quick strides to reach her side. 'It is not that. It is just that it is cold out tonight and you should not get a chill, especially in your condition.'

'It is not that cold,' she said, although she had been shivering while waiting for him.

'Why did you wish to see me, lass?' he asked.

'Today Mrs Summerfield and I went round to all the tenants' houses and the farm workers', and the wives all said the same about you. That you took care of their needs. That you were a good man, and one of the maids said that many of the young women around here would like you to be their husband.'

He dipped his head. 'I never knew that.'

'She said it was so.'

'And why did this make you wait for me?' he asked.

'I want to know why you picked me. You wanted to court me. At least you once wanted to. I want to know why.'

'Why?' He paused to think. 'I am not sure why. You are pretty and sweet-tempered. You do not come from here and I find that captivating.'

She felt her cheeks burn. 'But you changed your mind about me, because of the baby, correct? I want to know for certain, and I promise I will never trouble you again if you tell me the truth.'

He looked directly into her eyes. 'I never said I lost interest in you, because I have not.' He touched her arm. 'I still want to court you, and I hope in time you will want to marry me.'

'You would marry me knowing I carry another man's child?' She could not believe it even though she had come to this place to hear those very words.

'Of course I would,' he said. 'I figure I can give the poor bairn my name and there would be no one to question it. If you want to pretend you are a widow and the baby is your dead husband's, no harm done. It is very nearly the truth.'

Her eyes widened. 'That is what Mrs Summerfield would say.'

'Come to my cottage,' he said. 'I'll make you some tea and warm you up. You do not have to answer me now, but let me show you what sort of house I have and what sort of life you would live.'

She was too shocked to say anything, but she walked with him to his cottage.

The next morning Amelie woke at the first light of dawn, filled with regret. She'd intended to welcome Edmund home from the market. She'd planned to erase these days of her foolish insistence that he tell her each and every feeling he had towards her, but then he'd been so evasive and secretive that her temper had been piqued. Imagine checking figures when he'd been away all day and when matters had been strained between them.

She resolved to turn over a new leaf and stop being so high-handed about trifles.

But a return to sleep eluded her. She slipped out of bed

and went into her bedchamber for a wrapper. She put it on and decided to get some fresh air to clear her mind and to help her rid herself of these worries. She wanted things the way they were on those few days of bliss when she'd begun to believe they might eventually be happy.

Amelie left her room and descended the stairs. She could hear the faint sounds of the house stirring, servants rising to begin the day. She had no wish to meet any of them and feel compelled to explain her early morning wanderings, so she hurried through the hall to the conservatory, still empty of plants.

She noticed that the conservatory door was not locked, an oversight she must mention to Lloyd and Mrs Wood.

Not that it mattered much. In London, perhaps, or even in the country where Northdon House was, but not here. There was nothing much worth stealing in the house and even if there were, the farm's people were not so hungry they had to steal. On the contrary, they were well cared for.

She crossed the lawn and took one of the paths that led up a hill. On her way she noticed a man and a woman walking toward the house. As they came closer she saw it was Sally and Mr Reid.

Sally saw her and blanched. 'Mrs Summerfield! I can explain!'

'It is not how it appears, ma'am,' Reid said.

She ought to be appalled. She knew ladies of the *ton* who would fire a maid for less. Certainly those ladies would have fired Sally long ago. Amelie did not even care if it was exactly how it appeared, that they had spent the night together.

She was merely happy for them.

'Nothing happened, I swear it!' Sally cried.

Amelie directed her gaze at Mr Reid. 'Tell me only what your intentions are toward Sally, sir.'

'Why, to marry her,' Reid said. 'That has been my intention nearly from our first meeting.'

She turned to Sally. 'Will you marry him, then?' If Sally said no, Amelie still would not desert her. Sally and her baby would be secure; she'd see to it.

A rapturous look came over Sally's face as she glanced at Mr Reid. 'Oh, yes, ma'am. I will marry him. We'll have the banns called as soon as we can.'

Amelie smiled. 'Then you need say no more. I wish you happy.'

'Oh, Mrs Summerfield!' Sally hugged her, behaviour unheard of in a maid. 'It is all going to be fine now!'

How lucky Sally was. She would have a devoted husband...and a baby...and a good life, like the rest of the tenants' and farm workers' wives.

Amelie hugged her back, feeling a thousand years older, although Sally was probably very close to her age. 'I am happy for you both.'

Chapter Twenty-One

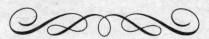

Amelie walked the rest of the way back to the house with Sally, leaving Mr Reid whistling as he headed to the farm building.

Sally rattled on about their plans, about how they had stayed up all night discussing them, about how lucky she felt to have met this good man.

'His house is just what it ought to be,' Sally said. 'Very cosy and neat, but I think it will be very pretty with new curtains and such…'

Amelie only half listened to her.

She was happy for Sally, happy that Sally would get what Amelie had not. A respectable marriage. A baby. A home that was hers alone. A man who adored her.

They entered the house and walked together up to Amelie's bedchamber. Sally kept talking, all the while helping Amelie to dress. When the girl finally left with instructions to get some sleep, Amelie walked to the connecting door to Edmund's room. She leaned her forehead against the cool wood and prayed she could somehow make amends for all her foolishness.

She promised herself she would trust Edmund. He'd always done right by her.

She took a deep breath and knocked on the door.

'Come in,' she heard from the other side.

She opened the door.

Edmund was almost dressed. The footman who had been assigned valet duties was helping him on with his coat. Edmund looked over at Amelie guardedly.

She placed a smile on her face. 'Good morning!' she said cheerfully.

The footman greeted her with a smile and a nod before leaving the room.

'Good morning,' Edmund said then.

'I have so much to tell you!' she said. 'Some of it I must tell you before breakfast, because it is a secret.'

He waited.

She told herself not to be daunted by his reserve. She'd brought it on herself, after all.

'It is exciting news!' she went on. 'Sally and Mr Reid are to be married.'

His face turned stony. 'Mr Reid?'

'Yes.' She turned to the window, because Edmund's demeanour disturbed her and she did not want to give in to discouragement the way she had before. 'Mr Reid took a fancy to her almost at first sight. And he knows about the baby. He even knows that Sally is not a widow.' She glanced at the door, turning nervous because he was not at all acting as she expected. 'Shall we go to breakfast?'

He nodded and moved to escort her.

'But you mustn't tell anyone, because they will decide when to announce it.'

'I will tell no one.'

She peered at him. 'Are you not happy for them?'

He shook his head as if to rid it of a thought. 'Forgive me. I was thinking about something else. I hope they know each other well enough.'

What an odd thing for him to say. 'We did not know each other at all,' she murmured.

'No,' he said. 'Of course we did not.'

'Do you know something about Mr Reid that means he and Sally should not be wed?' Sally should not be surprised the way she'd been surprised about Fowler.

'I know nothing for certain,' he said. 'But if I hear something, Sally should know I will say so.'

Amelie told herself to be contented with that response as they walked down the stairs to the dining room. Edmund seemed a world away. Sunlight streamed in the sparkling clean windows of the sitting room next to the conservatory, where the breakfast buffet was set out. Bread for toasting, slices of ham, kippers, eggs, butter and jam. Such a contrast to their first morning. There was even a footman in attendance.

They selected their food and Amelie sat across from Edmund at a small table she'd found in the attic. The footman poured coffee for Edmund, tea for Amelie and retired from the room.

Edmund was lost in his own thoughts.

Amelie disliked the silence but was determined not to ask about it. Instead she said, 'Would you like to hear about my visits with the tenants' and farm workers' wives yesterday?'

He at least looked up at her and almost smiled. 'Yes. I do want to hear it. Did it go well?'

'I think it did mostly,' she responded. 'Some of the wives were cautious and polite, but no one had any complaints to speak of or anything they required that was not provided them. They credited Mr Reid with managing their needs very well.'

'Mr Reid,' he repeated almost in a whisper.

'Mrs Peet absolutely sang his praises, and the maid we took with us agreed with her.' She lowered her voice. 'I cannot help but feel Sally is fortunate. Indeed, we are all fortunate he is here.'

'Yes.' It seemed he turned distant again. 'Fortunate.'

She had to speak. 'What is it, Edmund?' She leaned toward him. 'Something is troubling you. Can you tell me what it is?'

'A problem I need to sort out,' he said. 'I cannot speak of it yet.'

It must involve her in some way. Why else not tell her? 'I—I am sorry for my ill temper lately.'

He reached over and clasped her hand. 'It is not that. I will work through this problem, I promise.'

'Is it with the farm?' she asked.

'Not with the farm precisely, but do not ask me more. It is too soon for me to talk of it.'

In other words, it was a secret.

'What will you do today?' she asked.

'I need to meet with Reid,' was all he said.

Edmund found Reid in the sheep pens.

'Good morning, Summerfield!' Reid looked particularly cheerful this morning. And why wouldn't he? He'd become betrothed. 'We are preparing for the tupping—the mating—that is next on the schedule. There is always something.'

'I need to speak with you, Reid,' Edmund said. 'Alone.'

Reid's happy mood fell, Edmund could tell, but he tried to cover it over with a false cheer. 'Aye! As you wish. Give me a moment.' He gave some instruction to the men in the sheep pen and climbed over the fence. 'Shall we go in my office?'

Reid kept up the light pretence as they walked to the building where he kept his office. In the sunlight Edmund could see the dark circles under his eyes and the worry lines on his forehead.

Once there, Reid asked, 'Would you care for tea? I can build a fire and put the pot on.'

'Do not go to the trouble.'

'Will you sit at least?' A hint of testiness entered Reid's voice.

'I'll stand.' Edmund knew from the army that a man had more authority when he stood.

Reid rested against his desk. 'What is it?' he asked in a serious tone.

'I think you know,' Edmund said, watching the man carefully.

Reid laughed drily. 'I do not know. I have no idea.' He paused, then asked. 'Unless it has something to do with Miss Brown? I assure you my intentions are honourable towards her. I want to marry her, and she has agreed to have me.'

'My wife told me,' Edmund responded. 'This does not concern Miss Brown.' Although it would seriously affect her.

'What is it then?' Reid could not quite pull off a guileless expression.

'It is about the money you are embezzling from my wife's father.'

Reid tried to appear outraged. 'Embezzling? That is absurd.'

'You pay less for the sheep than the receipts state and you sell sheep for more than you record. Those profits go into your pocket.'

Reid straightened. 'I told you yesterday that you were mistaken. You heard wrong is all.'

'No,' Edmund said. 'I know what I saw, what I heard. The figures in the ledger do not fit with what the other breeders told me about last year's prices. Yours were consistent. You sold high and bought low. Every time. Do me the honour of not taking me for a fool.'

'I deliver a profit from the farm,' Reid said. 'Lord

Northdon makes good money from it every year, and each year we do better.'

'You also steal profit from the farm, do you not?'

Reid glared at him. 'You saw the books. Before I came the farm was making a pittance. One bad year and it would have gone under. Now it makes him money.'

'Explain what I saw, then. Those are profits you are not recording.' This was a card he hated to play. 'If you do not explain this, Reid, I will have to let you go.'

'Before the tupping?' Reid's voice rose. 'I need to be here!'

'Then explain about the money.' Edmund insisted. 'Or leave today.'

Reid turned away and waited so long to speak that Edmund thought he would actually leave.

He finally turned back. 'When I came here the farm was a shambles. It was in danger of failing. Worse, its workers were living in deplorable conditions. Roofs leaked. Fuel was scarce. In winter their children were getting sick from the cold. Grain stores were infested with vermin. Deplorable conditions!' He shook his head. 'If the farm failed the effects would stretch further than the farm. The village depends on us. The other farms on the estate depend on us. There would be a lot of people put in dire circumstances. So the farm had to prosper.'

'How does this lead to embezzlement?' Edmund demanded.

'Do me the courtesy of letting me explain in my own way,' Reid snapped.

Edmund inclined his head. 'Go on, then.'

'I applied to Lord Northdon several times for the funds to put things on a solid footing. I sent all the details. Every time I was refused.'

'Lord Northdon refused you?' Northdon did not seem to lack generosity or good sense.

'So his man of business, Mr Frye, said. It was he who proposed this plan—'

'The man of business devised the plan?' Could this be true?

'Aye,' Reid said. 'It was not the solution I thought best. Mr Frye said to skim off the top in all transactions. He said he could keep Lord Northdon from knowing about it for the price of forty pounds per year.'

'You went along with this, though,' Edmund accused.

Reid threw up his hands. 'What choice did I have? I knew if we poured more money into the farm and its tenants and workers, we would reap the rewards of it. And I knew if the farm prospered, the village would prosper and the other farms would not be hurt. I knew in the long run Lord Northdon would make more money.'

'But it is embezzlement just the same, Reid,' Edmund said.

Reid made a sweeping motion with his arm. 'But look what we've done. Everything on the farm is in good repair. The workers' needs have been attended to. As a result they work hard. Everyone goes along with this, because they know everyone benefits. How could I not do this?'

Edmund sank down in a chair. This was even worse than he thought. If he exposed the scheme, many people would be hurt.

Reid looked down at him. 'I can prove to you that I kept none of it for myself. I have another set of ledgers that show where every penny has gone, all back into the farm or to the workers when the need was legitimate.'

'How many people know about this?' Edmund asked.

'Everyone,' Reid said. 'That is why you received such a cool welcome, you know. We all expected you had come to cause trouble. To change things. To go back to the way it was when everyone struggled. But then you didn't do anything. Nothing but work and that put you in good stead.

When Mrs Summerfield helped harvest the hay, that was even better. We thought we were safe.'

Edmund rubbed his face. 'What is to be done now?'

Reid sat, as well. 'Might we not merely go on as before?'

Edmund looked at him. 'I do not see how. The money belongs to my wife's father. How can I turn a blind eye to it?' And how could he allow that man of business to extort money from a scheme he'd devised?

'You must find a way, or these people will suffer.' Reid looked defeated.

What was Edmund to do? He did not exactly have any clout with Amelie's father. In fact, he was quite sure his father-in-law would do the opposite of whatever Edmund recommended.

Edmund stood. 'Let me think about this. Go back to the sheep. Do what needs to be done. I will tell you first what I decide.'

Reid nodded and rose to his feet. The two men walked back to the sheep pens, but there Edmund left him and continued to the house.

What was he to say to Amelie about this? He could not put her in a position that required her to act against her father.

From her bedchamber window Amelie watched her husband and Mr Reid walk from the direction of the sheep pens to the building where Reid had his office. Even from this distance she could tell something was wrong. There was tension in both their gaits, and they were not speaking.

Her guess was the tension had something to do with whatever had upset Edmund the night before and preoccupied him this morning.

That he would not tell her bothered her. It must have to do with the sheep or the sale or perhaps with Mr Reid himself. Edmund had avoided answering her when she'd asked if it was about Mr Reid.

Amelie watched them until they disappeared into the farm building. She rubbed her forehead and turned around quickly to stride into Edmund's room. Even though one of the footman acted as his valet, she liked to straighten his room and fold his clothes.

She heard a sound from outside and glanced out the window. A carriage passed through the gate and was making its way towards the house. She watched it come closer, and as it went around a curve in the road she gasped.

The crest on the side looked like her father's.

She took off her apron and dropped it on one of the chairs. Her father would not like her looking like one of the chambermaids. She ran down the stairs to the hall, where the new footman sat, waiting for something to do.

'There is a coach coming!' she said.

He stood. 'A coach? What do I do?'

'Come outside with me to meet whoever it is.' She opened the front door herself, and he followed her outside.

'It is my father's carriage, I think, but I don't know why he would send it.'

'Your father?' the footman said. 'The lord that owns the farm?'

'Yes.'

The carriage pulled up, driven by the same two coachmen who had brought Amelie and Edmund here only a few weeks ago. She could see that the passengers were men, but she could not tell who they were.

The footman glanced at Amelie, looking uncertain.

'Put the steps down, open the door and assist the passengers,' she told him. 'You will do splendidly.'

He nodded.

The first man out of the carriage was her father's valet. Her father must be one of the passengers, then. The valet glanced at the house and shivered with disgust. He sighed, looked heavenward and waited to assist her father.

The next man was Mr Frye, her father's man of business, a short, portly man who always creaked when he walked from the stays he wore under his clothes. He spied her and bowed.

'Miss Glenville,' he said with a flourish.

She curtsied. 'Mrs Summerfield, sir, as well you know.' The man was more pompous than the highest society matron. She'd never liked him.

Last came her father. Amelie ran up to him and he gave her a big hug. 'Amelie, my dear,' was all he said.

'Why are you here, Papa?' she cried. 'Did something happen to Maman? Or Marc or Tess?'

'Nothing like that.' Her father patted her hand.

The footman was looking disoriented again. She stepped closer to him. 'Gather their baggage and carry it in.'

He nodded.

She spoke to the coachman holding the horses. 'You remember where the stables are, do you not?'

'Yes, ma'am,' the man said.

'The stablemen should see to your needs nicely.' She hurried over to her father and the other two men. 'Come in, please. The footman will see to your bags.'

She led her father and Mr Frye into the drawing room. 'Please sit, Papa. I'll see to refreshments.'

She stepped back into the hall, where the valet was looking around disdainfully.

The footman came through the door juggling three bags and a basket.

She hurried up to him but spoke in tones low enough that the valet would not hear. 'Leave these and run to find Mr Summerfield and Mr Reid. I saw them walking to one of the farm buildings. Tell them my father and his man of business are here.'

'Man of business,' the footman said in disapproving tones. 'Do you want Mr Summerfield and Mr Reid to come here?'

She did not know. 'Just tell them the men are here. They will know what to do. But hurry!'

'Yes, ma'am!' He ran off.

She turned to the valet. 'Come with me.' She led him through the servants' door leading to the kitchen. 'Mrs Wood!' she called. 'I need you.'

Mrs Wood appeared in the hallway.

Amelie spoke right away. 'My father and his man of business have called unexpectedly. Please see we are served refreshment in the drawing room and see to Hines, here. He is my father's valet. We will need rooms prepared for them.'

'Your father.' Mrs Wood frowned. 'Very good. We shall attend to it.'

Amelie hurried back to the drawing room.

'I am sorry. I was delayed,' she said. 'We shall have refreshments in a few minutes.'

Her father remained standing and was looking around the room. 'I had forgotten how austere this place was. More like the house of a tenant farmer.'

It was good he'd not seen it before they'd hung the paintings.

'It is plain,' she agreed.

'Where is your husband?' Her father said the word *husband* with great disdain.

'Out tending to farm business, of course.' Her brows knitted. 'Papa, why are you here? And why is Mr Frye with you?'

He walked over to her and put his hand on her arm. 'It is about business, Amelie. It is nothing for you to trouble yourself over.'

She was already troubled over it.

'Something your husband should have been alerted to,' he said scathingly.

Her father never gave Edmund a good word.

She lifted her chin. 'He already knows about it.' It must be whatever was disturbing Edmund.

'He does?' Mr Frye looked surprised. 'He knows about the fraud and embezzlement?'

Amelie felt the blood drain from her face.

Chapter Twenty-Two

At that moment, Lloyd brought in a tea tray, and they stopped talking. He set it down on the table and left.

Amelie poured the tea. 'How do you take yours, Mr Frye?' she asked.

'Three teaspoons of sugar and milk,' the man said, reaching for one of the biscuits Mrs Stagg had included.

Amelie sat, but mostly so they would. Her mind was spinning. What fraud? Who was embezzling?

Her father was restless in his seat. He finally stood again. 'Perhaps you should send someone to find Summerfield and summon him here.'

'I already did,' she answered. 'He will come unless he is involved in something that demands his attention.'

Mr Frye also stood again. 'What could be more important?' He mirrored her father's tone and demeanour.

Amelie fixed a gaze on him. 'You do not know the workings of a farm, do you, sir? Some tasks cannot wait.' She turned to her father. 'Edmund is handling the matter, do not fear.'

'He sent for the magistrate, then?' Frye asked.

The magistrate. Who was to be arrested? 'I said he is handling it, Mr Frye.' She faced her father again. 'Tell me what you know.'

He shook his head in dismay. 'I cannot believe he worried you over this ramshackle business, but since you know, maybe you can tell me what he plans to do about it.'

'Tell me what you know,' she repeated. 'And perhaps I can.'

Her father pointed to his man of business. 'Mr Frye discovered it.'

Mr Frye eagerly took up the tale. He cleared his throat. 'When I learned that you and Summerfield would be coming here, I carefully examined the records.' He smirked. 'To make certain I was prepared in case I was needed.'

As if Edmund would need the likes of Mr Frye, Amelie thought.

'Some anomalies made me suspicious, though,' Mr Frye went on. 'I have convincing proof that Mr Reid is embezzling significant sums of money every year.'

No. Amelie felt this blow deep in the pit of her stomach. Not Mr Reid. Please, not Mr Reid.

Her father's eyes flashed. 'If he knew about this, why did he not write me immediately?'

She met his eye. 'Why should he write to you, Papa? You gave him permission to act in your stead. Let him act. He will resolve the matter.'

'Resolve the matter?' Frye scoffed. 'Arrest the fellow and send him to the gallows.'

'Arrest who?' Edmund walked through the door, followed by Mr Reid.

Amelie's heart pounded in her chest.

He stood tall and faced her father and Mr Frye with boldness, but Amelie noticed the stiffness of his shoulders.

Edmund inclined his head to her father. 'Good day, sir. I hope you are in good health.'

'Of course I am in good health,' her father snapped. 'What has that to do with anything?'

'This other gentleman is Mr Frye, my father's man of

business,' Amelie told him, not trusting her father to have the courtesy to make introductions.

'I met Mr Frye when we made the marriage settlement.' Edmund said. He looked Frye up and down. 'Good day, sir.'

Frye turned red and sputtered, 'We shall see if it is a good day.'

'I am surprised you came, Frye,' Edmund went on. 'Given all we know.'

'I insisted he come,' her father said.

'Papa—' Amelie did not want to ignore Reid standing there '—may I present Mr Reid, the steward?'

'Humph. I am surprised *you* came, sir,' her father said to Reid. 'When you must know we are here because you have been embezzling funds from me all these five years.'

No! Amelie could not have misjudged Reid so completely, could she? Could she not trust the character of any man she met? Poor Sally. Amelie had practically thrown Sally at Mr Reid.

'Yes!' Frye pointed a finger at Reid. 'Mr Reid defrauded you and embezzled from you.'

'What did he do, precisely, Mr Frye?' Edmund asked.

Mr Frye looked smug. 'It appears he made it look as though the sheep sold for less than they really did and that he purchased new stock at a lower price than they really were. I believe he used that principle in buying and selling everything.'

'I wonder how you could tell that from your records,' Edmund remarked in a casual tone.

Amelie stood straighter. How would that show up on records?

'Mr Reid has a tale that is a bit more detailed than Frye's,' Edmund said. 'And he has the records to prove it.'

A panicked look flashed through Frye's eyes, but he

lifted his chin. 'You cannot tell me anyone will believe a hill farmer over me.'

'A hill farmer with good records.' Edmund turned to her father. 'You are a reasonable man, sir. Listen to him.' He nodded to Reid.

Reid cleared his throat. 'Sir, five years ago I repeatedly asked for more funds to improve the farm. When I came on, it was in a poor state. I appealed to you through Mr Frye, who said you refused. I indicated how dire the situation was, and it was he who suggested the scheme he described—'

'I never did!' protested Frye.

'Go on,' her father said.

'I felt I had no choice, sir,' Reid said to her father. 'If the farm failed, all its people would be out of work. The village would suffer. The other farms, too. I could not let that happen. You had good land. Good buildings. You had the foundation of good stock.'

Perhaps Amelie had not misjudged Reid. Whatever he'd done, he sounded as though he'd done it for the farm and its people.

As he talked she stole glances at Edmund, who looked in total command of the situation, unless you saw the stress at the corner of his eyes.

Shame on her for doubting him, for not trusting him. He never failed her. Never.

Reid went on. 'If you want to inspect the books, sir, I will show you everything. Where every penny went, including the forty pounds per year paid to Mr Frye.'

'Paid to Mr Frye!' Her father swung around to his man of business.

'It is not true,' Frye said, but his voice turned weak.

'Will your books show where every penny went?' Edmund asked Frye.

Frye returned a panicked look.

Her father frowned. 'I believe I would like to see these books, Reid.'

'They are in the library,' Edmund said.

Her father swiftly crossed the room to the door. Reid followed him.

Edmund walked up to Amelie. He touched her arm. 'Would you wait here with Frye? I'll have Rogers stay in the room with you. I want someone to watch him, and you are the only one—'

She covered his hand with hers. 'You do not have to explain.' She smiled at him. 'Not this time.'

He touched her face and walked out.

By the time the three men returned to the drawing room, Mr Frye was seated in a chair, quivering in fear and muttering to himself that he could not go to prison, that he could not die on the gallows.

Her father walked up to him directly. 'Here is what you will do, Frye, if you wish to avoid the gallows.' His voice vibrated with anger. 'You will return to London. You will get my affairs in order so they can be turned over to a reputable replacement. You will pay back the money you have stolen in payments from Reid. Then you will leave London, and I had better never hear of you or see you again. The only reason I spare your life is to avoid the scandal that would surely ensue.'

Frye rose from his chair with difficulty, but he nodded vigorously.

Edmund added, 'I'll have a man drive you in the wagon to Keswick. You can get a coach back to London from there.'

Edmund glanced over at Rogers. 'Can you manage it, Rogers?'

Rogers smiled. 'Oh, aye, sir. I'll see to it.' When Frye

reached the doorway, Rogers seized his arm. 'Stay with me, sir.'

'Would you like to see the farm now, Lord Northdon?' Reid asked her father.

'I would.' He started for the door but turned. 'Are you coming, too, Summerfield?'

Edmund glanced at Amelie before he followed her father.

She watched him leave the room, wishing for just a moment or two alone with him, enough time for her to tell him she loved him.

After the tour of the farm, Edmund and Lord Northdon left Reid at his office and walked back to the house.

'The farm is well-run, do you not think?' Edmund said. There was nothing like showing it to make the point that Reid's money had been well spent.

'Impressive,' Lord Northdon said. 'But do not suppose this changes anything.'

Edmund went cold inside. 'What is your meaning, sir?'

'Reid still embezzled money.'

Had Northdon not seen the sense of everything? Reid's acceptance of the embezzlement scheme had saved the farm. Northdon had made money instead of losing the entire estate.

He halted. 'Sir, you can't jail Reid. Think of the farm. Breeding is about to begin. You would be throwing away the profits Reid has produced for you.'

Northdon started walking again. 'I agree. Reid ought to stay.' He paused for a long time. 'You should go.'

'What?'

'I want you to go,' Northdon repeated.

'You wanted us here, now you want us to leave?' He and Amelie did not need to be uprooted again. They needed time together.

'As you know,' Northdon went on, 'I have no liking for you and the way you ill-used my daughter.'

'Much has happened since then,' Edmund said.

'This is not a suitable life for my daughter!' Northdon threw up his arms. 'In such a house. Managing servants who would do better working in the fields.'

'This is your property.'

'I did not remember how rustic it was.' Northdon waved a hand. 'And I did not want to send Amelie here. I wanted her to stay with her mother and me. She may have been ruined for a good marriage, but she can at least enjoy a pleasant life.'

Edmund's anger grew. He was a villain in this man's eyes—a bastard—and there was no changing that. 'Speak plainly, sir.'

'I mean I want to take my daughter home. Alone. I want you to leave her. And if you do not, I will call the magistrate and have Reid prosecuted, jailed and hung.'

'No.' Edmund could manage to say no more.

'I am absolutely determined.' Northdon's voice was firm.

'This is impossible.' Edmund fumed. 'Either I ruin the lives of all these people or I hurt Amelie.'

'She will recover well enough when she is back home.'

No, she would not recover. She'd never trust anyone again.

'You cursed contemptible scoundrel!' Edmund shouted.

He strode off, making haste to put distance between himself and Northdon before he put his fist in the older man's jaw, but he waited for Northdon at the door to the house.

When Northdon came near, Edmund crossed his arms over his chest. 'I call your bluff, sir.'

Northdon's brows rose, but his smug expression did not change.

Edmund stared him straight in the face. 'I am going to

wager on you being a decent man. I'm going to wager that only a decent man would have produced a daughter like Amelie, a son like Glenville. Only a decent man would have defied society to marry a woman like Lady Northdon. I wager that you will not ruin a good man like Mr Reid; you will not impoverish this farm and its people and its village's people just to hurt me. I wager that, even though you detest me, you will not hurt others merely to revenge yourself on me. So I defy your threat.'

Northdon pursed his lips, but Edmund thought he saw a moment of acquiescence, even respect, in his eyes. 'It is a great risk you take.'

'I do not need this farm,' he said. 'I do not need you and your money or even Amelie's dowry. I can well support my wife myself. I can and will prosper.' He leaned forward for more emphasis. 'But I need Amelie. I need her the way I need air to breathe. I will not leave her, not unless she wants me to go.'

Northdon tilted his head. 'Ah, but suppose she does want you to go. Suppose she would prefer to return to the comfort and loving arms of her family. Would you let her go then?'

The idea of it was like a fresh sabre cut, straight to his heart. 'If Amelie wishes for me to leave her, I will leave, but only if it is what she desires.'

'Then let us ask her.' Northdon pushed past him and walked into the house.

They found Amelie upstairs in the bedchamber that the maid was readying for Lord Northdon.

'We need to speak to you, Amelie,' her father said.

Amelie glanced at Edmund with a questioning expression. He had no answer for her.

She turned to Jobson. 'Are you finished in here?'

The maid glanced at Lord Northdon with a scornful

expression. Edmund supposed the servants already knew Northdon had come intending to arrest Reid.

'I'm done, ma'am.' Jobson curtsied and left the room.

Amelie's eyes slid towards Edmund again before she turned to her father. 'Well?'

It was Edmund who answered. 'Your father wishes you to make a choice.'

'What now, Papa?' Amelie said, exasperated with her father.

Her father's eyes twitched. 'I had forgotten this house was so ramshackle. Like living in a tenant's hut. The servants are deplorable. You've been used to finer things, better service and more comfort. You certainly have not been required to work in the fields.'

Someone told him she'd helped with the haymaking? How unfortunate.

'What is this choice?' she asked impatiently.

He responded, 'Come back to Northdon House with me and resume the life you were born to.'

'Edmund does not wish to live at Northdon House.' Why was he bringing this up again? 'That was settled back in London.'

Her father gave her an intent look. 'I meant for *you* to come home.'

Her stomach clenched. 'Without my husband, you mean.' She turned to Edmund. 'Do you want me to leave with my father?' She quickly added. 'And do not answer by asking me what I want. Just answer me.'

He held her gaze but did not speak right away. Finally he said, 'No, I do not want you to leave me.' His voice was low, but she felt it pulsate inside her. 'I will not prevent you, though, if you desire to leave.'

She closed her eyes and inhaled. Edmund always told

her the truth. *He did not want her to leave him.* She could trust that.

She swung back to her father. 'What are you about, Papa? Why are you trying to separate me from Edmund? I love him, Papa.'

Her father lifted his chin. 'How can you say that? He defiled you.'

'He did not defile me, Papa. Why can you not understand that? That night was a beginning for us—a lucky one, Papa.' She stole a glance at Edmund but could not let her gaze linger lest her emotions spill over. She turned back to her father. 'Are you making me choose between here and Northdon House? Because I want to stay here. Or are you forcing me to choose between Edmund and you and Maman? That would pain me to the quick, but my choice must be Edmund. Do you know why? Because Edmund would never force me to make such a choice.'

Her father's head bowed.

She lowered her voice. 'Make yourself comfortable, Papa. Hines will come to tell you of dinner. We keep country hours here.' She walked out the door, hearing and feeling Edmund following her. Her feelings for him were raw and acute, and she feared she would burst if she let them loose.

He seized her arm and pulled her into an embrace. They held on to each other as if a violent whirlwind threatened to blow them apart. Perhaps that was what had almost happened.

'Amelie,' he murmured. 'Do you truly love me? Do you want to stay with me?'

She hugged him close again. 'Of course.'

He released her but only enough so he could gaze into her face. 'I have not said it to you, because I thought you would not want to hear it, but I love you, too, Amelie. I believe I started to love you the instant we met, but I knew I was not good enough for you.'

'Good enough?' she cried. 'You are the best man I know, the most honourable man I know. You are always there when I need you. You never lie to me. You always do what needs to be done.'

The door to her father's bedchamber opened, and he stepped into the corridor.

Edmund's grip on Amelie tightened, and she braced herself for whatever her father would say next.

'Wait a moment,' her father said in a quiet voice.

He approached them as they stayed rooted to the same spot.

He looked directly at Edmund. 'Summerfield, my daughter is correct—my son even tried to tell me—you have behaved honourably ever since that—that one transgression. I, on the other hand, have behaved abominably. I am not going to have anyone arrested. I'm not making anyone choose between one thing and another.' He extended his hand. 'I apologise to you, sir.'

Edmund released Amelie and hesitated only a moment before accepting the handshake.

'Oh, Papa!' Amelie had feared her father might never see Edmund's worth.

Her father lifted a hand. 'I need to make amends—'

Edmund interrupted him. 'Your apology is enough, sir.'

What other man would be so generous? Amelie's heart swelled with pride.

Her father shook his head. 'An apology is not nearly enough. I almost drove away my daughter! You stopped me. So, I want to give you something. I want to deed you this farm, if you would like it. Or its worth, if you would prefer. Call it a wedding present.'

His valet appeared in the corridor carrying folded clothing. He halted, brows raised.

Amelie pulled Edmund away. 'Thank you, Papa! We will leave you to Hines and talk about this at dinner.'

Her father smiled wanly. 'As you wish, Amelie. It should always be as you wish.'

Amelie led Edmund to his bedchamber.

Once inside he put his arms around her. 'I knew your father was a decent man.'

She hugged him tight. 'What do you wish to do, Edmund? Do you want the farm?'

'Your father and I agree on one thing,' he said. 'It should be as you wish.'

'I should like to stay here,' she said. 'But if you prefer, I will go to Brussels with you, Edmund. I will go anywhere with you.'

'We stay here, then.' He kissed her forehead. 'It will be our home.'

She sighed. 'Our home.'

He held her again. 'Ah, Amelie. If it weren't for the baby, I would say my life is perfect. With you.'

'We will have more babies, Edmund.' She pulled away and made him look at her. 'We will be a family.'

Epilogue

August 1816—Brussels, Belgium

Edmund found Brussels much the same after a year, but also much altered. The buildings stood as majestically as before; the *parc* was as beautiful, but no soldiers in varied-colour uniforms walked down the streets or strolled through the shrubbery. There was no tension in the air, no fear of what was to come.

Edmund and Amelie had just left Lady Summerfield and Count von Osten, Edmund's stepmother and her lover. The visit had been a pleasant one. Lady Summerfield greeted him as warmly as ever, as if he were her son instead of her late husband's bastard. She also welcomed Amelie and genuinely seemed to delight in her, taking her aside for a tête-à-tête. Edmund and Count von Osten talked over their investments, and Edmund had the chance to tell them both about the farm. They left, promising to come to dinner in two days' time.

The afternoon was brisk and sunny, so they walked back to the Hotel de Flandre from rue Sainte Anne, where Lady Summerfield lived.

'I liked her, Edmund.' Amelie held his arm and they

strolled down the street. 'She is very charming but without pretence. I admire that.'

'I'm glad.' He put his hand over hers. 'I wish my sisters would let themselves know her.'

'In time perhaps,' she said.

They walked past familiar buildings, crossing familiar streets.

'Oh, my goodness.' She suddenly stopped. 'Do you know where we are?'

They were at the entrance of an alley. 'This is where that ruffian dragged you,' he said.

She clung to him tighter. 'Where you rescued me.'

He slipped a kiss onto her temple. 'I should like to thank that fellow.'

'Thank him!' She gave him a playful shove. 'He was horrid! I am grateful you came along when you did!'

'As am I.' He hugged her. 'We have had an eventful year.'

'Most of it lovely,' she agreed.

They resumed their stroll.

It, indeed, had been a lovely year for the most part. After Amelie's father's unreasonableness forced them to admit their love for each other, their days and nights had been more splendid than he could have imagined.

'Who would have thought we'd end up on a sheep farm!' she cried. 'Or that I would love it so.'

'I dare say Reid will keep it running well without us for a couple of months.'

She rested her cheek against his shoulder. 'I miss it.'

'I miss it, too,' he admitted.

She squeezed his arm. 'We did rather well this year, with all that happened, did we not?'

'We did, indeed.' Who would have believed a bastard son would earn the love of a viscount's daughter? Or live on a sheep farm and be happy over it?

She stopped suddenly and turned to him with an odd look on her face. 'I need to tell you something.'

He held his breath. Their life had become so perfect he'd worried that it might all come crashing down. 'What is it?'

'I'm not sure yet.' Now she was being cryptic.

He braced himself. 'Not sure of what?'

A glimmer of a smile tinged her lips. 'Of—of whether I am to have a baby. I think so, though. I haven't been sick but I feel different and—well—I counted the weeks since—'

He cut her off. 'You think you are with child?'

She nodded, smiling widely now.

He uttered a whoop of joy, picked her up and swung her around. Who cared if they were on the streets of Brussels?

'But I am not sure yet!' she cried.

'You are sure enough to tell me.' He could not contain his grin.

'Do not set your hopes on it,' she said more soberly. 'I might be wrong.'

He tilted up her chin and placed a kiss upon her lips. 'Then if you are wrong, let us see if we can still make it happen.'

She laughed. 'Shall we make haste?'

Their leisurely stroll became a dash past the Cathedral of Saint Michael and Saint Gudula, through the Parc de Bruxelles and on to the hotel where their love truly began.

* * * * *

MILLS & BOON

MODERN

Power and Passion

Prepare to be swept off your feet by sophisticated, sexy and seductive heroes, in some of the world's most glamourous and romantic locations, where power and passion collide.

MILLS & BOON
True Love
Romance from the Heart

Celebrate true love with tender stories of heartfelt romance, from the rush of falling in love to the joy a new baby can bring, and a focus on the emotional heart of a relationship.

Four True Love stories published every month, find them all at:

millsandboon.co.uk/TrueLove

MILLS & BOON

Desire

Indulge in secrets and scandal, intense drama and plenty of sizzling hot action with powerful and passionate heroes who have it all: wealth, status, good looks…everything but the right woman.

JOIN US ON SOCIAL MEDIA!

Stay up to date with our latest releases, author news and gossip, special offers and discounts, and all the behind-the-scenes action from Mills & Boon...

 @millsandboon

 @millsandboonuk

 facebook.com/millsandboon

 @millsandboonuk

It might just be true love...

GET YOUR ROMANCE FIX!

Get the latest romance news, exclusive author interviews, story extracts and much more!